W9-ASZ-311

RANDOM
HOUSE

LARGE
PRINT

THE
LAKE SHORE
LIMITED

THE LAKE SHORE LIMITED

SUE MILLER

RANDOM HOUSE
LARGE PRINT

Published in the United States of America by Random House Large Print in association with Alfred A. Knopf, New York.
Distributed by Random House, Inc., New York.

Cover photograph by Trinette Reed / Getty Images
Cover design by Carol Devine Carson

The Library of Congress has established a Cataloging-in-Publication record for this title.

ISBN: 978-0-7393-7765-9

www.randomhouse.com/largeprint

FIRST LARGE PRINT EDITION

10 9 8 7 6 5 4 3 2 1

This Large Print edition published in accord with the standards of the N.A.V.H.

FOR ZOE

LESLIE

BECAUSE IT WAS still afternoon, because she was in a strange room, because she was napping rather than sleeping ("I'll just lie down for a bit and see what happens," she'd told Pierce)—because of all this, she was aware of herself as she dreamed, at some level conscious of working to subvert the dream she was having, to make it come out another way, different from the way it seemed to be headed.

She was trying to get to Gus, that was the idea. Somehow she knew that he was far away and by himself, that he was in trouble. It was one of those dreams of turning wrong corners, of ending up in nightmare neighborhoods or in twisting empty corridors, of searching in vain. A dream of haste, too. Yes, now she understood that she was late, terribly late. She was trying to run, but her legs were thick and heavy, hard to move.

Oh, this is classic, she thought, floating over the whole mess. **This is so predictable.**

Let's not, she thought.

And it worked. For here was Gus, suddenly, conjured by her, **shoved** into the dream where he wasn't yet supposed to be—she still had miles to go. He looked younger than he'd been when last she'd seen him in life. He was smiling fondly at her.

"I'm sorry to be late," she said. This came out oddly because, she realized abruptly, she was weeping.

"Oh, you're always late," he said, carelessly, affectionately; and she woke up.

It simply wasn't true, what he'd said—she was never late—and this accusation, even so lightly made, this was the part of the dream that left her most disconcerted. She lay in the wide bed, the sensation of weeping still with her—in her throat, her chest—and looked around the room. The hotel room.

They were in Boston, in an expensive hotel overlooking the Public Garden. She had booked it. She had even specified the floor—high up enough to be looking across into the trees. It must have been four-thirty or later, she thought. It was dusky outside and the room was deep in shadows. She could hear voices in the hall, the women who turned down the beds, most likely. They were lingering, chatting out there. It was a language she couldn't understand, full of guttural sounds. Portuguese maybe. A jewel-bright stripe of light glowed at the bottom of the door. One of them laughed.

She was alone in the room. Pierce had gone to the Museum of Fine Arts, to a show she had read about in the paper and suggested to him—she wanted him to have something to do in the city that he enjoyed, too. It was a show of Japanese prints called the Floating World, prints of the life of the theater and the world of courtesans from the eighteenth and nineteenth centuries. Apparently it included some never-before-displayed erotica, described as fantastic in its inventiveness. It was on account of this that she'd recommended it to Pierce. Just his cup of tea, she'd said to him.

"You're sure you don't want to go?" he'd asked as he was about to leave. "You're not drawn by the prospect of those immense **members** being waved about?" He swung his arm wide. "Poked here and there?"

"I get my fill of immense members at home. I don't need to go to the MFA for that."

He had smiled, surprised at her, and then taken a formal bow before he exited, wearing his old tweed overcoat. She had told him recently that he looked like a panhandler in it—and he did, even when he was wearing the fancy leather gloves she'd given him for his birthday, as he had been today.

He didn't care, he'd said. "And we could always use the dough."

He would be back soon, she supposed. She should get up and try to make herself look more presentable.

But she didn't right away. She lay with her eyes closed, thinking of the version of Gus she had invented in the dream. Why do we alter them in the way we do? Why make him so young, so happy?

Erasing it, she supposed. The way he'd died. The awfulness of it. Its solitariness, as she thought of it, though he'd hardly been alone.

Gus was her brother, younger by fourteen years. He would have been forty-five now if he'd lived. He'd died six years earlier. For the most part she'd stopped thinking, or even dreaming, about the moment of his death, the exact way it happened, which she was grateful for. But she still dreamed of him, and she was grateful for this, too. In this after-noon's dream he seemed to have been in his early twenties—handsome, smiling, teasing her. That was his age at the point in their lives when they'd been closest. Before then she hadn't paid much atten-tion to him, he was so much younger—four years old when she went off to college, eleven when she married.

But a few years after that, when Gus was still in high school and she and Pierce were first living in New Hampshire, their parents divorced and things changed. Their father moved to California and dis-appeared, though for a few years he still called her occasionally late at night—midevening his time—loaded, weepy, full of useless and temporarily felt love. The first few times he did this she had stayed on the phone with him as long as he wanted to talk.

She had imagined finding some way back to the affection that had existed between them when she was a girl.

But nothing happened as a result of the calls, nothing changed. They began and ended the same way each time, as if he had no memory of the one before. And probably he didn't. Probably he had some vague notion when he woke the next day that he'd talked to **someone** he knew. Maybe he even remembered it was Leslie. But he clearly remembered nothing specific—not the promises to visit, not the pleas for forgiveness. In the end she started turning off the phone when she and Pierce went to bed.

Their mother moved into a one-bedroom apartment after the divorce, and Gus slept on a daybed in the living room. When he went away to college, she gave the bed to the Salvation Army and bought a real couch—she was tired of not having what she called "a decent place to entertain"—and that became Gus's bed when he was home. She was dating by then, and often didn't come back to the apartment at night at all, so Gus would wake alone in the morning, fix his own breakfast, and start calling his old high school friends for company.

Pretty quickly he stopped going home on school vacations and began to come instead to stay with her, to stay in the house just across the river into Vermont that she and Pierce had bought a few years after he got the job at Dartmouth-Hitchcock. They gave a room over to him, and he slowly began to accumulate stuff in it—books, sports equipment, records and tapes and posters. After college, he'd gone to work in Boston, but he still came home regularly—home to Pierce and Leslie's house.

It was over these years that Leslie came to know him, to love him as a person, not just as the cute little brother. She understood that some of this had to do with her inability to get pregnant, for those were also the years when she and Pierce were trying, and failing, to have children. She was, she supposed, depressed most of that time. At any rate, she felt she was learning how deeply life can disappoint you, how all that's good can become bad—for she and Pierce had turned away from each other then, and why not? when the most joyous, intimate connection between them had become enforced, more or less a topic for public discussion with doctors, with nurses—a matter simply of successful or unsuccessful function.

Unsuccessful, as it turned out.

And here came Gus, so sunny, so full of his boyish eagerness for life, so assured that all would always be well for him, that luck would follow him everywhere. He had a friend from college, Peter, who was also working in Boston, and he sometimes came up with Gus on weekends, or for holidays. "The fun boys," they called themselves. And they were fun. The smallest things delighted them. Her maternal fussiness, which Gus had once stopped by imitating a hen's clucking back at her. The response of an orderly, careful friend when they called to ask him to join them at a bar: "You mean . . . **now**?" When one or both of them were visiting, Leslie would stay up late playing Yahtzee or Monopoly, watching Johnny Carson, drinking, laughing.

Lying in the gray fading light of the hotel room now, she was remembering going for a walk with Gus in a snowstorm around midnight one night over a Christmas holiday. They had been talking in the living room and seen the flakes suddenly thicken dramatically in the lighted air outside the windows. "Let's go," he said, and without hesitation she pulled on her boots, her parka, her mittens, and stepped outside with him. She could feel it again now, she could call it up so clearly, the sense she had then of being enclosed in a private world with her brother—the flakes a kind of particulate blur, the ground beneath them turning quickly white, the rest of the world silenced and remote. **I am so happy,** she had thought. And part of that was the dearness to her of Gus, and the sense of how precious she was to him. When she had come in later and gone upstairs to her bedroom—her and Pierce's bedroom—it felt musty, closed in, the noise of Pierce's slow breathing in sleep somehow oppressive.

All of this, she saw now—and actually knew even then—borne of loss. Made possible by their parents' moving off separately into their lives, by Pierce's retreat from her during these years, by her own feelings of failure and the resultant wish to live once again with a sense of possibility. Or near a sense of possibility, at any rate. Near Gus.

"Possibility." She whispered the word aloud into the twilit air of the hotel room. And smiled, looking up at the shadowed ceiling, at the steady pass of headlights across it. "Possibility." What a funny, crotchety-sounding word for something so humanly necessary.

But was it necessary? She turned on her side in bed. Weren't there people, everywhere, who lived without it? Who didn't imagine anything other than **what was**?

She thought not. She thought everyone needed it—some sense that things would be better, might be better, soon. Or one day. She thought of immigrants, the way they worked two or three jobs to make something different possible for their children. It seemed one always wanted better for one's children. That was surely one version of it—possibility. Perhaps one wanted better for oneself, too. Perhaps even for one's religious group: the world converted to Christianity. The caliphate restored, spread. **One hundred virgins waiting for you.**

She sat up. Her mouth tasted sour, fuzzy. She fumbled for the switch to the lamp on the bedside table. When it came on, the window snapped to black, and here it was, the lushly carpeted room—the heavy, striped curtains at the window, the solid, dark, expensive-yet-undistinguished furniture, furniture such as no one would ever have in a real home.

She got up and went into the vast marbled bathroom. She brushed her teeth. Afterward she took a long look at herself in the mirror over the double sink, and then at her image reflected, multiplied smaller and smaller, in the full-length mirror hung on the opened bathroom door behind her. She turned this way and that.

The image she was used to, the one that faced her over the sink and the countertop, seemed much as it had for years. Different in some ways, of course—her hair was almost all white now, and she was heavier, certainly—yet still recognizably herself. But in the unfamiliar angles, the reversed versions she could see reflected again and again in the doorway mirror, she recognized what she didn't usually have to confront—that she was getting old. Her face was set and sagging. The flesh of her neck and arms looked tired, crepey. Her hips were shapeless. Worst was that she was increasingly looking like her mother—her mouth drawn down sourly into an inverted U, the flesh at her jowls pouched. This bothered her more than anything.

She thought of her mother, of taking care of her in her old age. When she'd gone to visit her, to take her for a walk or a drive or out to lunch, her mother would have dressed herself carefully, she would be wearing makeup, her eyes done heavily and with an unsteady hand that made her look, Leslie always thought, like the David Levine cartoon of the elderly Colette.

Clearly the point of all that effort was to look attractive, and, most of all, to look attractive for Leslie. She wanted to be pleasing to her daughter. She imagined that they'd reconciled, she assumed that Leslie's thoughtful caring for her was a sign of that.

She was wrong. Leslie held every small kindness she performed for her mother against her. Every single generous act was a kind of dagger. A **shiv,** Leslie thought.

How mean she was, really! She didn't have the courage to act on it, but she was. She didn't like it in herself.

Now she went to the closet by the door to the hall and got her coat. She had to search the room's surfaces for the plastic key card. It was on the bureau, under her purse. She would buy some flowers. A big bouquet for the room, to make it feel more theirs. Pierce would like that—she could picture his surprised face, opening in delight. And then it occurred to her that she should get something smaller, too, something she could easily take with her tonight— perhaps rosebuds, she thought. Rosebuds for Billy, for after the play.

She stepped into the thickly carpeted hall and pulled the door shut after her. Silently she made her way to the elevator, every noise muffled. You could kill someone in here, and no one would hear it. The notion made her smile.

Downstairs, though, the lobby was busy, noisy,

and alive. Over its bustle, Leslie could hear the tinkle of the cocktail piano floating in from the room where people sat having tea or drinks. Someone was playing "Mountain Greenery."

The cool dampness struck her as soon as she stepped outside. She loved this—the heaviness of the air in Boston, the smell of the sea. Tonight there was a fine mist of rain not so much falling as floating in the air. It was fully dark now, the early dusk deepened by the weather.

She walked slowly down Newbury Street, congested with people getting out of work or shopping, stopping for a drink. She had to weave her way around them sometimes, the groups of three or four walking abreast. The storefronts threw their beckoning light onto the glistening brick sidewalks. The bars were full, their soft lights warm, inviting. Leslie walked past them slowly, trying to imagine what such a life would be like. To sit, as she saw a woman doing now, perched on a bar stool in a crimson suit, turned sideways, her long legs on display, chatting to the two men who stood behind her, each in a suit, a tie. How did it feel? The woman threw her head back to laugh, either in pure pleasure or in the wish to convey pure pleasure, and the men shifted slightly, or so Leslie thought. It seemed to her they looked, for a moment, predatory. But then she was past the window.

The flower shop was in the next block. Leslie came down the short flight of stairs from the street and opened the heavy glass door.

It was cool, almost as cool as outside, and full of the fresh scent of greens, of flowers. There were several outsize bouquets set out on tables, but most of the flowers were separated by type in tall galvanized buckets staged around the room. There was no concession to the season—she saw tulips, delphiniums, hyacinths, long arching branches laden with lilacs. The two girls working in the shop were busy, one talking to a woman, leading her from one cluster of flowers to another, naming them. The other shop-girl was wrapping some amazing long-stemmed fringed tulips for a man. Leslie met her eye and the girl nodded very slightly, acknowledging that she'd seen Leslie, that Leslie would be next.

She moved around the room by herself. Lilies, she was thinking. They had yellow and pink ones, but also a bucket of immense, fragrant Casa Blanca lilies, and those were her favorites. So, for the hotel room, lilies, and maybe this bell-shaped blue flower clustered on a long stem—she thought it might be a kind of campanula.

And then what for Billy? In the refrigerator she saw roses, tall ones in every shade except blue and black, it seemed, but her eye was caught by the smaller ones, sprays of tightly held little flowers just beginning to open, several in a pink so pale as to be almost flesh colored. Almost exactly what she'd imagined beforehand.

When it was her turn, she announced her choices. The girl, very pretty in a plain gray sweater and black skirt, pulled the lilies and campanula—

Prichard's variety, she said—out of their buckets and held them up, dripping, in a loose arrangement for Leslie to see.

"Yes," Leslie said. "They're beautiful."

She had to wait while the girl wrapped them, while she cut the rosebuds slightly shorter and inserted each stem into its little plastic water holder. Then she tied their stems with a broad green grosgrain ribbon and wrapped them, like the larger bouquet, in clear, shiny cellophane.

Walking back, Leslie had a sense of largesse, of generosity, enriched by the heady scent she carried with her. When she passed the bar where she'd seen the girl in the red suit, she looked over. One of the men was sitting next to her now, and their heads were close together, talking. The other man, the one who'd lost, as she thought of it, had disappeared.

In the hotel she stopped at the concierge's desk to ask for a vase to be sent up to the room, and then she got into the elevator with two women, possibly her own age—she wasn't good at guessing that anymore. They were expensively dressed, perfectly made up and coiffed. They both had hair of almost the same color, the ashy blond that women going gray or white often chose. They cried out at the flowers' beauty and bent over them to breathe their perfume.

The women got out on the third floor, and Leslie rode up the rest of the way alone. She walked to the room down the broad, empty hall. The crinkling of the cellophane was the only sound.

When she opened the door, she could hear Pierce

in the shower. The air in the room felt humid. She laid the flowers down on the bureau top. She hung up her coat and then his, which he'd thrown across the bed. His shirt he'd draped over a chair back. His pants were neatly folded over that. He was singing tunelessly in the bathroom, though she thought the song might be "Shipoopi." He'd been whistling it at home earlier today. He'd said he couldn't get it out of his brain for some reason, though he'd never even liked it.

She went to stand by the window. From here she could look down at the people walking along Boylston Street or disappearing into the Public Garden under the trees, bare trees for the most part—the oaks were still thick with leaves. The moving figures were anonymous, sexless. Just dark shapes, full of mystery for Leslie.

A woman from housekeeping interrupted her dreamy state. Leslie took the vase from her at the door. She filled it with water in the little bar sink, and then unwrapped the bigger bouquet. When she'd arranged the flowers, spreading them in a wide arc, she set the vase on the desk. Then she took the cellophane off the rosebuds, too. It had occurred to her she couldn't take them wrapped as they were to the play—they would make too much noise.

Pierce emerged in the hotel's white bathrobe, his flesh slightly pinked from the heat of the water. He stopped at the lily arrangement. "Ah," he said. "So this is where you were. Lovely." He smiled at her.

Then he picked up the bouquet. "And what's this?" He waggled it. "Someone getting married?"

It was true, she thought. It did look like the kind of bouquet a bride would carry. Had she been thinking such a thing? She could feel herself blushing. "It's just something for Billy, to congratulate her— on the play, you know."

"That's more than generous of you."

"Oh, I don't think so."

"It is. Don't argue." He was going through the bureau drawers, getting out clean underwear, a fresh shirt, dark socks.

"I do argue. It's just . . . courteous, really. A new play opening, that's something to celebrate. And we're old friends. We should probably do more, when you think about it."

"When **you** think about it."

"You disagree?"

"Ah, Leslie, I don't know. I don't care, in fact. It's generous. It's like you. And it seems unnecessary to me. Maybe it's time you . . . let her go, as it were."

He unfurled his shirt. The creases where it had been folded were sharp on the expensive fabric he liked the feel of. Odd, the things Pierce cared about and didn't care about.

"I'm not holding on to her." Her voice sounded childish and defensive, even to her own ear.

"I didn't say you were."

"Well, that would be the opposite of 'letting her go,' wouldn't it?"

He looked over at her, his face not unkind, but distant. How clearly he saw her! How well he knew her! Sometimes she hated him.

"There are all kinds of possibilities between holding on and letting go," he said.

"Oh, 'possibilities,' " she said.

He looked at her again, and then away.

She watched him as he shed the robe, dropping it onto the bed. He was so casual about revealing his body, so offhand! But he could afford to be. He took good care of himself. He was tall and big-boned with a handsome, hawkish face and hair barely touched with gray, and though his flesh, like hers, was creased and stippled here and there, underneath it he was still firmly muscled. He worked out several times a week.

"Wouldn't you say asking Sam along is a way of letting go?" she said.

"I thought you said you'd asked him along because you wanted to see him after all this time. Because you thought he'd enjoy the play."

"Well, and also I thought it might be a kind of signal from me, if Billy needed one."

"What do you mean? What kind of signal?"

She shrugged. "Just that it would be more than okay by me if she got involved with someone else. Not that I'm fixing her up, just that I would understand if she were interested in someone else. It might be time."

"Time!" He snorted. "I suspect she's long since been 'involved,' as you put it, with someone else.

Multiple someones, would be my guess." He was buttoning his shirt, looking at himself in the mirror. "I don't think she needs your permission for that."

"Still, she might need my permission to acknowledge it to me, or publicly. And I suppose that is part of why I asked Sam. **And** I thought he'd like the play. **And** I wanted to see him myself."

"Okay," he said. He disappeared into the bathroom, but left the door open.

"How was the show?" she called.

He stuck his head out around the door frame. He was grinning. "Very interesting. **Very.**" He waggled his eyebrows up and down. "I'm sorry you weren't there. Though first I had to make my way past more kimonos than you could shake a stick at."

She smiled.

As she started to change her own clothes, she was thinking about Billy. She was nervous, a little, about seeing her. That was always true, for reasons she didn't care to examine too closely. But this time she was also nervous about seeing her play. Pierce had said something about it—that he was surprised she wanted to see it, given the subject matter.

Oh, she would see anything of Billy's, she had said. And this was a different setting, a different idea entirely.

The last time she'd seen Billy had been more than a year earlier, in New York. A year. So much for holding on to her. She should have reminded Pierce of that, of just how long it had been.

Billy had gone to the city for an awards ceremony, and Leslie had taken the train down from White River Junction to have lunch with her the next day, to congratulate her. She'd won a prize for her writing. Not, she'd said at lunch with Leslie, for any particular play, but for a body of work. She'd given this a funny emphasis, she'd smiled at Leslie as she'd said it.

"But what's the joke?" Leslie had asked. "You do have a body of work."

"I suppose so." She sat back, frowning. "But that's just so not the way I think of it. To me it's always just . . . the next play, and the next, and the next. Each quite separate from the last. It's strange to think of them as being part of any kind of a whole." She had looked off, down the quiet street. "I can't imagine it, actually—thinking that way about your own work." They were sitting at one of three tables on the brick sidewalk outside a little restaurant in the West Village. She lifted her shoulders. "Though maybe that comes along, when you've done enough. You sort of look back and say, 'Oh, so **that's** what I was up to, all along.'"

"But it's never just one thing you've been up to, is it?"

Billy laughed. She had a nice laugh, Leslie had always thought this about her. She remembered the first evening she'd met her, when Gus brought her up to Vermont. They were sitting outside in the backyard. Pierce had told a joke, and then Gus and Billy had each told several, and part of the pleasure of listening to them was hearing Billy's surprised-sounding, delighted laughter after each one. It seemed **generous** to Leslie. It made her like Billy even before she knew anything about her.

"Well, **I** don't think so," Billy said now. "But it seems the critics may. 'Oh, here she comes, doing that again.' When for me each one feels completely different."

"But I suppose what you expose is your . . . your temperament, in the end."

Leslie had startled herself, saying this. She hadn't quite realized that that's what she thought. But as she spoke, she understood it, that she'd recognized something about Billy, something that surprised her, when she saw the plays. In fact, she'd only seen two before the one they were to see tonight, but they definitely had shared some quality. Hardheadedness, she'd said to Pierce later. Toughness, he thought. Surprising, they both felt, when Billy in person was so accommodating, so easy.

Oh, every now and then with Gus you caught a glimpse of it—a flash of irritation at something he said, a cool withdrawal for a while after he offered an opinion that she apparently found questionable. And there was that one time when they were talking about movies they'd seen lately and he was describing one he'd liked. Where had they been? Some restaurant, she thought. Probably in Hanover, one of the times Billy and Gus came up to see them.

Gus's face was lively as he talked, but Leslie noticed that Billy seemed not to be responding to him. She looked impatient, actually. When he had finished, she said, "You should probably provide attribution for remarks like that, dear heart."

Gus's face changed. Closed up.

After a moment, Leslie asked, "Remarks like what, Billy?"

Billy turned to her, cheerful, even impish. "Remarks lifted wholly or in part from someone else's **brain,**" she said.

After his death, though, there hadn't been anything like that. She'd been stunned, nearly dumbstruck, in her grief. And her grief had seemed never ending. Even at their lunch last year she had spoken of it. They had almost finished, the table's white paper was dotted with red wine stains and translucent circles where drops of olive oil had fallen on it. Leslie could feel sharp crumbs under her arms where she rested them.

She had reached over and touched Billy's hand, lightly. "How are you doing?" she asked. They came to this point each time they saw each other.

"Oh, I'm fine," Billy said with a carelessness that seemed deliberate to Leslie.

"I'm so glad," Leslie had answered. (**You see, Pierce?** Even then she had wanted to give Billy permission. **Move on,** she had been about to say, hadn't she? Something like that. **Live your life.**)

Then Billy had said, "But I will never get over it. I won't." Her voice was fierce. Angry, even. Leslie was startled. Billy had raised her hand then to hold off whatever she might have said in response.

Well, of course Leslie would never get over it either, but at this point she could finally think of Gus without the anguish she'd felt for years. In fact, she often thought now that the pleasure she'd come to take again in her own life had brought him back to her, somehow. This play tonight—she could imagine how thrilled he would have been to be going. And where that thought would once have been a cause for the bitterest grief on her part, now she felt it as connected to her enjoyment of the evening—she felt she was going **for** him and, therefore, in a sense, with him. She stood in front of the mirror, holding her necklace in her hands, not seeing her own reflection. She was thinking of Gus, of how vital, how alive he'd been. Her own return to life, to **aliveness,** was in honor of him, she felt. Everything she noticed, everything she did, he was part of.

Pierce didn't understand this. He thought she was being morbid when she continued to speak of Gus so often two years, three years, after his death. He had said she was dwelling in it. She'd stopped trying to explain that it had changed for her, that she felt it differently. But by now she'd stopped talking about him at all to Pierce unless he brought up Gus's name first.

Now Pierce began to sing again, breaking the

spell. She raised the necklace to her throat, held it in place. Would it draw attention to her neck, or deflect it? Pierce crossed behind her, and she asked him.

He paused, gazed critically at her, tilting his head. "Wear it," he said.

Completely avoiding the question. How like him! She fumbled with the clasp, finally got it, and then went into the bathroom to apply her makeup. As she used the eyeliner, the shadow, the words to Pierce's song were running through her head. "Little old Sal was a no gal, as anyone could see. Look at her now, she's a go gal . . ."

"Do you want to walk?" Pierce asked from the other room.

"No. There are those brick sidewalks, and I'm wearing high heels."

"So?"

"So they get stuck between the bricks. You risk falling. Let's take a cab." She ran the lipstick over her mouth and blotted it. There. She was done. She looked at herself critically. It helped, she thought. A bit.

In the elevator, she asked him, "Are you looking forward to this?" She was watching his reflection in the shiny brass doors.

"I'm sure it'll be good, but you know how I feel about the theater."

She did. She'd heard it many times. Practically every time they went to a play. They were all **over**

the top, too much. What he hated, basically, was that the theater was theatrical. He preferred movies, their naturalism, the fact that people could speak as softly as they did in real life. And there was no spittle flying around either—that was very important to him.

"And I'll be glad to see Sam, of course." He turned to her and smiled. "And Billy." The doors had opened, and they were crossing the lobby again.

Outside, the doorman signaled for a cab, and she and Pierce got in. At the corner, they turned right, into the theater district, such as it was. But these were the big theaters, the ones for touring musicals, or **The Nutcracker** at Christmas. Billy's play was at a new, small theater in the South End. Leslie looked out the window, turned away from Pierce. It was nice of him to have said he looked forward to seeing Billy. She knew he had mixed feelings about her, feelings he'd been more honest about before Gus died. Afterward, her obvious pain had silenced him.

The cabdriver said something, something she didn't understand. She looked at Pierce, frowning, questioning. He gestured, shook his head, and she looked back at the driver just as he spoke again. He was wearing one of those earpieces that were telephones, she saw it now.

The language he was talking was unrecognizable to her. Another foreign tongue. As she relaxed back in the seat, she thought of how small, how parochial, their world was, hers and Pierce's. A New

England village, forty-five minutes from a New England university town. Far, far away from this new, polyglot version of America.

They turned down a dark, narrow street in the South End. Leslie looked up at the lighted windows in the old bowfront town houses they passed. Billy lived here, in this neighborhood, in a parlor apartment with high windows like these. It was just about as different from the place she had lived in with Gus as it could be. But Leslie thought that was probably the point. Some of it, anyway.

The cab pulled up at the curb outside the restaurant. After Pierce paid, they got out and crossed the glistening brick terrace to its entryway.

Inside it was light and warm, a haven against the dark rainy night. The walls were a buttery yellow, the wood trim everywhere a dark green. Leslie had a sense of familiarity and comfort whenever they came here, and they always came here for dinner on their infrequent trips to Boston. There were dozens of newer restaurants that she routinely clipped reviews of, that she attempted to persuade Pierce to try, but he always insisted on Hamersley's. In this case, though, it made practical sense—it was only steps away from the new theater, the one where Billy's play was being performed. And now that they were here, she was glad, as usual, that they'd come.

It was early for dinner, so early that the tables were only about a third full. They nursed their before-dinner drinks—dry vermouth on the rocks for Leslie, vodka for Pierce. Always the same. They'd joked more than once that between them they had the fixings for one terrible martini.

She started to try to explain to Pierce the feeling she'd had in the cab, listening to the driver speaking a language she didn't recognize on his cell phone. She mentioned the women talking in their slightly-more-familiar-sounding-but-still-unidentifiable-foreign language in the hotel hall.

"Your point being?" he asked.

"Oh, I don't know. How insular our lives are, I guess."

"In some way, I suppose." He sounded begrudging.

"How are they **not,** Pierce?"

He looked down at his vodka. After a moment he said, "Well, don't we know **very** well a kind of economic cross-section of people? More than you would in a city, I think. I mean **because** it's a village. Because we haven't sorted ourselves out economically by neighborhoods. And we also know very well a lot of people across the generations for the same reason—the kids running around, plus our ancient neighbors, too." He shrugged. "It's a kind of trade-off, I suppose. I'll take it."

Case dismissed. She felt a little rise of irritation at him.

But now, as if to apologize—or maybe to remind her of her attachment to the world they lived in, he asked about the Christmas book sale she was organizing at the town library.

This was sweet of him, and in response to that, she

made him laugh by describing how the old ladies on the committee had whisked away the donated books they were most interested in. But she had taken one, too, she confessed, and started reading it. Was liking it. A novel about the life of the office, told, amazingly, in the first person plural.

They talked about how unlikely a subject for a novel this was, office life. Pierce mentioned a Joseph Heller book that he'd admired years earlier, another **office** book. Then he started talking about what he was reading now, a book predicting economic disaster looming for the country.

All the while Leslie was intermittently thinking about the evening to come. The play, of course, but then the drink with Sam afterward, Sam and Billy. Billy had said she'd probably be a little late. The play was still in previews, and she had told Leslie on the phone that if there were notes the director wanted to go over, she'd want to sit in on that. So she'd arrive last, most likely. Leslie could imagine it, seeing her again across some room, so small, so lost-looking and waiflike.

"A waif with a spine of steel," Gus had said. Of course that was true, too. She was driven, she was competitive.

But Leslie had seen the other side of her at Gus's memorial service—her white skin almost gray, her lips bitten—actually bleeding at one point. Leslie had given her a Kleenex to blot the blood. She hadn't cried, at least not that Leslie saw, but she was so silent, so inheld, that it had frightened Leslie. She hadn't wanted to leave her alone. She had asked her to come up and stay with them for a while, but Billy had said no. She said she needed to stay in Boston, to work. She needed to settle into her new apartment. Leslie had seen it a week or so before the service—a big empty space. She had only a bed, and a desk to work at. She hadn't taken anything from Gus's apartment. She said she couldn't, she wanted to start over. Leslie had hated to think of her there, alone, but Billy was absolute. The spine of steel, indeed.

Pierce was talking happily about a patient of his, an eight-year-old boy whom he'd been treating for Ewing's sarcoma. He'd been in a cheerful mood for weeks because of what was pretty clearly this child's remission. They spoke now, as they occasionally did, of the strange serenity and maturity of kids with cancer, of the way it changed them and their families. Of the gift it could sometimes seem— unsought, unwelcome of course, and yet real and remarkable.

When she had met Pierce, he was already well along in his residency in a field—pediatric oncology—that she would have tried to dissuade him from if she'd known him earlier. It seemed too sad, too hard, to her. And as she began to think of him more seriously, to imagine being married to him, she worried about how this work might affect him—and therefore her—over time. How could he do it every day, she'd asked him. Accept the fact that so many of them, these beautiful little children, would die?

At first he had explained his choice to her in ways that seemed simply logical, reasonable. He talked about the children who survived and the extraordinary satisfaction they gave him. And even with the ones who didn't, he said, there were the rewards of giving the families as much time with their kids as possible.

Only later, when he knew her much better, did he speak of what he saw as the beauty of the whole experience. He said that: **beauty.** He seemed almost shy, talking about it—big, jovial Pierce. She was touched by that. He spoke of the sense he had of being witness, over and over, to something spiritual in its nature, even when the children died. He said that it seemed to bring forward all that was brave and selfless in everyone involved, even the children themselves. He said he felt privileged to be any part of it.

They had this conversation at his parents' vacation house in Maine. The two of them had been swimming briefly in the unbearably cold water. They were lying on the warm wooden planks of the dock in their wet suits. Pierce was turned to face her. He was squinting into the sun as he spoke—frowning, searching for words. The dried salt water had whitened in the creases by his eyes. She had never seen him so serious. She hadn't known that he could be.

And even sometimes now when Pierce irritated her with his jokiness, what seemed his unwillingness to take almost anything seriously, she had only to call up the way he had spoken of his work that day, how he had looked—or to think of the way he was sometimes emptied, silenced for days after a patient's death—to be reminded of her deepest feelings for him. She'd seen him then as wise, as deep. She'd had a sense of his having a greater understanding of death, of the price of love, particularly parental love, than she had. And of course all that was true of him.

But he was also only Pierce. That was the thing she'd had to learn. He was the person he seemed to be—dismissive, flippant—as well as the person who understood how pain can change you. The surprise of this two-sidedness was something that still, always, had the power to wound her. She guarded herself against it, she supposed, the way she guarded herself against everything difficult or painful—by being loving, by being solicitous.

But how she had counted on him after Gus's death! To understand her grief, to allow it, to come into it with her. His compassionate, dispassionate sense of the familiarity of what she was going through—in spite of all that was extreme about the circumstances—was what she leaned on. Maybe she had even counted on him to expect her to emerge from it eventually, in the same way he emerged from his sorrow each time one of the children he had come to love died.

As she had. Hadn't she?

She was sitting on a little banquette against the wall, facing Pierce and the room behind him. While they talked, she'd been watching it slowly fill up, the well-dressed couples being led in, the parties of businessmen, sitting, looking at the menu, chatting.

And all along a group of people was slowly assembling at the large round table directly in back of Pierce, calling greetings to one another as they drifted in by ones and twos, embracing, catching up. As their mass grew, Pierce turned several times in his chair to give them hard looks. He didn't like it—their noise, their obliviousness of how it might be affecting others.

Even as she and he ordered their meal, as their first course was brought to them, these people were all still standing, moving around their table to talk. Their voices were loud and cheerful.

She leaned toward Pierce and said, "It's a family reunion, don't you think?"

"What luck!" he said. Or she thought that's what he said. It really was quite noisy.

They didn't try to talk for a while. Gradually the party sorted itself out, sat, and began to quiet down, talking now in twos and threes; and she and Pierce began to talk again too.

But as she had watched the family gather together, laugh together, she was thinking about Pierce, about **his** family—three older brothers and a younger sister. His parents were still alive, too, as ridiculously lighthearted, as willfully oblivious of difficulty as ever, jolly stereotypes straight out of the sentimental Dickens. The reason Pierce could be so irritated by this family's noise was that he was just that privileged, too, she thought. Because he had such a family—welcoming, loud, traditional.

Oh, there were wrinkles. His next older brother had had four wives, and one of his divorces was so messy and drawn out that it resulted in his losing almost all contact with his kids until they were grown. And no one was exactly certain of the parentage of either of his sister's two children—probably including herself, Pierce thought.

But his family's ease together, their fondness for one another, these were things he took for granted. A big family such as this one next to them—such as Leslie had wanted to make with him—this was not the miracle to him it was to her. It didn't seem a precious gift to him or seemingly to any of the others in it. They were all, like him, offhanded in their generosity and inclusiveness, so much so that the first time she'd visited, she had trouble sorting out the multiple guests from Pierce's siblings. And she herself was welcomed just as carelessly and warmly as those guests were. As Gus had been, too, eventually.

Gus. She thought of their own sad growing up—the loneliness, especially for him. The long bitter silences between their parents.

Now Pierce was asking her what she'd read about the play.

"Well, they say it's not as experimental as her earlier work."

"Ah," he said. "Good."

She waved her hand and pushed her plate slightly away. She'd finished. Or she'd eaten all she could. If they were at home, she would have asked for a doggie bag. Just as well. Pierce made fun of her for that, for her frugality.

"And the story is this terrorism stuff," he said.

"Right. Actually I tried not to read too much about it. I like a little sense of not knowing what's coming. Just what I told you—a wife maybe caught in a terrorist attack, and the family sorting out various **issues,** I guess you'd say"—she made a face—"whatever they might be, while they wait to hear."

"But it's not 9/11."

This was not a question. Pierce already knew this. He'd been careful to establish this when she proposed coming down to see the play and Billy. But she said no. Again. "No, thank goodness. She didn't write it that close to the bone."

No. She hadn't written about Gus.

When they were through, when Pierce had paid, they gathered their coats from the girl in charge of the coat check and went outside. It was raining now, and Pierce raised the umbrella over them. She took his arm. You could see the theater almost as soon as you stepped out of the restaurant. It had a silvery, space-age front, from which an unattractive dark blue marquee projected. In white letters, Billy's play was announced: THE LAKE SHORE LIMITED. They walked slowly down the wide brick sidewalk toward it.

There were people milling around under the marquee. The glass doors opened and shut, opened and shut, as the couples, the groups, drifted inside. Standing still in the midst of this activity there was a man—no raincoat, no topcoat—a tall man, in a grayish suit, with his hands in his pockets, his shoulders hunched. From half a block away, holding on to Pierce's arm, walking carefully so as not to catch her heels between the bricks, Leslie could tell it was him, it was Sam, and she felt the little jolt of pleasure that seeing him always brought her. A **frisson,** she thought.

There was a time when she'd been half in love with him. She remembered—she often remembered—an afternoon when they'd taken a walk together, when he'd kissed her. The only time he had. They'd been picking blackberries, and he tasted of them. When she'd sat down for dinner that night with Pierce, he'd asked about the long scratches on her arms, scratches from the blackberry canes. She'd lied to him. She said she'd been pruning the roses. She didn't want him to know about any part of it. It was hers alone. She was almost sad when the scratches healed.

———

She had met Sam when he and his wife Claire bought twenty acres of farmland in Vermont to build a house on. Leslie sold them the property. She was working as a real estate agent then, one of a variety of jobs she had held over the years.

She'd gotten into this pattern in her midtwenties, early in her marriage—just after they moved to Vermont. Her first job had been running the office of a local small press, but then pretty quickly she was also doing some editing for them. After that she managed a bookstore. For a few years she was a kind of glorified secretary and bookkeeper for a local opera company, then she worked in an art gallery. But what she was really doing all of that time was waiting for the life she'd envisioned for herself to start—a life of motherhood, of family. By the time she'd given up that hope, she seemed to have made a habit of changing her job every four or five years, and she'd decided she liked that. She liked the variety. She thought of it as a way to come to know a good deal about the smallish world immediately around her, to know people in its various corners.

By the early nineties, she'd more or less backed into real estate. A friend of hers who had her own small agency was shorthanded and suggested that Leslie get a license and join her, so she had. This was the way things happened with jobs, with work, for Leslie.

She enjoyed selling real estate, she found. She took pleasure in meeting new people, in helping them.

And she discovered that she was curious about houses—how they were built, how they'd been renovated and decorated. Many of the homes that she was dealing with were old, they had interesting histories, colorful past owners. She liked researching this kind of thing, and it made her a good salesperson, not surprisingly.

When Claire called, she asked Leslie about prices, about the differences among the small towns in the area. She and her husband were interested in land, she said, a minimum of ten acres so they wouldn't have to think about neighbors. Her husband, Sam, was an architect. He would design the house. It would be a large, gracious place, a place to which both of them could bring their almost-adult children from their previous marriages.

They arranged a time to get together a week or so off. This would give Leslie a chance to look around for what they wanted. Claire knew Woodstock, so they agreed to meet there for coffee before they went exploring.

Leslie was sitting on a bench outside the restaurant when they drove up in a pickup truck with a long aluminum stepladder rattling in the back. They both got out at once, swinging themselves down from the high seats.

Claire was so striking, with her white-blond hair pulled cleanly off her face into a bun at the back of her head, that Leslie hardly noticed Sam at first. She was looking at Claire's high, rounded forehead and strong features. Her face was very lined, but this only accentuated the drama of her sculpted head, her deep-set, almost-hooded eyes. She was **arresting,** Leslie would have said, describing her to anyone else.

She extended her hand, saying her name, and Leslie took it. Of course, her grip was firm, cool. She turned to introduce Sam, who was standing behind her. When Leslie looked at him, her first thought was that he must be quite a bit younger than Claire. He was tall, a nice-looking man with a long, slightly crooked nose, a narrow face, and floppy brown hair just going gray. He wore wire-rimmed glasses, a scholar's glasses. She had always considered these an affectation. Later she would learn from him that it was the weightlessness of them he liked. That the pressure of any other kind of glasses on his nose gave him a headache.

He had a lively face. There was something avid in it—eager for life, ready to be amused. He and Claire were dressed alike, as if in a uniform—crisp jeans and light khaki jackets with multiple pockets.

They drank their coffee, and Leslie told them about the properties they would look at. Two were old farms, their fields growing over with pine and maple saplings and thick brush. The third was mostly in woods, which would offer a great view if cleared. "Of course," she said, "the trees are almost all second growth up here, so even the woods were **once** somebody's farm." She was aware of a kind of pride in talking about this: her world. "In the middle of what seems just forest, there are stone fences crisscrossing everywhere. Somebody's ancient field, somebody's property line. Some claim we don't know anything about anymore."

"So much for the illusion of ownership," Sam said.

Leslie laughed. "Well, precisely. But I'm in the business of selling that illusion."

Leslie paid, though Sam had taken his wallet out. "Don't be silly," she said. "This is part of my job."

Claire came in Leslie's car—the noise of the ladder had bothered her all the way up, she said—and Sam followed in the truck. While Leslie drove, they talked. Leslie learned a great deal about Claire, about her life. She and Sam had been married for two years. Claire taught some combination of ethics and political science at Harvard; Leslie couldn't quite figure it out. She talked about her children, about living in Cambridge. Leslie was dismissive about her own life, and Claire didn't seem inclined to press her for details. In the rearview mirror, Leslie could see the green truck behind them, sometimes dropping back, sometimes pulling closer at turns, at stop signs. Sam's face retreated, then approached, sober and blankened in his solitude.

At the first farm, they all got out to walk the boundaries. But the ground was muddy—it had rained the night before—and Claire wasn't wearing boots. They'd only gone a hundred yards or so when she turned back.

Sam and Leslie hiked on together, Leslie going

ahead in the wooded parts, pointing out the fallen limbs they'd have to step over, holding back the branches, the thorny whips that might have caught at them. Sam asked questions, mostly about the land—the old farm, its history—but also about her. Leslie found herself talking easily about her life, her "pickup life," she called it.

When they got back to where they'd parked, in the open field next to the tall stand of lilac bushes that marked the location of the original house, Claire got out of Leslie's car, where she'd been waiting. Sam went to the truck and got his stepladder out. He told them he'd be a little while; he wanted to check some of the possible sight lines.

They watched as he lurched away, bent a little to the side carrying the ladder. Claire said, "Ah, Sam. This is what he believes in."

"What?" asked Leslie. She looked over at Claire, at her stern, noble profile. There was a little smile playing on her lips.

"That it actually makes a difference—what you look at, the space you live in, **where the windows are.**" She said this last with a heavy emphasis, as if Leslie must of course agree with her that it made no difference at all where the windows were.

This was odd, Leslie thought. It made her uncomfortable.

After a few minutes of standing around, shuffling their feet with their hands in their pockets, Leslie suggested they get in the car. She ran the engine for a while every now and then to warm them up. Their conversation seemed suddenly desultory and empty to Leslie. She was struck by how much easier it had been to talk to Sam. They could see him out in the overgrown field from time to time, his head and upper body appearing above the apple trees or the spindly maples, the short scrubby pines. He seemed to have a small camera with him—at any rate, he occasionally lifted his hands in front of his face and turned this way and that, as if to frame a picture or a view. Sometimes he seemed to write something down.

Sam came by himself the next time, to look at the place he'd liked best once more, and then two other new ones she thought he should see. When he and Claire made an offer, Leslie dealt with him exclusively. When they negotiated back and forth a bit, he was the one she called. He came alone to the closing, with a power of attorney to sign Claire's name. Leslie didn't see Claire again for a year and a half, until the house was almost finished.

As they were leaving the closing, Sam asked her to have a drink with him to celebrate. She was charmed and agreed, and then was even more charmed that he was talking about a bottle of champagne that he'd brought along with him in a cooler in his truck. They drove to the site, and he opened the bottle and poured them each a glass—he'd brought these along, too, tall, expensive glasses that chimed when they touched them together. They sat in the truck and sipped champagne and talked easily and loosely, jumping from the names of builders Leslie knew of, their strengths and weaknesses, to his neighbors up and down the dirt road, to his kids and Claire's, to Pierce and his work. They finished the bottle as the sky turned the chilly purple of a quick winter dusk. He took her home as it grew dark—she was too tipsy to want to drive. He stayed for dinner with her and Pierce.

After that, though, when he came up to walk the land, to interview contractors, to supervise the building of the house, Leslie saw him mostly by herself—for lunch, for coffee, for a walk through the house as it took shape. He did come over to her house for a drink or dinner with her and Pierce several times—Pierce enjoyed him, and Leslie would have said they were all becoming good friends. But occasionally she would be aware that she hadn't mentioned seeing Sam when she could have, perfectly easily. And when Sam told her that he and Claire were going to divorce—this just months after they'd moved their furniture into the finished house—she didn't tell Pierce about it for several weeks. She held on privately to some sense of excitement, of possibility, in the news, even while she knew nothing would change in her life because of it, or in Pierce's.

And although that was all in the past now, and probably for Sam nothing memorable—a vague feeling of sweetness and perhaps melancholy to their friendship—Leslie had a sense of renunciation in introducing Sam to Billy, a sense of giving up a thing of private value. She could never have talked about any of this to Pierce, of course. But then she couldn't have spoken of it clearly to anyone. She herself could barely grasp the conflicts among her own feelings in regard to Sam, or in her impulse to bring him and Billy together.

And in the end, she told herself, it would probably turn out that they'd all spend a pleasant evening together, and that would be that. This notion she had of offering a dear and valuable thing of her own to Billy would turn out to be misplaced. And perhaps Pierce was right—perhaps Billy had already begun again with someone else. Perhaps, as he'd also suggested, more than once. Perhaps there was a lover in her life right now.

But that didn't matter. It couldn't hurt anyone. And she wanted to do it. She didn't know why, exactly, but it was what she wanted.

"Ah!" Sam cried, seeing them. He stepped quickly across the space under the marquee. Before she could lift her arms, he had her face in his hands, he was **in charge** of it, turning it to plant a kiss very close to her mouth, now on this side, now on that. He smelled of wool, of the wet air, of some complicated gingery men's cologne or aftershave.

Now he was embracing Pierce, a bit sideways, patting his back as he did so. They were all saying things at the same time: **How wonderful, how well each one looked, it had been too long.**

As they began to move together toward the glass doors, they were trying to remember exactly how long it had been. Two years? Three? Remember the time he'd stopped by after skiing? Was that it, the last sighting?

Pierce went to get the tickets at the call window, and Leslie and Sam waited, talking. He was asking her about their weather—the dry fall, the lost leaf season. He seemed awkward, a bit shy. Maybe he was feeling something like the sense she had of disjuncture in all this.

When Pierce came back, they went together up the wide carpeted ramp to where there was a bar, people crammed in front of it ordering drinks. Leslie stood leaning her back against the wall while the two men plunged into the crowd. She watched them for a moment and then looked around her. It seemed a younger crowd than typically went to the productions in the larger theater connected with this new, more experimental one. The woman standing next to Leslie, talking with her friends about a concert of some sort, had a little diamond stud in her nose and a bluish tattoo of unidentifiable swirls that climbed down her neck and then into her sweater.

Now Pierce was by her, touching her arm. He handed her the white wine he'd ordered for her, and she sipped at it. It was sharp and cold, unpleasant. She hoped their beers were better.

Sam was saying something to Pierce about his work. Things had dried up a bit with the mortgage crunch. Two of the private houses he'd started on were on hold for now, but there was another larger project he'd gotten that would take their place—a library at a small private college north of Boston. He talked about the way he envisioned it.

Leslie had only a few sips more of her wine. The crowd in front of the bar had thinned. The men finished their glasses of beer and the three of them ambled in and found their seats. Leslie sat between Sam and Pierce. Both of them helped her arrange her coat behind her on her seat. They all began to leaf through their programs.

Leslie was reading a history of the theater's development when Sam said, "Wait." She looked up and met his eyes.

"Isn't the playwright here . . . wasn't she your brother's lover?" he asked. He had the program open to the page where Billy's bio appeared, hers and the director's, both with dramatic photos.

Leslie could feel herself flushing. "That's right," she said. She leaned over and looked at the photo more closely to give herself time to regain her composure. "She doesn't really look very much like that, though."

"I thought I remembered the name." She could feel his eyes on her. "I think I met her at his service."

"Yes, that's right." She looked at him. "I forgot that. That you might have met her then."

She turned back to her program and pretended to read on. She was remembering the service, remembering Billy that day, and now Sam.

Just before the lights went down, she thought she saw Billy come in and take a seat on the far aisle, down near the front. But the house went dark then, and she couldn't be sure. She had changed her hair, if that's who it was. It was short, sculpted around her head, with thick bangs. It made her look a bit like Louise Brooks.

As the curtain went up and the stage was revealed, the audience let out a little sigh. She'd noticed this before at a play. She thought of it as the noise of the suspension of disbelief: **Ah! Here it is, what we'll give ourselves over to for a few hours.**

The set was a living room, its couch facing the audience, the chairs at either end of the couch turned slightly forward, too, like most stage living rooms. **As though we were the fireplace,** Leslie thought. The fireplace, looking back. It was supposed to be the living room of intellectuals, you could tell by the jammed bookshelves. In places a few books were actually wedged in sideways across the tops of a shelf of vertical ones. Stacks of them sat on the little tables scattered around.

There was a large, high window at the back of the set and a balcony running along the left side of the stage above the living room, a balcony lined with more bookshelves.

And then there was a movement up there, and she focused on him: a man, sitting at a desk on the balcony, bent forward a little, reading or working at something in front of him. He drank some coffee and set the cup down in its saucer, the clink of china on china loud in the silent theater. It seemed a little too long to Leslie, these moments when nothing was happening, but then the phone rang and she jumped, so she supposed it had worked, if that was what was intended.

The man raised his head and took off his glasses, rubbed his eyes. He sat waiting through three rings. A woman's voice came on, gracious, smooth, and said, "You've reached Elizabeth and Gabriel. Leave one or both of us a message." None of that silly stuff about the beep, Leslie thought. She should do that at home.

Now another woman's voice, louder than the one they'd just heard, louder and less patrician, younger perhaps, began to speak. "Gabriel, it's me. Gabriel. Pick up. We have to talk. This is important."

A pause. The man—Gabriel, it must be—tilted back in his chair and looked up at the ceiling.

"Gabriel? Pick up. Please. Please pick up."

Gabriel got up and started down the spiral stair that led from the balcony to the living room, holding on to the rail. For a moment he stood motionless at the back of the stage.

"Gabriel?" the woman said. There was a loud sigh, and she hung up.

He came forward to a side table where the phone

sat. He pushed a button on the machine, and the message came on again. He stood listening, gazing out over the invisible audience. He was frowning, thoughtful. He was a slender man, perhaps fifty or so. He was dressed the way the owner of all those books would be—baggy corduroy pants, desert boots. An academic, Leslie assumed, though without the requisite tweed jacket. Otherwise he looked just like the Dartmouth professors who meandered the streets of Hanover.

Now he pushed another button on the machine, erasing the woman. As one can in this new world, she thought. Who had it been? A lover? A lover he was done with, maybe.

As he stood there, perhaps thinking about returning the call, there was a knocking. "Dad!" someone called, the voice sounding urgent, a man's voice. "Dad, are you there?"

Gabriel seemed frozen. He was clearly torn. He started to cross the stage, stopped. But then a look of puzzlement, or curiosity, passed over his face, and he stepped to the right rear of the stage, which Leslie couldn't quite see from where she sat. Evidently he opened a door there, because suddenly a young man burst into the room, trailed, after a few seconds, by a woman. He was talking loudly as he crossed to the front of the stage. He turned back from there to his father, to Gabriel. He was still talking, question after question. Why hadn't he answered the phone? He'd called four or five times. What the hell was he doing? Did he have any idea what was going on in the real world?

The woman with him was pretty in a pale, washed-out way: minimal stage makeup, long, straight blond hair, the kind of role Sandy Dennis would have played in Leslie's youth. She was standing by him now in front of the couch, trying to shush him, to calm him down.

But he wouldn't be silenced. He turned to her, he yelled at her, too. She stepped back, as though she'd been slapped. She and Gabriel exchanged a look. She was embarrassed by this, by being treated this way in front of anyone else. Leslie had a quick half memory of her parents, her father shouting, her mother silent, shamed.

Gabriel had by now come forward almost to the center of the stage, too, and he stood next to the couch, impassive, waiting, letting his son's ranting pass over him, as though this behavior was familiar and perhaps tedious to him. Leslie was inclined not to like him, he was so condescending. But then the son himself was overbearing, so maybe it was a natural response. Or a little dance they did together.

"Have you listened to the news?" the son was saying. "Or have you been sealed up here all morning in your . . . precious cocoon? Do you **know** what's going on?"

The woman—the son's wife, Leslie assumed—had sat on the fat upholstered arm of the chair on the left side of the stage.

Gabriel answered calmly, "I don't. But you will tell me, no doubt."

The younger man shook his head in exasperation. He knew this patronizing calm all too well. He had a full head of curly hair, which flopped around with his quick motions. He was darker than his father, and shorter, squatter. It could have been cast better in that regard, she thought. He turned to the woman. "He will never change. Why do I let you persuade me that it's even worth trying, with him?"

The couple had an exchange, voices lowered, intense, while the father crossed to an arrangement of bottles and glasses on a ledge among the bookshelves and poured himself a drink. Leslie came fully into disbelief here: she knew no one who kept bottles and glasses in the living room. The scene should have happened in the kitchen, she was thinking. Though it would have meant changing some other things.

"Just tell him," the woman was saying.

The young man turned to his father. He cleared his throat. "If I may interrupt your privacy, then," he said, a grim, unpleasant smile on his face.

Gabriel had come forward again with his drink. "Please," he said. "Do."

And then it came pouring out. The details of a bombing on a train, the Lake Shore Limited, as it pulled into Union Station. Questions, corrections, flew. The young woman was clearer about things than her boyfriend. Or husband? The father came farther forward and sat on the couch, setting his glass down on the coffee table. His face was unreadable as he asked his questions, as he listened. What became clear slowly was that his wife was supposed to have been on the train, returning from a trip. No, he hadn't heard from her. He looked frightened. Though he hadn't been picking up calls, and there were a few hang-ups.

Were there survivors? he wanted to know.

Yes, the son said. There were a couple of cars that blew up completely, and most of the train derailed, but people climbed out and some walked away. Many were hurt, some gravely, according to reports. And of course there were many dead.

Gus, Leslie thought. It **was** about Gus. His face came to her, the face from her dream earlier in the afternoon. She was sitting up very straight now. Pierce's hand had come over and was resting on hers.

Suddenly the younger man said, "I can't believe you didn't go to the station to meet her."

Gabriel's hand waved, dismissive: this wasn't important. "We agreed I wouldn't."

"I can't believe that."

Gabriel tried to persuade him this was irrelevant. That their concern should be Elizabeth now. He kept asking more questions. What time? How long had it been? Was there anyone to call?

The son explained it all again. Said he had been calling. Leslie's heart felt heavy in her chest.

Gabriel got up now and went to the back of the

stage. With his back to the audience, he poured himself another drink. He asked if either of them wanted one. The wife said she did. He poured another glass and brought it to the front of the stage, to her.

The young man—Alex—was silent, incredulous, watching this. When his father sat down again, he started to talk. He didn't mean to interrupt this, this **party**—his voice was laden with sarcasm—but they needed to think about what they were going to do.

Gabriel, the father, looked at him for a long moment.

The son looked back, defiant. "I can't believe you," he said again.

"In what sense?"

"Every sense! I can't believe you didn't go meet her."

Gabriel set his drink down. He spoke patiently, as if to a child. "Your mother and I had agreed she would get herself here. This is what we always do. Why should her travels, or mine, for that matter, when I travel, discommode both of us?"

" 'Discommode'?" The younger man was almost shouting. The woman got up, went toward him. A few people in the audience laughed. " 'Discom-mode'?"

"Alex . . . ," the woman said. She reached a hand up to his arm.

"No!" He jerked his arm away. "You pretentious fuck," he said to his father. He turned to his wife. "He's such a fuck. Such a jerk."

"Alex," she said, pleading. "This doesn't help, it doesn't help anything."

"Okay then," he said more calmly. "Okay, let me just ask. How come you weren't answering the phone? Huh?"

"I was working," Gabriel said. "I don't answer the phone when I'm working."

"Oh yeah. Work. The thing you do instead of living."

"It **is** living."

"To you, it is. Only to you."

The son started to pace, railing against his father—how absent he'd been in the young man's childhood, in spite of the fact that he was home most of the time. The things he'd missed—performances, recitals, sports events. The Great Pooh-Bah, he called his father. The Wizard of Oz. He stopped behind the couch, bent a little forward, his hands resting on its back. "The **nothing** behind the screen," he said bitterly.

Then he stopped. He seemed to gather himself. After a long moment, he came forward and sat down at the other end of the couch from his father. He started to tell a story, a story about how, as a boy, he used to love it when he got a splinter, because he was allowed then to interrupt his father at his desk, and his father would get out his kit, his tweezers and his needle, and hold Alex's hand, or his foot, and speak to him in a loving voice while he extracted it. He said he sometimes ground a splinter in deeper when he got one, so it would be harder to get out, it would take longer, and he would be able to believe for that much longer that his father actually cared about him, that he loved him.

Leslie remembered this story. This was Billy's story, Billy's story about her own father, the academic, the great man. She had called him that same thing once: **the Great Pooh-Bah.**

Onstage they all sat silent for a moment. Then Gabriel said, "Well, I did, love you." He sounded sad, as if he were mourning a precious thing lost long ago.

"Bullshit, Dad. I was calling you today, and you were screening my calls." The son laughed. "Let that be a metaphor. Let that be a metaphor for the way things are between you and I."

"Me," Gabriel said, distractedly, almost under his breath.

"What?"

" 'Between you and me.' Is correct."

The young man laughed again, bitterly. "Jesus," he said. He got up, pulling his cell phone out of his pocket. "Know what? I'm going to call around some more and see what I can find out. I'll take it to the bedroom so I don't **bother** you." He exited by the door on the left side of the stage, the one Leslie could see.

Gabriel and the woman sat for a long moment. He finally said, "Want another?" raising his glass.

"No," she said.

"No, I don't either," he said.

"Why isn't it you? Calling," she asked after a minute. She had such a small voice. Feathery, slightly nasal.

He shrugged. "Alex will find out what there is to find out. He's better at that than I am, anyway."

"But you're so . . . detached."

"No, I'm not," he said.

"But you seem to be. You seem so . . ." She was frowning. Her hands rose a little, then dropped. "You know, I've always defended you to Alex. Because I felt like I understood you. It seemed to me that you and I were a little bit like each other. Quiet." She smiled, a wistful, Sandy Dennis smile. "Quieter than Alex and Elizabeth, at least. Though that's not so hard, I guess." She gave a quick little laugh. "Less . . . overtly passionate." She paused a moment, then went on. "I remember once when we were all in Massachusetts, and they were having one of their long, great intellectual arguments, about . . ." She waved her hand. "Something. Nothing." She made a face. "**Gender** identity. Something like that. Or the Iraq War." She shook her head. "Something where you've heard both sides of the argument so often that it sets your teeth on edge. And of course Alex was being provocative, and Elizabeth was amused and above the fray, both of them loving it, almost . . . feeding lines to each other. And it just, exhausted me. Their commitment to it. It was so, stupid, really. And I remember going out onto the porch, and you were there, and we sat for a while just watching the water, with their voices rising and falling, and you said to me, just, 'More of same.' Do you remember? 'More of same.' And we both laughed. It didn't seem necessary to talk, even."

It was an offering, Leslie saw. An offering of love to him. The young woman wanted him as her father. Perhaps also, without recognizing it—that would have to be the case—as a kind of lover, too.

"But now I wonder . . . is it that you don't care about her?" She was leaning toward him. Her face was earnest, open. "About . . . anyone?"

"No, that's not it," Gabriel said, softly.

"Not what?"

"It's not the reason I'm so . . . calm, if you will."

Now he got up and went to the back of the stage to set his glass down. He turned, faced forward, and started talking. Elizabeth, he said, wasn't at all sure she wanted to stay married to him. Nor he to her, "in all candor." He kept talking as he walked slowly forward until he was standing at the back of the couch, speaking to the young woman, but looking over her head, straight at the audience. He talked about their slow withdrawal from each other over the last years, describing scenes of absence, of emptiness. He called up a time at the Massachusetts house when they had guests, and each of them, but particularly Elizabeth, was lively, was charming and talkative; and then the moment the guests' car was out of sight, they turned silently away from each other. He smiled, a strained smile. "Back to our corners. 'Show's over, folks.' "

He said the reason she'd gone off by herself to the summerhouse now was to think about all this. "And my assignment was to think about it also. Which I've done."

"And?"

"And what?"

"And your decision?"

"My decision . . . doesn't much matter now, does it?"

"But you must have felt, like, **one** way or the other."

He smiled. Laughed. It sounded like **Heemp!** to Leslie. "As you've said, I'm not a decisive man."

"But this is . . . your life. You have to know what you want."

"That's your take. Your version. In my version, I can do either thing. I can stay with Elizabeth, if that's what she wants, or I can leave."

"If that's what she wants."

"Yes."

"But what do **you** want?" Her arms lifted slightly. She was frustrated. He was irritating in his chilliness. Leslie didn't get him either.

"I don't see that it matters, now."

"God!" She spun away. "I see why Alex gets so infuriated." She picked up her glass and took a quick swallow.

"Good."

"Good! Why?"

"Because Alex needs you to see that. He needs you on his side. And I don't, my dear."

She was suddenly angry. "No, you don't need any-one on your side."

"That's right."

"Not even Elizabeth."

"I would be in trouble if I needed Elizabeth on my side. She's not. She hasn't been for a good long while."

"So it doesn't matter to you if Elizabeth is dead, it doesn't matter to you."

Leslie saw that Alex had come to stand in the door-way to the living room. He stopped there. Neither of the other two had noticed him.

"It would matter enormously to me. Enormously. But it might not change my life—what would have been my life." He paused for a moment, then said, "It might not change my theoretical life, let's say."

Alex stepped forward. "That's the only kind of life you have, Dad—theoretical."

Gabriel started, and turned to him. He smiled, sadly this time. "This would be your mother's per-spective, too."

The younger man snorted, began to talk again, but the woman interrupted, wanted to know what he'd learned.

He turned to her. He said they'd started pulling out the dead and seriously injured, that more people had arrived at hospitals, either in ambulances or on their own, that they weren't releasing names. They'd set up an information center for the families.

Everyone was silent for a moment. Then Gabriel

went to the back of the stage and turned on a small television set wedged into the bookshelves. There was a man talking, interviewing someone you couldn't see. The voices were speaking of who might have done this. The younger couple moved back and stood watching too. They listened for a few moments to the speculation. There had already been several claims of responsibility.

"Imagine wanting credit for it," the young woman said. She shook her head. "What a world."

Alex began to talk about their intention, their motivation. Trains, the Midwest: new territory, new methods. "Fuckers," he said.

"But perhaps this is how it's going to be," Gabriel said. He turned the television off. "It will be something that just **happens** from time to time." He brought up John Kerry, he said maybe he had been right when he said during his failed campaign that terrorism was like crime, something ineradicable, something to be managed, rather than eliminated. He described being in Paris with Elizabeth the fall after the Metro bombings. "We traveled everywhere together by subway—by Metro." He paused for a moment, and Leslie thought that he must have been remembering Elizabeth as she was then—perhaps even tenderly, it seemed for a half moment; but then he cleared his throat and went on to say that 9/11 wasn't different from that, really, except in scale. Alex and he began to talk about it in the abstract, theorizing about the likelihood that these terrorists had actually intended to blow up the station, too, the possibility of their being from Morocco, like the Madrid bombers, and the reasons for that; or Pakistani. Or Al Qaeda. There was something comical in this easy turn to theorizing on the part of the men, and the audience seemed to recognize this—there was mild laughter here and there.

While they were speaking this way, the woman was walking slowly back and forth across the stage, her face full of reaction to each of them, now bitter amusement, now disgust. She sometimes tried to interrupt with a phrase or two, but they paid her no real attention. They had moved to the front of the stage as they talked, facing each other for the most part, and she claimed the back of the stage, watching them. Finally she came to a halt, dead center, in front of the big stage window. "For God's sake!" she shrilled, hands on her hips. They both fell silent and turned to her. "This is Elizabeth we're talking about." Her voice quavered. She dropped her arms.

They were all quiet for a moment. Then she said softly, pleadingly, to Alex, "Your mother."

He turned a little away from her, almost a flinch.

She looked at Gabriel and said, "Your wife."

They were frozen in this tableau for a few seconds. Then the doorbell rang. As one, they turned in that direction, then looked back at each other—a kind of wild, frightened expectancy in their faces. The stage blacked out. The curtain fell.

The room filled with applause that ended quickly as the house lights came up.

Leslie bent over to pick up her purse. Over her back, in the sudden hubbub of people talking and getting up, she heard Sam say to Pierce, "Well, quite an ending—for the first act, in any case."

"Yeah," Pierce answered. They were all standing now. They moved into the aisle among the others inching back to the lobby. Pierce kept his hand on her elbow—a kind of sympathetic connection, she felt. She was grateful to him, but she was far away. She felt confused. Around her, she could hear others talking, speculating, commenting on the actors, on the arguments.

Some weren't. Some had shed the play quickly, were on to their own lives. She heard a voice say, "I wish I'd known it was going to rain today. I didn't bring an umbrella to work."

In the lobby, Pierce went to get the drinks this time, just for him and Sam. Leslie didn't want anything. She and Sam stood together.

"Is it hard, watching this?" he asked. His face was kind, concerned.

She dipped her head from side to side, equivocating. Then she said it. "Yes. Yes and no."

"The yes I get. The no is . . . ?"

She shrugged. "It has its own complexity. Its own . . . life, I suppose." She paused. "But of course, it makes me think of Gus. Mostly of that time before we knew for sure that he was on the plane.

When we still had hope, even though we pretty much knew."

"But even then, the husband's—the father's— ambivalence is so unlike anything you might have felt."

"Well, of course."

"Or the playwright either. Billy, right?"

"Yes. Billy. No, she wouldn't have felt that either." But where did it come from, then? This is what Leslie didn't get. So much in this play, as in the others she'd seen, came from things she knew about Billy, about her life. Why would she have imagined a thing like this? It seemed so ugly, so awful, really.

"Still, it's well done," Sam said. And they talked about this for a bit, about the actors, about certain moments they'd liked, others they hadn't quite believed. Leslie made her point about the liquor, the glasses, and Sam agreed. Pierce came with the drinks, and Sam asked about Pierce's work, and then hers.

She tried to make a joke about it, about not having work. The truth was, she didn't want work anymore. She hadn't wanted it since Gus died. She had been **stopped** for more than a year after that. All she could manage was to stay at home and grieve. And then, when her grief had eased a bit, she wanted just to concentrate on each day—to see friends and play in the garden and read. To make a kind of closed-in, sheltered life for herself and Pierce.

Oh, she did a kind of work, a little. She filled in

from time to time at the real estate office when things were busy—doing a showing, managing a closing. And she'd gone back to doing the other things she'd always done—volunteering at the public school, working on the zoning board in their town, swimming almost every day in the Dartmouth pool. This seemed to be her life. It was just the way it had happened with her, to her. It was what she had chosen because of what had happened. Or it had chosen her.

She and Pierce had talked about it occasionally, about whether this was all right, whether she should be doing more. She was remembering this as the men chatted. Whether she ought to try to get a job, whether she was too young for this kind of life. "Maybe we should buy some old inn and run a B and B," she had suggested once, only half joking. He had pretended to gag. It was only then that she realized she had been asking him whether he would come with her into what she thought of as this new life—and that he was telling her no. No. He needed work he cared about, he needed to be in the world, to feel his life mattered in that way.

The lights dimmed once, and Pierce and Sam threw their plastic glasses away. They started to walk back into the theater. Sam was telling them about another play he'd seen here earlier in the fall, a one-man show, "Which usually I hate. That it's done at all is really the point. You know, you're called upon to find it amazing. But this was different."

Pierce asked how, and Sam kept talking, but Leslie, who was ahead of both of them, couldn't hear him. They sat down. She opened her program and was partway through the bio of the actor playing Gabriel, a man named Rafe Donovan, when the lights dimmed.

The curtain went up on the scene exactly as they'd left it, the three actors standing frozen, looking at one another. Then Gabriel broke away to answer the door, and the other two moved closer together, as if to face whomever, whatever it was, as man and wife. As a couple, at least.

It was a woman. She burst in just as Alex had, full of recrimination about Gabriel's not answering the phone, and then froze, seeing the other two. Leslie recognized the voice—it was the woman who had called and left the message earlier. She was younger than Gabriel by at least a few years, and attractive, if not really pretty. Dramatic in her looks—long thick hair, dark coloring.

Gabriel introduced her as a friend, Anita. There followed a scene of awkwardness and growing embarrassment, of slowly dawning awareness on the part of Alex and his wife that Gabriel was somehow involved with this woman. Again, there was something amusing about this, and laughter here and there in the house.

When Gabriel finally acknowledged the relationship, Alex smiled bitterly and said, "So this part of your life is not so theoretical, right, Dad?"

Then he turned to the other woman, to Anita. He said, "Well, then . . . Anita, is it?"

She nodded.

"What have you come calling for, then? At this particular time. On this particular day. Are you here to celebrate with him when he gets the news: he's free! Or to commiserate with him. 'Ah shit! She's alive.' "

Anita looked in confusion from one of them to another. Gabriel lifted his shoulders. He couldn't help her.

She turned to Alex. "To be with him," she said. "Whatever the news is, to be with him."

Her voice was so raw and honest that Alex was silenced for a moment. But then he jerked into motion, picking up his coat, coming around the couch to take the younger woman by the elbow, talking all the while, saying, "Fine, fine, you be with him, someone should be with him, let it be you. For Christ's sake not me, not me anymore. No matter what happens, not me, ever again." They were at the back of the stage, by the door. He turned briefly to look at his father, said nothing, and they were gone, the door slamming behind them.

Gabriel and Anita stood looking at each other, a little shamefacedly. Then he came around from behind the couch and sat down on it.

"I'm . . . I'm sorry," Anita said. "I shouldn't have come."

"No, you shouldn't," he said.

She drew her breath in sharply. She was wounded.

"What if Elizabeth had been here?" he asked gently.

"I said I was sorry," she said.

After a moment, he said, "So, what did you think of my boy Alex?"

She half smiled. "Somebody should have taught him better manners."

"At the very least," he said.

She came and sat on the couch, close to him. He turned his body to her, making a distance between them.

He looked at her. "I think you should go," he said.

"I want to be with you."

He shook his head, his face hardened. "I can't have you here with me. I have to do this alone."

"You don't. Have to." This was a plea, Leslie thought. Whining. She didn't like this woman.

"I **want** to do this alone, then."

"I don't believe you."

"You should."

She sighed. She looked away. Then back at him. She said, "Just answer me one question."

He shifted on the couch, impatient, not looking at her.

"Gabriel? Just one."

"All right," he said.

"Tell me honestly. When you heard, didn't you feel any sense of . . ." She stopped. After a moment, she shook her head. "Forget it."

"Joy? Possibility? I felt that. A sense of release. Is that what you're asking?"

She nodded.

"Of course. Of course I did. Instantly. 'It's over. She's gone.' "

He stood up and started walking toward the back of the stage. " 'I'm out of it. I'm out of it without hurting her. I can be bereaved: **Oh, it's so terrible, what happened to Gabriel. Did you hear? Oh, poor Gabriel. Poor man.**' All of that." He made a fist and struck the frame of the window. Anita started. She looked frightened for a moment.

"While my son was here, telling me what an awful, unfeeling person I am, I was being that person. That unfeeling. No. Worse than unfeeling: that **calculating** a person. And I'll have to live with that. That that is what I am, who I am. That I was, at least for a moment, glad that Elizabeth—a person I used to love better than I loved myself, a person I still care for and respect—glad that she wouldn't be around anymore." He laughed, horribly. "The first stage of grief: **'Oh, goody.'** "

"Gabriel. It's only human. To want . . . to . . ."

"Anita, please, don't. Don't . . . excuse me. Don't forgive me. You need to, to want to go on. But that doesn't help me, don't you see? It doesn't matter to me, honestly. Your forgiveness. It's of a piece with my own greed for . . . freedom. A new life."

"It's not greed, what I feel."

"It's what we all feel. We want. Then we want

more. It's the human condition. And when we stop wanting, we feel dead and we want to want again."

"But that's what you said you felt with Elizabeth. Dead."

"Yes."

"And with me, you felt alive again. You said so."

"Yes. But it was wanting. Wanting what I didn't have."

"Me!" she cried.

He came forward again, not looking at her. She was waiting. Finally he did turn to her. His face was sad, kind. "Ah, well," he said.

"Me!" she said, with anger this time.

"The idea of you anyway, Anita." And then, compassionately, "Anita."

"Don't say my name! Don't say my name that way."

"I can't help it. It's the way I feel your name now."

She sat very still for a long moment. Then she said in a small voice, "You're letting me go, aren't you?"

"How can I keep you?" His voice was strained, but gentle.

"Why can't you keep me?"

"Because I want Elizabeth. I want Elizabeth to be alive."

"It's not a deal. An exchange. It doesn't have to be one or the other." He didn't answer. "You said you wanted to end it. You wanted to be free."

"I can't be free unless she sets me free."

"But if she's dead . . ."

He moaned, loudly, and turned to face her. "If she's dead, then I'm Gabriel, the widower. That's who I am. That's who I'll be. I have to . . . enact that, for her. I have to honor her. I can't be free. I can't be glad. She was my wife. She is my wife."

"And if she's alive?"

"If she's alive, I'm glad for her life. I have to be glad for her life. I have to be a person who is glad . . . that she's alive. I will be glad she's alive." He sat down again, but in one of the chairs this time. Not near her. "I can't be . . . that other person. The person Alex thinks I am."

"This is ridiculous," she said suddenly, angrily. "This is like fucking Henry James."

A sad little smile moved on his face. "I don't think you'd have much of a chance at that." A few people laughed.

"It's not funny, Gabriel."

He looked exhausted all at once. "No. It's not. Really."

She watched him. Then she said, "And what about me?"

He shook his head. "I'm sorry."

"But you said you loved me."

"I'm sorry, Anita. I am sorry. But the terms have shifted. You see that, don't you? Everything has changed. My life. Life itself."

"But you said you wanted me."

"I wanted you."

"In the past."

"Yes. Past tense."

She got up and moved around. She looked teary, about to say something. Then, abruptly, she was in motion. She grabbed her bag. She went quickly upstage. She stopped. Slowly she said, "You're one, stupid, fucking son of a bitch."

He nodded, over and over.

She left, slamming the door even harder than Alex had.

Gabriel sat motionless for a long moment. He was facing the audience. He was faintly smiling—a sad smile, it seemed to Leslie. But why? She didn't understand him, what he was feeling. He got up and slowly moved around the room, straightening books on the tables, picking up a glass, that strange half smile still on his face. He carried the glass back to the liquor shelf and set it down. He was frozen for a long moment, standing there, looking down at his hands. He turned and went back to the window. He stood with his back to the audience, looking out.

And then there appeared on the stage, at the back of the stage where the door was—the door that Leslie couldn't quite see—a gray-haired woman, a woman Gabriel's age. There were vivid bruises on her face. She was wearing a coat over her shoulders, a coat that she shrugged off onto the nearest chair. Now they could see that her arm was in a cast.

She saw Gabriel and stopped. She spoke his name softly, a question. "Gabriel?"

He turned quickly, startled. His mouth opened

slightly. They were frozen this way for a long moment. Then his head dropped back and his hands rose to his face and covered it. You could hear a ragged intake of breath. Another. Finally, he lowered his hands; they dropped to his sides. His face was twisted. Tears gleamed in his eyes, on his cheeks. "Elizabeth," he whispered in a choked voice. They stood like that, facing each other. He began to step toward her, his hands rising, just as the curtain fell.

After a beat or two of silence, the applause started. **I should be clapping, too,** Leslie thought.

The curtain rose again. There were the actors, in a row onstage. They held hands, they stepped forward. They were smiling, except for the Gabriel figure. The applause roared on, and now Leslie was part of it, though she wasn't sure what she felt. The actors stepped back, they dropped one another's hands. The Gabriel figure, Leslie saw, used this moment to wipe his eyes. Then the two men, Gabriel and Alex, stepped forward and bowed, first to the audience, then to each other. They gestured back at the three women, who came forward and bowed with them again.

They all held hands again, they bowed once more in a row and were backing up together as the curtain came down. Just before it touched the floor, you could see their line break up—their legs, their feet, moving away from one another. The applause continued for a few more seconds, and then, when the curtain stayed down, it stopped.

They were silent for a moment. Pierce leaned toward her. "You're okay?"

"Of course," she said. "Yes." But she could feel that her heart was beating heavily. Something in the ending, in Elizabeth's safe return, or in the way the Gabriel character had said her name, had moved her, she didn't quite understand why.

But the play had been unsettling to her generally—the complications, the ugliness in it. She didn't understand what Billy was saying, what she intended. She had been thinking she might say afterward to Pierce and Sam, **There was not one person on that stage you could like,** until those last moments when she felt sympathy—was it sympathy?—for Gabriel. Or even before, she was thinking now, before, when he tried to explain himself to the woman. Anita. She closed her eyes for a moment. Pierce held her coat up for her, and she turned away from him to put her arms into the sleeves. She was facing Sam. He was looking at her, a worried, kind look. He said, "So, what do you make of the ending?"

She shook her head. She didn't know. She wasn't ready to talk about it.

"He stays," Pierce said, in his big assertive voice. "That's clear. He's made his choice."

"Then why is he weeping?" Sam asked Pierce.

She looked back at Pierce. He shrugged. "I don't know."

"Maybe he doesn't know," Sam said.

"Relief, maybe," Pierce said. "That she's alive."

They filed out, Leslie ahead of both of them. She could hear that they were speaking to each other, still about the play, she thought, but she kept her head bowed; she watched her feet make their way up the tilted floor.

As Sam leaned over her to hold open the glass door to the street, the cool, moist air enveloped her. It was still raining. She took a deep breath.

"Where to?" Pierce asked. "This place we're meeting Billy."

She pointed out a little corner restaurant about half a block away. Pierce opened the umbrella, and they started in that direction.

After a minute Sam said, "He didn't look glad. He looked . . . tormented."

Back to the ending.

Pierce was looking at her, worried, so she smiled at him. She knew she needed to shake this off, she needed to talk.

"Here's what it is," Sam said. He paused, and then said, " 'He asserted modestly.' "

"You can assert immodestly to us all you want," Pierce said. "For all the good it'll do you."

"It's that he doesn't know what he wants."

"Then why is he crying?" Leslie asked. Why was he? But now they had to go single file to get out of the way of a man walking three dogs, and when their line reformed, neither of them took up her question. It seemed to have vanished. Maybe they hadn't heard her. She wasn't sure she wanted to listen to them offer their notions about the play anymore anyway. It was something she needed to think through for herself.

They crossed the street to the restaurant. Pierce held the door open for her, and she stepped in, into another world: background music, loud voices. Instantly she was worried about Pierce, his reaction. Was it too loud? Would he be irritated? They had to stay. It was the place Billy had suggested.

A tall blond waitress came, dressed all in black but for a big white apron that fell from her waist to her ankles. She led them to a high table facing out the window toward the dark street and the rain. Pierce and Sam sat at the short ends of the table, and Leslie sat at the long side, looking back the way they'd come, toward the theater. The chair for Billy sat empty next to her. She could see that a few people were still standing under the marquee, waiting for rides, perhaps, or maybe just talking.

The restaurant was small, the walls dark, a warm cave in the rainy night. Around them, the hubbub of talk, of clinking silverware, and under it all a plaintive voice singing to a regular, bluesy beat.

Another waitress came and took their drink order—they served only wine, to Pierce's annoyance. She left menus for them. Pierce started telling Sam about the erotic Japanese prints. He was funny, describing the Tuesday afternoon art patrons, women mostly, moving decorously around, seeming

to consider with equal studiousness the prints of
women in elaborate robes moving through formal
and stylized gardens or theaters, and the ones that
involved people screwing in inventive and unlikely
ways, their faces impassive. "There weren't many,"
he said. "Only five or six. But all of them very . . .
convincing, I'd say. Very thorough." He raised his
eyebrows for Sam's benefit. "And just where everything came together, **as it were,** there was always
just the subtlest drop or two of some clear, shiny
substance **so** carefully painted on." He grinned,
widely. "Hotcha!"

Sam laughed, shaking his head at Pierce, at all that
was predictable, she supposed, about his energy, his
enthusiasm.

They started to talk about the difference between
erotic art and pornography, what the line was. The
wine came and they clinked the glasses, **To friendship,** and drank. They talked about their first experiences of porn, at what age, how it had affected
them. Leslie tried to do her part in the conversation,
and she was amused by them, and interested, but
she still felt far away. She was aware, too, of waiting
for Billy, of the usual anxiety about that, mixed with
something indefinable left over from the play. Un-
easiness, she supposed. That was probably it. What
you didn't understand made you nervous. That was
all.

They talked about contemporary movies, how
close to porn some were, and yet finally, Sam said,

the closer they got without crossing that line, the more dishonest they seemed. She was watching him, his face, the slight squint of his eyes behind his glasses as he thought through his point. She was feeling tender toward him.

And then she saw Billy outside, a small figure all in black, her face a white circle under her umbrella. She stood on the corner opposite, waiting to cross. She had a huge bag slung from her shoulder, big enough to carry her life's work, it was so enormous. She **had** cut her hair. Her face shone beneath the straight, thick bangs. A car passed, two, and then she started across the street.

"Here's Billy," Leslie said, gesturing at the window. The men turned and just then she remembered: the flowers! She'd forgotten them back in the hotel room when they left, her gift to Billy—she could see them in her mind's eye, the tight, perfect, fresh bouquet, lying on the bureau.

But then the door opened, and as she got down from her chair to start toward it, Billy saw her and her grave face was suddenly transformed by her open, surprisingly sweet smile.

RAFE

THE JOKE WAS that they'd found an angel to play another angel, though he told them that his name was just plain Rafe, not Raphael.

"And those guys are both archangels anyway," the director said. Edmund. "Gabriel, Raphael. They're both archangels." They were sitting onstage, most of them at a big table, some in scattered chairs around the periphery.

"Pardon my French, but what the fuck are archangels?" This was somebody whose job he wasn't sure of. A sound guy, maybe. Or electrics.

"The head honcho types in heaven, I think," Edmund said.

"Just one plain old angel would be good enough for me, thank you very much." That was the stage manager, Ellie. She had her computer set up on the table and was typing into it, even while she was talking, notes on what needed to get done.

Edmund had laughed. "An angel. One would do. Yes indeedy. But where, oh where is he?"

Rafe sat and listened to the horsing around, feel-

ing mostly relief. He'd gotten the part. He needed
the part. He needed to stay busy, to stay away from
the house. He needed to be in this world, where
everything else fell away. Where only this was real—
what happened on the stage and how you made it
happen—and reality was irrelevant.

It was Edmund who had asked him to read.
They'd worked together years earlier, but Edmund
had seen him recently in **Uncle Vanya** and liked the
rueful quality he projected. This is what he'd said on
the phone.

"Yeah, well, I'm your go-to guy for rue," Rafe
had said.

Edmund was short, fat, balding, seemingly mild.
Everyone knew better. He was in control always.
He shaped everything by asking his gentle, persistent questions. He had a full beard, and his hands'
almost-relentless attention to it was part of how he
talked. He stroked it, pulled at it, twirled its ends.
He had done all of these things while Rafe was reading, and Rafe had found it hard to ignore.

Among the other slacker-looking people who had
been sitting around or drifting in and out while Rafe
was reading—costume people and sound people
and set designers and builders, gofers of one kind or
another—was a person so small he took her at first
for a child, and almost made a remark. It would
have been one of his usual pointlessly sarcastic
things: "Is someone here **baby**sitting?"

But he didn't, unaccountably. And luckily, he supposed, as she was, of course, the playwright, though he didn't find that out until a week or so later.

So, rue. Well, the passage he'd read was from the first act, a section in which his character, Gabriel, is explaining to his daughter-in-law, Emily, drink in hand, the state of his marriage, the complicated reasons for his calmness in the face of the terrible news his son has just brought him. Or the potentially terrible news.

What he says is that he and his wife have withdrawn from each other over the years. He says that neither is really fully alive or real to the other. "Maybe you know how it is when you're tired and don't feel like having sex," he says to Emily. "You know, you undress carefully, you expose only a little flesh at a time, so as never to be fully naked, never to seem to be issuing some kind of invitation with your body, God forbid. Maybe"—and Rafe had smiled here—"you don't know how that is. Lucky you. But even so, maybe you can imagine this: that there's a later stage you can reach when you don't bother with even that formality because there's no possibility either one of you could ever feel invited by the other's nakedness." He had paused. "Well, there's a parallel thing that happens emotionally after you've lived too carefully around each other too long, always hiding some part of yourself. **You stop caring.**" He'd dropped the smile here, let his whole face fall. "In just the way your bodies are dead to each other, so is everything else. There's nothing you can say that will charm the other or, for that matter, hurt the other, because nothing you say is ever of any importance at all. Your conversations remain polite, **fully clothed,** as it were, at all times. And in the end, with us, they were so pointless that we literally stopped speaking."

He had shrugged. "I remember having friends drop in on us in the summerhouse in Massachusetts. I remember that we were laughing and talking up to the minute they left. Elizabeth had told a story about a student of hers who would come to office hours and start to cry the moment she crossed the threshold into her office. It was a victory, she said, when by midsemester the girl got halfway through a conference before the waterworks started.

"I remember watching her talking about this and thinking how lively she was, how attractive. She has a way of telling stories—well, you know it—a way of saying, ' "Da-dum, da-dum, da-dum,". . . **says she,** "Da-dum, da-dum, da-dum," . . . **says I.**' That nice inversion that makes it seem that you're listening to an old familiar tale. A nursery rhyme. Or even a song. I remember thinking . . . I guess just thinking her name: **Elizabeth.** Startled by her, you know, as though she'd just come back from a long trip away. Or maybe as if I'd just come back from a long trip away.

"Anyway, we stood by the car saying good-bye, and then we stood in the driveway waving." He'd been smiling a big false smile as he said this, and waving, a monarch's regal slight turning of the hand this way and that. "And the **moment** the car turned into the road"—he dropped the smile, made his voice hard, brisk—"she turned one way and went inside, and I turned the other way and went in the other direction." He gave a short, mirthless laugh: "Back to our corners." He held his hand up, palm forward. " 'Show's over, folks.' "

They'd liked this. They'd asked him to read a few other shorter speeches. He was hired, amid the jokes about his name.

In the car on the way home, he let himself start to worry about Lauren. He'd been around most evenings for a while—ever since **Vanya** closed, actually. He thought she might miss that—his getting dinner for her, helping her with it, getting her to bed.

But if she had a moment's pang, he didn't see it. What she said was that it might actually be easier for the Round Robin to make time for her in the evening than it was for them in the day.

The Round Robin was what they called the group of friends who had, for the moment, taken on Lauren's care. Later they would need to pay for someone, later they would need professionals, but for now one of Lauren's friends, Carol, had summoned these others, friends of Lauren's or friends of Carol's who knew about Lauren, and they made her life—and his, too, he recognized—possible.

They didn't all come into the house. One shopped

for them, one took Lauren to the hospital and to doctors' appointments. But most of them helped her—helped them—in more intimate ways: cooking for them, feeding Lauren, taking her to the bathroom, getting her to bed at night when he was working.

She had welcomed this, because her main wish was that he be freed of all these tasks so that he could see her as a woman still, not an invalid. This is what she'd said to him, weeping, one night early on after the diagnosis was made, when they were still trying to ignore the symptoms—the broken dishes, the orange juice that slopped onto the table as she poured it. The trembling, the falls, the bruises. She said that she didn't want to become an illness to him. That she wanted, most of all, to stay real to him as a person, as a woman, as his wife.

"As my sexy wife," he'd said. He'd brushed her hair back off her face, thumbed away the tear sliding down her cheek.

Later she didn't weep anymore. Later she joked about it. "Don't you think it's weird, this newfangled business of naming everything? Megan's Law. Amber Alert. Lou Gehrig's disease."

"But there's Halley's comet," he pointed out. "Maybe it was ever thus."

"Still. A **disease,**" she said. "If it's his disease, why do I have to have it. 'Lou! Lou! Come back! You forgot your dis**ease!**' "

By then they weren't making love anymore.

They'd met in college, when Rafe was, as he put it later, "basically priapic." It's what had drawn him into acting as an undergraduate, he'd told her all those years later. He assumed the women would all be beautiful and sexually liberated.

He was wrong in this assumption. Some were beautiful, some were not. Some were liberated, some were not. But most of them had no desire to sleep with him, a lowly sophomore. They were interested in the older actors, in the directors, in their teachers.

Lauren was his lab partner in biology, and she **was** interested in sleeping with him. Very interested. For a few weeks in their sophomore year they had frantic sex together through long late afternoons in his dorm room, the noise of his roommates' lives on the other side of the door the background to their marathons. She was then still a little chunky, she wore glasses that she ceremonially removed before their exertions began.

They tried everything they could think of. She was the first person who ever gave him a blow job, who ever licked his balls, put her finger up his ass, let him do the same to her. She showed him how to flatten and widen his tongue to give her more pleasure, she corrected the way his mouth pulled at her nipples. Finally he had found her almost mannish, as he thought of it, in her willingness to experiment, her seemingly coldhearted enthusiasm to try the next forbidden thing. He tired of her. He tired of it. It was as though she were working from a text, he told her later when he met her again, when he fell in love with her.

Oh, she had been, she assured him. It was the way she'd done everything then. By the book.

Their second meeting happened twelve years after their first, when their real lives had begun. Though sometimes he thought now that perhaps they hadn't yet begun, even at that point. Perhaps the present was the real part, the true test, and all the rest of it mere preparation.

Either way, they were both happy in their work then, single, in their early thirties, still living in Berkeley, which is where they'd met the first time around, where they'd gone to college. She came to a benefit for the repertory company he was with, after a performance of their ongoing play, **Bosoms and Neglect.** Rafe was Scooper, and he was still in costume and makeup, as were the other two players, so that they could easily be recognized by patrons who might want to schmooze with them, whose asses they had been instructed to kiss as enthusiastically as possible.

At first he'd taken her for one of these patrons. She looked expensive. She was tall and slender. Her brown hair had been streaked silvery blond. She wore dangly silver earrings and a big silver cuff on one wrist. Her heels were very high, her legs miles long and nicely shaped. She had on a black sleeveless dress, and her bare shoulders were like sheeny knobs jutting out of it. He wouldn't mind kissing **her** ass, he thought.

He proceeded to start to do so, repeating the things they'd been told to say to the patrons, the questions they'd been instructed to ask: how lovely of her to come, the theater so appreciated her support, had she been to other performances?

She stood smiling at him for a long moment, and then she said, "You don't have the foggiest who I am, do you?"

Uh-oh, he thought. Someone really important. "I'm sorry, I don't." He gestured, shook his head. "I'm kind of the village idiot at these affairs. Please help me out here."

"Lauren Willetts." She tilted her head slightly. Her hair swung over and kissed her shoulder. Her eyes were steady on him.

He was looking right at her and he didn't remember.

"Lauren Willetts," she said slowly.

Nothing.

She opened her purse, fished in it, took out some thick glasses, and put them on. "Lauren," she said again.

"**That** Lauren?" he said. My God. Ugly duckling to swan of swans.

She took the glasses off. "Have there been so many other Laurens?" She was smiling.

He looked her up and down. He could feel himself starting to get hard, remembering. He laughed. "None quite like that one."

"Though you ran away from her, as I recollect it." She raised her finger, scolding.

"Well, she was scary."

"Was that it?"

"And a little . . . heartless, I guess."

"But you were, too, of course."

"Yes. Well. I guess I expected that I had the patent on heartlessness then."

"I was infringing, as it were."

As quickly as that, he was tired of banter. "Listen, are you here with someone?"

She laughed again. "A friend."

"So I couldn't take you home."

She shook her head. "You could call me, though."

And again she fished in her bag. She brought out a little embroidered envelope and extracted a business card from it.

LAUREN MARGOLIN, it said. TECHNICAL CONSULTING.

He looked up at her. "Margolin."

"Yes."

"You're married."

She shook her head. "Not anymore, I'm not." She walked away. He watched the rolling motion of her buttocks, the alternating wink of her long muscled calves below the black dress.

Someone touched his elbow and he turned, smiling. But distracted. And he was distracted until he saw her again, and then he was distracted until they had sex again, which happened almost immediately. And then he fell in love with her.

In the early days of this second time around, they talked a lot about their other, younger selves, and how the strangeness of their affair then had made this one inevitable. How, the minute each of them had realized who the other was, they wanted to redo what they'd done, but differently. Once more, with feeling. "Or maybe a couple of times more," she said.

Many, many times more, it turned out.

It was both like and then unlike the way he remembered it. She was as strong and as wild as ever. Rafe had never had such an athletic, experimental lover. But this time it seemed they were driven by something deeper within both of them, something that perhaps had to do with the wish to revise old vulnerabilities. To make up for what seemed wrong-hearted or emotionally truncated in the first experience.

But there was something about the first experience that compelled them, too—its very limitations, its sad desperation. Rafe sometimes felt swept by a tender sorrow after they'd made love, sorrow for something they might have had then, when they were so hungry and needy, but hadn't. Something that gave even their most ordinary couplings now a sense of depth, an inexplicable element, a pentimento.

After they'd been living together for about a year, she got a job doing tech stuff for an NGO based in Boston, so they moved to Cambridge. Rafe had to more or less begin his career again, but his connections in Berkeley had connections in Boston, and eventually he landed in the repertory company he preferred in town. They lived marginally, though every now and then Lauren got an independent consulting job that made them suddenly very flush. Then they'd take a vacation in the Caribbean, or rent a house in Vermont for the summer, or stay in a good hotel in New York for a week and see plays and hear great music. Once she bought him a Joseph Abboud suit. Once she bought herself a Jennifer Bartlett print.

They got married. Time passed. They moved a few times as apartments in Cambridge got more expensive, inching their way east and south, closer to MIT, to the river. Their old ardor became intermittent. She accused him of being withdrawn. They fought occasionally about his acting, the way in which he lost himself in it. She said that sometimes she hated seeing him in a play. "It makes me mad, how alive you are onstage when you have so little energy for me." She had an affair that she told him about.

He had one.

They resolved not to tell each other about their affairs, which, after all, had nothing to do with their marriage, with who they were together.

But he couldn't stand living with her and not knowing who she might be thinking of in those moments when her face went blank—what she might be imagining then. He left.

He moved to New York, to see if he had what it took. That was the way he put it, to her and to others. Later he was sorry for this, because he had to acknowledge that when the question was framed that way, the answer had to be no.

He got some walk-ons, occasionally a small speaking role, but he was a little too old for most leads, too good-looking in a sort of has-been way for most character parts, too unknown, too unconnected. And maybe, just maybe, he didn't have what it took.

Then there was his life, the way he had to live in New York—though for the first eight months or so, it was fine. He was essentially house-sitting then, paying a token amount each month to stay in the rent-controlled, gracious apartment of friends who were in Rome on a fellowship for a year. The women he had over were impressed. Even when he told them the truth of his situation, he implied that he would be looking for the same kind of place once his stay on West Eleventh Street was over.

But it was all downhill after that. He was in one roommate situation after another for a while, and then he found a strange flat on 112th Street with a dark, speckled linoleum floor, worn through in places. It had a tiny bedroom off the even tinier kitchen. The plastic shower stall had been installed sloppily—it tilted—and water collected at its front lip. You had to slosh it back manually toward the drain when you were through showering, something Rafe didn't always bother doing. There were mice. He thought of the apartment as temporary—but what would change in his life to allow him to move? He didn't let himself consider this for very long. But because he thought of the place this way, he did nothing to fix it up. He bought only the furniture he had to. He was mostly dating younger women during this time, because they were the only ones who were tolerant of his situation: middle-aged actor, no dough, serious aspirations. But even they found the apartment unattractive and depressing.

And then he fell in love, with a woman almost his age. A painter. The friend of old friends. She was a Southerner, and this was new and exotic to him. She was big, his height or even taller. Her hips were as wide as her vowels, her flesh everywhere soft and abundant. She had family money and a small apartment she kept in the Village where she stayed for a couple of months at a time. She drank a lot, she told dirty jokes, she was smart and gregarious. She needed to be among people. After his work was over, he would meet her at a party somewhere, drink fast to catch up to her, and they'd go back to her place and fuck until one or the other of them essentially passed out.

She was generous with friends and with him. She paid for everything. She bought him gifts. She took him on trips—Key West, New Orleans.

And then one day out of the blue she asked him quietly, innocently, "Lookee here, why don't **you** invent something for us to do?" They were in bed. It was Monday morning. The theater was dark today.

"Because. Because, I suppose, **you** are the mother of invention."

She frowned, uncharmed. "No, really. Why don't you . . . plan a trip for us. Buy us a ticket to Paris France for four days." **Fowah dayze,** she said.

"I would, Edie. If I could afford it. Either the days or the dough."

She rolled onto her side, facing him, her elbow bent, her head resting on her palm. Her big breasts lay one on top of the other. He reached for them, but she brushed his hand away. "You're really an odd duck, aren't you?" she said, her voice not friendly. "Most men your age in the arts have either made it, or they've found another line of work so they can have a little money."

He didn't say anything.

"How have you managed to **slide** along the way you have all these years?"

"I don't think about it much." This was not true. "And then, when I was married, my wife made considerably more than I did, so we got along fine." He felt embarrassed, so his voice sounded stiff and fussy.

She got up out of bed and pulled her bathrobe on. It was a deep ruby satin kimono with a large dragon embroidered on the back. "Well," she said. "Yuck."

And that was that. It was over, quite abruptly. No answering his calls, no calls from her, no more parties, and no explanation at all. He was on his own. It was up to him to figure out the reasons it had ended. He could think of quite a few. Still, it seemed unfair to him. Rude, really.

But wounded as he was, he didn't have long to dwell on it, because at exactly this time, Lauren started to write to him. What she said was that she had collapsed into a dark depression, she was in intensive therapy. She wanted him back. It had all been her fault. She'd been wrong, she said, to have started the affairs. She had been angry at him but unable to say that. Far from being irrelevant then, her lovers had had everything to do with their marriage. And his having lovers right back had made her more angry, and she'd had more, and on it went until a while after he left, when she realized what she'd done and how angry she'd been all along. How terrified of expressing that she was, how low she had fallen since then.

Now she was slowly working on being more honest—with herself and, she hoped, with him. Would he let her try again?

At first he said no. It felt to him as though it would be a capitulation, an admission of failure in the wider world, of defeat in love, of being old and used up.

But she was persistent, nearly intoxicated, he would have said—he **did** say it to her later—with her sense of self-discovery, with what she felt was her increased ability to love, to love him. She called and wanted to talk. She kept him on the phone for hours. The letters she wrote him ran to five or six pages.

Well, timing **is** everything. He came back. To Boston, to Lauren—though he returned in a kind of defeat, though he was still half in love with Edie. But Lauren was so happy that she barely noticed his melancholy, his absence. And slowly he came out of it. Their lovemaking was new and fresh and sweet, and she wept afterward. She wept to think of what she'd done to their marriage. She wept because she was so happy he'd come back. She wept because he was wearing boxer shorts, which he'd never done before, and she assumed they were the preference of another woman. (She was right: Edie had bought him a dozen pairs and made him throw away his graying jockeys.)

The warmth of her joy over his return, of her grief over what she'd done, was a balm to him. Slowly he recovered from his sense of failure, his pain at Edie's abrupt turning away from him. Lauren loved him. He had never been so devotedly loved. How could he not enjoy it? How could he not subside into it?

"Who ever gets **three** chances to love?" she asked him one night. "**We** have all the luck."

They were happy again. Once, a while after they'd gotten back together, a good friend asked, in a joking way, "How did this **happen** anyway?" and Lauren said, only a little in jest, and not without pride, "Oh, I abased myself. Repeatedly."

"Is it a good part, my sweet?"

"It's the lead. It's a biggie." He was putting on her makeup for her. Friends were coming over.

"But good?"

"Very good. Very complicated guy. Not entirely nice. Look up." She did, and he ran the eyeliner on her lower lids. "I'm onstage the entire time. It begins with me and it ends with me."

"As I do."

He looked sharply down at her. She was smiling at him, her newly goofy smile, slightly out of her control now.

"You know," Edmund said. They were alone in the theater, sitting at a table in the middle of what would be the set, going over his lines with infinite and tedious thoroughness, Edmund's specialty. "It might well be that he's doing as much recollecting of Elizabeth here as he is arguing about how we should think about terrorism."

"So the emphasis should be on the memory of her, of that time in Paris." This was a question, as he said it.

"I'm just saying," Edmund answered, "that they might have been having a kind of a nice vacation there together."

Rafe reread the lines, going a little slower over

the memory of Elizabeth, as though he were suddenly, surprisingly, seeing her as he spoke, calling her up.

"Unh-**huh,**" Edmund said, nodding and nodding and twining his fingers in his beard. And then, just to confound things, "Of course, he's also trying very hard not to think of her situation right now—the train, the bombing, et alia. Trying to stay in that theoretical world where he's so comfortable. So maybe the idea is that as he's making this argument, the John Kerry argument, this memory more or less"—his hand circled in the air in front of him— "catches him unawares, so to speak."

Rafe read the speech again, thrusting quickly through the lines about John Kerry's perspective, in full argument mode. Then he paused for a moment, looking down. "I mean, I remember the time when Elizabeth and I were in Paris for four months, that sabbatical year." Now he spoke more softly. "We traveled everywhere together by subway—by Metro." He looked up, off in the distance for a second, then back at Edmund. "And it didn't matter that there'd been a bombing in the subway only a few months before. One lived one's life, one hoped to have warning, but it was simply there, a possibility."

"Yup, yup, yup, yup," Edmund said. "That's the way. See, this sets up a kind of pattern that helps with the ending, the way he takes her back. You know, that all along he's had this . . . awareness, of her, of what he had in loving her."

Rafe was marking the script, flipping back to the earlier speech, making notes.

"Okay, let's do it again," Edmund said.

Afterward, they went out for a drink. They were sitting at the noisy bar in funky old DeLuxe, each with a beer. Edmund tipped his head, bent closer to Rafe, and said, "He's kind of a funny guy, your Gabriel, isn't he?" On the television, behind him, the Bruins, dark blobs on white, looped smoothly over the ice.

"How so?" Rafe asked. **I'll bite.**

"Well, he plays it pretty close to the vest, don't you think?"

"You think?"

"Do you?" Edmund's pale eyes behind his glasses were steady on him.

Rafe swiveled on his seat for a moment. "Well, I was thinking he doesn't really know what he feels, actually. He knows he doesn't feel what he's supposed to feel, but he's not sure what he does feel, don't you think?"

"Hunh." Edmund sat for a long moment, staring down at his beer. He looked up. "Well, I think if it hadn't happened this way, if it had ended some other way—maybe even if she'd had, say, a heart attack, he might have been able to be glad." He frowned, he pursed his lips. "No, I don't mean that," he corrected himself. "Not glad. But certainly . . . relieved, to be out of it somehow without inflicting pain. People do feel that sometimes," he said gravely to

Rafe. "It ain't nice, but it's so." He had another swallow of beer. "But this, this is . . . national. It's like 9/11.
It's political. It has its claims, doesn't it? In that there
is only one politically correct response to this. Humanly correct. And that just isn't where his heart is."

Edmund sat up. "I mean, think of it as if it **were**
like 9/11. Think if you'd been about to ask someone
for a divorce, and they upped and died then. The
ambivalent reaction to such an event, the complicated one, is shocking to people. No one wants to
hear it. It's . . . repulsive. It's unpatriotic." His fingers
nestled into his beard. "It's small. It's personal. It's
unworthy. Such a truth needs to be suppressed. **He**
needs to be suppressed." He banged his fist on
the bar.

They both sat, not speaking for a moment. Rafe
had some beer.

Edmund said, "Think what a crumb he must feel
like."

That was it, Rafe thought. That Gabriel was trying to figure out a way **not** to be a crumb, but still to
be honest. He wanted somehow to be **honorable.**
That's what he was doing in that last scene with
Anita, figuring that out. That's what was slowly happening to him.

He was about to say something to Edmund about
this, but when he looked over at him, Edmund had
turned away to see how the Bruins were doing.

They'd been back together for about two years when the symptoms started. Of course at first they didn't think of them that way. Just mishaps. She was dropping things, she began taking long naps, naps that left her limp and somehow more fatigued. Sometimes she had a funny garbling of her speech, so that she'd stop and take a deep breath. She'd say, "Allow me to rephrase that," and repeat something with carefully precise enunciation of each syllable.

They thought mononucleosis, or Epstein-Barr, and she had a few tests, which revealed nothing. It seemed to go away for a while. Over the summer she was herself again. In early August they took a trip to Saratoga Springs. She bought an extravagant hat on the main drag, a hat that would have been worthy of the Queen Mother, as she said. They lost more than one hundred dollars at the track.

On the way home, they stopped to stay a few days with her mother in southwest Vermont, near Bennington College, where her father had taught.

Her mother, Grace, was a poet. A poet manqué, she called herself, because she hadn't written for years. She said she'd stopped writing because she came to the abrupt realization that there already **was** an Edna St. Vincent Millay. She said to be a poet manqué was better by far than being a poet because it got you out of the house.

He'd seen pictures of her mother as a young woman. She'd been beautiful, in a Garboesque way—a little androgynous, a little too strong-featured for contemporary taste. Lauren had inherited some of that.

Now she was a wreck, really. Her hair had gone iron gray, cement gray—a bad color, the color of battleships. Her nose, which had been strong and beautiful, was beaky, the nostrils too large, hairs visible in them. She'd been a lifelong smoker, and it showed. Her skin seemed shadowed by nicotine, the long deep creases in her face and around her neck were slightly embrowned. She still smoked occasionally, luxuriating in it, but she made herself go out of her own house to do it now. The news about secondhand smoke had devastated her, and she was determined to do no more harm to her family and friends than she'd already done. She would come back inside smelling strongly of tobacco, chewing gum to make herself less odious.

It had taken Rafe a while to get used to her. He'd grown up in suburban Chicago—the aspiring suburbs, as he put it. Not Winnetka, not Oak Park. His parents were holding on tenaciously, but marginally, to a version of middle-class life that wouldn't have included anyone like Grace. It was she who'd given the young Lauren the copy of **The Joy of Sex** that had been their cookbook in their sophomore year. "You should love your body," she had said on the occasion of its presentation. "Love what it can bring you."

She'd been a student of Lauren's father at Bennington. It was a scandal. She got pregnant and he divorced his wife of almost thirty years and married her. Lauren's half brothers were older than her mother. One of them, Frank, had died the summer before this visit, at seventy-six. The other, Pete, came over with his wife the night before they left.

"Hey, bro," Lauren said. She was sitting in a chair with her back to the kitchen door, but she'd turned a little when she heard them come in.

Rafe watched as Pete bent over her from behind and kissed the top of her head. His hair was skimpy and white above her face, his skull shiny through it.

"And now"—she stood up, shoving her chair back—"I will embrace you." She rocked him in her arms. "Oh, oh, sweetie Petie."

Pete was still rumpled and blushing a little when he shook Rafe's hand. "Why do you never look any older, Rafe?" he asked.

"It's a part I'm playing," he said to Pete. "I'm called on to be about thirty-two."

"Well, you're a damn fine actor."

Lauren was hugging Pete's wife now. Natalie. Small, with bright, improbably orange hair.

Grace was standing off to one side, waiting her turn at all this embracing. **In the wings,** he thought.

They went out on the porch and drank martinis, made by Pete, as always. The cat scratched at the screen door, and Natalie let him in. He twined himself around everyone's legs, then settled by Gracie. They talked about Frank, Pete's brother. He'd stayed mad at his father after he left his first wife. He wouldn't enter the house until after the old man had died. "He missed out on a lot of fun," Grace said.

Rafe had heard the stories. They all drank when Lauren was little, "like fish," she said. "Exactly as though it was the medium they lived in." When they were good and drunk, they played games, the games she might have played with other children if any had lived nearby. Sardines, kick the can, red rover. Later word games, board games, guessing games. Botticelli, charades. They wrote operettas and performed them. They danced. They sang. Lauren had once said that it was as though the confusion about the generations had addled them all, made them all about fifteen, max. "When I went to college, I was bereft," she said. "I looked around and couldn't figure out where the fun was. Thus, sex." She made one of her dramatic gestures. "A party you could have with only one other person."

Now, sitting on the screened porch, they were talking about the retirement community Pete and Nat were about to move to. Nat said, "Pete will be one of three men there. Three men, and I think about forty women. They'll all be waiting for me to die so they can make their move."

Grace went out on the stone steps to smoke a cigarette, followed by the cat. She held the door open for him. The breeze was such that the smoke blew back over all of them through the rusty old screens. "Come on and smoke back in here, Momma," Lauren said. "You're upwind out there, anyway."

But Grace wouldn't. She moved farther away. They could see her drifting around among the old apple trees. Pete offered to freshen up their martinis. "I couldn't," Lauren said, and her hand went over her glass just as Pete was about to pour. Rafe shook his head.

"There's no sense in Nat and me pacing ourselves," Pete said, filling their glasses. "We got to do everything in a hurry now. Time is closing in on us."

"You'll outlive us all, Pete," Rafe said.

Pete snorted.

Grace came in, trailing the mingled odors of nicotine and Juicy Fruit. They should eat outside, she'd decided. It was too beautiful. So while she fixed their dinner, they all deconstructed the table Lauren had set inside earlier, traipsing back and forth, in and out, with dishes and glasses and silverware and napkins and candles, setting the wooden table on the stone terrace. An old apple tree stretched its gnarled branches above it. Lauren found two citronella candles and lighted them, so there was that to remember later, too—that lemony, camphory smell.

The sun set slowly and dramatically in the west as they ate. They sat in near silence for half an hour or so when they were finished, watching the clouds change color.

"Thanks for that, Gracie," Pete said as they pushed their chairs back in the near dark and started to clear the table. "You sure have a way with a sunset."

Rafe and Pete did the dishes. From the living room came the thin, touching music of the scratchy 78s Grace still owned. Someone had stacked up the enormous old record player, and one by one, heavily, the records dropped and the needle moved across them. When Pete and Rafe came in from the kitchen, Grace was kneeling at the open cabinet doors, selecting new discs, and Lauren and Nat were dancing to Lil Hardin Armstrong.

When Lauren saw him, she let Nat go and came to him, lifting her arms. They did a two-step, and then jitterbugged to some swing tune by Duke Ellington. Pete and Nat were dancing too. "The Sheik of Araby" came on. They all tangoed. Then came Fred Astaire and Esther Rollins and Lee Weaver.

Pete and Nat were pooped. They had to go. "You danced us into the ground," Nat said.

Gracie and Rafe danced a bit more, and then Rafe danced four or five songs with Lauren while Gracie went out to have a smoke. She came back after a bit and sat on the couch, watching them. They were both sweaty, panting and laughing. Finally the record player clicked off, and no one moved to put on any more. It was only about ten-thirty, early by the standards of yore, as Lauren pointed out.

They all sat and talked for a bit, quietly. Then Gracie said, "I have something I need to tell you." She stopped and made a mischievous face. "And it's not, you'll be relieved to know, that I'm pregnant." It was that she was giving the house up. She was going to join Pete and Nat at the retirement place.

The house was already on the market—she would need the money for the entrance fee—but she'd asked them not to put a FOR SALE sign up by the driveway until after Lauren's visit.

"I feel so awful about this," she said. "I'd always planned to leave it to you, but it's nothing but an albatross at this point. I haven't kept it up worth shit."

"Oh, Momma," Lauren said. "Don't, don't feel bad. If this is what works for you, this is the right thing."

"And you know we're stuck in Boston," Rafe said. "There's really no way we could have taken it on, a second home."

But Grace needed to be penitent about her failures awhile longer. They listened, they reassured her, the women hugged one another, and then they all said good night. Lauren started to put the records away, but Grace turned on the stairs and said, "Don't. Don't bother with that, darling. I like to do that in the morning. It's like having the fun all over again."

They went to bed, and Lauren wept a little. "My sweet old house," she said. She smelled of Ivory soap, which was the only brand Gracie ever bought.

In the middle of the night, a complicated, several-stage **thud** waked him. It was pitch-black, and he couldn't remember where he was for a moment. Then from somewhere below the bed—from the floor—came Lauren's voice. "Did I wake you?" she whispered.

"Yes," he said. "What's happening?"

She laughed. "I seem to have misplaced my **knees,** Rafe."

That was the real beginning. In the morning, she couldn't walk. He had to carry her downstairs, and after breakfast, he helped her to the car. She was dismissive, for Gracie's sake. She'd pulled something dancing, she said. "You and Pete can apparently pretend to be seventeen with impunity, but not me."

Each of them hugged Gracie for a moment. They promised to come back soon. Gracie in turn promised she would save everything in the house Lauren might conceivably want.

They drove back to Boston. They were mostly silent. He helped her into a rest stop on the Mass Pike and waited anxiously outside the women's room.

When she emerged and spotted him, she laughed. "You look like a mole-ster, hovering there," she said, using her own favored pronunciation of the word. But he'd seen her inching along the wall, and when he reached for her, she almost fell into his embrace. She leaned hard on him all the way back to the car.

After that there were more tests, and then late in the fall the terrible diagnosis. The doctor was kind and patient. He answered everything honestly and said three or four times how sorry he was.

"It is fatal, yes, invariably," he said, in answer to Lauren's question. "But there is variability in the length of time it takes. Look at Stephen Hawking."

They didn't speak going to the car, starting to drive home. It was a sunny day, a beautiful day. Irrelevant gold and red leaves blew across the street in front of them. She said abruptly, "**Look** at Stephen Hawking."

"Swanee . . . ," he started.

"No. Shut up. Stephen Hawking is like a . . . disembodied **brain,**" she said. "Stephen Hawking has a mechanical voice. I am . . . I **am** my body. I can't live without a body." She was sobbing. "I don't want to live without my body."

He spotted a parking space. He pulled over and reached across the console and the stick shift to her.

He held her awkwardly, spoke to her: he loved her. It would be all right. He was with her. He was aware of the stick shift poking his side. He would stay with her. There was nothing that could happen to her—to them—that would make him love her less.

"And sex?" she whispered. "What about sex?" Her eye makeup was streaked down her face. Her mouth was twisted.

"As long as you want me to make love to you, I will want to make love to you."

A lie. The first of many.

The little playwright was in the first row, watching him and Serena Diglio, who was playing Anita, go through their scene at the end of the second act.

"I have to do this alone," Rafe said.

"You don't, have to."

"I want to do this alone," Rafe said.

"Hold it," Edmund said. They both looked over at him. "Does he? Does he want to? Is he telling the truth here?"

There was a silence. Then Rafe said, "So, less conviction?"

"Well, maybe he's mostly trying to convince himself," Edmund said. "Okay, sorry. Go ahead."

"I want to do this alone," Rafe said, more slowly.

"I don't believe you," Anita said.

"You should."

"Just . . . answer me one question."

Rafe turned away, impatient, as he and Edmund had agreed he would be.

"Gabriel? Just one."

"All right."

"Tell me honestly, when you heard, didn't you feel any sense of . . ." She paused, shook her head. "Forget it."

It seemed to Rafe that Serena was overdoing this a little, that she was too desperate, too pleading, too early on. But Edmund said nothing, so he said his line, and they moved on.

When he came to the self-pitying lines, " 'Oh, poor Gabriel. Poor man,' " his voice was thick with contempt for himself, and for her. Maybe **he** was overdoing it, he thought. But Edmund was still just watching.

She went on. She blew a line, and Edmund gave it to her. **It's not greed, what I feel.**

"Oh, right," she said. "That's a funny one to forget."

"Yup," Edmund answered.

She took a breath, her face changed. She said the line.

He answered with his lines about wanting as the human condition, about feeling dead without it.

"But that's what you said you felt with Elizabeth. **Dead.**" Her voice was shrill.

"Yes," he said.

"And with me, you felt alive again." She was begging him: **You** said **so.**

He hadn't thought of it this way. He had heard her being more assertive. So he said his line more sorrowfully. "Yes. But it was . . . wanting. Wanting what I didn't have."

"Me!" she said. Now assertive.

He took a step back from her. He could see Edmund nod. "Ah, well," he said. He had his distance again.

"Me," she insisted.

And then he began his long, slowly developing explanation, something he wanted to be discovering as he went along, in just the way he and Edmund had talked about it—they'd agreed that he was actually feeling his way into his position as he spoke. When he got to his passionate declaration at the end, that he would enact whatever he was called up to be—the widower, the glad husband—at that point, they had agreed, he **had it;** his feelings had caught up to what he was saying. He'd caught up to himself.

Then her cry, "But you said you loved me."

Edmund stopped her. He didn't like it. "You sound like a spoiled little girl, Serena." He pitched his voice high and whining: " 'You **said** I could have some candy.' "

She was nodding, looking sheepish. "Yeah, I hear that. But I'm not sure how I should say it."

Rafe sat down while Edmund and Serena talked about it. He looked over at the playwright, sitting in the second row of seats. Billy Gertz, her name was. Wilhelmina, she'd told him. Yes. That had been their exchange at the meet and greet.

"Billy," he'd said. "Short for something, I bet."

"Wilhelmina," she'd said back, in a stern voice with a German accent, pronouncing the **W** as a **V.**

Now she was slouched deep in her seat, making notes. She had her glasses on. Her head barely rose over the back of the seat. She could have been a precocious fifth grader with a thick bowl haircut.

She looked up at him, and he met her eyes. She smiled, raised her hand for a moment, and then went on writing.

"Okay, Rafe," Edmund said.

He stood up and took his place, and they went over their last lines together. He liked the way Serena said her last line, yelling at him. It sounded full of rage, but you could hear her sorrow, too. She overdid slamming the door, in fun. The set shook. Someone backstage protested: "Hey!"

"Sorry. Joke," she called, coming back onstage.

They sat down and talked for a while with Edmund, who had suggestions for both of them. Gestures. Emphases. Praise, though, too. He knew how to balance these things, crafty old Ed.

When he was done, he looked down at the playwright. "Anything for these guys, Billy?"

She shook her head. "I might give a few things to you for them tomorrow."

"Okay then," Edmund said, turning back to them. He clapped his hands. "Be off with you."

Serena went backstage, where she'd left her stuff apparently, and Rafe came down into the house to get his jacket. Billy was standing up, shoving things into the big bag she seemed to carry with her always.

"I'm a bit at loose ends," he said to her.

"**Are** you now?"

"Do you fancy a drink?"

She slung her bag up onto her shoulder. "Hmm. I think so. Yes. I think that's the very thing I fancy."

"You smell boozy," Lauren said. "Brewer-y."

"Ah! You're awake."

"I woke up when I heard you come in."

Garbled gook, they called it, the way she spoke, but he understood every word. He'd grown into it with her. He leaned over and kissed her. "I had a drink—several drinks, not to put too fine a point on it—with the playwright after work."

"Fun?"

"Yeah, I guess you'd say. She's nice."

"What did you talk about?"

"Actually, Swanee, we talked a lot about the play."
This was true, surprisingly.

Or not surprisingly. Though Rafe often stayed out in the evenings, away from Lauren, what he did then was drink and talk. He had the perfect life, he often thought, for someone married to an invalid. There was a semisteady supply of fresh blood to listen to his tale of woe. Or of fresh ears. Ear after ear after ear. Just when everyone might have been getting tired of him and his sad story, the play would be over and the faces—the ears—would change.

Not that he always told the sad tale. Tonight, for instance, he hadn't mentioned it. They had, in fact, talked about the play. And then about Billy. Her life, her history. Why she'd left Chicago, which was, he pointed out, a great theater town.

"Yes, but the problem with Chicago is that what happens in Chicago stays in Chicago."

"Boston's not so different."

"Boston's different."

"How is it different?"

"Because this play is leaving Boston."

"Hey, can I come, too?" he'd asked, and she had laughed. She had a good laugh—snarky, quick.

He asked her about the play—where the idea had come from.

"Oh, I dunno. Worcester?" she said. She was drinking Stoli, neat. He was having beer.

"No, really."

She shrugged. "I guess I was thinking about 9/11. You know."

"So this is really a 9/11 story?"

"Well, another version thereof. The train version. They seem to like trains, don't they, those nutty old terrorists. Trains and buses and subways." She made a little moue. "It seemed . . . I don't know. A way to reinvent it."

"And changing it to Chicago?"

"Oh, I guess that was my imaginary way of"—she gestured—"bringing it home, as it were. **My** home. I grew up there. Sweet home Chicago."

"Inflicting it on the Second City."

She nodded.

"Though we've got a pretty small sampling of Chicagoans here," he said.

"Well, but isn't **two** what it always comes down to? Isn't that where things are felt? In drama. And in life, for Pete's sake? **Chekhov**"—she drew herself up— " 'The center of gravity residing in two, he and she.' " She slumped a little, back to normal. "That's it, don't you think? The question we all ask of the big event? How am **I** affected? How are **you** affected? 'Where were you when you heard?' " She'd made her voice breathless, avid. "Or 'I knew someone who knew someone whose husband died.' And then there's '**My** husband died.' Or 'my wife.' "

"Thus, Gabriel and Elizabeth."

"Yes, that particular he and she."

"And who are you, in that story?"

She turned away. She tipped her glass this way and that, and then she looked up at him. "That's their story, it's not mine." She lifted the glass and had a tiny sip.

"But you made it up."

"I imagined it, yeah. But please, please, give me some credit. Give the imagination some credit. No one really does. No one believes in it anymore. Everything always has to be autobiographical, somehow."

He thought of Lauren, working on her memoir. Kept alive, as he saw it, by recording her own slo-mo death as it happened to her. She wanted to make use of it in some way, she said.

"So this isn't autobiography," he said now to the playwright. "You're not either one of them."

"Nor Alex or Emily or Anita. No. Or, I am, but maybe about equally all of them." She grinned quickly and looked about ten years old. "Which means I'm also none."

"And you just imagine what it would be like, each situation and each character."

"That's my job. Imagining them, imagining what they say and why they say it and how they say it."

He took a swallow. "So how do you imagine it was on 9/11, for the people who were waiting?"

She was silent for what seemed to him a long moment before she answered. Finally, she said, "Well, that all depends, doesn't it?"

"On what?"

"Ah. Well, I guess how . . . you know, how some people embrace disaster. Zoom right into the worst scenario: Oh God, it's my wife! And others think, Well, she could have gotten out. Or, Maybe he was late to work. Or, She could have missed the train. She'll call."

"Denial."

"I suppose." She took another tiny sip of Stoli.

"Like, I guess . . . yeah," he said. "I'm remembering all those posted notices, you know?" She looked at him. "Sort of as though the victims might be **lost** somewhere. Might just be having a tiny bit of trouble remembering how to get home. What was that but evidence of the way people can just find reasons, or ways, not to believe a terrible thing?"

"So do you think that's part of Gabriel's response?" Billy asked.

"No. Actually I don't, no. I think he believes she's dead, right away. Because I think that's the kind of guy he is."

"Well, then, if you think so, that's who he is. So, what difference will that make in how you play him?"

"Well, it's not quite like **The End of the Affair,** is it? Did you see that?"

"I saw it, I read it. But I don't know what you mean."

"Well, Gabriel's not like the woman in that story. He's not about to pray for her return, the way she did for her lover. To make a deal for her return. He just . . . it's just something that makes him examine himself—his own responses. What he wants, most deeply." He lifted his shoulders. "Maybe that's the contemporary version of religious conversion—**self**-examination."

She laughed, and he did, too.

"So how would **you** say the last line?" he asked.

"The last line being 'Elizabeth'?"

"Yeah. What are my choices, as you see them?"

She made a funny face and lifted her hands. **How would I know?**

"I mean, is he glad? Is he . . . feeling trapped? What?"

"Sure." She dragged the word out. "All of the above."

He grinned. "You're no help, are you?"

"You're the actor, dear heart." She was smiling now, too.

He lifted his glass. "Indeed I am," he said.

"Ah, you're married," she said. She was pointing to the ring on his finger.

"Yes. Very."

She exhaled through closed lips, a dismissive noise. "There's married and there's not married. No such thing as **very.**"

"You're wrong there."

"Well, if you're so very married, why are you here, having this drink?"

She didn't say **having this drink with me,** he

noted, but that's what she meant. And he didn't know the answer to that. But he said, "I often have a drink after work. My wife goes to bed early."

"Ah."

And that was as close as he'd come to the sad tale, tonight. A little bit later, she'd swung down off the bar stool and said she had to get home to walk her dog. He'd watched her out the window as she crossed the street, a little figure, all in black, disappearing quickly into the dark of Union Park, the fanciest of the little private parks studding this neighborhood of Boston. He'd stayed on by himself, talked a bit to the bartender about the Red Sox—who they might sign, who they'd let go—and then he drove home.

Now he lay next to Lauren in the dark. She was motionless, quickly back in her deep sleep. Dreaming, maybe. Dreaming of the way she used to be.

A few weeks ago he'd been getting something for her from her desk, and he'd read the top page of her memoir in progress. She was describing a dream she'd had, a dream of running. "In my dream, my body worked perfectly. My breathing was unstrained and full and slow. My legs were weightlessly muscled. My knees rose high in front with each step, my heels kicked high behind me, everything was smooth and effortless. I woke to the sound of my own laughter, as grateful and happy as we are when we conjure some long-dead friend or lover in our sleep and get to talk with them or touch them once more."

Now she lay propped up on her pillows in her drugged sleep next to him, her body immovable as a dead woman's—only her labored, thick breathing attesting to the life it still held, captive.

A month or so after they got the diagnosis, Grace had called and asked them if they'd take her cat. The house had sold, and she was moving, but she couldn't take the cat with her. Belle-Vue had a no-pet policy. She'd tried giving him to a younger friend, but the woman's son turned out to be allergic.

Rafe's first impulse was to say no. He and Lauren were still in a fragile state, one or the other of them likely at any time to begin to weep—though Lauren had already begun, too, to sometimes make a quick, biting joke about it. But he said to Grace that he'd talk to Lauren and get back to her.

Lauren wanted to take him. She would be home more of the time, and Marsh—short for Marshmallow—would be nice company. They decided Rafe would drive over and get him, and while he was there, break the news to Grace that Lauren had ALS. Lauren said she knew this was a rotten thing to ask him to do, but that she couldn't possibly do it herself: "I'd just as soon take a knife out and **stab** her about a dozen times."

So Rafe set out on a Monday morning in mid-December. It was snowing, but the really heavy stuff wasn't supposed to start until nightfall, by which time he'd be at Gracie's, safely off the road. And by the time he headed back, after breakfast on Tuesday, the roads would have been cleared.

There was something hypnotic about the drive. There was almost no traffic on the Pike, so Rafe didn't have to think much about what he was doing. The snow came at the windshield steadily, and the wipers kept a constant rhythm. The road gradually turned white. He stayed in the one lane where there were tire tracks. Occasionally he passed a plow, throwing up wet clumps of brownish slush. He was relieved to be away from Lauren. He had the sense mostly of that, of being on the road, **going away.** He listened to music, he kept his mind empty.

Route 9 across Vermont was slow, busy with local traffic and occasionally slippery. Twice he scared himself with a long skid. When he got to Bennington, he stopped and had a drink in a bar. There was a giant television mounted high on the wall in the corner with the volume turned off. Men in football uniforms ran this way and that. There were two couples lingering at tables, having finished lunch a while earlier, he supposed. The snow fell steadily on the empty street outside the plate-glass window. He had another drink. He wanted nothing more than he wanted to stay there and have one after another until he was shit-faced, but after those two, he paid up. He stopped at a liquor store in town and bought a bottle of Johnny Walker Red, and then he drove to Grace's.

The field around her house was unreasonably beautiful. The day was still, no wind, and the snow had collected evenly on every branch of the twisted old apple trees, of the swooping birches bent low under it; it had settled thick and white on the dark green of the mammoth pines at the bottom of the meadow. He sat for a while after he cut the engine, thinking about missing this, thinking about losing it, about losing Lauren, losing Grace, losing Pete and Nat. It seemed more than he could bear, this beauty, and all this loss.

He saw Grace's face, blurry and white, moving across the living room window. He got out of the car. The snow was about a foot deep, soft, light. He retrieved his overnight bag from the backseat. As he came up the walk, she opened the door.

"My favorite son-in-law," she said.

"Hello, Gracie." They kissed, she held him and patted his back heartily, as if she were burping a baby. She was wearing jeans and a flannel shirt. Her hair smelled a little oily.

While he went to hang his coat up, he looked around. The rooms were nearly bare, but he'd expected this—she'd given away or sold everything but what she was taking with her to the retirement place, and they'd been consulted every step of the way. Earlier in the fall, before Lauren was diagnosed, he had come over in a rented van with a friend and taken some stuff back to Boston—an old chair Lauren liked, books, china and linens, boxes of photographs, silver, candlesticks, the worn quilts she'd grown up with.

Now their voices ricocheted around the rooms, their footsteps sounded hollow and ominous on the naked floors. Grace had some boxes she wanted him to bring downstairs, and he did that. Then he got the snowblower out of the garage and cleared the front walk and the porch—Tim Holloran would come by when the snow stopped, late tonight or early tomorrow, to plow the driveway out.

When he came back in, it was already getting dark. He could smell meat cooking—roasting beef or pork. He went into the kitchen. He'd resolved to tell her before dinner. He couldn't sit across the table from her and eat and make small talk and then spring it on her.

She was peeling potatoes at the sink, her back to him, her arms and hands in steady, tight motion.

"Come have a drink with me, Gracie," he said.

"Can't," she said without looking up or stopping what she was doing. "I want to get this stuff going. Then I'll get looped."

"I need to talk to you. Come on and have a drink now."

She looked sharply at him and set the peeler down at the sink. "I don't like the sound of this," she said.

"No, it's not good."

She wiped her hands on a dish towel and came over to the table. She sat and he poured a tumbler full for each of them. She had a swallow, and then she said, "You're not splitting up again, are you?"

"No." They were almost at right angles to each other. "No, this is about Lauren." He didn't look at her. "She's been diagnosed with a disease." He heard a little intake of breath. "A wasting disease." He'd decided on these words a few days ago, after Lauren asked him to do this.

"A wasting disease? What disease?" She pushed her glass away.

"It's ALS."

She shook her head.

"Amytrophic lateral sclerosis." He pronounced it slowly. "ALS. Lou Gehrig's disease. Remember when she was having trouble getting around last summer? When I had to carry her?" Her eyes were unwavering on his face. He tried to meet them. "Well, that was a sign of it."

"I've heard of this disease," Grace said. "But I don't know what happens to you. What will happen?"

"She will get weaker, progressively. She will need . . . help. She may, in the later stages, even need help eating, or breathing."

Gracie's mouth opened. Then she said, "So, she's going to **die** from this."

"She will." He was looking down at his hands.

"How long does she have?"

He shrugged. "I guess it's different from case to case, and for that reason the doctors won't say, at this point. But we've read about it, and it could be three years. Maybe five years. It's certainly a few years off. She's still able to do most everything now."

"But . . . this is so terrible." Grace's face was awful to look at.

"It is," he said. He reached over to take her hand.

She drew in a deep breath now, and expelled it. "I believe I'll go upstairs for a bit." She shoved her chair back.

"Take this." He filled her glass almost to the brim, and handed it to her.

She took it. At the door, she turned partway back. "You might get the potatoes on, sliced, in boiling water."

"Okay," he said. He was near tears. He wanted her to go, so he could cry. For her, for Lauren, for himself.

She must have sensed this. Or maybe not. At any rate, she said, "I'm so sorry for you, dear, having to tell me this."

"Well, I'm . . . sorry, too."

But when she left, he didn't cry. He drank some more scotch, he peeled the potatoes and put them on to boil, he checked on the roast. He saw the baster sitting out on the counter next to the stove, so he basted it, just in case. This was how he'd been functioning for weeks now. **Oh, this foot? You put it down in front of the other one.** Now he moved his chair over by the window and sat, his drink in his hand, watching the slow fat snowflakes descend.

He didn't hear Grace come down, but suddenly music blared forth from the living room—horns and voices from the thirties or forties.

He turned, and she was in the kitchen, the cat trailing her.

"We're not having any vegetables," she announced. "The hell with them. Just meat and potatoes, that's all I feel like doing tonight." She went to the oven and opened it.

"Then that's all I feel like eating," he said.

She took the roast out of the oven and set it on the counter. "And we'll drink."

"I'm ahead of you there," he said.

"Have you been drinking?" she asked. She was at the sink pouring the steaming water off the potatoes. "I mean, in general?"

"Not so much. Lauren thinks it makes her speech worse, plus she's on some med for depression, which means, I guess, that she's really not supposed to." He had another sip of scotch. "But tonight is different. Let's get wrecked."

"I am wrecked, whether I drink or not. But yes, let's have a few. Let's get blotto."

He set the table while she mashed the potatoes. She put the food on the table and went back to the living room to restack the records. They ate, listening to the music, and then it stopped. They talked in a desultory way, always about Lauren, about the disease. Grace wanted to help. She spoke of coming for a week or so each month, once Lauren needed her. She seemed, so quickly, to have taken it in, to have accepted it.

But as they stood side by side, doing the dishes,

she stopped and turned to him. "How will I go on living, after she dies?"

He couldn't think of an answer. He just stood there, and then he shook his head, and she went back to the dishes.

Later, they danced a little, and then he helped her pack up the records—Lauren had said she wanted them.

In the night, he heard Tim Holloran plowing the driveway, he saw the headlights of his truck rake the ceiling. When he woke again, to a muted light, his mouth was dry, and he had a headache. Aspirin, and then coffee helped.

He packed the car. Grace had more stuff for him to take than he'd counted on. The cat would have to ride in his carrier in the front seat. He took two bananas and left without eating breakfast. Maybe the roads would be plowed, maybe they wouldn't, but he couldn't bear to stay any longer in the emptied house with this flattened, silent version of Grace. And he thought it was likely that she wanted him to go, that she needed to be alone.

As he turned at the bottom of the long driveway, he saw that she was still standing where he'd left her, watching him out of sight.

The first preview performance had only a few glitches. Annie, the actress playing Emily, dropped her glass of fake bourbon and it broke, and Bob—

Alex—flubbed a line but covered for it nicely. Rafe felt he gave an off-kilter emphasis to "Elizabeth," his last line—the play's last line. It seemed to him, just after he'd said it, that it sounded as though he didn't recognize his own wife.

No one was interested to discuss this with him at the bar afterward, where most of the cast and some of the crew had gathered for a celebratory drink. A few spouses were there.

He talked to Billy. Just as she was about to turn away, she asked him, "Hey, where's your wife, to whom you're so very **married**?"

"I told you, she goes to bed early."

"Every single night?"

"She's an invalid, actually. She's not well."

Her face fell. "Oh, I'm sorry."

"Yeah, well, we're sorry, too."

"But I'm sorry also because I was sort of . . . teasing you, and that's, that's just . . . inappropriate."

He knew what she was saying—that she'd been flirting, that she'd been teasing him sexually. "Ah, it's okay. I miss being teased."

"I suppose one would."

"One does."

Later, as things were breaking up, he found her. "Want some help walking your dog?" he asked.

"You can come along if you like. My dog actually mostly walks himself. And it's a quick walk at night. Strictly business, as it were."

They went halfway into Union Park and up the

steps of one of its grand brick bowfronts. She let them into the front hallway where a staircase rose splendidly and vanished into the upper reaches of the house. She opened one of the double doors into what once must have been the town house's parlor.

A black shape bounded forward out of the dark toward her. The dog was enormous. As she spoke to it enthusiastically, it rose on its hind legs and rested its front paws briefly on her shoulders. Its head was almost at the height of hers. Its tail was wagging frantically. They seemed to be smiling at each other.

The dog dropped and then came to Rafe and poked him with his nose once, approximately in the groin.

He asked her what the breed was, and she said she'd been told a mix between a Newfoundland and something else maybe even bigger. "Though what **that** could be, I don't know."

"He is unbelievably huge," Rafe said.

"Yes. I thought I'd get the least appropriate dog for a person my size that I could find." She turned away. "Let's get your leash," she said conversationally to the dog.

She stepped into the dark room, and Rafe and the dog followed. The parlor was vast, high-ceilinged. He saw double pocket doors, partially pushed back, and beyond them another room and windows.

The dog stood patiently while she hooked the leash to his collar, and they went outside. They strolled down to the corner, where patrons still lingered in the glass box of a ground-floor restaurant, and then they walked slowly back. The dog must have lifted his leg twelve times.

She asked him if he'd like to come in for a drink.

"I've had a few."

"One more, then."

He hesitated. "Sure," he said. "Sure. Why not?"

"**That**'s what I like," she said. "Unbridled enthusiasm." She was unlocking the front door.

"Sorry," he said.

Inside, she turned on a lamp and disappeared into a galley kitchen off the parlor. She brought out two glasses and a bottle of wine. "If you'd open it," she said, handing him the corkscrew, "I'll put some music on."

While he peeled the casing off the bottle and twisted the corkscrew in, she squatted by a wide console and loaded some CDs into a player. Piano music, jazz, suddenly blared in the room, too loud.

"Oops," she said, and turned it down. He didn't recognize the tune or the player.

She came and sat at the other end of the long couch. She put her feet on the scarred coffee table. It was round, it looked like an old oak dining room table someone had cut down. Books and magazines were arranged in piles on it.

He handed her a glass and lifted his own. "Cheers," he said.

"To us," she said. "To the first real performance."

After one sip, he set his glass down. He really

didn't want any more. "Weren't you intimidated, writing about 9/11?" he asked.

"Well, of course, it's not 9/11, it's the Lake Shore Limited."

"Yeah, yeah," he said. He leaned back. "I happen to know it's 9/11. I got it straight from the playwright."

She smiled at him, tilting her head. "Yeah, you did." She breathed in, loudly. "The thing is," she said, "I have great creds."

"Nine-eleven creds?"

"Ah-huh. I'm a kind of almost widow." She looked over at him. "A lover died."

"Oh, I'm sorry."

"Well, I appreciate that." She sat silently for a moment. Then she smiled, a little bitterly, he thought. "But it gives me impeccable authority. Almost as good as Rudy Giuliani's."

He laughed. "And are you thinking of running for president, too?"

"I have a life that's as close as I want to get to a public one. And after 9/11, it was too public, for a while."

"Were you beleaguered?"

She looked at him sharply for a second. "Nice word. That would be apt. I was, briefly. They quoted me in his little **Times** piece—my name, that I lived in Boston—and after that, for a while, I got calls whenever they wanted a statement, a response from, you know, a bereaved relative, or quasi-spouse. Fiancée, I was called, officially. Though that wasn't true. But that came from his sister, so I didn't correct it. And then his sister, of whom I'm very fond, she wanted me to be with her at various functions. Memorial things. It was hard to say no, so I didn't say no. And I had to talk to other people on those occasions, too. His sister actually wanted me to have some of the **money** when it came." She sighed deeply.

"People think they know what you're feeling." Her voice was softer, suddenly. "What you must be feeling. And because it's easier not to expose yourself, what you're truly feeling, you don't disabuse them. You go through the motions for them. That's why, I think, I wanted to write the play—about a man who doesn't feel what he's supposed to. Who has an entirely too-confused response to it for lots and lots of reasons. So he can't show . . . anything, almost."

"Well, that helps me, actually. Thinking about a couple of things in it."

"Good. Anything that helps."

They sat, listening to the music. Or he was listening to the music. He looked at her. "But what were **you** feeling, that you weren't supposed to?" he asked.

"Oh, I don't know. I just didn't feel . . . It's not important, really. I was . . . It's just, there's this set of things everyone expects of you. That's all."

They sat silent for a moment. Rafe felt strained, a bit. He asked, "What was he like? Your, almost fiancé?"

"He was . . . good. He was sweet."

Rafe made a face.

"I know. But he was. He was kind, sweet. He was a little younger than I was." She swung her knees up sideways onto the couch and turned so she was facing him. "He was a prep school English teacher. I went to the memorial service at his school, and to a boy, to a girl, his students were weeping. Straight through it. There wasn't a dry eye in the house, except for me." She laughed, lightly. "I was always more than a little aware of my great unworthiness around him."

"Well." He nodded several times. He was thinking of his own unworthiness, of the variety of ways, daily, that he failed Lauren.

As if she'd read his thought, she asked, "And your wife? What's she like?"

He shrugged. "She was wired. Funny. Lively." He shrugged again. "Great legs."

"You're using the past tense."

"Yeah, I am. Even the legs are a little . . ." He thought of them—white, flaccid. "They've lost what I've learned to call **tonus.**"

She was silent for a moment. "You seem very distant from her."

He thought she sounded sad about this, perhaps compassionate. At any rate, not judgmental. He had a sudden sense of relaxing with her. "I am, of necessity, very distant from her. She really is . . . her real intimacy, at this point, is with the illness. And I, to keep going, I have to more or less ignore the illness.

We're at cross purposes. I think she feels . . . that I've left her alone with it. And I suppose I have."

"And the illness is?"

"Lou Gehrig's disease. Stephen Hawking," he said. He smiled. "Or, as she calls him, Fucking Stephen Hawking.

"She's writing about it, you know." He nodded. "Yep. A memoir. She's got some elaborate voice-activated software. I've seen a bit of it here and there. I think she'd like me to want to read it. And I don't. It's the last thing on earth I want to read. While she's alive. Maybe I will after she's dead. I'll read it and weep, as they say. For now . . ." He shook his head. "Yeah, I keep my distance."

The CD had changed. The piano was slow now. Some old Fats Waller tune, he thought. Probably he and Lauren had the original version on one of Gracie's 78s.

"But you love her."

"I loved her. And because of that, I love her. Yes."

She looked at him, her head tilted. "You must be very lonely."

He laughed, quickly. "I need to get a dog, I guess."

She smiled. "It works, you know. A dog. To a degree."

"We have a cat. Though he's more my wife's companion."

They sat quietly for a few minutes. Then she said, "Would you like to make love? Since you can't have a dog." She was smiling, her lips slightly parted.

"I would," he said. He looked directly at her. "I'm not sure I can." He smiled, too, but ruefully. "This hasn't been the most erotic lead-in I could imagine."

"You never know," she said, and leaned forward to set her glass down on the table.

He followed her back to the two pocket doors. As he stepped into the darker room, she spoke to the dog, who had started to follow, too. "Stay, Reuben."

He dropped instantly and laid his head on his front paws. A worried moan escaped from him.

"Get real," she said.

She slid the doors shut. They were in a smaller room, maybe half the size of the living room. It would have been the back parlor before the house was divided. Tall windows opened onto a closed-in space behind the house, some sort of yard. There were nineteenth-century gas lamps dimly glowing through the branches of the trees, and their faint light fell into the room. There was a bed against the wall, made up, with a patchwork quilt on top.

They undressed on opposite sides of it, like a couple who've been married for years. She lifted the covers and got in on her side, moving to the middle of the bed, turned toward him. Her face was in shadow, but he could feel her eyes on him.

He slid in toward her, and they were touching. Her body was small—so much smaller than Lauren's—and tensed, muscular. He moved his hands over her limbs, her buttocks, her breasts in a kind of astonishment. Everywhere she was quick and alive, responsive. Her muscles jumped under his touch; her tendons were like tight wires. She radiated heat, energy.

He could have wept.

He was hard, almost right away. "I don't have anything," he said. His breathing was audible, quickened. "A condom. I don't have one."

"I do," she answered. She rolled away from him and reached out to the bedside table. He heard the drawer open. She turned back and moved over him, swinging a leg up, then straddling him. He could see in the dim light that her breasts were surprisingly plump. She settled herself on his thighs, and tore the condom package open. She was expert with it, stroking him with warm hands while she also unrolled the sheath down over him. He moaned in pleasure.

She rose up onto her knees and moved forward. He watched what her hands were doing, holding his stiff penis, easing it into herself. When she was fully lowered onto him, when he was completely inside her, she arched her back and began to move herself slowly up and down. Her buttocks and her thighs tightened rhythmically with her motion.

He held her hips and helped her move faster. Her breasts jounced. He was wild with excitement. He started to come, much too soon, too fast. As he pushed into her harder, longer, she answered him with her body, and she rode him steadily until he was through, until they both slowed, and then he stopped. She sat, panting for a minute. Then she laughed, a short exhalation. They stayed like this, breathing hard. Billy was still moving, a gentle rocking.

He slipped out of her, finally. She lay down on him then, closing her thighs around him, moving her hips a little from side to side. Their breathing evened out. They rested for a bit, and then she moved up on his body. She kissed him. He held her. Her legs were open across him. He could feel her knees pressed in on either side of his rib cage and her warm dampness on his belly. A little while later, she slid off him, and they lay next to each other.

He turned on his side to look at her, to touch her. Her eyes were black in the dark room. How small she was under his hands, and perfect. And yet the full breasts, the thick dark bush. His fingers brushed over her nipples, and they stiffened.

"There's something I didn't tell you," he said. His voice was hoarse.

"Uh-oh."

"No, I like your play. That's all."

"That's all?" She laughed. "It's close to everything."

"I'm glad I got around to saying it then." He was touching her everywhere now—her breasts, her nipples, her hips, her abdomen. He couldn't get enough of the way she felt.

"Strange, then, that an act of sex is what loosed your tongue." Her voice was dreamy.

He slid his hand down her belly and pushed two fingers through her thick curly hair into the slick warmth of her. Her eyes had closed. He found her clit with his thumb and began a circling motion on it. Now she opened her eyes. She was breathing faster. "It must be that the fabulousness of . . . same, reminded you."

"No doubt." He played with her for a while, spreading her wetness with his fingers to make everything slippery, everything easy.

He slid down on the bed. He spread her legs wide apart, opening her for himself with his fingers, putting his face down onto her, onto her taste, her smell, using his mouth, his tongue. Her hips began to move, pressing up against him. He moved his fingers over her clitoris, he held it pushed up so he could pull on it with his whole mouth. She moaned. He thrust his fingers in and out of her.

She cried out sharply over and over when she came, raising her hips off the bed, pushing herself convulsively against his mouth, his face. As she finished, her motion ebbed, and finally she lay still. He turned his face to the side, feeling the soft fur, wet now, on his cheek. He kept his fingers in her, moving them slowly in and out. "Oh," she said. "This is so **sweet.**"

He laughed lightly. After a little while, he moved up so that he was lying next to her. He helped her pull the covers over both of them. He slept for a while. He woke. The clock's red numerals said 2:12.

When he got up to leave, she stirred and got up, too. He'd thought she was asleep. She pulled on the robe that had been hanging on the door to the bathroom and came out with him into the parlor. The dog rose when the doors opened and stood, alert, waiting to see what would happen next.

She crossed to the hall door with Rafe. "This was so lovely," she said. She was almost whispering.

"It was." He kissed her, bending down to meet her tipped-up face. He'd forgotten again how small she was.

"I love your mouth," she said. "Thank you for your mouth. Among all the rest of your very nice things."

He didn't know what to say.

She stepped back from him. "Are you going to be worried about this?" she asked gently.

He didn't answer. His shoulders rose a little.

"Rafe, this was two lonely people consoling each other. I was lonely. I feel wonderfully consoled. That's what I hope you feel."

He nodded. He spoke. "Yes. Yes, I do. Indeed I do."

"Please, please don't **worry** about this. You strike me as a worrier. Don't . . . let me—or this—become a worry. I won't be. I'm not. It's not. It was just for now, just for us. Our one-night stand. Just a wonderful onetime event. Wonderful for me, at any rate."

"No, for me, too," he said. He kissed her, and her

arms came around his waist. She rested her head on his chest. He cupped it there for a few seconds, liking the way the smooth cap of her hair felt.

"And that's that," she said softly. "Isn't it?"

"Yes, it has to be," he said. "Thanks. Thank you for saying that."

She stepped back and curtsied.

As he opened the door to the hall, he looked back at her. She was standing with the dog just beyond the slant of hall light that fell in. She looked like a child, but a mythical child, a child in a fairy tale, guarded by some large wild animal—a black bear. A griffin. She raised her hand as he left.

The night air was cold, and the streets were empty, except for the occasional cab and a pedestrian here and there. His car had a ticket, which he shoved into the glove compartment. There were several others in there—he'd have to pay up soon, or he'd get booted.

He drove up Mass Ave, almost the lone car. Every single light turned red for him, all the way. He didn't mind. He wanted it to take forever, getting home. He knew what was awaiting him—the sense of shame, the sense of having wronged Lauren. But as long as he was in transit, only **on his way,** he could hold that off, he could be just **here,** his body awake to itself for the first time in more than a year, his vivid sense memories—of Billy's body opening to him, moving in response to him—not yet what he mustn't allow himself.

At the Mass Ave bridge, he looked over at the

lights of the city, the purple spokes of the Zakim Bridge, its reflection doubled, spangled in the choppy water of the river. He drove past MIT. He turned south on Pearl. The streets of Cambridgeport closed around him, sleeping, silent. At home, the porch light had gone off.

Inside, he took his shoes off. Marsh came to him and leaned against his leg. He bent down and stroked him. In the dark kitchen, he washed his face. He took off his shirt and washed his upper body, too, shivering in the cold. The bones of his bare feet clicked against each other as he moved into the living room. He left his jeans on a chair.

But when he opened the bedroom door and felt the weight of the warm, moist air, heard the noise of the humidifier whirring, he didn't want to go in, he didn't want to lie down next to the motionless form that was Lauren. Gently he closed the door again and went to stretch out on the couch, pulling the old afghan from Gracie around himself.

At five, Lauren called out, her voice panicky.

She was angry, he could tell as he helped her out of bed. She didn't even grunt hello, she wouldn't meet his eyes.

When he helped her lower herself onto the toilet, she said, "You **have** to come home."

"I was home," he said. "I came home. I didn't want to wake you, but I was here." Even though this was true—partly true—he felt like a liar saying it. He **was** a liar saying it.

"But I didn't **know** that." She started to cry. She hadn't cried in a long time. "I have to know I'm not alone," she said.

He bowed his head quickly. "Yes, you're right," he said. He fumbled for a Kleenex. He wiped her eyes, her nose. "I'm sorry, Lauren. I'm so sorry." He was imagining how it must have been for her, the physical terror of abandonment as well as the other, the idea of what he might be—must be—doing. What he'd **done,** for Christ's sake. And always the possibility—could she think it?—that he simply wouldn't come back, ever. Probably she could think it, yes. And that's what he deserved.

When she had peed, when he'd wiped her, he supported her back to bed and lay down next to her. Marsh came in and jumped up onto the bed, walking back and forth across them until he found a good spot, curled against Lauren's side.

Rafe told her a long story about barhopping with Edmund and Serena.

She said she was sorry. She shouldn't have let herself think about him the way she had. But she'd been so alone, so scared.

He stroked her hair, her face, he held her hands. He felt the quick-flickering memories of Billy's body, of his hands on her, but he kept the same hands slow and comforting on Lauren. He whispered to her, saying her name, saying he loved her, over and over, until they both fell back to sleep. They didn't wake again for more than two hours.

That evening, friends came over for dessert and coffee and brandy. This was how they'd solved the problem of entertaining now that Lauren could no longer cook—or for that matter really even eat in public. It also made the evening shorter and less tiring for her.

They talked about the Sox, about Ben Affleck's new movie, set in Dorchester. The topics jumped around. The problem was that even these good friends—and Mary was one of the people in the Round Robin: she saw Lauren once every two weeks or so—even they had trouble understanding her speech now. Mary knew enough to keep her eyes on Lauren while Rafe translated, but Victor openly turned to him every time Lauren started to speak. Gradually she stopped trying.

It was amazing to Rafe, given Lauren's immensity in his own life, how quickly she was simply **erased** socially, even for him. They talked on without her, around her, as though she weren't there.

Once she said something clearly. They were speaking of Norman Mailer's death, and she said, "He was an asshole."

They all laughed, and Rafe felt a pang, looking at her face, to see how pleased she was to be understood, to have amused them, even with this minimal, crude remark. Lauren, one of the most amusing people he knew.

"How can you say that?" Victor said. "He wrote at least a couple of really great books." Victor taught literature at BU.

"I don't care," she said, and Rafe began to translate again. "He emerged in an era when most men were assholes about women, and he didn't bother to notice that about himself. Just the opposite. He embraced it. He argued for it."

But after this moment in the conversation, they moved on. Mary asked about Rafe's play, and he told her that it seemed to be starting off well. No, it hadn't been produced elsewhere, but it was going out after this run.

"Ah, so will you go with it?" Victor asked.

"No." He shook his head, and looked over at Lauren quickly. Her eyes were unmoving on him. "No, I stay put. I have a couple of other things in the works."

They talked a bit longer. Lauren was completely silent now, and finally Mary looked at her and said, "It is getting late. Work for all of us tomorrow, no?"

They stood up. They gathered their things. They both bent to kiss Lauren good-bye, and Mary said, "See you next Thursday, right?"

Lauren nodded, and Mary and Victor ambled conversationally with Rafe to the door.

He came back and got her into bed. She was exhausted. He cleaned up. Then he had another brandy and read through the second act of the play, thinking of what Billy had said about her reasons for writing Gabriel as he was, thinking about what Gabriel felt and what he didn't.

He thought of Lauren. The memories Gabriel had of Elizabeth, he thought—bright, funny, difficult, exciting—must be a bit like his memories of Lauren. Submerged, but always there, under the Lauren he lived with, the Lauren he took care of, or tried to. Just as Gabriel's remembered Elizabeth was somewhere under the distant woman he lived with.

It had taken him this long to see that the play was about him. Denial, indeed.

He set the script down and allowed himself to think about Billy. Her conversation. He remembered, too, the way she came, the way her small strong body moved convulsively in the dim light of her bedroom. He reached up for the lamp next to the couch and turned it off. He was aroused, but he didn't touch himself. He told himself it wasn't likely they'd sleep together again. He didn't think he could. He had felt too awful about Lauren. Admittedly only afterward, not during, but he knew he couldn't bear another morning like this last one— the way she'd felt, the way he felt.

Billy had seemed to sense those feelings rising in him just before he left. She'd been kind, given everything. He shook his head: what a lugubrious fuck he'd become. In several possible senses of the phrase.

He sighed and got up. He undressed. He went into the bedroom and got into bed next to Lauren. She didn't stir.

The next evening, when he came into the living

room to say good-bye, Lauren said, "We shouldn't try anymore." He must have looked startled, because she said quickly, "Socially."

He sat down. "Look," he said, "I know it wasn't good last night. But that was my fault. I let it happen. I should have made it easier for you to be part of it."

"No," she said. "Don't say that. It's too much for you to manage it all." She turned in her chair a little, as though she were uncomfortable. "After all, I have friends. I can talk to them." Her head moved slightly, a gesture toward the kitchen, where Carol, who'd come to spend the evening with her, was washing dishes, the water running steadily. "I can make it work, one on one. And that's the way I want to see people from now on."

"I don't agree with you."

She smiled. "That's too bad. 'Cause that's the way I want it."

"I think we should keep at it. Keep trying."

She gave an exasperated moan. "I don't **want** to keep trying. That's just it."

"Okay," he said. He stood up, looking at her. After a moment, he said, "If you change your mind, though . . ."

"I won't," she said.

He put his coat on.

"Poor you," she said. She was smiling again, a smile that almost worked, and reminded him of her as she'd once been.

"**Not,**" he said, smiling back.

"Yes," she said. "It's such hard work, being Lauren's hubby."

"I love you."

Tears sprang suddenly to her eyes. "It must be awful, then, to sometimes wish me dead."

He was shocked. He came over to her, knelt by her chair, and reached up to her face. "I never wish you dead."

"Ah, **liar,**" she said clearly. "I sometimes wish me dead, so I know you must."

The answers came to his mind, all the things he had said so often. That no matter what, she was always the same to him, that he loved her, that he loved her no less now. That he cherished every moment with her. That, as he had just finished saying, he never wished her dead.

He didn't say any of them.

After a moment, he said, "None of that is important."

She seemed almost startled for a few seconds. Then she said, "I know."

When he turned at the door, leaving, she said, "Do well tonight."

They seemed a little off, a little slow in the first act. The day away from it, maybe. For himself, there was a sense of bringing new information to Gabriel, Billy's information. And somehow—he felt this in an inchoate, unreasoned way—all of his own experience these last few days, with Billy, yes, and with Lauren, too.

In the second-act argument with Anita near the end of the play, the long argument over what Gabriel felt he should do and feel, he was hearing the exchange differently, responding differently. It changed her responses. It could have been bad, but he experienced it as a kind of **clicking,** the moment he always looked for in acting, with each role—when he felt the full meaning of the play in every line. Like a mathematical proof, he'd sometimes said of this feeling, trying to explain it to a friend. Or a piece of music. It was of a whole to him, like that. He felt as he said Gabriel's lines that he was truly understanding them. He had the sense of **being** Gabriel—Gabriel, accepting the implications for him of Elizabeth's fate, whatever it was to be. Accepting the randomness of terror's reach into her life as **his** fate. Choosing **this**—acceptance—over what suddenly seemed paltry in the possibility of his own action: the mere saying yes or saying no to his marriage. And he was experiencing this not as passivity, but as a kind of daring risk taking, necessary to him. He was excited, speaking the lines.

He could feel Anita's surprise and confusion, but that, too, seemed real to him, the best reading possible.

After she left, he moved slowly, almost wonderingly, around the set, as if all of it were new and remarkable in some way. As if he were a new

Gabriel, looking freshly at everything—his hands, the empty glass, the books he touched. He stood staring blankly into the blinding light behind the window upstage, smiling slightly to be feeling it—what he felt.

When he heard his name spoken, he turned and had the shock of seeing Elizabeth, Elizabeth come back to him—hurt, but alive. It was like a blow: the news of his life, of his own fate, arriving. He could feel the tears starting. He wasn't ready for them, he hadn't known they would come. He covered his eyes for a few long moments.

Then he realized what he had to do. He dropped his hands to let her see his weeping face—this was, after all, his gift to her. He stepped forward, toward her, and in a voice barely above a whisper, said his last line. Her name. **Elizabeth.**

BILLY

WHEN THE CURTAIN FELL, Billy sat unmoving though the applause and its gradual fading, through the audience's getting up and starting to talk, through the beginning of their slow shuffle out. Her heart was thudding heavily in her chest, it had been all through the last moments of the second act. She was nearly breathless at the end. She felt she was seeing **Gabriel,** exactly who he was, who she'd wanted him to be in that moment. As she watched him, she understood what she'd intended in a way she hadn't before, even when she was writing it.

The stage direction next to Elizabeth's name—the last spoken word of the play—had been "Joyously. Sadly." Rafe had managed to convey both those things tonight, joy and sorrow, and as the scene unfolded in front of Billy, she felt intimately connected to what he was making of it—as though he'd understood not just the character, but also, somehow, her.

She shut her eyes and saw his face again in the moment when he dropped his hands to show Elizabeth what he was feeling—his head tilted back, the tears running down his cheeks, his mouth opening to speak. It was Gabriel up there. She hadn't seen Rafe at all. She hadn't thought about what he was doing or not doing.

The spell was broken when the curtain rose for the applause: there was Rafe, his face still wet with tears. She felt almost stunned with gratitude to him. She wanted to see him, to speak to him. To say thank you. To offer him her pleasure in what he'd done. Maybe even to say she was sorry.

Sorry for what?

She wasn't sure.

The way he'd looked as he'd left her the other night came to her—the untransformed Rafe. She had sensed that he was already heading into guilt and sorrow, feelings that probably always lay in wait for him in his sad life with his wife. Instantly she'd thought that it was a mistake to have slept with him—that they shouldn't have done it.

They: no way. She was the one who had made it happen. It was she, **she,** who shouldn't have done it.

But now she was glad she had. She had been glad doing it, too, but that had been private, purely sexual. She'd been lonely, sexually lonely. It had felt like water to her thirst. But she was glad now because it had brought her—and him—this moment on the stage, she was sure of it. Something had opened in him, had changed. Something that made Gabriel say his wife's name as though it were a blessing and a penance at the same time—to be welcomed, to be suffered.

She stood up. She threaded her way through the last stragglers, heading toward the front of the theater. She mounted the steps and pushed the curtain aside. As she moved backstage, she heard voices and, turning, saw Edmund and Nasim, one of the lighting guys, onstage, talking. For a moment she was almost startled to see anyone else there, in Gabriel's living room. She spoke Edmund's name.

He looked over to her, and instantly his wide face opened in a grin. His head had already started moving up and down: yes.

"Did you see it?" she asked him. He nodded more. "Wasn't it fantastic?"

"Yep," he said. "It sure was." His hand rose and caressed his beard in pleasure.

"Where is he? Where's Rafe? I wanted to speak to him."

"Gone. Absent. He must've left about the second the curtain came down. He was so out of here."

"Hey," Nasim said. "I'm gonna check out this lightboard problem, see what's going on."

Edmund turned to him. "That's the ticket," he said.

Billy had come onstage, too, and now she sat on the arm of the overstuffed chair. "Why?" she said to Edmund. "Why did he leave?"

"I think he was . . . upset by it in a way." Edmund lifted his shoulders. "I suppose he sorta stunned himself, too."

"You told him how amazing it was, I hope. Before he took off."

"I did. We all did." They sat for a moment, smiling foolishly at each other.

"God, I was just so . . . moved," she said finally.

"It was fantastic."

She let a little silence gather. Then she said, "I should have slept with him much, much sooner."

His face changed. "Billy, you didn't!"

"Nah." She was shamed, suddenly. "Nah," she said. "Just kidding."

"Good! 'Cause, you know, his life is . . . really complicated."

"I know. I know. He told me about it."

Edmund watched her. She knew he couldn't tell whether she was lying or not. He shook his head. "It could really do some . . . bad, bad stuff to him," he said.

"I know. I was kidding." But his face was stern. The scary Edmund, the one they all dreaded. "It was funny, Edmund," she insisted, trying to make him happy again.

"Only **mildly** funny," he said.

"I apologize then." She put her hand on her heart for a moment. "I only said it 'cause I was just so . . . thrilled. It's actually almost embarrassing, I'm so happy. For him, and for me."

"For us."

"Right. For all of us."

Now Edmund set his bulk down on the couch,

grunting a bit. Here they were, the two of them, relaxed and happy in Gabriel's sad world. Incongruous.

He was frowning suddenly. "The big question is, will he be able to do it again?"

"Oh, now that he has it, I bet yes."

"Yah? But without that sense of surprise, maybe." He took his glasses off and began to polish them with the hem of his immense and shapeless T-shirt. It said SONOMA JAZZ FESTIVAL.

"But we were the only ones surprised," she said. "I mean, who else knew he'd never done it before?"

"Well, he was surprised, too, that's the thing. He surprised himself. That'll be hard to replicate."

"Oh, try not to be such a pessimist, Ed."

"Hard for me," he said. He put the glasses back on, and his pale, washed-out eyes got big again.

They sat in silence for a moment, both staring off at nothing. Billy sighed. She needed to get going. She stood up and began to pull on her coat, her **bat coat,** as she thought of it. It was black, it had big, loose arms, like wings.

"Want to get a drink?" Edmund asked. "Celebrate?"

"Can't. I'm meeting friends."

"Oh." And without missing a beat, "Well, maybe I could join you."

Billy imagined it quickly, the impossibility of the group. "They're kind of special, old friends," she said. "We'd be pretty boring to you, I think."

". . . 'she said, brushing him off.' "

"I adore you, Eddie, you know that." She reached out and touched his cheek. The fur of his beard was surprisingly soft. "I hope you're as happy with yourself as I am with me."

"Oh, I doubt it."

She laughed. "I know. But do it, Ed—get happy." She picked up her bag. "I'll see you tomorrow, anyway."

He bowed his head ceremonially. "Good night, then, Wilhelmina."

Billy walked back out through the empty theater, empty but for the cleanup crew moving around in the rows of seats, picking things up. She turned at the opened doorway to the lobby and stood looking back at the slope of the seats, at the closed curtain, remembering it again—her Gabriel, his visible sorrow and joy and the way she had felt connected to that, to both feelings. Had felt, somehow, **comforted** by them, she realized now.

As she stepped outside into the chilly rain, as she put up her umbrella, she was aware of a dragging reluctance about this next part of her evening. She just didn't want to do it, to go and be with Leslie and Pierce and whoever their pal was. It was partly her usual hesitation about Leslie, fond as she was of her. But it was also because she was so stirred by the play tonight. She wanted to hold on to that, to think it through.

Instead she would go and sit and make the smallest of small talk with the person she most would have liked to talk to honestly about everything—but never had. And never would, she was certain of that.

The day Leslie called, Billy was at home alone, working. When she heard Leslie's voice at the other end of the line, she experienced immediately what she'd come to recognize as the usual mix of feelings about her. The pull of the old affection, and then the wish to be free of that pull. But when Leslie said that she and Pierce were coming down to see the show, Billy had said only how glad she would be to see them. She offered the name of a place to meet afterward. Then, just as it seemed that the conversation was over, that the next step would be to say good-bye and hang up, Leslie said, "I think we'll bring a friend along, too."

"Great," Billy had said.

As soon as she hung up, she started to worry about the play, about how Leslie would receive it. It wasn't about Gus and it wasn't about herself, but the feelings behind it were ones she understood because of Gus and herself. Leslie would probably wonder about that. She might even be wounded by it. Billy had wounded a number of people with her work, but she didn't want Leslie to join the club. There was something so open, so recklessly generous about her that it made you want to shield her from anything painful.

It was only a while later, fixing herself a snack before she headed to the theater for another rehearsal, that it occurred to her that the friend Leslie had spoken of might be a man, a man she was planning to **introduce** to Billy, in some old-fashioned sense of the word.

Surely not. Surely it wasn't a man. And even if it was, surely there was no sense in which an "introduction" would be made.

But standing in the kitchen, eating her crackers and cheese, Billy had thought, **How strange would that be?**

She walked slowly through the misty rain down Tremont Street, trying to make the short trip last as long as possible. But of course the lighted windows of the restaurant had been visible from the moment she started out, and she was there in only a minute or two. As she waited on the corner for the cars to pass so she could cross the street, she could see Leslie and Pierce at their table, leaned in, talking to the third person, who was, indeed, a man.

Okay. Okay, maybe that would make things easier. A stranger, to let some air into this evening, to keep them all turned away from the topic at hand. The topic always at hand between her and Leslie.

She had barely stepped through the door—she was just shaking out her collapsed umbrella—when Leslie was embracing her, engulfing her in the

citrusy scent she always wore. She was saying something, something about flowers. Billy didn't understand right away. She felt as confused as if she'd been
waked from a deep sleep to a conversation already
under way. But apparently, yes, Leslie had bought
some for her, some flowers, and then forgotten
them. She was apologizing for this.

Billy smiled. "Leslie, I wouldn't have known anything about it if you hadn't told me. Don't tell me,
for God's sake."

"But I could kick myself."

"Well, don't. It was such a sweet thought, I'm glad
you had it."

And then they were at the table, being introduced.
Sam, the stranger's name was. He stood up—
unfolded himself slowly and for what seemed to
Billy like a long, long time. She felt like laughing.
Leslie couldn't possibly be fixing them up. It would
be ridiculous, the way they'd look next to each other.
It would be a kind of visual joke.

Leslie sat down. Billy had to clamber up onto her
chair—it was high, bar-stool height. She slung the
big bag she was carrying over the post at its back.
Leslie was still talking about the flowers, telling the
friend, Sam, about forgetting them. Pierce, meanwhile, had started to speak to Billy, congratulating
her on the play. After a minute or two, they were all
turned to her. The Sam guy began to add his questions to Pierce's. **How had she thought it went
tonight? When was the official opening? Had**

there been reviews yet? Billy answered politely, fully, but nervously. As she slid her coat off, she felt the man—Sam—helping her, easing her sleeve away so she could extract her arm. It felt good, this small kindness. Maybe it would turn out that he'd be a refuge of sorts.

The waitress came over, tall and blond and cool, unsmiling, a tiny diamond blooming in the outer flesh of one nostril. Billy asked for water and red wine. Pierce ordered a plate of cheeses for the table.

After she left, they turned to Billy again. More questions. It made her feel jittery, more jittery than when she'd been walking over. When the wine came, she lifted it immediately and had a swallow. What she wanted was not to be at the center of things here.

She asked Sam where he lived.

Brookline, he said.

"Oh, I lived there when I first came to Boston!" she said. She talked about the apartment she had then, the horrible cats she was sitting for. They figured out where his house was in relation to hers. They talked about restaurants they liked, and the bookstore. They were both fans of the Coolidge Corner, the independent movie theater.

Movies. Always good. And it worked tonight, too. Pierce had seen **No Country for Old Men** recently and wanted to talk about it. He said he didn't know what to make of it.

This was so un-Pierce-like that Billy was curious: why not?

She was turned to Pierce, listening to his explanation of what was unreasonable in the film, when she saw Rafe's pale face float by outside. He was hatless—no umbrella, his collar turned up, his eyes squinted against the rain. He didn't look in, he didn't see her. She had the impulse to get up, to go to the door and call to him, but of course she didn't. She sat, nodding, being polite, listening to Pierce.

Leslie, who hadn't liked the movie at all, said the best thing about going was the moment buying the tickets when she got to say, "Two seniors for **No Country for Old Men.**" Billy had turned to her when she started to talk. As she laughed now, she glanced over at Sam, at the end of the table. He was watching her with level, appraising eyes, as though he'd noticed her quick mental trip away, perhaps had seen where she'd gone in those few seconds.

But then Pierce was suddenly pointing to the back of the room. "Good Lord, what kind of place have you brought us to, Billy? It looks like a . . . an, **abattoir,** for God's sake."

The others turned and looked toward the far end of the room to what they apparently hadn't noticed when they came in: past the tables and the big square chopping block, the three wide refrigerators sitting side by side, lighted brightly from within. Their clear glass doors revealed chunks of bloody, raw meat stippled with fat, hanging sausage links, indecent-looking birds—naked, plucked.

"Yes," Billy said. She curtsied her head to Pierce. "A charnel house, for the edible dead."

"The Oedipal dead?" asked Leslie, incredulously.

Billy laughed. "E-di-ble," she said. "Though who knows? Who knows how the capon feels about the hen?"

"Isn't there a joke that begins that way?" Sam asked.

"There should be," she said.

"I'll be working on it."

His face had a worn quality to it. She liked that. A **used** man, she thought. She turned to Pierce, said, "It **is** called the Butcher Shop. In its defense."

"Very original," Pierce said. "I don't think it would quite fly in Hanover. All those naked carcasses. Too much unbridled mortality for a polite college town."

"I like being reminded of mortality," Billy said.

"You're younger than we are," Pierce said. "We don't."

Billy smiled. Leslie smiled back at her, and for a moment she felt a spark of the warm connection that had once lived between them. It unnerved her. She had a little more wine to drink.

As if she were feeling the connection, too, Leslie leaned forward. "I like your hair," Leslie said. "Cut that way."

Billy's hand went up as if of its own volition and touched her hair. "I'm dyeing it now," she said. **Completely irrelevant, Billy.**

Leslie sighed. "I probably should be, too. Mine's gotten so white."

"But it's a **beautiful** white," Billy said. "Pure as the driven snow." She could hear the nervous, jazzed quality in her own voice. She hoped no one else could.

It seemed not. Pierce and Sam had started to talk across the table—they were at opposite ends—about the approaching primary elections, the odd assortment of candidates in both parties. Leslie said she and Pierce had gone to see Hillary Clinton in Hanover and were impressed.

"I can't vote for Hillary," Billy said. "Not after the Iraq vote."

"For Christ's sake, Billy," Pierce said. "Everyone voted for the war."

"Well, clearly a majority did. But not everyone."

"Who didn't?" Leslie asked.

"How soon they forget," Billy said. "Your buddy Patrick Leahy. My buddy Ted Kennedy. Paul Wellstone. Barbara Boxer. A bunch of the good guys."

"Mikulski did, too, I think," Sam said. "And Chafee."

"Right." She looked at him appreciatively. "And a couple of others. It wasn't a done deal at all. It really mattered, how Hillary voted."

"But didn't she sort of have to, really?" Leslie asked.

"Hillary?"

"Yes. Because of being a woman. Not to be a wimp."

"Not to be a woman, anyway," Sam said.

"But I **hate** that! It's so strategic." Her voice was too loud. **Pull it in, pull it in.** She lowered it, spoke calmly. "No, I'm for Obama. Ever since that convention speech. Plus he's my homey—from Hyde Park, just like me."

Sam offered the preposterousness of Mitt Romney as a candidate, and Pierce joined in trashing him. They moved on to Fred Thompson, and he got it, too. Billy started to relax a bit. She had the sense of an opening up of the evening, a kind of freely moving conversation spurred by politics—she loved politics, for this and other reasons—so she was surprised when Leslie was suddenly standing by her chair, lifting her coat from it, making excuses for herself and Pierce. She was tired, it was past their bedtime. **No, no, Billy and Sam must stay,** she said. Pierce was standing now too, pulling out his wallet, joking about how expensive the hotel was, saying that they had to get to bed as soon as possible to get their money's worth.

Sam and Pierce argued briefly about the money that Pierce tried to set down, but Pierce won—he simply wouldn't take the handful of bills back. Billy slid off her chair while Pierce helped Leslie on with her coat. Then she was lifting her face to Leslie's cheek, to Pierce's—and they were on their way, one last wave before they were out the door, into the dark night.

Leaving Billy and what she supposed was her **date.** She got up onto her high seat again. They were silent for a few seconds. Too long. "If we're going to stay," she said, "I'd like another drink." She knew this was a bad idea. She'd had almost no supper, hours earlier—half a tuna-fish sandwich consumed standing in the kitchen, Reuben watching the slightest shift of the hand holding the bread.

"Are we going to stay?" He was looking at her, truly asking.

"I suppose we should. We've been instructed to, anyway."

He laughed and raised his hand to signal the waitress.

When she'd come over again and taken their order, he turned to her. "Now that I've got you alone," he said, "let me ask you about the play."

"Okay."

"Would you say it had a **happy ending**? We were arguing about it."

She couldn't tell if he actually cared or was just being polite, so she didn't know whether to try to explain it to him, what she had wanted, and then the surprise of how it had gone tonight. What she said was "Maybe. I guess I don't really think of it as an ending, anyway. More a beginning, maybe."

"A lot of maybes there." His eyes were unreadable through his old-fashioned spectacles. "But then I suppose it's not really fair, is it, to ask the playwright what the play means."

Billy thought this was generous of him. She'd been evasive and he was being generous. She should be generous. She said, "It's fair enough. And it's probably time the **playwright** worked up a quick, deft explanation for wider consumption. Hey, what **is** my play about?"

"And?"

The waitress came then, with their wine.

Billy leaned back as she set their glasses down. And then she proceeded to do a little housecleaning, picking up around them a little, taking away Pierce and Leslie's glasses and silverware, their napkins, giving the table a quick swipe with a towel.

"A clean slate," he said when she'd left.

They didn't speak for a moment or two. Billy had a sip of wine and glanced around the room. It was getting late for a Tuesday night. There was only one other table still occupied, and two couples at the bar, plus a lone drinker chatting to the bartender. He was someone Billy saw a lot by himself in the bars in this part of the neighborhood. **When you're by yourself in these same bars,** she reminded herself.

She looked at Sam, apparently pondering his wine. Everything felt awkward, suddenly. She needed to do something, something to make it easier. "What's Leslie up to, do you think?" she asked. "Has she **donated** us to each other?"

He looked surprised for just a few seconds. He said, "It felt something like that, didn't it?"

"So are you in any sense **hers** to donate?"

He raised his shoulders, his eyebrows. **Who knows?** "Are you?" he asked.

She considered it. "Well, maybe **she** thinks so. I was her brother's . . . girlfriend, I suppose you have to say. Though that's such a ridiculous word. **Fiancée,** by her lights. So she feels, I guess, a combination of things about me. Affection, I believe, as I do for her. But also worry. Responsibility." She had some more wine and set the glass down. "I don't mean I think she owes me any of those things. But that's who she is. What she's like. As you no doubt know, if you know her." He nodded, a slight smile on his lips. "The deal is, Gus was supposed to love me forever, according to her. To take care of me. He died. Now who will do that? I think that's some of it." She pointed at him. "Now you," she said.

"Me what?"

"Now you explain why she thinks she can give you to me."

"That's easy," he said. "I'm an age-appropriate single man. An old friend. It's not so surprising she'd try to fix us up."

"But you didn't know about it."

"I didn't. She said a friend had a play being performed, would I join them, and perhaps we'd all have a drink together afterward."

She felt more comfortable suddenly, knowing he hadn't been in on it, hadn't agreed to it. She looked at him appraisingly. "So, are you more an old friend of Pierce's, or of Leslie's?"

"Both." He looked a little sheepish for a second, she thought. What was **that** about? "More Leslie. I met her first. I know her better." He was frowning, considering something. "She was kind to me when my marriage was falling apart. She and Pierce both were. But more Leslie, yes."

"When was that?"

"Oh, it was years ago. My wife and I built a house together near them in Vermont—I'm an architect— and before it was even finished, the marriage was collapsing. Leslie had sold us the land—she was working in real estate at the time—and as it turned out, she was more interested in the house than Claire, than my wife, was. Interested in the process, in the design, in the building of it, and so forth. We saw a lot of each other over that year and a half or so. I was up there every few weeks." His face had changed. She had the quick thought that it was like Gabriel's—Rafe's—when he was remembering Elizabeth. "I suppose you could say I had a kind of . . . crush on her. Though that makes me sound like a ten-year-old." He dipped his head, smiled ruefully. "Which I might have just about been for a couple of months after my marriage ended." He looked at her. "But nothing ever happened between us."

"You don't need to tell me that."

"Well, it didn't."

"I mean, I think I know that. Or at any rate, it seems—it would seem—unlikely to me that Leslie would be unfaithful to Pierce." She gave a little snort. "Talk about codependency."

"Aka love."

"I take your point." She was enjoying this. Him. "It is a hideous word, isn't it? 'Codependency.' " She took some bread from the plate Pierce had ordered and spread it with some soft, blue-veined cheese. "Wordlet," she said. She pushed the plate toward him. "Phrase. How long were you married?"

"That time? About four years, total." He started to help himself to some bread and cheese, too.

" **'That time.'** There were other times?"

"One, other time." He looked up at her quickly. "My first wife died."

"Oh, I'm sorry." Again. "**That** will shut me up."

"No. It was a long time ago. And you?" He sat back, bread in hand. He seemed relaxed, physically. He'd turned his body to the side, his legs stretched out. And out and out, she thought.

"Marriage?" she asked.

"Yes."

"One. Young. Disastrous. A bully." Her husband's face went by, sneering. "I thought it was romantic, fool that I was, to be married to a complete jerk."

"You would have to explain the romantic part of that to me."

"Oh." Billy remembered herself then quickly, the way she had thought about it, getting married to Steve. It was hard to believe she'd been so dumb. "The difficult man. You know. Women have been sold a bill of goods about difficult men. Heathcliff. Rochester. Marlon Brando in **Streetcar.** Well, Marlon Brando in anything. **On the Waterfront.** God." She took a bite of the bread and cheese. "**One-Eyed Jacks,**" she said with her mouth full.

"Your character tonight was difficult."

"Gabriel?" she said. She shook her head and lifted her hand to tell him to wait. When she'd chewed and swallowed, she said, "I think his wife may be more difficult, actually. That he's become difficult partly in response to her. Or so I saw it."

"Well, you're the writer. Isn't the way you see it necessarily the truth of the matter?"

"Yes. But also no. I mean, I write it a certain way. I think of it a certain way. But then it can change depending on who the actors are, how they say things. How they feel them. Depending on who's directing it, even. Maybe especially that." She thought of Edmund, his face, frowning at her about sleeping with Rafe. She thought of Rafe. Suddenly she wanted to explain this to Sam, what had happened on the stage, how miraculous it had seemed to her.

"Like tonight." She leaned forward a little, elbows on the table. He shifted slightly, as if in response to her. "Like the way Rafe—the actor, the guy playing Gabriel—said that last thing: **Elizabeth.** It was, to me, fantastic. I mean, I wrote it, of course. I even wrote how I wanted him to say it. But in the end, it's just a word." He was watching her attentively. "Not even a word, actually. A name. And he said it . . . perfectly. Wonderfully. It was . . ." She gave a little half laugh, an expulsion of breath, and his face lifted. "I felt, 'So **that**'s what I meant.' It was so clear to me all of a sudden. A revelation." Suddenly, absurdly, she felt almost tearful. This embarrassed her, and because of that, she made her voice tough and said, "Maybe I should sleep with him before every performance."

Sam's face changed. He sat up straighter. "Well," he said. He cleared his throat. "Yes. I guess you should."

"Oh, Christ," she said. She reached over and almost touched his sleeve. "I shouldn't have said that." Her lips tightened. **I will grow old and die,** she thought, **still doing this foot-in-mouth thing.** She thought of Edmund again. "I said it earlier tonight, too, to someone else. Apparently it's a **line** I'm trying out."

He looked at her for a moment, and then he smiled. A tentative smile, at best.

And she realized that he thought she'd been joking. Joking about the whole thing. She couldn't let him think that. "I mean, it **is** true. I did sleep with him." She watched as his face changed again. "Not that it meant anything." She sighed, and shook her head. "I mean, it did mean something, but it didn't . . . change anything, for him or for me." She met his eyes, neutral behind the glasses. Waiting, it seemed. She lifted her hands, slightly. "We were lonely. We slept together. Once. But I made my little unfunny **joke** because I really, truly am so grateful for the way he said that line, the last line, tonight. It seems to me it's what I meant, but without knowing that I meant it. That he was able to make it contain . . . so much. Love, yes. But capitulation, giving up, giving in. Loss." She was remembering the moment again, she saw Rafe's face. "Sorrow for himself and for her. And relief. Love. Did I say that? A kind of joy." She shrugged. "I don't know." She stopped. After a moment, she asked him, "Didn't you think all of that was there?"

"I did, yes. I think so. But I would have thought . . . you intended it. All that."

"Well, now it seems so clear, I must have. Or I would have wanted to. But it was Rafe who saw it. Who read it that way. Who made it contain that." She brought her hand down on the table. "**God,** I love the theater."

After a moment, he said, "Well. We certainly seem to have covered a lot of territory here."

"Mea culpa. You've been a model of restraint."

"I've been an open book. Not that I wanted to be."

"Not so! You've told me the bare minimum. The number of marriages and the way they ended."

"And Leslie."

She waved her hand. "Leslie."

"No, actually I think I was too dismissive of it to you. Since you've been so honest . . ."

"So excruciatingly honest," she said.

He nodded. "I guess I should say about Leslie that what I felt, for a while—for a long while, actually—was that I loved her."

She looked at him. "Oh," she said. Surprise, surprise.

"While knowing I wouldn't do anything about it."

She kept her voice light. "Well, who wouldn't love Leslie? **I** love her. There's nobody gooder." Was she jealous? She couldn't be jealous. She didn't even know him, this too-tall man.

"That's what I felt at the time. How good she was."

"Look, if that's the worst thing you've done . . ."

"That's not what I meant, of course."

"Of course it's not." A silence fell. Behind Billy someone was talking on a cell phone, too loudly, about an argument she had with someone, reporting each side. Now she was saying, "So I'm like, 'I don't think so.' And he was like, 'Do I care? Do I even care?' "

Billy said, "What **is** the worst thing you've ever done?"

He laughed.

"No, what?"

"Really?"

"Sure. Why not? While we're covering territory. While we're embarrassing ourselves. You should do your share."

"I suppose it would have to do with my kids."

"Aaah! Kids." But why was this news? It was always like this. People and their complicated stories. Anyone over thirty or so. Hers, after all, could rival his.

"Yeah. Three boys. Men, I should say. Who . . . they had, in various ways, a hard time with their mother's death. My first wife's death. Not surprisingly. And then with the marriage to Claire. And then with the end of **that.**" He dipped his head on the word in emphasis. "I think it's why I've . . . I've tried to keep my life simpler since then. Though of course it doesn't matter at this point. Now that they're grown. But I would say that I just . . . I didn't know how to help them when they were younger. And what's worse, I'm not sure I'd be any better now."

"Mmm. But they survived."

"Of course. They're fine, in that sense. But scarred, I think. Damaged."

"Oh, who in this wide world worth their salt isn't? Why would you wish otherwise for them?"

"I don't, really. But I think what I wish is that I had made it easier for them, that's all. That I'd been more, attuned to them, or useful to them somehow."

His face was so thoughtful that she felt bad, she felt she'd been cavalier. "I'm sorry," she said. "I was glib. Again. I'm a little nuts tonight, I think. Wired. For many complicated reasons." She took a deep breath. "Anyway, I know—or I assume—that it must be hard, to feel that way about them."

"Well, I almost never do. Only occasionally." He turned forward in his chair. He smiled, suddenly. It made him younger. "But enough about my sins. What's the worst thing **you've** ever done?"

Many possibilities arose, and she was silent for a

long moment. Then she said, "Oh, my life is a bot-
tomless pit of worst things. I slept with the actor.
And he's married."

"Well, he's in charge of that."

"Mm," she said. She thought of the way Rafe had
looked, slouched next to her on the couch. The way
he'd moved on her in the half dark of the bedroom.
"I kind of seduced him."

"I say it again: he's in charge of himself."

Billy looked at her wineglass. She had some wine.
She looked at him. He met her glance, steadily. After
a few seconds, he said abruptly, "Why are we talking
like this? I don't know you. I don't even know you."

"Well, I have a theory about that. Naturally."

"**Do** you." He smiled, expectantly.

"I think it's because of at least two things. One,
that you saw the play, so in fact you think you **do**
know me. People always think that."

"Do they?" he said.

"They do. They extrapolate. And I'm sure you
have, too."

"I'll never tell. And the second thing?"

"The second thing is that I told you that I fucked
Rafe. That broke the ice, all right."

"Don't say that." He made an odd face, displeased,
as though he'd smelled something off.

"What? That I fucked him?" She was surprised.

"Yes."

"Why? It's how I think of it. And would say it. I
do say it. So please, don't be fastidious because"—

she drew herself up—"you think I'm a lady, or something. It's my business, after all, **not** to be a lady. To know how people speak. All the very unladylike things people say. How they think."

"I suppose it is," he said. And after a moment, "You're a little . . . difficult, yourself, for me."

"Why?"

"Oh, your life is so different from mine. Mine is . . . has been, I guess you'd say, regulated. The kids, the marriages, the house, the office. Those things."

"Well, that is different from mine, yes. Lots. But, why does that make **me** difficult? Maybe you're the difficult one."

"I might well be." They were quiet for a minute. "I think all I meant was that you're used to a more . . . to a wilder life, I think. Less regular."

"Ah." She laughed. **"La vie bohème."**

"Well, yes. Compared to mine."

"You couldn't be more wrong. I wouldn't be up to it. It's more **la vie** boring, I'm afraid. Most nights I'm in bed by eleven with my dog and a cup of tea." She had a sudden fond image of her bedroom, Reuben lying on the quilt, the pretty old gas lamps out in back. "Up at seven. Alone, all day long." She shook her head. "It's pathetic, really."

"But then there's being in the theater, being with other people."

"Yeah, once every couple of **years.**" Then she nodded. "But you mean sex, don't you? **That** kind of being with other people."

"Probably. Probably I do."

"Everyone has sex. You don't need to be a bohemian for that."

"No, I don't suppose you do." They sat silent for a moment. He was moving his hand over the table-top. Now he leaned forward, one elbow on the table. "You and Gus seem an unlikely pair," he said.

"Did you **know** Gus?" This possibility hadn't occurred to her.

"Not really. I met him once. At Leslie's. But . . . wasn't he much younger than you?"

She laughed. "Oh, I wouldn't say **much.**" Then she remembered what a child he had often seemed to her. "I don't know. Maybe I would. But after all, I'm six years older now than I was then. And he would be, too."

"But he also seemed . . . I don't know. Well, you seem like you're very different . . . types."

"We **were** very different. It was . . . it sometimes made things not so great between us. There were times . . ." She looked out the window at the dark, at the lighted marquee down the street.

"Times?" he prompted.

She looked back at him and met his steady gaze. "Oh, nothing."

"Right. I suppose we should save some information for next time."

"Oh. There's going to be a next time?"

"Well, I'd like it." When she didn't answer right away, his eyes behind the glasses changed. "And we more or less owe it to Leslie to have, say, coffee together, or dinner or something."

She sat still for a moment. What had she been doing here? Was she incapable of conversation without inviting someone to put the moves on her, even someone she had no intention, no possibility, of getting involved with? She pushed her glass away. There was a half inch or so of wine in the bottom of it. "I have to go, actually," she said. She slid off the seat.

"Oh, look," he said. "I didn't mean to be pushy, or make assumptions . . ."

"No," she said. "No, let's. Let's have coffee or something. It's just, you know, I have to get home. I have a dog."

He stood up, too, to get his wallet out of his back pocket. He was signaling for the check.

The waitress came over right away—she had probably been waiting for them to leave so she could finish up her shift—and he gave her Pierce's money, and his own. Billy was beginning to rearrange her possessions. "Do you need change?" the waitress asked.

"No, that's fine," he said. "Keep it."

He stepped behind Billy to help her on with her coat. There were a few awkward moments when she couldn't find the sleeves—she could feel him moving the shapeless thing around, trying to help. Then there he was. She slid her arms in.

Outside the rain had stopped. It was colder.

He asked if he could walk her home, but she said she was fine, that she was just steps away, really. He talked about the time when it wouldn't have been fine in this neighborhood. He was trying to hold her there, she could tell. He said he'd call. She nodded and extended her hand. They shook. She smiled up at him. "Well, then," she said, and turned and walked away.

She felt certain he was watching her go, but she didn't look back.

She had a headache the next morning. She lay in bed for a while feeling sorry for herself, remembering the things they'd talked about the night before. The line about sleeping with Rafe. God. **Twice** she'd said it. Why? Why, Billy? In particular, why the second time, with Sam? Had she been trying to attract him? To repel him?

Both, she supposed, she was in such an agitated state.

And maybe because she'd drunk the second glass of wine. The wine she'd had to calm herself down. The wine she'd felt she needed because she'd been a little crazy, a little vulnerable, after the play. Because it always upset her to see Leslie anyway, and here she was being presented by Leslie with a new man. Clearly, yes, being **introduced.** Because she'd liked him, the new man, and wanted to resist that.

But why had she wanted to resist liking him?

Because she didn't want to sleep with Rafe and then a few nights later with someone else. Because he seemed ready to like her, and she didn't want a "nice, age-appropriate man," as she remembered him calling himself, in her life. She liked being alone. When she wanted company, she could usually find it in people she met at work.

Because it was so complicated, with Leslie's having set it up, with all that would mean in terms of Leslie in her life. Gus.

Because she needed to be alone. It was better for her to stay alone.

Because of Gus. Because of Gus.

Billy still had a picture of Gus somewhere in her desk. Correction: of Gus and Leslie. It had been taken long before she'd met him, actually. He was probably only about twenty-five in it, so Leslie would have been about forty. Her hair had been dark then, and it fell thick and straight to her shoulders. She wore a sundress with wide straps. Gus's arm was around her waist. He was barefoot, in khakis. He was grinning at the camera unselfconsciously. Leslie was looking at him, at his profile, looking at him in the way Billy had seen her look at him dozens of times in life—lovingly, admiringly. Behind them the flowers of Leslie's garden made a deckled blur in the sun. Billy knew the exact spot where they were standing.

She liked to think of Gus as he was in the photograph—admired, adored. She liked to think of Leslie as she looked in the photograph too: young, pretty, happy.

This was the picture she'd chosen to keep when she put everything else into a big plastic bag—all the other photos and the letters and the odd things he'd given her—and set it out on the curb along with the other stuff she left behind when she moved out of Gus's apartment.

Billy had never started an affair with anyone in quite the way she did with Gus. Effortlessly, she would have said. Maybe thoughtlessly. Certainly quickly. She was surprised, even delighted, by the ease of it. This, perhaps, should have been a danger signal, but she ignored it. **Maybe it's my turn for something unanguished** was what she thought.

Her specialty before had always been sunless men. Dark, punishing, punished men. Men full of ambition and bitterness. She had fled Chicago, in fact, from such a man. Oh, certainly, there were professional reasons for the move, too. The job she'd gotten at BU, her feeling that she needed to leave the city she'd always lived in in order for anything big to happen to her, the sense that she was mired in familiar patterns in her work. She was not without ambition herself. But she was also very happy to escape from Tom, from his stalker-like unwillingness to let her go. He had wept; he had cursed her. He had telephoned her as many as fifteen or twenty times a day. He had appeared on her doorstep at two in the morning, angry, bitter, pleading.

And suddenly, almost as soon as she moved to Boston—light and air: along came Gus.

She met him in May, on the slow ferry to Provincetown, about a month after she'd moved from Chicago—this charming, perhaps slightly younger man who started talking to her about the book she was halfheartedly reading. Partly because he was so pretty, partly because of their destination, she assumed he was gay. She was always making mistakes like this, misunderstanding other people, particularly other people in relation to herself. She had done the other thing, too, assuming some gay man was straight and, what's more, interested in her. But the result of her mistaken assumption about Gus was that when he started to kiss her, she was so surprised that she uttered a little involuntary shriek.

She made a sexual joke of it later—she shrieked when he entered her for the first time. And then occasionally after that, just to make them both laugh, she shrieked when he did anything for the first time.

They started to see each other, at first every two or three weeks. After a little while, more like once a week. It was he who was pursuing her, trying to make something happen—she could feel it. And she decided to **let** it happen. She was having a good time.

There were other reasons, too. She didn't know very many people in Boston yet—she was lonely, a bit—so she was pleased just for the company. And she loved being in bed with him. It was as though sex were a sport he was very, very good at, and easy and joyful in doing. She told him so.

"But that's the way it's supposed to be, isn't it?" he asked.

She laughed.

She couldn't believe it when he wanted to take her to meet his sister. He kept pressing her about it, almost from the start. It seemed ridiculous, this wish of his. His **sister,** for God's sake.

But he brought it up so often that she said yes, finally.

They drove up to Vermont on a Saturday in late July in Gus's old yellow Volkswagen Beetle, the windows open because you couldn't turn the heater off. As they slowed down to drive into the little town where Leslie lived, Billy looked around and thought how preposterously perfect it was—the sunlight filtering through the tall maple and oak trees on the town green, the white houses arrayed around it. Billy saw children playing on the green as they pulled into Leslie's dirt driveway.

The house itself was old and quirky and sweet, its windows wide open to the soft air moving through it. Inside, the floors tilted, the ceilings were low. They stood for a long moment in the front hall.

Billy watched the curtains at the living room windows lift and fall. When no one appeared, Gus leaned into the stairwell to the second floor and called Leslie's name.

"Oh!" someone said. They heard rushing footsteps above them, and then Leslie came down the narrow staircase, emerging into their view feetfirst on the steep ladderlike stairs. Billy was startled as she descended by how different Leslie was from Gus— soft, almost plump, where he was buff, dark where he was blond. And there was something grave, something serious, about her, which you couldn't have said of Gus, though when she turned from embracing him to hold out her hand to Billy, her face opened in a smile of dazzling warmth. "Billy," she said. "I think I would have known you anywhere." Her hand itself was warm, her grip firm. Billy liked her immediately, just as Gus had promised she would.

They sat in the side yard, and Leslie brought out a tray with a pitcher and served them lemonade. Just as she finished pouring their glasses, one of the children across the road called loudly to another, "That's not the rules." And another answered, "Yeah, well, the rules stink."

"So true," Billy said, and Leslie laughed.

The shade around them was dappled, shifting when the breeze moved the trees. From where she sat, Billy had a view in one direction of the green and the playing children, in the other of the garden—wide swaths of tall, arching plants in pale colors. Leslie peppered her with questions about herself, about where she'd grown up and how, about how she started writing plays. But she talked about herself, too, about her family and Gus's. Late in the afternoon, she got up "to do something about supper," she said, though it would turn out she'd already done a great deal about supper. She came back after a minute or two, the screen door smacking shut behind her, and handed Billy and Gus two small tin buckets. She asked them to pick a few cups of raspberries from a patch she had in the backyard, behind the flower garden.

When Pierce came home from the hospital, he served them gin and tonics under the trees, and Leslie came and sat with them again. Billy didn't quite **get** Leslie and Pierce together, they seemed such an odd pair. Leslie fell almost silent around him, and he seemed entirely comfortable about that, about occupying center stage. Gus kept him going, too, asking him questions, almost teasing him sometimes. They told jokes for a while, in turn, and Pierce laughed loudly after each one, even his own. Billy liked that, someone who laughed at his own jokes.

They moved indoors for dinner, just in time to escape the bugs that had started to descend. There was cold soup to start, a minty puree of peas, and then sliced lamb and potatoes. The dark slowly gathered around the house. About halfway through

the meal, Leslie lighted the candles on the table.
There was something lovely, something ceremonial,
in the concentrated, graceful way she did it. When
Billy looked away from her, the windows were suddenly black. The reflection of the candles swayed
and leaped in the warped, uneven old panes of glass.

Leslie cleared off the dinner plates—Gus got up
and helped her—and then brought out pound cake,
with ice cream and a seedless raspberry sauce.

After dinner, Pierce went up to his study to do
some work. Gus and Leslie and Billy carried the
dishes to the kitchen. Leslie wouldn't let them help
her wash them, so Gus took Billy for a walk, **to spy
on the neighbors,** he said. They made a slow circuit
of the green. Amazingly to Billy, no curtains were
drawn. She and Gus could look freely through the
windows at what seemed the mild and pleasant
activities of the townspeople: television, reading.
Some families were still sitting around tables in their
kitchens or dining rooms. As Gus and Billy walked,
a group of boys on bikes swooped past them several
times in the dark, doing wheelies, yelling at one
another, their white T-shirts all you could see of
them at a distance. The air smelled green and fresh.

They lay down on the grass of the town green. It
was cool and dampish against Billy's back. Above
them, more stars than she would have thought possible glimmered and shone. A distant cluster was so
thickly strewn that it looked like spilled powder.
Someone called for a child to come in, a faint call
that sounded full of grief to Billy: "Louey. Lou-ey."

A car drove past, its headlights raking over the white houses, the trees—and then it was gone and everything was dark again. Billy said, "I know why you wanted me to meet your sister."

"Yeah? Why?"

"Because you wanted to append this whole scene, and Leslie, too, to yourself. To add this . . . dimension, whatever it is—sweet Americana—to my sense of who you are."

"I'm not so devious as you think I am. I just thought you'd like her."

"I do. What's not to like?"

When they got back, the house was silent. There was just one lamp on in the living room. Leslie and Pierce had gone to bed.

Gus and Billy turned the light off and felt their way up the creaking, narrow stairs to the bedroom that had been Gus's when he was in college. It had a ceiling that sloped radically. Over the bed was a skylight. Looking up, Billy could see the moon just appearing. The stars were made faint by its bright light, and the night sky looked blacker behind it.

She took the first turn in the bathroom and then slid between the cool sheets. She could hear Gus brushing his teeth, peeing. He came back and stretched out next to her. He smelled of peppermint and a flesh smell unique to him, faintly grassy. He started to touch her breasts, but Billy said, "No. Gus."

After a moment, he asked, "Why?"

"They'll hear us."

"We'll be quiet. We'll make stealth love."

"I can't, Gus. It's too close. They're too close." Was that it? Billy wasn't sure.

They lay there, whispering in the silvery light. After a while, from across the hallway, through the walls, they faintly heard a light, repeated crooning—Leslie's voice. Pierce joined her after a few moments, first a soft rhythmic call under her song, then getting louder, rising above it, as they each—both—swam toward a climax. A definitive climax, though all of this had been muted, perhaps out of the polite hope that they wouldn't be heard. Slowly they subsided into silence. After a minute or two Billy heard their voices in sleepy conversation, a few low alternating murmurs.

"Hmm!" said Gus, when all had been quiet for a while. She could see that he was grinning. His teeth looked dangerous in this light.

"Interesting," she answered.

"Kind of a precedent, wouldn't you say?" He turned on his side to her again.

"Gus, no. I mean even more now I'd feel self-conscious. It would seem so . . . competitive."

"Oh, and that's something you never indulge in."

"I just can't, Gus."

She lay awake a long time after Gus had dropped off. The moonlight moving across the bed kept her from sleep, but she was also conscious of a slight discomfort she was feeling about him; she wasn't sure why.

No, here's what it was. Gradually, over the course of the afternoon and evening, he had come to seem **young** to her. Too young. Not grown up. It had to do with Leslie, with the way he was around Leslie. He seemed so easily to take from her. He had described her to Billy as being like a mother to him, but this was something you'd grow out of in the back-and-forth struggle with a mother, she thought.

In the car the next day, driving home, she said, "I would pay money to have someone adore me the way your sister adores you." She had her bare feet propped on the dash to escape the warm air pumping steadily in from below it.

"You don't need to. Ta-da! Here I am."

"Not the same. You are aware of certain, shall we say, flaws."

"I can't think of a one," he said.

"You see? You have to joke about it."

Over the next year, they went up to Vermont frequently, usually once a month or so. Often Billy and Leslie sat up late together after Pierce and Gus were asleep. In the warm weather they sat on the screened porch off the dining room; and then—in August and September, as the nights grew rapidly cooler, and then cold—they were inside, in the low-ceilinged living room. They moved easily from one thing to another in these conversations—plays and movies, books they liked, cities they'd traveled to.

Leslie asked about her awful first marriage, about her childhood as the daughter of a distinguished man.

"A great man," Billy said. "Or so we were instructed. By our mother, poor invisible woman. And, of course, by him, himself." She felt at ease talking about this with Leslie, though she'd never discussed it with Gus. "A bigger narcissist I never met. The Great Pooh-Bah, I called him. Behind his back, of course."

Leslie in her turn talked about Pierce and the way they met, about her and Gus's ugly growing up. About their mother's irrational anger—once she'd seen scratches on Gus's face, she said, and he'd told her it was nothing, that their mother had slapped him because he'd left his bedding on the sofa after he'd gotten up, and her ring had caught in his flesh and torn it.

"**Nothing,** he called it." Her voice was full of pain. Her mouth tightened as she shook her head.

She spoke of how amazed she always was by Gus's lightheartedness. "I feel as though we divided up the way to respond or react to our family along very tidy lines. I took in all the hard, mean stuff. I noticed it. And I know that's made me the kind of person I am," she said. "I also know what kind of person that is. I know how I like things—orderly and calm— and I understand what's not very brave about that, what frightens me when that feels threatened."

They were having this conversation outdoors, on

the porch. It was dark, and their voices seemed almost disembodied in the night air. Perhaps they wouldn't have said so much otherwise.

"Honestly, though," Leslie said, "I don't know where Gussie's temperament comes from. He's so . . . carefree, really. My father might have been a bit that way when he was younger, but by the time Gus would have been aware of him, he wasn't much of anything but a drunk."

When work started for Billy and Gus in the fall— Gus at the suburban prep school where he taught, Billy at BU—they were so busy that they agreed they wouldn't see each other at all during the week. Billy was teaching two courses that were new for her, and Gus, of course, had classes every day, and lessons and papers to go over most weeknights. They usually spent a day of every weekend together, though, sometimes in the big apartment Billy was subletting in Brookline, occasionally at Gus's smaller place in Somerville. They explored the city or slept late; they cooked together and saw plays and movies, they listened to music. They made love. They drove up to see Leslie and Pierce. All of it seemed easy, unfraught.

Almost all of it.

Occasionally Billy would feel Gus's attentiveness to her as stifling, his willingness to change his mind about anything she had a strong opinion on as weak.

Where were his own feelings? His own passionate convictions? She'd withdraw from him then, and sometimes be silent, sullen, disliking herself for this but unable to control it. Or she'd stay away from him for a couple of weeks—once, for almost a month—making up some excuse having to do with her need to work. Which was always true, there was so much she was trying to get done.

Every now and then, too, she would have the uncomfortable awareness she'd experienced the first time she'd seen Gus with Leslie—the sense of him as undeveloped, little-boyish. And seeing that, feeling that, would make her conscious of her distance from him, conscious of the way in which she was almost using him. **Passing the time,** as if with a pleasant, momentarily engaging diversion—the equivalent of the popcorn and ice-cream dinners she sometimes indulged in when she was alone.

But then he'd do something winning, say something funny. Or she'd remember his terrible childhood and excuse him for everything. Or she'd suddenly be turned on by his physical beauty and they'd spend an afternoon or an evening in bed, making each other come over and over.

She didn't love him. She knew she wasn't going to love him. She knew, too, that it was different for him. Once he had said to her, "I think I'm falling in love with you, Billy Gertz."

She had felt almost sorry for him then, it had seemed so adolescent to her—the claim of someone who wants reassurance that his feeling is returned before he'll truly announce it. She had made her voice light, though, when she answered. She said, "Oh, don't do that. It's more fun the way it is."

When there were problems, it was mostly a matter of this kind of thing, Billy aware of her distance from Gus and reacting to that by being irritated with him for pushing in closer or with herself for not taking her own life more seriously, for wasting her time and, therefore, as she reminded herself occasionally, his time, too.

Occasionally though, very occasionally, Gus would find something about Billy or her life that bothered him. Sometimes he complained of the way she disappeared into her work, the way she was distracted and only half there when she was in the midst of some project. He didn't like it when she went out with other men, which she did every few weeks, sometimes in a group, sometimes with just one person. These were colleagues, she pointed out to him. Other writers, people she was getting to know as she moved more into the Boston theater community.

Once it was because she used a private joke of theirs in a play she was working on—the little shriek she'd given when he kissed her for the first time. She was sitting next to him during a reading of this play, an evening of staged readings of faculty work. She thought to turn and watch him when the moment arrived. He laughed, but his face fell quickly. She could tell he was hurt.

They talked about it the next night. He got to

Billy's about six. She had been alone all day, work-ing, except for a trip to the grocery store to pick up things for dinner. Gus had gone out to his school for an important soccer game—he coached the team. All the teachers at the school coached something or led some extracurricular activity. Billy couldn't believe this at first, this **mens sana in corpore sano** crap, but she supposed it made sense if you were try-ing to keep a bunch of adolescents in line.

She had thought from time to time through the day of the way Gus's face had looked at the theater. She thought of that, and of the slight sense of strain, of politeness, between them afterward. They'd gone home separately, though that had been the plan all along on account of his need to get up early. They were sitting now, having finished dinner. Billy was drinking wine, Gus beer. She was still wearing the apron she'd put on to cook in, a dowdy but com-pletely protective affair she'd been given by her grandmother years before. Gus was wearing a blue-and-white-striped shirt, open at the neck, and he looked fresh and youthful. She felt at a disadvan-tage, she realized. She felt plain.

They'd been talking about the reviews of a movie they thought they might see the next afternoon, but they'd fallen silent.

She said, "You were startled at the play last night, I think."

"Hmm?" He frowned at her.

"Yeah. When Jay moves in to kiss Elena and she makes her little noise."

He was looking down at his glass, avoiding her eyes.

"**My** little noise," she corrected herself.

He looked up quickly. "**Our** noise, I would have said."

"Meaning you felt it was . . . private. Between us."

"Yeah, I sure did." He nodded many times, rapidly. He was unsmiling.

"I'm sorry," she said.

"But it **was** private, wouldn't you say?"

"Well, it still is."

He expelled his breath sharply, a mock laugh. "Explicate."

"Well, you are not Jay, you are not a guy who makes his living gambling, a guy who's betraying his wife. And I'm not Elena. I'm not . . . dependent upon the kindness of strangers."

"But you gave them something that happened between us. Something private."

"But for them to do it makes it something else." She had leaned forward on the table, but he still wouldn't look directly at her. "It's different with them. It means something different. It's not our noise when they make it. When she makes it. It's transformed."

"Not transformed **enough.**"

"What. You think people are going to say, 'You know, I bet that happened between the playwright and that cute boy she was sitting next to'?"

"I don't care what they say. I care about me, about us. About you not using us." Gus, angry. A surprise.

But she was angry right back. "I use **me,** Gus," she said. "I use me up. I need all of me, and if you're with me, that means I use you, too. I use everything. How could I not? And what I don't use, I don't use because it doesn't work. Not because it's sacred." Her voice had risen. "Nothing is sacred. That's just the way it is."

They sat in silence for a minute. Billy could hear that her own breathing was a little rapid. She consciously slowed it down. She changed her voice, made it playful. "If you can't stand the heat, as they say . . ."

He looked at her. He smiled suddenly. "Ah, Billy," he said. "Spoken of course by a woman wearing an apron. You came with props. Not fair."

Was it fair? The use she made of everything? Billy thought about this often. In her first play she'd used her miserable youthful marriage, in particular the mocking way her ex-husband used to speak of their domestic life. "Mr. and Mrs. **Married,** and their little married apartment and all the little married things they're accumulating." Within a few weeks of their wedding, he seemed bitter with regret, he was incapable of kindness to her. There was virtually no loving gesture she could make that didn't beckon his irony. Having suffered through that for three years, she felt she'd earned the right to make use of it however she wished.

In particular she'd used a fistfight they'd had.

She'd started it, actually. She'd punched him first, a downward chop with her fist on his moving mouth, intended simply to stop the ugly, ugly words emerging from it. Purely by reflex, he punched her back, with all his strength. He had sixty pounds on her. She actually rose up into the air before falling, crumpling against a wall. It was like living through a cartoon scene. All that was missing, she told a friend later, were stars and planets circling around her head.

The fight choreographer had a good time with it, and it was convincing onstage. The actress wore a black eye for the rest of the play and told a series of cheerful and increasingly loony lies about its origin, lies she was meant to be believing, at least in part. It was a kind of absurdist work, one act, about self-deception, and it ended with the couple singing "Tea for Two" in pretty, closely entwined harmony.

She had written it in a rage once she got started, and she couldn't have argued to Gus that she transformed things very much in that particular case. Maybe the tone, maybe the humor, which had been entirely absent as she lived through it.

But it wouldn't have made any difference to her ex-husband. He had moved away by then, to work in Phoenix. It was a certainty that he hadn't seen it, since its only performances were in a small experimental theater on the North Side of Chicago. The sad fact was that almost no one saw it.

The second play was nearly as directly drawn from life, and it did make a difference to other people in Billy's life. It was about a family gathering, a Thanksgiving holiday, five grown children returning from their lives to stay in their childhood home for a few days. The father was a professor, retired, reduced almost to invisibility by his wife, a woman with a need to be at the center of every situation, it didn't matter how. Whatever method was at hand—knowing more than anyone else, being more sexually provocative than anyone else, talking more than anyone else. If necessary, being more wounded than anyone else—in one scene the turn from dripping contempt to anguished tears was accomplished within seconds by the actress playing her.

In the course of the play, each of the adult children in turn was sucked into the orbit of this monstrous character and changed. The oldest brother, a doctor, got into a futile and increasingly childish argument with her about tuberculosis, in which she would not concede that he might know anything more about it than she did. One of the daughters was called upon to comfort her about his cruelty in arguing with her at all. She got drunk and was seductive with the youngest son. Together the two of them made fun of the second daughter, who pretended not to be hurt, who actually laughed at herself with them. And through it all, the father's polite blindness to the cruelty and manipulation involved provided a kind of cover for the mother's behavior, asserted the lie that this was a normal, perfectly pleasant family gathering.

And of course this had been Billy's family, with the gender of the parents reversed—in her case it was her father who was the narcissist, and her mother who receded so much as to be invisible. But the change didn't fool anybody in Billy's family—all of whom were then alive except her mother, three of whom lived in Chicago and came to the play. The result was that she was estranged from them for a long time afterward and still not reconciled with her father when he died some years later.

He had called her after he saw the play to offer a critique of it. She had defended it, defended herself. At one point he said, "You know what your problem is, Billy?"

Well, Billy knew what some of her problems were—she'd been in therapy enough through the years—but she doubted her father had any of these in mind. "No," she said.

"Your problem is, you think you're better than everyone else."

Billy laughed. "Doesn't everyone?" she said.

He hung up.

She hadn't worked so closely to her own life since then, not through a fear of wounding people or losing them, but because she was just less angry. As a result of this, her plays were less angry, too—less accusatory, she supposed. She worried about this a little. She had felt that what made her work interesting, what made **her** interesting, was her rage. She was concerned that without it she would become ordinary. That's what she saw as having happened to her siblings. The strain of pretending things were all right in their family had made all of them less than they might have been. She'd escaped that by being angry, and it made her wonder what would happen to her and to her writing as that anger dwindled.

Basically, she discovered, what happened was that her plays became less eccentric. More conventional, anyway. "Deeper," "wiser," the critics said. She began to have a wider audience. More success. Sometimes, though, she missed those early, angry plays and especially the heat with which she'd written them. She had to work harder now—at the writing itself, and at figuring out why she was writing. She would never have acknowledged that to Gus, but she knew, even as she was making her passionate argument to him about her need to **use** everything, that her anxiety about all this was connected to the ferocity of her defense of herself to him.

Starting in March, ten months after she met Gus and three months before the owners of her sublet apartment were due to return and claim it, Billy began to look for another place to rent. The sublet had been cheap because she'd had cat-sitting responsibilities for two unfriendly, sneaky white cats who were completely uninterested in her until they heard the whine of the electric can opener. Now as she went through the listings at BU, as she read the ads in the Sunday papers, she was appalled by how expensive housing with no strings attached was in Boston—far more so than Chicago had been. By June she hadn't found anything she liked that she could afford.

In the end, she let Gus persuade her that she should move in with him for the summer. Her idea was that she'd keep looking, that she'd find something for September, which was the next big turnover date in this academic town. Gus's idea was that he could convince her to stay on, which she knew but pretended not to know. In any case, on a sunny Wednesday in early June, he and a friend of his drove over to Brookline in an Econoline van, loaded it with Billy's worldly possessions—mostly books and papers and clothes—then drove to Somerville and carried everything up to Gus's apartment, to the room he'd cleared out for her to work in.

She spent the first few days, while Gus was still teaching—gone from early in the morning to dinnertime—fixing this space up, setting up her computer, laying out her notebooks and the plays she liked to have around to look at while she worked. Then she had a couple of days where she did work, and worked well. **This could be okay,** she was thinking. She actually liked the room, which looked directly into a lush tree. And she liked the noise of the kids playing in the street in the afternoons. The street in Brookline had been expensive and empty and silent. If there were kids, they were somewhere else, taking lessons.

At the end of the week, Gus persuaded her to come with him to his prep school's graduation ceremony. "It's pretty," he said. "You'll like it."

It was pretty. It was held outside, on a stage erected on the vast green at the center of the campus. The audience sat in rows on folding chairs set up on the grass. The women—mothers and grandmothers and sisters—wore big hats in straw or white, in bright colors, to protect them from the sun. "It's like finally getting to go to the Kentucky Derby," Billy said to Gus. "It makes me miss the horses, though." The graduating girls, dressed in white, each carried a red rose, and the boys with their white jackets had roses in their lapels. Billy actually got teary as they were given their diplomas and loped across the stage so triumphantly, so hopeful and unaware of what was coming at them.

Afterward, while Gus went to congratulate his students, she moved around anonymously, eavesdropping, as she loved to do in any crowd, making mental notes for herself. She kept catching glimpses of Gus through the milling people. He was talking to different groups of the graduates, joking around—teasing the girls, jockeying with the boys, punching the odd kid's arm, laughing and completely at ease.

And then, at one point, looking across the lawn

through the thinning crowd, she saw him and didn't recognize him. It took her more than a second to realize the kid she was looking at was not a student. Was Gus. She stood there, staring at him. He was moving his head around in a strange way, clearly imitating someone, and then he laughed. The boys around him laughed, too; their little group broke up for a moment, and then reassembled.

Why, he's a boy! she thought. **He's their age.**

She had a moment of shock, followed quickly by revulsion. But the revulsion was at herself, for not having known this before. Or for not having let herself know it. She'd seen it, she'd been aware of it—she acknowledged this to herself now—but she had gone along, even so. Because it was easy, because the sex was good, because she was busy in the rest of her life and Gus was someone she didn't have to think about.

What a terrible thing to do, to use someone in this way. To use someone's love.

And Gus loved her, she knew that. Whatever love meant to him, that's what he felt for her. It was there in his admiration, his attentive noticing of whatever she did. It was there in the way he watched her responses to things, echoed her opinions. All the things that irritated her, if she were honest. Which she hadn't exactly been, had she?

She felt stunned by it all, and overcome with anger at herself. In the car on the way home, she barely spoke. Gus was high on the event, though, so it didn't matter. And then when he fell quiet—in response to her, she supposed—she turned the radio on and the Red Sox were playing, and he was happy enough listening to that.

After this, all the things that had sometimes charmed her about Gus—that he was good and kind and considerate and sweet, that she liked making love to him, that she liked looking at him, that he was funny and smart—didn't matter much anymore. Or didn't matter enough. What she saw now were the things that bothered her, that had always bothered her. But new things, too. She saw that he had no deeper dimension, no darker side. Or none that was available to her, anyway. For instance, it was as though he'd simply pushed away from himself any awareness of what was troubling about the way he'd grown up. Billy had gotten a more honest picture of this from Leslie in the long late evenings they sat up talking than she did from Gus. And the fact was that Leslie had cared to look at it, painstakingly. Had tried to try to understand it. She recognized that her own need to be kind, to be calm, was an almost-conscious response to what had been difficult and ugly in her growing up. And she understood that her response was a limitation as much as it was a strength.

Gus didn't see his growing up as sad. Or he wouldn't see it that way. He once called it "irregular" to Billy.

"Irregular, as in **ouch**," Billy said.

It got worse after the graduation. Gus was on vacation. Billy wasn't. She needed to work, but Gus wanted her company, he didn't see why she had to be at her desk every single day. It was summer. Why wouldn't she come with him to the Vineyard? To Vermont? To western Massachusetts? To a play, for God's sake? To Williamstown, to see a play, the very thing she cared about most.

She came to feel that in some way he didn't think of what she was doing as work. Oh, he admired the plays—or said he did. But he didn't seem to make the connection between them and her need to be alone at her desk for four or five hours a day.

She started to go to her office at BU to write. It was kind of a dump. It looked out over an air shaft; it had unpleasantly bright fluorescent lighting. The paint was old, and there were water stains on the ceiling. But it was private. It was quiet. Very quiet now in the summer, when most of the faculty disappeared from the warren of offices around hers that housed them in the academic year.

Most of all, there was not Gus.

It was on the way there on her bike one morning that she realized she had to end it. It wasn't just that she needed to find her own place, to move out. She needed to tell him it wasn't going to work at all, ever. That it wasn't working now. It was early, around six-thirty. Traffic hadn't yet thickened, and there was hardly anyone out besides the joggers. She was pedaling along the river, watching someone in a scull moving smoothly upstream, watching the steady quiet lap of the water into the tall grasses on the riverbank. She stopped her bike. She looked up at the Boston skyline and the graceful cable ribs of the Zakim Bridge. This is what she loved, this, being alone, being sentient only for herself. She didn't want Gus noticing her noticing things, admiring her, ignoring all that was unpleasant about her, insisting on his version of who she was.

She would tell him. She would.

Not now, though. It would be better to wait until she had her own place—it would be too awkward living with him once he knew, too hard for both of them. But she would tell him.

The relief she felt at acknowledging this, at making a plan, was sharp and clear, as though some months-long fog she'd been living in had lifted. The gulls above the treetops wheeled and cawed, white against the blue sky, and Billy had a sense of almost-giddy happiness for a moment. When she got to her ugly office, she sat down eagerly and started to read through what she'd written the day before. She would have her life back.

As though he sensed this—and surely it must have made some difference in the way Billy behaved, she felt so much lighter—Gus seemed to want to draw closer. Only a few weeks after this, she arrived home one afternoon and opened the door to find him sitting on the living room floor playing with a puppy, a medium-sized black puppy, but one with enormous paws. It was for her, he said. A present.

He'd clearly been planning it for a while—he had a crate set up in a corner of the living room, and he said he'd hired a dog walker who would come each day mid-to-late morning. He would walk the puppy early, he said, before he left for school, and again when he got back—long walks. Billy would only have to come home around two or three, as she did every day anyway, and walk him then. Just a short walk.

As she sat down, silenced by surprise, he went on, nervously. He introduced the dog. He was a mutt, Gus said. His mother was a Newfoundland, owned by another teacher at school. She had no idea what the father was.

Billy looked at the puppy. He was chewing on a large rawhide toy Gus had bought for him. He was, of course, completely, heartbreakingly winning. Gus was smiling at him. She felt a pang of deep anger at Gus, and then pity, too. She wondered whether he was at all aware of what she had instantly felt were the complicated motivations behind this gift.

She knew she should tell him no, and she knew that saying no to the puppy was part of the larger no she needed to say to him. She looked at him. She could tell by his face that he was at least a little ashamed he'd given the dog to her. Ashamed, because it was such a terrible way to try to keep her attached to him, to try to make her stay.

The puppy stood, wobbling a bit, and frolicked unevenly over to her. She held out her hand, and he lowered his hind quarters and started licking it.

"What shall we call him?" Gus said, and she sighed and gave in.

That was in August. Billy was still looking at apartments when Gus was getting ready to start back to school. She had a lead on one in Cambridgeport, another sublet, but it wouldn't be available until January, when the family, academics, was taking a leave, so she was still scanning the housing lists at BU almost daily, checking the Sunday notices in the paper.

On September 11, Billy woke early. She'd waked once before, actually, when Gus got up to leave for the airport, but she'd pretended to be asleep that time. This time she couldn't do that. The puppy was crying. Reuben. She'd named him Reuben. She peed and brushed her teeth, she got quickly dressed and went into the living room. As soon as she saw Reuben, she gave over to him again, just as she had the day of his arrival. He was charming, even beyond the charm most puppies have. His winning awkwardness on account of his size, his sad brown eyes, his immense paws, the rounded shape of his head, his long pink tongue, the clean way he smelled—everything about him gave her pleasure. He was in his crate now, the crate he was already almost outgrowing. He was making a noise that sounded like an old woman keening.

Now he saw her and he yipped. He began scratching frantically at the floor of his crate. She picked up some plastic bags and the keys and the leash from the hall stand. She came and unlatched his door. He sprang out and ran to the front door of the apartment. When she opened it, he thundered downstairs and stood impatiently by the outer door. She heard a little anxious cry in his throat. "Good dog," she said, opening the last door.

He almost fell down the porch stairs in his haste. As soon as his feet touched the sidewalk, he squatted and peed.

She lavished the praise on him that was part of his training, patting him, scratching his long, floppy ears. Then she hooked the leash to his collar and they started out, around the three-block circuit that constituted the walk she took with him twice a day.

It was a perfect day—cloudless, mild. There were many fine things about having a dog, all of which she was reluctant to admit, but one of them was simply how much more frequently she got outside. She knew, of course, that this wouldn't be the pleasure it was today come January or February, but for now Billy liked it.

Especially today, when Gus was gone. Today, tomorrow, Thursday. He wouldn't be home until late Thursday night. He was flying out to Los Angeles this morning. His father had died—Leslie had called on Sunday with the news.

It was strange for both of them. Neither wanted to go. They hadn't seen him in years. There was the second wife to deal with, and she was also what Leslie called "a high-functioning drunk." But Gus had been named executor of his father's will and there was a service of some sort Wednesday, so they agreed they ought to be there. After the call, Billy and Gus had sat and talked about it with more affection and friendliness than they'd been able to muster in months. Than she'd been able to muster, anyway.

It couldn't have been worse timing for him—his school started this week. But he'd called the headmaster and the chair of the department right away. He'd spent all day yesterday—Monday, the first day of classes—at the school. He'd met with his kids and outlined the special projects he wanted them to work on over the three days he'd be gone.

And this morning he'd left the house at five-thirty to get to the airport on time while she pretended to sleep.

She felt his absence as an enormous relief. Three days of not acting as if she didn't know it was over. Three days of not having to sit through dinner with him. Three days of not feeling angry at him and then at herself for allowing the whole thing to happen, for ignoring all the ways it should have been clear from the start that it wasn't going to work. Three wonderful long mornings of work without having to bicycle over to BU.

And in the afternoons she would get herself organized to find an apartment. She had to. It might be too expensive, it might be in a crummy neighborhood, but she needed to do it. After she and Gus had gone to bed Sunday night, she'd lain there next to him as he slept, planning it—the lists she'd check, the neighborhoods she was interested in.

When she got back home from the walk with Reuben, she fed him, and then she made coffee for herself, coffee and toast, and went out onto the back porch to sit. Reuben padded behind her and lay down by her feet. She would take him with her when she left, she had decided this already. After all, he was hers. He'd been given to her. He'd been given to her to make it harder for her to leave, and harder it would be. But in an odd way, it had strengthened her conviction that she needed to do it.

She sat with her coffee, her feet propped up on the porch rail, and looked out through the trees at the other rooftops in the neighborhood. Gus lived on the middle floor of a triple-decker just over the line into Somerville from North Cambridge, near the commuter line he caught every day to go out to teach. The houses here were only a few feet apart, sometimes just the width of a narrow driveway. Most had aluminum siding. In front they all had little yards, scraps of lawn or gravel or dirt, many of them protected by chain-link fences. But the backyards were deep and lush with trees. You could almost forget you were in a city. Looking out now, she thought how she would miss this. As though he understood what she was feeling, the puppy heaved a great sigh.

She finished her coffee and went inside. Reuben followed. She put him in his crate and looked at the clock in the kitchen. Seven-thirty. He should go out again in a couple of hours. She went into her study and turned on the computer.

At about quarter to eight, her cell phone rang. She opened it and looked at the number. It was Gus. She felt a quick tug of the irritation she had been trying to stay in control of, and closed it without answering.

She worked well. She was trying to shape up the play about Ray and Elena and his big con, fussing with the beginning of the second act, which had seemed expository to her. By the time she stopped to walk the puppy again, she'd made what she thought was good progress—she'd put into dialogue about a third of what had existed as stage directions or notes to herself.

Reuben was asleep. He woke as soon as she touched the door of the crate. She took him quickly outside. Again, he peed as soon as he reached the sidewalk, and she gave him a treat.

The streets were quiet. The kids must all be back in school, she thought. As she rounded the corner by the Ell-Stan Spa, the little convenience store that marked the beginning of the tiny local commercial strip—a Laundromat, a pizza place—she noted that there were six or seven people clustered inside, all standing, all watching the wall-mounted TV. On it she could see a talking face, and then the screen filled with roiling, tumbling smoke. She thought immediately of Waco, those terrible images of the fire. It must be something like that, something awful that had happened somewhere out in the wide world.

She turned Reuben around and walked quickly back to Gus's. Inside, she went immediately to the second bedroom, Gus's office, where the tiny TV was. She turned it on just in time to see a replay of the collapse of the South Tower, the billowing dust and debris, the strange tribe of ghostlike people coated with white emerging from the thick rolling cloud—running, looking behind them, terrified.

She watched for a long time in stunned horror as the events unfolded and unfolded, and then were played over and over again. At some point maybe several hours later, she paid attention for the first time to where the planes were coming from, where they were going. It occurred to her then that Gus might have been on one or the other of them.

It couldn't be, she thought. It was too unlikely.

She found her cell phone and played his message. "Hi, sweetie. We're getting on the plane, so I just wanted to hear your voice for a second. You must be walking Rube. I'm thinking of you. I'll talk to you tonight."

She played it again. Then she hit RETURN CALL. There was no sound on the other end of the line. Nothing.

Frantic now, she went through the papers on his

desk, looking for a note, something he might have jotted down about the airline, about the flight number. She couldn't find anything.

She was going too fast, that was it. She made herself stop, she went through everything more slowly. Here were his papers, his innocent papers. Plans for the semester. Notes, quickly scribbled about what the students could do while he was away. Bills. A postcard from a friend traveling in Europe over the summer, with a detail from a fresco by Fra Angelico reproduced on the front.

There was nothing about the trip, the reservation, the airline.

She tried to call Leslie at home. The phone rang and rang, and then a message came on in Leslie's calm, modulated voice. After the beep, she couldn't think what to say, so she hung up. And then remembered abruptly that Leslie would be on her way west, too. She had been planning to fly out from the little airport in New Hampshire. Manchester, that was it. Manchester on a connecting flight to some hub probably, and then the final leg from there to Los Angeles.

She tried calling a few airlines—American, United, Delta—but she couldn't get through. Everything was busy. What would she have asked anyway? She wasn't certain what time he was leaving, she didn't know whether it was a direct flight, or even what the airline was. There must be thousands of people in exactly her situation, trying to learn something.

She tried Gus's school. Maybe someone there knew something.

That line was busy, too.

She played his message again.

On her way to the bathroom, she saw that Reuben had left a puddle in the hall. How long since she'd walked him? She couldn't remember. Where was he, anyway? What time was it?

She went in the kitchen and looked at the clock on the stove. One-thirty.

When she was done in the bathroom, she went into the living room. Reuben was back in his crate—he'd gone there on his own. He was asleep, his head sticking out through the open doorway, resting on his paws. She didn't wake him until she'd cleaned up the piss. Then, bending over his crate, she spoke his name. He sprang to instant eager life, and she took him out for another walk. The streets were still silent—everyone, she assumed, indoors by the television, by the telephone. Except in New York, where everyone was panicked, on the move.

At two-thirty, Leslie called. Her flight had been canceled and Pierce had driven her back home. She was calling to ask whether Gus had actually left, to say that one of the planes was Gus's. She'd heard the number and recognized it—they'd conferred about flight times and she'd written it down.

When Billy said yes, there was a little moan on the line, and then silence.

"Leslie?" Billy said.

Leslie's voice was uneven when she spoke. She

said, "He must be dead. I think there's no way he can't be dead." She breathed audibly, unsteadily. "Oh, Billy, I think it's true. I think it is," she said. She started to cry, and then tried to check herself.

Billy wasn't sure what she said back. She was sorry, she said that. "I can't believe it." She said that.

Leslie said she had kept hoping that he wasn't on it, that he somehow didn't make it, but she'd tried his cell and there was no response. And he would have called, surely, if he could. If he were alive.

"No, he called," Billy said.

"He called?"

The hope in her voice was painful for Billy to hear. "He called when he was getting on," she said quickly. "Just when he was getting on."

Leslie started to cry again. "Oh, what did he **say**?" It was hard to understand her.

"He said just that. That he was getting on. He said he'd talk to me tonight."

"Oh. Well." She was pulling herself together. She blew her nose. "I'm so glad you got to speak to him."

"Yes," Billy said, feeling already how false a position she was in.

"I know . . . I know," Leslie said. "This is . . . a terrible time. To talk. But we will . . . I will call you, if I hear anything. I'll call. Anything."

Billy said yes. Yes, she'd call, too.

About half an hour later, the phone rang again. Billy almost jumped. It was Leslie. Her voice was stronger. She thought Billy should come up to Vermont. That she shouldn't be alone. "Alone with this," is what she said. If she didn't want to drive, Leslie would arrange for a car to bring her.

"We could help each other, don't you think?" she asked.

Billy couldn't imagine anything she wanted to do less, but she kept her voice calm as she said that she wanted to stay in the apartment—that's the way she put it. She had the puppy, she said. She just wanted to stay here with him.

When she got off the phone, she turned the television off. She went into the bedroom and lay down. The images from the towers played over and over in her mind, inescapably. She couldn't remember which was the South Tower, which was the North. Which was Gus's plane. She thought of Leslie's voice, breaking. She thought of him, the way it must have been—the disorder, the panic and the chaos in the airplane. The understanding you would have— how long before?—of what was going to happen. And then surely the instantaneous death. Surely.

Or perhaps not.

Her stomach gurgled. She hadn't eaten, she realized, since early in the morning. She got up. Standing in the kitchen, she ate a few bites of an apple. She set what was left carefully down on the counter, walked into the bathroom, and threw up. She stayed there, kneeling over the toilet, until her knees began to ache.

A while later, she walked the dog again. She fed him. Then she took him downstairs and walked him once more—she'd done things in the wrong order, she realized. She should have fed him before the first walk.

There were people out now, at the end of the day, moving around, standing in clusters on porches, on the sidewalk, talking to one another about it. An old woman walked toward her on the sidewalk. When their eyes met, she said, "Isn't it terrible." Her face was anguished.

"Yes," Billy said.

Back in the apartment, she went to Gus's desk. She sat down. She went through his things again. She picked up the smiling photograph of herself he'd set in a clear plastic stand and looked at it for a long time, then dropped it in the wastebasket. She turned over the Fra Angelico postcard. On the back, in scratchy black ink, it said, "The things we are seeing! I hope you will too one day. We are drinking it in, along with what we are actually drinking in. Theo and Nina."

She had no idea who Theo and Nina were.

There was so much of Gus's life she didn't know. Who would take care of all this? Who would it belong to? Who would dispose of it? Who was in charge of Gus now?

Leslie, surely.

Not me, Billy thought. And she started to cry for the first time.

She walked the puppy once more after dark, and then she brought him into bed with her. It was about ten. He hadn't been allowed to sleep with her—with her and Gus—ever before, and he was confused. He stood up several times and came and planted himself by her head, panting his hot breath on her, his tail wagging.

She spoke sharply to him each time, and finally he lay down, his bulk curled against her rump. She could hear his breathing change when he went to sleep. She lay awake a long time. Twice she got up to pee. Once she cried, silently but long enough that, when she stopped, her face felt swollen and thick, she couldn't breathe through her nose. The last time she looked at the red digits of the clock, they said 1:10.

Reuben woke her a little after three, mewling, scratching the pillow close to her face.

Gus had done the nighttime walks until now. Nighttime, early morning, the one before dinner, the last one before bed, all to show Billy how easy a puppy would be, how easy it would be if she just stayed with him.

She pulled on her jeans and a sweater, slid into some sandals, and they went out into the hallway and down the stairs. The moment she heard the outer door click behind her, she knew she'd screwed up. She'd locked herself out. In her mind she could see the key on the table. On the table where it should have been but wasn't, next to the leash and plastic pickup bags. Where it wasn't, because she'd been careless today. She hadn't followed Gus's orderly patterns, she hadn't put things back where they belonged. Here, here was the price.

Reuben peed. She sat on the porch steps for a while. The dog watched her attentively for clues as to what was happening. Finally she got up and started to walk with him. A big walk. Might as well. One or the other of her neighbors in the house would let her in, but it would be hours before she could decently ring either bell.

She walked through the dark, dead streets. Everything was quiet, except for here and there the bluish flickering light in a bedroom or a living room—someone awake, someone unable to stop watching the events again and again, someone finding consolation, perhaps, in the theorizing, the expert opinions.

She walked south and west, over into the streets of Cambridge, toward Harvard Square, thinking she would go to the river, she'd sit in the grass there until the sky was light. As she walked, she thought reasonlessly, uselessly, swinging between a deep disbelief—the sense she had that nothing like what had happened could possibly have happened—and the horrified imagining, over and over, of how it would have been for Gus, slicing into the building, crushing it and being crushed.

In flight from any of that, she made herself think of the most practical issues. She wondered if the rent was paid up, where Gus had left the car, what she would do with all his belongings. She would move out, she knew that. She couldn't possibly stay. It was Gus's place. She didn't belong there.

It occurred to her with something like relief that she hadn't talked to anyone about splitting up with Gus—anyone except the one old friend in Chicago whom she e-mailed and called regularly. It would make it easier for her to get through it, to go through the motions of grief, which is what she'd have to do.

No! It would be more than that, more than **motions.** Of course it would. She did mourn Gus. Her throat ached with sorrow for him. It was awful, truly awful. That he'd died. That he **wasn't,** anymore. The way he'd died. The cruelty of it, the enormity of it, the randomness of it. The wrongness of it—for how could it be Gus's end? Gus, who was so sunny, so blameless.

She'd gone about a mile and a half—she was approaching Harvard Square on Ware Street—when she realized that the puppy was flagging, that, unconscious of him as she was, she'd more or less been pulling him for the last couple of blocks. She hadn't ever exhausted the dog before, she specialized in such short walks. It was Gus who did the walks that really exercised him, that wore him out.

As soon as she stopped, he sat down. He sat down in a way that suggested he would never get up, a kind of grateful and rubbery collapse. After a moment, when she didn't pull him up, he lay down on the sidewalk and put his head on his enormous paws.

She squatted by him and patted his head, stroked the softly curling fur of his body. His tail slapped the sidewalk. He turned on his side and grabbed at her hand with his mouth, licking, chewing.

"Not allowed, buddy," she said. She clamped his muzzle shut with one hand and, with the other, scratched his belly, stroked him for a long time, talking to him, sometimes crying for a minute or two. She had to use the edge of her sweater—why not?—to wipe her eyes, her runny nose. She crouched there until her legs started to feel numb. When she stopped and stood up, he sat up too, watching her face, his tail swinging in wild swoops, wanting more.

She started back north, toward home, and he pranced beside her for a few blocks, then slowed, then wanted to stop again.

She let him. She stood by him while he rested for a few minutes, and then she squatted and patted him again. In this way, Billy crying and petting him, Reuben resting, they retraced their steps slowly back to the house, Gus's house.

The sky was lightening when they sat on the top step of the porch. Reuben lay down and instantly slept. Billy was exhausted, too, she realized. She leaned against the post at the top of the stairs. It was cool against her skin. The flesh of her arms under her hands felt chilly. She thought of Gus in the plane again. She stopped herself. Somewhere a rooster crowed. Across the street, she could make out the big pink plastic flowers stuck into the earth of the front yard by the old woman who lived on the ground floor. So much for the bother of gardening.

She thought of her downstairs neighbor, how he might come out and find her. What would she say? She would tell him about Gus. She would have to. They'd known each other a long time. He owned the building and two others on the block. He knew all his tenants, but he especially liked Gus. He would be shocked and horrified. She would be, too, all over again. She would be, because she **was,** shocked and horrified.

But a part of it—a part of her, a part of everything from now on—would be false. Would be a lie.

Leslie drove down, by herself, on Saturday. Billy had held her off until then, but couldn't any longer—she was insistent. She wouldn't stay overnight, she said. She didn't want to impose, but she wanted to see Billy, she wanted to be in Gus's place, to look at his things.

Billy was shocked at the way she looked. The open, warm quality she had always conveyed was gone, as if erased, though she said the same words, the same **Leslie** kind of things. But she seemed, Billy would have said, smaller. Exhausted.

The worst moments, of course, were the very first, when she embraced Billy as though Billy needed comforting more than she did. "My dear," she said.

"Oh, my dear." She held on, almost rocking Billy for a long moment. Billy could hear, she could feel, Leslie's ragged intake of breath. When they stepped away from each other, she saw that Leslie was fighting tears.

But Billy was tearful, too, because it was awful that Gus was dead. That so many were dead. That Leslie was so visibly in pain. Leslie's gaze, resting on her, was soft, full of sympathy and affection.

That shamed Billy, and she turned away. She went to make some tea, and they sat in the kitchen and talked. Mostly just going over, as everyone did in those days—even those who weren't directly involved—how it had happened for them. How it was for Leslie at the airport, hearing about it and checking what she'd written down about Gus's plane. The terrible ride back home, listening to the radio. Pierce finally turned it off, she said, and that somehow made it worse, made it final.

Billy was aware of herself, of her responses, as she listened to Leslie's account, as she told Leslie about her day, about how slowly she came to realize that one of the planes might have been Gus's. She was conscious of trying to calibrate her grief, trying to hold on to a shred of honesty by not letting Leslie think she was overcome, or had been overcome. As soon as she could, she excused herself to walk the dog.

———

Over the next days and weeks, Leslie misunderstood almost every gesture, every word, Billy said. The more Billy tried to back away from being the grief-stricken lover—the more she deferred to Leslie—the more Leslie insisted she had prior rights. **She** should have the final say on whether the Boston service should be at the school. She would know better than Leslie the list of friends to be invited. She should go through Gus's things and choose what she wanted to keep. She should read at the service.

Her **no** to most of these things seemed only to confirm Leslie's sense of Billy's lostness in grief. Again and again Billy told herself that she would be as honest as she decently could. She would try not to lie, not to pretend what she didn't feel. But in the end it seemed to her that there wasn't a truthful gesture she could make. She felt cottoned in falsity. Her dry eyes were understood by Leslie as shock. Her finding the too-expensive apartment in the South End was a sign of her need to flee the place where she and Gus had been happy together.

Could she have told her the truth? Someone braver than Billy might have. But Billy knew Leslie took some comfort in believing that she had loved Gus, that she mourned him, so she said nothing. This was the least she could offer her, could do for her. It was, she slowly realized, the only thing she could do for her.

The service was to be held at Gus's school the first Saturday in October, in the chapel. Billy hadn't done any of the planning for it, and she felt bad about that—that Leslie, so burdened by her unequivocal grief, should have had to do it by herself. Of course, Pierce had helped her; there was that. And Leslie said that Gus's old friend Peter had helped, too, that he was "a godsend."

Billy did buy a new suit for the service, a dark gray suit. She assumed that this would be the only formal occasion in her life for remembering Gus, and she wanted her appearance itself to be a kind of honoring of him. The day of the service, she took her time getting ready. She applied her makeup carefully, she blew her normally messy hair smooth. About half an hour before Leslie and Pierce were to pick her up, she walked Reuben and crated him. Then she pulled a chair over to one of the curved front windows of her parlor apartment and sat looking out it for Leslie and Pierce's old Volvo—they'd never be able to find a parking place. When she saw them pull up and double-park, she grabbed her purse and went quickly to the door. As she closed it quietly behind her, Reuben let out an anguished cry, long and mournful. She couldn't stop to console him; she just had to hope for her neighbors' sakes that it didn't go on too long.

Leslie had just stepped out of the car on the way to get her when Billy emerged. She looked elegant, Billy thought—all in black, with a royal blue shawl thrown over the shoulder of her suit. Her face was drawn but beautiful, her hair pulled back simply into a ponytail at the nape of her neck, as if she hadn't wanted to bother arranging it. There was something immense, almost monumental, about her. Billy felt like a girl, a child, by contrast.

They embraced—quickly, because a car had pulled up and was waiting behind the Volvo, the driver watching them with what passed for patience in this environment. Billy got in the backseat, where the child belonged, after all. Pierce turned around to say hello before he put the car in gear and began to drive. His voice was without the exuberance that usually marked it. It was tender, the way he must speak to the kids in his practice.

Their conversation was polite, neutral. **How was the drive down? How's the dog? The new apartment? This is such a lovely neighborhood.** Pierce said his favorite restaurant was close by and Billy said she'd have to try it. Leslie asked about how the teaching at BU was going this year. It was a relief for all of them, Billy felt sure, to get on the highway, where the noise made conversation unnecessary.

At one point, though, Billy leaned forward to ask, "Is there anything in particular I should know about the service, or the reception?"

Leslie turned sideways, almost in profile. "I think it will all just move along smoothly," she said. "No surprises. Peter has arranged for some friends to talk, and the students wanted to do a choral thing. I think one of them will speak, too."

Billy was instantly swamped again by guilt about

this, that she hadn't offered to speak, or do anything else, in fact.

"The headmaster's in charge, for which I'm grateful. Mr. Willis. He put it in the paper and had someone contact every single person I listed. He's been wonderful."

Leslie turned away, but not before Billy saw the tears well in her eyes. Sitting back again, she felt small and ashamed, ugly.

They drove in silence, not even Pierce feeling compelled to talk. The trees had thinned out a bit—their leaves would begin to fall in earnest soon. For now they were at their most intensely beautiful, the colors on the hillsides astonishing. They turned off the highway onto the winding, almost-country roads. They drove by the old houses set far apart from one another, their lawns sprinkled with the fallen leaves, the new, low light dancing through the trees. They passed eight or ten bicyclists moving in a group at the side of the road, sexless and insectlike in their busyness, their gleaming helmets. Billy saw a yard sale in front of an open barn, an odd collection of possessions. There were dishes and chairs, two iron bedsteads leaned up against some old trunks. A small crowd of people was milling around, examining the boxes of things. Billy thought of the things she'd set out on the curb in Somerville, things that had been part of her life with Gus.

They drove down the main street of the little town. It was lined with shops and restaurants, thick with people out doing Saturday morning errands. At the end of this strip, they turned onto the side street where the school buildings began. The dorms looked like simply more of the white Georgian houses of the village, but then the campus suddenly opened up and you saw the larger new administrative buildings arranged around the central lawn with its crisscrossing pathways. The sky was a grand painted blue behind the vivid trees and white buildings, behind the green of the glistening grass. Billy felt a sharp pain in her stomach, something like nausea, something like stage fright. She dug her fists into her midriff. It would begin now, her performance.

Pierce parked in the visitors' lot, and they walked together on one of the paths to the chapel building. Its narrow white steeple pierced the blue sky. Mr. Willis, the headmaster, a man only a little older than Gus, stood in its entryway, perhaps waiting for them. He was in his shirtsleeves, but he had a tie on. He greeted them and led them back to a private room. Gus's friend Peter was already there, Peter and his pregnant wife and another couple Billy had met once. She waited her turn beside Leslie and Pierce to be greeted. She and Gus had had dinner with Peter and Erin two or three times. Now she murmured something: Thank you, she would call, yes, if she thought of anything they could do. Leslie was working so much harder, talking about Gus, remembering that Peter and Gus had once tried to hitchhike back to Boston when they'd missed the bus. That quite by chance she'd seen them when she was out doing errands, that she'd ended up driving all the way down with them, calling Pierce from a restaurant near an exit to tell him she'd be home late that night. "Do you remember?" she asked Peter. He nodded.

"Imagine," Leslie said to Billy, to the group, "me doing **anything** on a lark! But that's what it was like with Gus."

As soon as Billy could, she told Leslie she was going to go and sit in the chapel.

"Oh, Billy—oh, of course," Leslie said. "I understand completely."

Don't, Billy wanted to say. **Don't understand.** But she said nothing of the kind. She said nothing at all.

The chapel had no religious symbols or decoration. As Gus had told her, it wasn't really a chapel at all. It was called that because all these old prep schools had at one time been sectarian, had started each day with a religious service and then made the daily announcements; so that the gathering for these announcements was still called chapel, and the place where you gathered was also called chapel. All anachronism, he had said. Like so much else about the school.

It was large, with enough pews for the entire school population. Tall, clear windows opened out onto the trees and lawns of the campus. A bank of flowers, mostly white, sat across the apron of the stage. A lectern was set in the midst of them. Toward the back of the stage, there was a grand piano, its dark, harp-shaped lid propped open.

Billy moved into a pew three rows back. There were programs set out along the seat cushions at regular intervals, each with a photo of Gus's face. Over and over, Gus, smiling, bright sunlight making him squint, his yellow hair windblown. She picked one up and sat down, holding it. The pew creaked under her.

She wasn't alone for long. In a few minutes, people began to straggle in, taking seats nearer the back, whispering, talking quietly. After ten minutes or so, a young man came down the side aisle to the stage and mounted the steps. He sat down at the piano, arranged some music, and started to play. Billy wasn't sure of the composer—Schubert, maybe. Then more quickly, the pews filled. Students, mostly, but also people Leslie's age, Gus's age. Billy knew none of them.

Leslie and Pierce came in with the headmaster and Gus's friends and took the first few rows. Peter's wife, Erin, was sitting directly in front of Billy. She bent forward, as if praying, but perhaps she was only reading through the program.

When the piano stopped, the headmaster stood and mounted the short flight of stairs to the stage. He greeted the room. The students—and, raggedly, a few others joining in—said, "Good afternoon," back to him. There was a moment of silence, and then he said, "We gather to celebrate the life of our dear friend Gus Forester. Lost, among so many others, in the cruel events of September eleventh. But Gus was ours, and so we especially miss him, and we know all too well what an emptiness his death will leave in our lives."

Somewhere in the room, someone began to cry softly, and here and there people were blowing their noses. Billy shut her eyes for a moment. The pews' creaking was a constant, the rustle of the programs, the shifting of people's clothing as they moved.

The headmaster spoke for a few more minutes, and then Peter came up and took his place. He introduced himself and talked, it seemed mostly to the students, about friendship, about his friendship with Gus in college and its irreplaceable importance to him. Gus's loyalty, his joie de vivre. He mentioned Leslie, and Billy saw her lift her hand to her mouth.

After Peter, a gaggle of students came up the steps and assembled themselves into two rows, the girls in front. The pianist did a quick introduction and they sang "Swing Low, Sweet Chariot." As soon as they finished, one of the girls broke down. She was instantly surrounded by the three other girls, and they huddled down the stairs from the stage, their arms around one another, and then down the aisle, past Billy, who sat dry-eyed, not looking at them.

One of the boys from the choral group had

remained onstage. He stepped to the lectern now and talked about Gus as a teacher and friend, someone who pushed for excellence in their work and made them care about it, too. He called him "one of the great teachers."

The headmaster came up again. He announced the Twenty-third Psalm, and they stood and read it together, the beautiful words of calm faith. Was Gus a believer? Billy didn't even know that.

The whole room sat down, and then Leslie got up and went to the steps, mounted them. Billy looked down at her own hands, folded on the program on her lap, resting on Gus's face in the photograph. She didn't want to meet Leslie's eyes, she couldn't watch her face.

Leslie carried a little sheaf of paper that she set down in front of her. She put her glasses on. The remarks were read, then, and as she started, Billy heard that quality in them—a bit formal, certainly composed. Leslie's voice wobbled, though, and several times she had to stop.

She talked about the age difference between her and Gus, about the joy he brought to her life, as a sister—almost as a mother. Near the end of the talk, she said, "How glad I am to think of him in the last year, so especially happy in his work with many of you here, and in his life, with the woman he loved so much, Billy Gertz."

Billy breathed in deeply and unclenched her hands. She saw the print of her fingernails in her flesh, dark crescents arcing across her palms.

There was a musical interlude, and then the headmaster invited anyone who wished to speak to add his remarks. For a long minute or so, it seemed no one would, but then a woman arose and introduced herself. There was the rustle of everyone turning to her. Billy turned, too. She was a tall, thin woman about halfway back, with a mass of long, wild graying hair. Her name was Augusta Sinclair, she said, "so of course, we were the two Guses. And somehow this was enough, in Gus's world, for us to be friends. Sometimes he would ask me, 'How is it in the alternate Gus universe?' and he always took time to listen to my answer." The other thing, she said, was how important his teaching was to him, how much he loved it and the kids. "And whenever I needed a shot of what I think of as **emotional caffeine** about my work, I'd find him, and that is exactly what he would give me. Actually, he gave me that in other contexts, too. I'll miss him very much." She sat down.

After her a few students spoke, and then an alumnus, a young man who "had to come," he said. Mr. Forester had changed his life, had made him understand that language shaped thought, clarified it. That if you couldn't say it or write it, you hadn't fully mastered it. "He was exacting, and I slowly learned to really, really love that. And it's brought me to where I am today." And then he said, " 'Explicate!' " and the room laughed.

The headmaster stood up again and announced a student's name. A young woman came up and read the 103rd Psalm, one Billy didn't know as well—about God's power, his generosity, and man's small-ness by comparison, God's pity on man. The girl's voice was strong, reading the lines. Near the end of the reading, she intoned, "As for man, his days are as grass. As a flower of the field, so he flourisheth. For the wind passeth over it, and it is gone, and the place thereof shall know it no more."

Billy thought of Gus, of course, but she thought, too—as almost everyone else must have—of the Towers, gone, the blank spot on the skyline where they'd been. That, **that** was how absolute his death was. All of their deaths. "The place thereof shall know it no more."

The noise of weeping spread around the room—that choked sound—and people blowing their noses. Then a hymn was announced, the words printed in the program. The piano played an introduction as they all stood. It was an evening hymn, "Now the Day Is Over," in a minor key. Billy knew it from the churchgoing days of her youth. The verses had been chosen carefully—no mention of Christ. The verse asking for comfort for "every sufferer, watching late in pain," was still there, though, and it made Billy think of Leslie. She felt her own tears starting, but stopped herself. They were sentimental tears, and she wouldn't allow herself them. The last verse they sang was about dawn:

When the morning wakens
Then may I arise,

**Pure and fresh and sinless
In Thy holy eyes.**

Gus. It seemed made for him. Leslie must have chosen it. The last note of the "Amen" floated in the air and then disappeared. Everyone sat down again.

The headmaster got up and asked everyone to come to a reception in the meeting room off the dining hall. The piano started once more, and the first few rows stood and began to file out. And then everyone was standing, the same noise as the rustling hubbub of a theater audience. There was a gradual increase in volume as they all began making their way out of the pews and down the side or the middle aisles, talking, greeting others, some of them simply wiping their eyes.

Billy stepped outside onto the steps in the bright sun by herself. Leslie came up to her. "Billy, dear," she said. "You're bleeding. You've bitten your lip." She fished in her bag and brought out a packet of tissues, from which she extracted one for Billy. Billy took it, touched her lip, held it out. A bright stain.

"So I have," Billy said. She was glad for it, and somehow glad, too, to have Leslie see it.

"Oh, Billy," Leslie said. "I wish there were some way I could help."

"I do, too," Billy said. The truth, for once.

Leslie kissed her, and then Pierce joined them as they started across one of the paths toward the dining hall.

The reception was in a smaller, more elegant room off the enormous student dining area. Tables had been pushed back against the walls, and an array of food was set out, mostly square sandwiches, the crusts cut off, and various desserts and fruits. One table had pitchers and several big, institutional urns—coffee and hot water, and probably decaf, too. Billy wanted nothing, but others were loading plates, and some were already holding them as they stood around, talking and eating.

Peter's wife, Erin, came up and launched herself into a conversation. She liked to talk. Billy had complained about it to Gus after their evenings with her and Peter, but now she was grateful. She felt at ease, briefly. Surrounded by Erin's gentle chatter, there was no need to speak. But then she moved off and Billy was alone.

"So, how did you know Gus?" someone asked her, politely. He had a plate of cookies he had held up to her by way of saying hello.

"I actually met him on a ferryboat," she said, ignoring the larger question behind the small one: **Who are you in relation to him?** "And you?"

He was a parent of someone on the soccer team Gus coached. He'd come to the games regularly and struck up an acquaintance. He spoke of Gus's drive to win, his pleasure in using his body.

"Yes," Billy said sadly, remembering the uses he'd made of it with her.

The head of the English department came up to

her and said, "So you're the famous Billy we all heard so much about."

"I suppose I am," she said. "At least, I don't think there were other Billys."

"Gus spoke of you so often," he said.

"Thank you. Thank you for telling me," she said.

Always she felt she should be saying more, that her silence, her failure to have been part of the service, were things that people would have noticed, would be thinking strange. But then she also told herself that this was self-important, that no one was thinking of her, that they were thinking of Gus—only of Gus.

She met two of Pierce's brothers, with their wives. Leslie introduced her to several old friends of hers, people who were there mostly for her, it seemed, as Billy spoke to them. Who hadn't known Gus all that well. They asked her about him, and then about how she thought Leslie was doing.

When Pierce touched her back and asked if she remembered what Leslie had done with her shawl— "Did she take it with her out of the car?"—Billy seized on this as an excuse to escape.

"I'll go look. Maybe she left it in the chapel."

"That would be nice of you. Thanks, Billy."

As she stepped out into the cooler air and started walking back across the green to the parking lot, Billy wondered if Pierce had noticed how out of it she was and was rescuing her. More likely Leslie had noticed and had sent Pierce over. Either way, walking alone for the first time today, she felt her body ease. She breathed in. The sky was so blue, as blue as it had been on 9/11, though the air was cooler, a kind of presentiment of fall in it. She started to think about what she might have said about Gus, if she'd spoken.

But no, she was only glad she hadn't. There were many good things she could have offered, of course there were, but she would have offered them to make things seem okay, and not because of the wish to honor him, to remember him.

But of course she would remember him. She would remember good things about him as well as the trapped feeling she'd slowly come to have living with him. She would remember him perhaps longer and with more pain than someone whose feelings were less ambivalent, less knotted. She would remember him every time she walked the dog, every time she saw an airplane glide through an azure sky, every time she saw Leslie, every September 11 of her life. She swore to herself she would. She would remember him, she was sure, long after she'd forgotten exactly what he looked like, or exactly why she'd felt she couldn't live with him anymore.

The shawl wasn't in the car. She retraced their steps to the chapel and went inside. It seemed enormous once more without people filling the pews. The pictures of Gus were scattered everywhere, even on the floor. She went to the pew Leslie had been sitting in. She could see the scarf, the brilliant blue corner of it, sticking out from under the bench. She gathered it in. It carried Leslie's perfume with it and, somehow, the sense of Leslie. She had loved her better than she loved Gus; she knew this. And she was as sad about Leslie, she realized, as almost anything else—sad that she would always dread seeing her, being with her, even while she missed all of that. She folded the shawl neatly and carried it out into the bright sunlight.

A couple was walking toward her as she crossed back over the pathway. It was Peter and Erin, she saw as they got closer. Erin was carrying her shoes. They stopped when they met. Erin explained she just couldn't stand up anymore. She pointed to her feet. Billy looked down. They were shapeless, unfootlike. "I need to get home and elevate them, ASAP," she said.

On an impulse, Billy asked if they could wait. They lived in the Back Bay, just a few blocks north of Billy's new neighborhood. It would be easy enough, then, for them to drop Billy in Copley Square. She could walk home from there in fifteen minutes. "I need to take Leslie her shawl, and let her know I'm going, but I'll be right back."

They said they'd wait by their car.

The crowd at the reception had begun to thin. Leslie was talking to two of the students. Billy held the shawl out to her, and Leslie turned from them.

"Where was it? Thank you so much!"

Billy told her. Then she said, "I'm going to excuse

myself now, Leslie. I just need to get home, and Peter and Erin said they could drive me." She knew how Leslie would take this, her announced need to leave, and she felt a certain sorrowful anger at herself for using the feelings she didn't have, but might have had—should have had—in order to make a getaway.

"This was hard, I know," Leslie said, sympathetically.

"Yes," Billy said. "And for you, too," she said. It felt lame, pathetic, whatever she said.

Leslie lifted her hand, dismissively. "I'll call you tomorrow, shall I?" she asked. "I want to be sure you're all right."

"I'll be all right," Billy said. "I am all right. I'm just, tired, I guess."

"Of course you are. And of course you'll be all right. I just . . . I miss you."

She was engulfed again in Leslie's embrace.

Peter and his wife let her sit in the backseat. They didn't seem to mind her silence. They talked to each other about Gus for a while, about the service, about 9/11, but then moved on to other things. She had a doctor's appointment coming up. She was going to ask about her feet. Their voices dropped. She said something about bleeding. Billy opened her window a crack and let the breeze and its rushing noise shelter her.

Instead of dropping her off in Copley Square, as she'd suggested, they insisted on driving her home.

It wouldn't be a problem, an extra five minutes, Peter said. When they pulled up in front of her building, he got out and came around. Billy was out of the car, was bent over Erin's opened window saying good-bye. When she stood straight, Peter held out his hand. She took it, and he folded his other hand over hers and said earnestly, "If there's anything we can do, Billy, you'll let us know."

Billy was sure he meant it, but it was also an easy, perfunctory thing to say, and her answer—to thank him, to say she would—was easy, too. They both knew she wouldn't call.

The parlor was quiet when she opened the door— no frantic greeting from Reuben. For a moment she was frightened—where was he? what had happened?—but then she heard him shift in his crate, and an anxious small whimper. As she came closer, she saw he was sitting all the way at the back of the crate, pressed against that wall. Then she noticed the smell and saw the turd heaped in the front corner. He hadn't been able to wait.

She went quickly into the bedroom and took off her suit and heels. Wearing just her slip, in stocking feet, she went into the bathroom for a roll of toilet paper and a towel. From under the kitchen sink, she got paper towels and rags and the bucket. She filled the bucket with soapy water and carried everything with her to the crate.

When she opened the door, Reuben didn't move to come out. She knelt on the floor. The smell from within the crate was awful. She made two wads of the toilet paper and picked up the turd, set it on the floor on some paper towels. Then she reached in, curled her fingers under Reuben's collar, and pulled him forward. She saw that he'd gotten shit on his haunch and leg, probably because the crate really was too small for him now. As soon as he was out, he crouched down to the floor in apology, looking carefully away from her, ashamed. His ears were flat. He turned over on his back, a supplicant for forgiveness.

She reached out and stroked him on his face, his enormous head. "It's not your fault, sweet boy. You're good. It's my fault. You're good. You're a good boy." Something in these words made her throat ache, brought tears up. Why? She didn't know. "It's my fault," she said. "You're a good boy. A good, good Reuben."

With tears blurring her vision, she dunked a rag in the soapy water and began to clean him up.

Sam called on Friday, three days after they'd met. The message was waiting when she got back from the theater. She stood for a moment listening to his voice in her dark living room, looking out the window at a couple moving past under the streetlight. Their voices were pitched loudly—a little flirty, a little drunk. Reuben was whining at the door. **Come on.**

"I wondered about our having the coffee we're

supposed to," Sam said. "Or maybe lunch. Or dinner, for that matter—on Monday. I think that's the
day theaters are famously closed. Let me know." He
left several numbers.

She got Reuben's leash and took him out. The
fountains in the private park at the center of the
street were turned off now, so there wasn't that
steady, pleasant sound—nature disciplined, as she
thought of it. It made a kind of emptiness. The
leaves were gone from the trees, and her view into
the parlors and the ground-floor apartments was
unimpeded. TV and more TV for the most part.
There was one dinner party still in full swing,
though, a group of men around a table, their faces
alive in the glowing candlelight, their chairs pushed
back or turned sideways, their voices a faint mur-
mur from the street.

They met one other dog, coming their way, much
smaller than Reuben but unintimidated by him,
and friendly. As the dogs circled and sniffed at each
other's private parts—easier for the small dog than
for Rube—she and its owner, a young man, passed
the leashes back and forth to avoid their getting tan-
gled. There was a kind of absurd intimacy to this
teamwork, their anticipation of each other's next
move for the sake of what amounted to terribly rude
dog behavior, but it made Billy feel accomplished in
some small, pleasant way. "Have a nice night," the
man said as they parted.

Outside the restaurant on the corner, the patio
chairs and tables, which had been stacked up and

chained together through the fall, had been re-moved. **The end,** she thought. The season of ease was over. She stopped walking. This was as far as they went at night. She gave the leash a little tug. "We're going home, Rube," she said, and he turned back, trailing her now. He stopped to sniff again at all the places he'd stopped on the way out, occasion-ally feeling it worth his while to lift his leg again and make a claim.

As they dawdled home, she was thinking about Sam. She was surprised he had called, actually. She had felt his interest in her as they talked in the restaurant—and hers in him, for that matter—but she thought she'd sent a signal at the end of the evening that she wasn't interested. Or that she wasn't **very** interested, anyway. **Of course, Billy, maybe the fact that you** were **interested jammed that signal.**

She remembered that awkward moment when he'd suggested they see each other again and she didn't know what to say. She remembered his face changing, looking surprised, then quickly almost blank, as he registered her withdrawal.

Inside, she got ready for bed without turning the lights on. She liked moving around in the dark. It wasn't really dark anyway, with the faded glow from the gas lamps. Reuben was already lying on top of the quilt on his side when she slid into bed. "Good night, sweet prince," she said. He sighed. His tail whacked the bed twice.

She lay looking out the windows at the bare trees,

at the shadows they cast inside. She wasn't sure what to do about Sam's invitation. He came from Leslie, and Leslie was the last person she wanted closer in her life, it had taken her so long to pull away to the extent that she had, to establish her distance. But she was drawn to Sam, as she hadn't been to any- one in a long time. As she had chosen not to be in a long time.

Her last serious relationship had been almost three years earlier, with another playwright—probably, as she thought about it later, reason enough for its not working out. But for a while she had thought it was possible it would, she had thought that her string of bad choices—God! her husband; all those gloomy, demanding Chicago guys; and Gus, poor Gus— that all that might be over.

The relationship had been five or six months old, and they were talking about living together, when Leslie called. She wanted Billy to take some of the money, the money the government had given to the families. It was a lot, Leslie said, much too much, and she didn't need it. She was going to give most of it away to charity, but she thought Billy should have some. Gus would have wanted it, she said. And it would make a difference in Billy's life, as it wouldn't in hers. "That seems right to me," Leslie said. "That it should go—at any rate that some of it should go—to someone where it would make a difference. Someone Gus loved."

Billy said no, and she and Leslie argued on the

phone, awkwardly, politely. Finally, Billy agreed to think about it, just to end the conversation. And she **would** think about it, she told herself—she would think about how to say no in a way that Leslie wouldn't argue with. That she couldn't argue with.

When she told David about Leslie's call, she treated it as something so out of the question as to be sadly, horribly funny. She thought he would laugh ruefully with her, that he'd help her figure out how to manage getting out of the situation.

"What are you talking about?" he said. "Of course you should take it. It would change your **life.** It would change our lives, together."

Billy was so startled that she could barely respond, but over the next few days, they argued about it, over and over, increasingly bitterly. It was he who spoke the line about **fucking Henry James** in one of these long, drawn-out sessions, the line she used in the play. She'd been silent in response. She didn't think of the answer, of Gabriel's answer, until much later, when she was writing it, when David was long gone. Her characters were always quicker than she was—the advantage of living their lives in the slow motion of her imagination.

It was in the course of these arguments that she understood that things weren't going to work out with her and David, that it was over. Another bad choice, another messy ending.

Since then her specialty had become the occasional one-night stand, and that only when she felt secure that the other person understood the rules, didn't want anything more complicated either. Rafe, for instance.

With Sam, this would be an impossibility. There would be no rules with him. This was something she just knew.

She groaned aloud and rolled over onto her side.

She lay there and imagined him here, in her house, or her bed, and understood instantly how much she didn't want that. She didn't want to go to his house, either, to see the way he lived. She didn't want to learn about him, to accommodate him. To feel him learning about her, accommodating her. And he brought with him, again, all the complexity of the connection with Leslie, the memory of Gus. At some point, with him, there would have to be the discussion about Gus. She didn't want to discuss Gus with him. She didn't want to discuss Gus with anyone. The closest she came to doing it now was the sort of thing she and Rafe had talked about, and that was as much as she wanted to say to anyone ever again about that part of her life. She couldn't go back there again. That way monsters lay.

"It's over, Rube," she said in the dark. He was still.

In the morning, she worked on her own stuff. Then she had some student scenes to critique and a grant application she'd been putting off finishing for days.

Around one, she walked Reuben for the second

time that day. When she came back, she went to the kitchen and got some takeout soup from Whole Foods from the refrigerator. While it heated, she played the message from Sam again. She thought about what to do.

Actually, she talked aloud about what to do. Like many people who live alone, she often talked to herself. And almost as often, she pretended to be talking to Reuben—speaking to him about what she was doing in the moment, or about the characters she was writing, or about her life. Her voice now was subdued and meditative. "I'm going to have to manage this, Rube." She stirred the soup, set the wooden spoon down on the counter. "I'm going to make him be my friend. My pal." She scratched behind the dog's ears as he stood next to her, looking up into her eyes. "I can do that, don't you think? I have lots of friends. Guy friends. Why not Sam?"

There were many reasons why not, but Billy ignored them. She called the number he had left, and he picked up after two rings, his voice neutral but somehow exciting to her. She ignored this, too. She suggested, instead of dinner or a drink, that they go for a walk with Reuben on Monday afternoon, at the Arboretum. "I never get to go there because I don't have a car."

"Well then," he said, "I'm happy to accommodate you."

She saw the squirrel just before Reuben did, and she knew, even as he took off, that it would be bad. Why hadn't she just let go of the leash? She didn't. She gripped the plastic handle even tighter—what a fucking idiot!—and braced herself.

Reuben weighed almost as much as she did. When he hit the end of the extendable line, he was up to full speed. She felt herself yanked forward, she felt herself falling. Here she must have let go of the handle, because as the ground leaped up to meet her, she could see Reuben across the field disappearing into the woods. Her arms were in front of her, her hands scraping the ground, but still she landed hard on her belly, and her chin whacked something. She cried out, she was crying out, even before the impact.

And then lying there, no dignity left at all, she started truly crying, it hurt so much. Sam was by her side almost instantly, crouched next to her. "God, Billy," he said. He was stroking her back. After a few moments, when she'd calmed down a little, he helped her to a sitting position. She turned her face away from him. She could taste blood, she could feel it in her mouth and leaking down her chin. Her tongue touched the inside of her upper lip. It was already swelling. Her wrist hurt in an ominous and ridiculously painful way. "Damn it!" she said.

Sam was wiping at her face with something—his scarf, his expensive, probably-cashmere-it-felt-so-soft scarf. "Okay. Okay," he said soothingly, as if to a child, and she realized she was making little grunts of pain.

She made herself stop. She rested her face against the scarf, against his hand holding the scarf. He was sitting down next to her on the ground now, she saw. Her own legs were straight out in front of her, the knees of her jeans smeared with black earth, her hands resting on her thighs, filthy. One of them held the other one, the broken one. Was it broken?

"You'll get all dirty," she said to Sam after a moment. It was hard for her fat lip to say the word.

"I'm not worried about that," he said.

They sat together, not talking. He had his arm around her. "Oh!" she said after a minute. "I'm just so **depressed** about this."

He laughed. She looked up at him—even sitting down he was so much taller than she was—and suddenly she was laughing, too. "God," she said, resting her head against his jacket, his shoulder.

She saw Reuben emerge from the woods, prancing sideways, trying to avoid the handle of the leash as it kept retracting toward him, as if it wanted to wrap itself around his legs, as if it were alive. "There he is, that criminal," she said. "I'm going to sue him." She started to stand.

"Here, let me help you up." Sam reached for her arm.

"Careful, careful, careful, careful!" she cried, turning her body away from him. "I think my wrist might be broken."

She held it out, supporting her hand. It was

swelling, turning red. She couldn't believe how much it hurt.

He bent over her, taking her other elbow, and helped her as she gracelessly rose to one knee and then heaved herself all the way up. When she was upright, he began to brush off the front of her coat, the knees of her jeans. She stood, letting him, holding the scarf against her mouth.

Reuben had come close by now and was watching them dubiously. "It's all your fault," she said to him. She pronounced it **fawt.** "You asshole."

"Think he gets that?" Sam asked. "Think he's experiencing remorse?"

"Oh, it's all right if he's not," she said. "I have enough for both of us." The plastic handle to the leash was dancing and jumping on the grass. "Could you grab that, Sam?" she asked. "I don't want him taking off again."

Sam picked up the handle, and Reuben turned his sober gaze on him.

"Will you be able to walk?" Sam asked.

"Yes. It's just my face and my hand. My wrist, I mean. My knees hurt, but they're fine."

"I think we should head back, then, and find an ER, or your doctor. Someone to look at your hand, at least. Maybe your lip."

"My lip is that bad?" But she could feel it was. Her tongue went there again. In the middle of the swelling, there was an open slice. The impact of her chin hitting the ground must have shoved her lower teeth into her upper lip, hard. Yes, her jaw felt achy.

"It's not good," he said.

They started back down the hill. With every step, every jolt, her wrist hurt. Sam was ahead of her on the path. He was wearing jeans today, as she was. It made him look less formidable. Lankier.

Had she thought he looked formidable in his elegant suit? Apparently so.

She watched his long, loping stride. Reuben moved eagerly alongside him, his new best friend, every enthusiastic step a betrayal of her.

They had to wait in the urgent care wing of her HMO. The intake person, a handsome, fat black woman, smoothly coiffed, bejeweled, thoroughly in charge, thought it might be half an hour. "Take a seat," she said. "They'll call your name."

There were two other people waiting ahead of Billy, one a Hispanic child with his father, looking listless, almost gray, and breathing phlegmily, probably contagiously. Billy settled herself as far away from him as she could, which meant she was very near an old man who sat almost doubled over, rocking rhythmically, as though to soothe some terrible internal pain. Sam sat next to her. They talked in near whispers. She felt compelled to apologize for perhaps the fourth time.

"Don't be boring, Billy. We've been through that. You'd do the same for me."

"I'm not sure I would. I might try to weasel out, somehow."

"There is no weaseling in an emergency. You'd do the same."

"Yeah, I suppose so." They sat. Glumly, Billy said, "This is making me so sad, being here."

"Because it hurts?"

"Not that. Just . . . the humanity." She rolled her eyes.

"Yeah. There's no escaping that." After a minute, as if to change the subject, he said, "I talked to Leslie."

"Did you?"

"Yes. She was the one who gave me your number. **Since you hadn't.**"

Ignoring the pointed quality in his voice, she asked, "And was she pleased you were going to call?"

He was silent for a moment, as if considering this. "I think so," he said at last.

"Why? What did she say?"

"She said that she hoped we'd be friends, anyway."

"No more?"

" 'Anyway,' she said."

"No, I mean, no more about me."

"Oh. A bit. Yes. She talked about you and Gus."

"I think I can assure you that Leslie knew almost nothing about me and Gus."

"But you were together a long time."

"Not so long. A year, more or less. But we mostly didn't live together."

"What she said was that Gus loved you. Wasn't that true?"

"Gus thought he did."

"If he thought he did, then he did, surely."

She said nothing for a long moment. She was suddenly remembering all her reservations about Sam, about getting to know him. She said, "I don't want to talk about Gus with you, Sam."

He looked at her, coolly, she thought. "I was just answering the question."

Billy felt awash in confusion. Finally she said, "You're right. I asked. But let's talk about something else now."

Perhaps he wanted to change the subject, too. Perhaps he saw how badly she needed to be distracted from her throbbing wrist. At any rate, he launched himself into his history with emergency rooms—the story of taking his kids to various hospitals over and over when they were young. He said she was lucky to be in the care of a pro like him—he'd seen it all. There was the time when they'd opened the back of the station wagon too fast, and Mark, the youngest, had tumbled out headfirst onto the pavement. "Concussion. Plus twelve stitches." Once Charley had chased Jack through a closed sliding glass door. Forty stitches in all. Mark had been showing off for a little girl in his class, jumping from a swing at the high point of its arc, and broke his leg. There were two broken arms, a dislocated shoulder, one fever so terrifyingly high he'd brought whatever child it was that had it into the hospital. And those were only the emergencies. There was lots of ordinary blood and gore, too.

Billy kept him talking, kept asking questions. She

liked his voice, she liked not thinking about her own pain. She liked the sense of him as a parent, taking care of other people, having survived it all, being able to joke about it.

Finally her name was called. She went into an exam room and sat on the padded table, the paper crinkling under her. The technician, a short, plump, cheerful young woman wearing a terrible perm and a flowered hospital top, took her temperature and her blood pressure—125 over 82. Billy always wanted to know, even though she had no idea what the numbers meant in terms of her health. "Is that good?" she asked. The technician said it was okay.

After she'd been alone for a few minutes, a very young man in a white jacket came in and greeted her. Dr. Cramer, his name was. He couldn't have been more than twenty-five.

"I don't usually look like this," she said, pointing to her face.

"That's a very good thing," he said. He listened to her sad tale while he washed his hands. Then came over to her and, without asking her, flipped back her upper lip in what she thought was kind of a rude way. He looked at it for a minute and said he thought there was nothing much to do about **that.** Ice, he suggested, though he added that it was probably already too late.

He asked who Sam was. Then his face turned suddenly grave, which made him seem even younger. "Do you feel safe with him?" he said.

Yes, Billy said. She did. It hadn't occurred to her how it would look—as if she'd been knocked around. They should go after Reuben, she thought. Reuben, who was probably sound asleep in the car out in the parking garage.

He moved her wrist, and she cried out. He sent her to X-ray. Sam came with her and waited for her to be called, and then waited longer with her for the film. He'd been reading an old **Newsweek,** and both times they sat together, he reported to her on whatever obsolete article he'd just finished. They talked about what the appropriate punishment for Michael Vick might be. They discussed their recently discovered ability to make new neurons as adults—who knew? Sam talked to her about his middle son, who probably **had** known—he was doing research on Alzheimer's disease.

When they got the films from the X-ray guy, they headed back to urgent care with them. By now Billy could feel that her knees were stiffening up. "I'm getting older by the second in here," she said, shuffling down the corridor.

"We all are," Sam said. "It's what hospitals are meant to do to you."

Nothing was broken, the young man said, showing her the picture of her own intact, shadowy bones lighted from behind. He gave her a splint that closed with Velcro straps and told her to keep her wrist elevated and iced. She asked for and got a prescription for painkillers, and she and Sam sat together in the pharmacy while it was being filled. She asked him why he was free on a Monday, a workday, and he explained the shape of his life to her—that he worked alone now, he made his own hours. That he'd had a partner for years, but they'd split up when the partner got more interested in developing projects on his own. "More speculative stuff. He's braver than I am. Or more entrepreneurial, I guess you'd say. It was a bit like a divorce, but without the rancor." He'd taken his jacket off and he was slouched in the waiting room chair. He seemed entirely comfortable.

" 'Rancor,' " she said. She looked at him. "Was there rancor in your divorce?"

He thought for a moment. "Not quite rancor. Something a little more like . . . disappointment, maybe."

"Who was disappointed?"

"We were both disappointed, I think."

"In equal measure, would you say?"

He laughed. "What's it to you?"

She shrugged. "I'm interested in narrative," she said. "How it went. How it was. What happened next."

"Well, I would say yes, in just about equal measure."

"That's a good thing," she said.

He didn't answer.

"Right?" she asked.

"A better thing is no disappointment."

"Well, **yeah.** But do you think that's possible?"

"Don't you?" It was in part his glasses, she thought, that made his gaze look so intense when he asked a question.

"No, I don't," she said. "I've managed to disappoint everybody."

"And been disappointed?"

She smiled at him. "In about equal measure, I would say."

They sat looking across at the pharmacy counter, where everyone—five or six people in white jackets—seemed very busy, but no one was being called.

"Who's 'everybody'?" he asked.

"You don't want to know."

"But I do. I'm interested in narrative, too," he said.

"Well. That's not part of the walk-in-the-Arboretum deal. That information."

"But neither is urgent care," he said.

"Point taken."

"Point **scored.**"

Finally her name was called, and she went up and got the pills. She took one immediately, bending over the water fountain in the corridor and then tilting her head back to wash it down. Sam admired her technique, called it birdlike.

By the time they pulled over to park, a half block from her apartment, it was getting dark. Billy was slouched against the window on the passenger side, already feeling more comfortable. "Oh drugs," she said. "I love them so."

"They are a blessing," he answered.

She thought suddenly of his wife, of how much serious pain he must have witnessed and had to help with. And failed to help with, finally. And yet here he was, indulging her, trying to make her feel better too. She had a pang of apologetic shame for her whining. "You've been swell today," she said. "Nearly as good as a drug yourself."

"That's almost the nicest thing anyone's ever said to me." They were getting out of the car. He opened the door to the backseat and attached Reuben to the leash.

"What was the nicest?" she asked. She felt afloat, detached from her body as she leaned against an elaborate little iron fence circling someone's front garden. The streetlamps were on. They started to walk, their footsteps seeming loud in the twilight.

"I wouldn't want to be immodest," he said.

"Oh, be immodest."

"Nah," he said.

Inside she hung her coat up and turned on the lamp on her desk and then the one by the couch. She flopped down on the couch. Reuben came and set his immense head in her lap. "Sweet boy," she said. She leaned over and smelled his fur. "I could kill you. I could kill you, my darling. You are a darling I could gladly kill." She leaned back, and a wave of sleepiness rolled over her. She felt it as that: a wave.

Sam was in the kitchen, out of sight. She heard things clunking around. This was exactly what she hadn't wanted, this intimacy, this invasion. "Want tea?" he asked. "Coffee? Wine? What else is here." He was being nice; she gave him that. She heard a cupboard open. "Cognac?"

"Sam, stop it," she called. "You're off duty."

"I have stopped," he said. "I'm going to have a cognac." He appeared in the doorway holding the bottle and a glass. "Want some?"

"I better not," she said. "I'm already a little tipsy from my drug."

"What about tea?"

She looked at him. She should tell him no. She should tell him she wanted to sleep. She said, "Tea would be awfully nice."

He went back into the kitchen. She heard the water running, then the clash of the kettle on the burner. She closed her eyes.

When she opened them, he was setting a cup down next to her. The windows were completely dark. Steam wisped off the teacup. "Whoa," she said. She licked her lips. "I was asleep."

"I know," he said. "You were snoring a little."

"No, I wasn't."

He lifted his hands. And his eyebrows. "As you wish," he said.

"What about the dog?" he asked, sitting down across from her.

"What about the dog?"

"Does the dog need feeding?"

"I'll do it," she said. "I'll do it later. He's flexible,

poor thing. He's had to be, since I'm his owner. And you need to stop being so . . . solicitous."

"I'm being mostly solicitous of me. I'm having a glass of terrific cognac." He stretched his long legs out. They reached half the distance between them. His face was in shadow, his head tilted up, resting on the chair back.

Billy leaned back, too, on the couch. "You're probably going to get a ticket."

He waved his hand: **Who cares?**

"Which I will pay," she said. "It's the price of living where I do, where nobody can park. I wouldn't have friends if I didn't pay their tickets."

"We won't argue about it," he said.

She tried some of the tea. Almost too hot, but not. She set the cup back in the saucer, her hand circling the warm china. After a minute she said, "I didn't want you to come here today. It's why I suggested a walk. Neutral territory."

"Why not?"

"Oh." She gestured around her. "It's all so kind of personal a place."

"Isn't every place where someone lives personal?"

"Not yours, I bet. I bet yours is lovely in a tastefully neutral way. Big. Gracious. Guest hand towels in the bathroom. In the lavatory. Monogrammed. Many bedrooms. Et cetera."

He was silent a moment. She closed her eyes. He said, "You're kind of a snob, you know it?"

"Am I?" She couldn't really see his face, how he meant it.

"In a sort of reverse way."

"But you're the one who thought I was too bohemian or something. That was snobby of you."

"We're both snobs, I guess."

"Perfectly suited to each other. Let's call Leslie."

She could see he was smiling. She closed her eyes again.

Later she would remember that he said something else—a few other things—and that she swam up several times from wherever she was sinking to say something back, but the next time she rose to full consciousness, he was gone. She was covered with the quilt he'd taken off the bed, and Reuben was asleep on the floor by her dangling hand.

She groaned and got up. She went into the bathroom. Bent over the sink, she splashed warm water on her face. She stood straight, grabbing a towel, and looked at herself as she dried off. Her lip was immense, fat, as though she'd been shot with an elephant-sized syringe of collagen. She leaned forward to the mirror and lifted it slightly to look at the cut inside. Standing back again, she saw that she'd lost an earring during this adventure. One of her favorite pair of earrings. This seemed important, somehow.

She felt tired, suddenly. Sad. Emptied out. Reuben was standing in the bathroom doorway, waiting for her. "Come on, old Rube," she said. "Let's get you some supper."

He turned and loped to the kitchen. She followed, more slowly.

Sam's glass and her cup and saucer were rinsed

and set in the sink. Reuben's leash lay coiled on the counter. Under it there was a note. She picked it up. **I walked the dog, but I couldn't spot his food. Sam.**

She made a noise. "What am I gonna do with this guy, Rube?" she asked. She suddenly remembered something that he'd said as she was dropping off. She thought she remembered it. He had been speaking again of how different they were, but this time he said, "I thought, Why not? Why not let someone so different into my life?"

Hadn't he said that?

She didn't want to be in Sam's life. How could she be? She didn't want to be in anyone's life but her own.

She picked up Reuben's dish from the floor. Her wrist hurt. She crossed the little galley. She knelt on the floor on her sore knees to reach under the kitchen sink for the bucket that held his dried food. Her view now was of the disorder, the mess hidden under here—the old rags, the dark, irregular shape of some dried-up liquid she'd spilled months ago, a stiffened rubber glove, palm up, supplicant, its yellow browning around the edges.

She felt suddenly teary. "I can't," she said aloud. "I can't do **any** of this."

SAM

"SAM!" SHE SAID on the phone, before he could tell her who was calling. It was Wednesday, late in the afternoon, the day after the play. He had tried earlier, but she and Pierce weren't back home yet. "It was so lovely to see you. Thank you for joining us last night."

"No, I was calling to thank you. You were kind to ask me."

"Well, we were both eager to see you after all this time."

"It was . . . it was good to catch up."

"It was."

"And to see Billy's play." It felt strange to speak her name to Leslie. Maybe just to speak her name to anyone for the first time.

"Yes." She seemed hesitant. Or equivocal in some way.

"Though it was tough. Tough for you, I'm sure." They'd talked about this briefly at the intermission. "Tough in some ways for me, too."

"Well, it was just a play." Her voice seemed subdued. "Billy has a right to whatever . . . topic. She wants."

"Of course," he said. "When I say it was tough, I don't mean she shouldn't have used it."

There was a moment of silence. She said, "Used Gus, you mean?"

"Actually, no. I wasn't thinking of Gus." He was confused. "I didn't particularly see Gus in there. I mean that she used 9/11. What she might have felt about living through 9/11."

"Ah!"

He thought she was about to say something more. When she didn't, he said, "You did see Gus." It was a question.

"Well, not right away. Not last night. Though I was, bothered, I guess you'd say. And then the more I thought about it, yes. I saw Gus, and I saw Billy. I saw how she must have felt about him—at least at some point. It made me very . . . sad."

He waited, but she seemed to be done. "I'm sorry, then," he said.

"Yes. But as I say, she has every right." There was something pinched in her voice.

"It came around though, didn't you think? The play?"

"How do you mean that—'came around'?" she asked.

He was sitting in his kitchen, in his house in Brookline. For some reason, he hadn't turned the lights on in here, so there was just the faint illumination from the hall coloring everything a twilit gray—the chairs and table, the countertop, the dishes from this morning standing in their rack. Outside, it was already dark, at four-thirty.

"Just that the character," he said, "the Gabriel guy, begins to remember his wife. Didn't you think that, in the second act? He remembers the way she was before things . . . soured between them. He remembers her, and he more or less, **decides** to love her again."

It was about me, of course, he wanted to say. As a joke.

He smiled to himself for a moment, but almost instantly he was recalling also the sudden absorption he'd felt in the events playing out on the stage, the sense of a complicated set of his own emotions being laid bare. During the last part of the play, the exchange between the Gabriel character and his lover, when he was acknowledging being relieved for a moment that his wife might have died—when he spoke of his shame about that—Sam had thought of his first wife, of Susan. Of how impatient he was sometimes in her long illness and dying, impatient for it to be over, just to be over, so that whatever would follow it—his **life,** he felt—could begin. He'd grown tired of pretending that all was well, that she wasn't incapacitated, that they weren't asking anything of the boys by going on as usual. For a long time after Susan's death, Sam wasn't able to let go of the memory of having those feelings. He simply didn't like himself.

But even earlier in the play he'd felt implicated.

Watching the son's anger at his father on the stage, he had flashed on Charley, his oldest son, his face distorted with contempt, saying about Claire, "What do you have to **marry** her for? Just fuck her. Don't involve the rest of us."

"Didn't you think that?" he asked Leslie now. "That it **turned**? That that's what the ending meant?"

"It would be nice to think that."

"Well, if that part was in any way about Gus and Billy, wouldn't that be a good thing? Wouldn't it be . . . loving?"

"If it was, yes." He heard the reluctance in her voice.

"But that's what I thought you said, that you felt it **was** about them."

"Oh, I don't know, Sam." Her voice was lighter suddenly, dismissive. "I've no idea what I'm saying, really." She laughed, a small pant of sound oddly amplified by the telephone. "The whole thing probably just went right over my head."

He wanted to help them both out of this. "We've gotten mighty serious here, wouldn't you say? When I was calling just to say thanks, and to ask for Billy's phone number, or e-mail."

He heard an intake of breath, quick, almost inaudible. "So you're going to call her."

"Isn't that what you intended?" He tried to make his voice genial, light.

"Of course it is." But he could hear her hesitation.

"No. Yes. I hoped you would be friends, anyway. She was . . ." There was a little silence. "Gus loved her, I think, very much." She said, "Just a minute, I'll get it," and set the phone down, with a clunk.

When she came back, half a minute later, she sounded like herself again—calm, affectionate. "God, I wish I were more organized," she said. "But here it is. I finally found it. Ready?" She read the number off. She said, "And of course I'll be interested to hear, whatever happens."

"Of course," he said, though he couldn't imagine reporting in to her.

"Give Billy my best."

"I will." He thanked her and they said good-bye.

After he hung up, he sat there for a minute or two in the half dark, thinking of her moving around in the house—crossing the hall into the living room, turning on the lamp by Pierce's chair, bending over to stir the fire in the fireplace. And then he realized he was imagining her as she'd been when he first knew her—tall, brunette, graceful—not the white-haired, almost-stout woman he'd seen the night before.

Like Billy, Sam had an image of Leslie that he held on to. Not a picture—a memory. A memory from a snowy day when he made the long trip up from Boston to check on the progress in the house he'd designed for Claire. He'd gotten within a mile of the site, driving on what was a dirt road for half the year but now was a gravelly strip of icy, brownish snow running between the white fields that fell sharply away on one side and the thick woods on the other. Almost as soon as he started up the last section, the point where the road lifted most steeply, he could feel the car losing traction.

Then it had none. The wheels spun uselessly. Within a few seconds, he had started to slide slowly backward.

He had a moment of anger, at himself mostly, for not having snow tires. He'd actually thought about putting them on, but no new snow had fallen in Vermont for the last few days and he'd assumed he could get by without them. So much for that notion.

He shifted into reverse and backed carefully down the hill until he could turn around in a neighbor's driveway, then continued down facing forward. When he got to where the road flattened out, he parked carefully just off to the side of it and called Leslie on his car phone.

She was there, in the real estate office. Her voice on the line was warm. She said yes, of course she had snow tires. Yes, of course she'd be glad to come and drive him up to the house.

She was walking ahead of him when they came into the living room. She stopped directly under the groin vault, the place where the two barrel vaults came together. Slowly she turned in a circle, her arms flung out, her mouth open. Her breath plumed like smoke around her. There were still snowflakes in her dark hair.

She faced him. "I see what you're doing," she said. Her eyes were excited. "This beautiful space. You **sculpted** it. It's just . . . spectacular. It's wonderful."

That was it. That was the moment, that look stamped on her face.

Claire couldn't have looked at him that way. She couldn't have said that, or anything like it. She was by then barely interested in him, let alone the house he was making for her, and every time he was with Leslie, it made him more aware of this, of how deep and unbridgeable the differences between him and Claire had come to be.

Leslie stood for the possibility of another kind of woman. She **was** another kind of woman. Over and over Sam found himself watching her, listening to her, and thinking how different she was from Claire—Claire, who was so much cooler in temperament, so much more critical in her approach to everything. He once used the word "creamy" to describe Leslie to a friend—a problematic word choice, as he knew. But he thought of her that way. Her skin had a white softness, a welcoming, pillowy kind of softness that seemed expressive of this quality in her generally.

It might have been that moment, then, when Sam began to fall in love with her. It might have been that image that triggered the period in his life during which he thought of her on and off through the day if he wasn't fully occupied with something else. **Leslie: the default mode.**

But there were other possible starting points. It might have begun earlier, maybe on the night when he was driving back to the Hanover Inn with Claire after they'd had their one and only meal as a foursome with Leslie and Pierce. She'd come up with him from Boston because he was getting ready to draw the kitchen cabinets, and she decided she wanted to look at the space for them, to have some say about their arrangement. When he'd told Leslie that Claire would be with him this time, she responded by inviting them both for dinner.

"Not the brightest bulbs in the chandelier, are they?" Claire had said in the dark car, her voice heavy with irony.

He didn't say anything. It had been a long, hard evening, though Claire had been at her most poised. But this was part of the problem for him—he felt this poise as a kind of absence. It was connected to the public persona she could call up effortlessly, and it was this Claire, the public, remote version of her, who had stridden into the little low-ceilinged hallway where Leslie stood waiting, smiling and extending her hand.

In contrast to her, everything about Leslie seemed slow and soft. She talked a little nervously as she took their coats and hung them up, as she told Claire, who'd asked, how old the house was, who had built it.

"And how long have you lived in it?" Claire said, smiling.

"Twenty-five years," Leslie answered. "Practically as long as the house is old." She smiled, lifting her shoulders in a helpless shrug. "Apparently we can't be budged. But come in, please." At her beckoning gesture, they'd stepped into the living room.

Just at this moment, as if on cue, Pierce entered it, too, from the kitchen. He carried a tray with glasses, with napkins and crackers and cheese. No bottles. He had already set those out on a long table between the two windows facing the town green—two bottles of wine and an array of hard liquor. There was a blue bowl there, too, filled with ice. It had been the same routine the five or so times Sam had come without Claire. Most of those times, though, he'd had just a drink or coffee before he drove back to Boston. Only twice before had he stayed for dinner.

Pierce, as always, seemed too big for the room, his voice too loud in the small space, too enthusiastic. He told Claire that he'd begun to believe she didn't exist, that she was someone "old Samuel here imagined, dreamed up out of whole cloth, as it were."

"As you can see," Claire had said, sweeping her hand in front of herself, down and then away in a dramatic gesture, "I'm very real." It made them all look at her, of course, at how beautiful she was in her austere way, at how long and supple her body was.

It was that beauty that had compelled Sam. He'd seen her at the twentieth-anniversary party of some friends, sitting at a table, talking animatedly, laughing, and he resolved he wouldn't leave until he'd at least met her. And here he was tonight, looking again at the curve of her cheekbones, at her shapely head, her long legs—everything they'd been beckoned to notice. But instead of feeling the impact of all that, Sam was seeing her in a new light. A part of him wanted to laugh, to cry out, **But you're** not **real. Not real at all.**

And as the evening went on, every exchange seemed a confirmation of this, even the small ones. At the dinner table, when Leslie started to talk about her garden, Claire plied her with questions, as though she knew something about gardening, as though she cared, when Sam knew how contemptuous she was of intelligent people **wasting their time,** as she saw it, in this way—she'd said these very words to him. She laughed too heartily at Pierce's humor, his jokes. She explained her own work to them—right now, a series of public lectures she was giving on the ethics of debt and exchange—in a tone that seemed to Sam just slightly condescending. She was **indulging** Pierce and Leslie, tolerating them in a self-consciously gracious way that Sam knew he was meant to notice.

"Oh, I'm **sorry,**" Claire said in the car. "I know they're your friends. I don't mean to dis them."

"Of course you do," he said quietly.

She let a moment pass. It was October, the Vermont night had turned sharply cold, and the car's heater revved and paused, revved and paused. Then she said, "Well, okay. I do. But you know what I mean."

"I don't, actually."

"Sam," she protested in annoyance, as though he were being childishly uncooperative, silly.

"I don't. You wanted to dis them." He looked over at her. "That's exactly what you did want."

She sighed in exasperation and crossed her arms on her bosom. The slide of her blouse, silk on silk, made a light, whispering noise. She looked out the window for a moment, and then she turned back to him. "No, it isn't." Her voice was flat. "What I **wanted** was for us to have a little fun together after a rather dull evening. Maybe, yes, at their expense, but that wasn't the point."

He didn't respond. He was tired of this, he realized—this thing they did: constructing a review of each social occasion immediately after it, always pointed, always critical. It seemed abruptly a kind of folie à deux to him.

She was smiling now. She wanted things to be okay. "The point, my love, was you and me."

She waited. He could see without looking over at her that she was watching him, wanting to have charmed him back into her orbit. He felt sorry for her, suddenly. He felt sorry for both of them. He said, "You don't have to try so hard all the time, Claire."

"For us to have fun?"

"Right." They were coming across the bridge over the Connecticut River into Hanover. The river was black below them. "And actually, I don't mind the occasional dull evening."

She faced forward, her profile beautiful and exacting. "There's the difference between you and me. I do. I mind it very much."

After a moment, he said, "But actually—again—I didn't find it dull."

"Hn. Another difference then."

They barely spoke as they got ready for bed at the inn, as she pulled on a black, sliplike nightgown he hadn't seen before. One she'd bought, perhaps, for this very night—a night in a hotel with no children around. It might have been an invitation, but if so, it was one she no longer wanted to make. This was clear by the way she was facing away from him as she put it on, the way she slid quickly under the covers and turned away from him in bed.

But it was an invitation he would have had trouble responding to, anyway. Because lying there next to her, breathing in the scent of her perfume, of her flesh, listening to the occasional braying of a group of Dartmouth students passing by the hotel, he was thinking back over the evening and seeing it as a series of images of Leslie. Leslie, as she turned to invite them into the living room, her arm extended. Leslie, as she leaned over the table to set a plate in front of him. Leslie, as she looked across the table at him, her soft mouth open a little, her eyes melting in the candlelight.

What was willed? What just **happened?** He didn't know. He couldn't tell if these experiences made something in him shift, or if he used them to shift things. Things changed, though. After this point, it seemed to him that an agreement had been somehow reached between him and Claire that they would turn away from each other into their own separate lives.

Oh, they were courteous to each other. They continued to have a full life together—the children, the evenings listening to music, the dinner parties, their active socializing, which he'd loved at first; he and Susan had been so limited for so long by her illness. But Sam felt more and more that there was no room for him to be who he really was with Claire. And he felt he'd lost a sense of who she was underneath that bright, poised exterior. Perhaps because of this, they no longer turned to each other after these evenings, or even during them, for confirmation of the other's pleasure—or the other's critical response. There wasn't the folie à deux that Sam had felt suddenly constricted by, but there was no longer the sense of their twoness, either.

Well, there was always a way for Sam to work longer hours on his projects, and that's what he did now. But strangely, he focused his energy on the house in Vermont. He recognized the perversity of this; he knew by now that he and Claire would probably divorce—how could they go on the way they were? But he told himself that the house was a gift he wanted to give her, a way to honor his first feelings for her and the hope with which he'd entered the relationship.

An apology of sorts, then. Also—he realized this—a kind of justification of himself, a way to try to make himself feel better about whatever part he'd played in the way things seemed to be heading. Detailing the elaborate trim on the vaulted ceiling in the living room, he had a sad sense of virtue. Drawing the built-in cabinets in the bedroom, he imagined Claire alone, finding pleasure in their design. As he worked, he made himself remember how he had felt about her when he was getting to know her—the headiness, the elation of their first months together.

But it was like a distant, fond memory. Like the way he thought of the girl he'd been in love with in high school, that irrelevant—the pleasure he took in her largely a matter, he sometimes thought now, of the kind of underclothing girls wore then: The long tease of the difficult hooks on the back of her white, nurselike brassieres. The rustling crinolines, the garters and stockings. The band of silky, fat flesh between her cotton underpants and the smooth stocking tops. Of course, there was Candy herself, but when he remembered her minky little face, her way of laughing through her nose, he felt only a kind of amazement at the entirely other version of himself the memory suggested—though oddly it also felt continuous with who he was now.

So with Claire, with the distance he felt from the person he must have been, loving her—a person who was, nonetheless, recognizably still the man sitting at this table, doing these drawings, fussing over these details, thinking of his love for her as something past, long gone.

And as he made one trip after another up to the site to make sure that things were being done exactly as he'd wanted them for her, he understood that all this care and attention were also a way to see Leslie, to be with her more.

These things were confused in his mind, then. It wasn't until much later that he teased it all apart, that he saw how much of his focus on Leslie had to do with the slow, painful ending of his marriage to Claire and with everything that wasn't working between them in those months. In the meantime, though, it felt like love, like an impossible version of love.

He had kissed Leslie, once. It was in late August of the following summer. He'd come up for the weekend with a rental van to load the few things of his he was taking from the house before it went on the market. He asked her to meet him there.

She was waiting with a picnic lunch when he arrived. They spread it out on a blanket on the porch and sat there, eating, talking, looking down at the valley below and the mountains beyond it, made blue by distance. He told her about the ending of things with Claire, the decision they made together that—as Claire put it—they'd run out of energy for each other. He told her how, having made this decision, they were somehow able to be kinder, more generous, to each other again.

"I'm glad for that," Leslie had said. "It must make all this"—she gestured vaguely, the house, the moving van—"easier."

When they'd finished eating, he helped her pack up the paper plates and napkins, the tin cups. She suggested a walk. She knew a field near here where there was a good blackberry patch. They left the rucksack on the porch and started down the old logging road that ran through the woods behind the house.

It was early fall. Wild asters grew at the side of the road, an airy, delicate blue or white. Here and there a maple flared hot red, almost fuchsia. Leslie was walking ahead of him. She was wearing blue jeans and an old white linen blouse, the collar fraying slightly. Her brown hair fell just over it. When she looked down at the ground to watch where she was going, the hair slid apart into two wings on either side of her neck, exposing the vulnerable knobs of her spine as they disappeared into her shirt—the white curve of that private flesh. He had the impulse to step forward, to stop her, to put his lips there.

Suddenly she was speaking. She said she sometimes wished she had the courage to tell Pierce, **This isn't good enough.** She lifted her shoulders then, her hands rose slightly, too. "But I don't, so that's that." He couldn't see her face, but her voice sounded full of regret.

They walked on in silence, both of them watching their feet on the rocky, pitted dirt track. He was thinking about what she'd said, about what it might mean about her and Pierce. He was excited by this glimpse into their lives together, by the sense of possibility for himself he saw in it.

Just then they started to pass an overgrown field to their right, a field studded with maple saplings and small pines. This was it, she said. The blackberry patch. "Let's see if the bears have gotten all of them."

They hadn't. Sam and Leslie moved around in the pale sunlight, picking the blackberries, eating them. The thorny canes caught at their clothes, scratched their hands. She was laughing about a bear that had come up on the porch of a friend, right outside the window where they had a bird feeder. As her friend and her husband watched, as their dog barked insanely and hurled himself over and over at the glass, the bear had leisurely, almost prettily, eaten every last seed. She imitated its dainty motion.

Sam had been standing close behind her while she talked. Now he reached for her and turned her to him. He kissed her. She stood still for it, waiting for him to be done, though her mouth—warm, sweet tasting—responded to him.

When she stepped away from him, she was shaking her head. Tears glinted at the lower rims of her eyes. "I can't, Sam," she said. "I don't, have the courage. Pierce and I . . . Pierce and I, **rely** on each other."

There were so many things he could have said then. He could have said, **Do you think that's a good enough reason for staying together?** He could have said, **But I love you.**

He didn't, though. He didn't because he mistrusted himself, because he didn't want to turn so quickly from Claire to her. He didn't because she seemed so sorrowful. Because he wanted to be sure he wasn't just desperate, or afraid of being alone.

He didn't because he knew he **was** desperate and afraid of being alone.

He said, "I know." They stood a moment more, looking at each other, and then not looking at each other in the sun-struck field. She turned away first, and they started back. He remembered her mouth, stained with berry juice, and her earnest dark eyes meeting his.

He thought that was the end of it for him. That he saw how things were for her, that he accepted it. But it wasn't over. There was still a day, months later, after the divorce was final, when he suddenly decided he should . . . what? Claim her? Ask her to run away with him? He wasn't sure.

It was the day after a disastrous visit from Charley, his oldest son. He'd told Sam he was going to get married, and Sam, worried about how young he was, about how young his girlfriend, Emma, was, wasn't enthusiastic enough, fast enough. Charley had still been clearly angry when Sam dropped him off at the Back Bay train station and watched him disappear through the doorway under the neon arch.

As he turned the corner at the intersection a block away, he noticed a parking spot in front of a Starbucks there. On a whim, he pulled into it. He went inside and ordered a cappuccino. He sat in the window, looking out, drinking his fancy coffee. He wasn't sure what he would do next.

The week before, Claire had called to say she was taking an endowed chair at the University of Chicago and would be moving in January. Sitting behind the plate glass, finished with his cappuccino, Sam had a sense of being suspended. Even the weather seemed vague and indeterminate. It was gray and misty, about to rain, but much warmer than it had been. People walked past in no rush. It seemed to Sam that he'd failed at everything he'd turned his hand to—his children, his marriage. It seemed that nothing had happened to him, nothing had happened in his life, for years. His sons, his ex-wife, they'd moved on; they were making choices and changing things for themselves, while he'd done nothing.

Behind him, there was the sudden shriek of the steamer frothing someone's milk. Outside, the rain began. In the midst of this, aware of all this, thinking too of his office, how empty it would be when he went there, remembering Leslie bent over the long bracts of the blackberry bushes in the fall sunlight, he knew abruptly what he wanted to do. What he would do.

He finished his coffee, he carried the paper cup and stirrer to the trash barrel and threw them away. He buttoned his raincoat and opened the door to the soft noise of the rain.

The car windows began to fog up as soon as he shed his coat. He turned the engine on, and the defroster. The rain drummed now, the fan whirred.

He drove east on Stuart Street and then turned south, heading to where he could pick up 93, the highway that left the city going north.

It was after dark when he got to Leslie's village. It had been a hard trip—rain so heavy he'd had to park at the edge of the road once, and a skidding accident he'd stopped to offer his help at. He'd sat with the young woman whose car was smashed up until help arrived.

His headlong mood had been tempered, altered then, in ways he wasn't sure of, and when he pulled over to the side of the road across the sloping front lawn from Leslie's house, he had already begun to doubt himself, to feel a sense of disconnection from the impulses that had brought him here.

He looked up at the lighted windows. Pierce and Leslie were in the front rooms of the house, Pierce in the living room, in the chair he always sat in, the one by the fireplace. He was looking down, perhaps reading. Leslie was moving around in the kitchen, clearly in the process of making dinner. He could follow her in motion and guess what she was doing at each step. When she disappeared through the doorway at the back of the room, she was in the dining room, perhaps setting the table. As she stood in profile facing the wall, leaning forward slightly, she was at the sink or the stove.

From the dark of his car, this is what he saw—the two of them, stage left and stage right, in their life together. And as he watched them, he was increasingly sure that he didn't belong here. He realized he wasn't going to do what he had planned to do. He wasn't going to enter, stage right, and try to change her life or his.

But he stayed for a while, he made himself look. Why? Later he thought it was so that he would remember it, exactly the way it was, and not delude himself again.

Leslie was busy in the kitchen for a few minutes, her back to the window, to Sam. Then she came toward the front of the house and stood in what Sam knew was the open doorway between the kitchen and the living room, maybe to say something to Pierce.

Yes, now he raised his head from whatever he was reading, he raised his head in the orangey light of the old lamp and answered her. He smiled.

She laughed in response and then went back to the kitchen, bent again over her work.

It was so ordinary, so unremarkable, but for Sam it

had the potency of a Vermeer. Something changed in him as he watched. He had a sense in himself, in his response, of mildness, of generosity, as though in some way he were responsible for what he was seeing—Leslie, at peace in her own old, frumpy house, with Pierce, whom she'd chosen, whom she'd chosen over and over. As though he were blessing it, its very ordinariness, by witnessing it. Or if not he, then something, some force in the universe that allots us just this much pain and no more. This much disruption. This much violent change.

He reached down and turned the key in the ignition.

He stayed at the Hanover Inn that night, too—it seemed to be the place where he went to experience the end of things. This time, though, he was strangely exhilarated. He felt a clean, absolute relief at acknowledging to himself that it was over. Or maybe that it had never been real.

A woman once said to Sam, "Well, I guess I must not be your type." Her tone was chilly. This was during a brief period a year or two after the divorce from Claire when he was going out with people he met through a couple of dating services. He'd driven this woman home after an uncomfortable dinner, and he'd just turned down her invitation to come in. She was right, she wasn't his type—though he didn't say that at the time. It seemed as though that might be dangerous, she was so pissed off. He didn't remember exactly what he did say—some polite denial. It didn't matter anyway. They both knew that they wouldn't be seeing each other again.

But it had made him consider the question of what his **type,** actually, might be. Did he even have a type? He couldn't answer the question. He seemed to be an omnivore when it came to women, except when he wasn't. They came in every shape and size and temperament, one unlikely type after another. His first wife had been preceded by a big, blond college girl, a hard-drinking premed who played lacrosse and could beat him arm wrestling. Then along came Susan, tall and quiet and pretty in her unstartling way.

There was a moment at their wedding when he did see her as a **type** suddenly. He couldn't avoid it. She had lined up for a photograph with her sisters, the bridesmaids. There they were, a row of women not only all wearing the same pink dress—all but Susan, in white—but displaying the same genes. They were all the same height or close to it, they were all slender, brown-haired, brown-eyed, with even features. The noses might have been slightly too long, maybe the chins were a little sharp, but all were pretty enough in a high-WASP way. Which is what they were—**that** type. And that was part of the attraction for Sam.

———

He and Susan had met when they were seniors in college. They married the month after they graduated, under a flower-laden bower in the enormous, sloping backyard of her parents' second home on Martha's Vineyard. A large open tent—a kind of pavilion—was set up in one corner of this yard, with a smooth dance floor that workmen had laid down in sections over the thick grass the afternoon before. A band played music such as neither of them had ever danced to, music no one would consciously have chosen. Wedding-band music.

Sam was intensely aware of his parents through the whole three-day affair. They'd driven out from Illinois, from the small farming town where he'd grown up. He knew they must be uncomfortable. He'd spot them occasionally, always together, smiling politely, looking strained, usually engaged in conversation with someone—his mother, anyway— and he felt unable to help them.

But every time he looked at them, he also felt a stab of anger. He knew exactly how they would talk about the whole thing when they got back home, how they would alter the experience in their reporting of it to manage the sense of dislocation or discomfort they'd felt living through it. Everything would become laughable in its pretentiousness— though they wouldn't use the word. They would make jokes instead: "Sam sure caught himself a fancy one." "I never seen so many people put away so much pricey liquor." "It must have cost a pretty penny." And the eyebrows raised to signal all the things they weren't saying.

The problem was that even then Sam didn't feel he'd escaped them sufficiently—their world, their way of seeing things, their rules. It seemed to him he was still **faking it,** four years after leaving home.

The rules of his college world had seemed like those of another country when he first got there, so different were they from the rules at home. Even the clothes he had brought with him were wrong. Sam sold them at the local used-clothing store within a few weeks of arriving on campus, and with the money from that and some of what he'd earned working at the grain cooperative over the long, hot high school summers, he bought several versions of the uniform the prep school boys wore—Levi's, not slacks; blue work shirts or Brooks Brothers button-downs; striped rep ties; two tweed jackets. This made him more comfortable in his body, but he was still so unsure of himself socially that he sometimes waited to hear other people's opinions before he announced his own.

Susan was utterly at ease wherever they went in the world—the world of school or the wider world. Sam watched her, imitated her, learned from her. This was the way you spoke to a cabdriver, a waiter. This was how you talked to older people at a party, to faculty after class. These were the forks you used for salad and these for the main course. This was the present you took when you were staying for the weekend, this was what you took to a dinner party. Sam wanted to know this kind of thing. He asked her questions. He took her advice.

She was charmed by this, by his open curiosity, by his eagerness to fit in.

And fit in he did, to a life arranged for him by her and her family—benevolent guides, as he saw them then. Her parents paid for the wedding, of course—**a pretty penny**—and the honeymoon to St. Croix. They paid for the apartment Sam and Susan lived in while they were in graduate school. They paid for Susan's library science degree. Sam had a fellowship to architecture school, so that wasn't an issue, and both he and Susan worked part-time through the academic year and over the summers. But there were lavish gifts, and they joined her family on vacations and holidays, sometimes on the Vineyard, once to Italy, several times to Bermuda or the Bahamas. Sam felt that not to do this would have been to deny Susan their company, their indulgence of her, all the things they could do for her, so he went along. He enjoyed it. He was a boy, greedy and glad for what he was learning, what he was being given.

He would have said that he and Susan were happy. Happy enough. Sex was an issue. This she wasn't able to teach him about, because she wasn't terribly interested in it. Sam was unsure enough of himself to feel that this might be his fault, and perhaps it was. But she seemed to enjoy it. At any rate, she liked the talking, the touching, that led up to it and that followed, and she never turned away from him, not until she got sick. It wasn't until much later, long after she'd died and he began to have other lovers, that he understood that she wasn't able to have an orgasm. That he realized that when she said, after sex, "I **think** I came"—as she often did when he asked—this meant she never had.

Charley arrived, unplanned, three years after the wedding, and a year after that Jack; then Mark, when Jack was two. A few months later, Susan found the lump in her breast. They removed it, and she had radiation and chemotherapy. This took almost a year out of their lives, but afterward she seemed to be in the clear.

But three years later there was a recurrence, and after that she was never well again. When she died, the boys were eleven, ten, and eight. Sam was thirty-five. He had been managing the household pretty much singlehandedly for years, though they had pretended for as long as they could that Susan was in charge.

It was during this period, her dying and afterward, that Sam had to grow up. That he had to learn to behave like a grown-up, at any rate, though sometimes he felt as frightened as he assumed the boys were.

But he didn't allow himself that. He couldn't.

As he couldn't allow himself his impatience with her, sometimes his anger. Anger that she insisted on the fiction that she could do it. That she rejected her parents' offer of household help. That she seemed not to notice how much she was asking of him, of the children. There were moments, hours, days, even, when it seemed just too hard to keep her going, to handle the boys and their fear, their acting out, to get some kind of dinner on the table night after night so they could maintain the semblance of a normal life. But he did it. He always did it.

Still, sometimes, suspended in this role, growing into it—because he did get better and better at it—he had the sense of having mislaid his true self, his real self.

And then she died, and slowly his life changed again. He had two women between her and Claire, each an astonishment to him in her way, neither of them a woman he'd chosen, exactly. They more or less **happened** to him. Both, apparently, his type. Or maybe neither. It didn't matter.

And then Claire. He had often thought that part of her appeal for him was that she didn't need taking care of. She was completely independent, competent, used to solitude.

Was that a **type**?

A few years after the split with Claire, Sam was having lunch with a friend of his from architecture school, Paulus Norton. Paulus told Sam he was planning to spend the summer in Truro helping his son build a house the younger man had designed—

architecture seemed to run in families, Sam had observed, except for his own. Paulus and Sam had worked together on small building projects in the summers during graduate school to make money, and he idly suggested Sam join him. A lark, he said.

Sam had been living alone in the big house in Brookline—the house he'd lived in with Susan, the house the boys had grown up in, the house he'd rearranged architecturally, several times. Even when he married Claire, even when he and the boys went to live in her big house in Cambridge, he hadn't sold it. He'd held on to it, he rented it out, he wasn't sure why—maybe because in some unconscious way he knew from the start that he and Claire wouldn't last.

At first he'd been glad to come back to it, alone. He'd never lived alone before, marrying as young as he had. He'd reveled in his solitude for a while. But increasingly now he was aware of avoiding it. He lived mostly in the office; he ate out; he stopped and had a drink somewhere after that or went to a movie or a bookstore. When he was home, he was restless and lonely.

This had surprised him. He was disappointed in himself that he wasn't more resourceful.

Paulus's project was a chance to turn away from all that, his disappointment with himself included. He said yes. By late June the project he'd been working on had broken ground—an addition to a house in Lincoln—and he loaded up his car and drove out to the Cape.

They lived like teenagers, like animals—Sam and Paulus, Paulus's son Chase, and a tall, silent friend of Chase's named Lex. They slept in tents on the ground for the first weeks, until the framed house could be used as a kind of platform. They got up with the sun and worked until it set, sometimes stopping for a while in midafternoon for a swim. Once every ten days or so, Sam drove into the city, took a shower, put on civilian clothes, and went out to Lincoln to go over things with the builder there. The next morning he'd dress in his work clothes again—laundered now and smelling of soap instead of sweat. He'd stop by the hardware store or the lumberyard for whatever specialty items for Chase's house they couldn't get on the Cape, and then make the long drive back out and start to work again.

After Paulus and Lex left in the fall, Sam stayed on with Chase, the two of them working shorter days, doing cabinetry and trim work. They didn't talk much. Chase seemed comfortable with that, and Sam tried to be. In the evenings, Chase would lie down with a book next to the woodstove they'd installed when the nights started to get cold. He was working his way through the Russians—he was on Pushkin at that point.

Sam wasn't able to settle down. He was itchy. He'd go to a bar, or he'd call one of the women he'd met over the summer.

There were four in all, people he'd thoughtlessly, heedlessly slept with. Through the fall, he juggled them, sometimes awkwardly. It helped that Chase didn't have a phone at the house, that Sam never gave any of them his cell phone number. It meant he could reach them, but they couldn't reach him.

They were every type, these women. Un-type-able. One was young, entrepreneurial, a wiry smart-ass blonde in her early thirties who'd borrowed the money to start her own small restaurant. Things quieted down for her once the tourist season was over, and she had lots of energy for Sam. Too much energy. Another was married to a fisherman. She ran the farm stand where he and Paulus bought fruit and vegetables and homemade bread in the summer. She was tough and touching, a little overweight, but very beautiful, Sam thought, in a sweetly sad, worn way. There was also the owner of a touristy bad-art gallery in Provincetown he'd met one rainy day in the summer trawling the streets with Paulus. She was tall and thin and stylishly dressed—she'd been a model. And there was a writer he'd met at a reading at the Fine Arts Work Center, a poet with long wildly curling hair that she used in sex, wrapping it around his cock, stroking his belly with it.

"I seem to be suffering from a bout of concupis-cence," he told Paulus on one of the nights he was in town. "I'm not sure what your kid is making of it all."

"Don't worry about Chase," Paulus said. "He's brilliant at not noticing things. And I'd like to say it's about time."

"But kind of typical of me, don't you think, to be doing this stuff assbackward." He was thinking of the wild group of young married couples that Paulus and his first wife had been part of, that Sam and Susan had been bemused observers of. In the mid-seventies these couples had a kind of ongoing drunken dinner party in which they slept with each other in various combinations, smashed up their marriages, and rearranged themselves—some several times over—as new couples, their hapless children shuttled back and forth as it suited their needs. Now they all seemed as settled and cozily domestic as Sam and Susan had been through those crazy years. "He has the morals of a billy goat," Susan had once said of Paulus. Which is what she would have said of Sam now, too, he supposed.

He wondered but didn't feel able to ask Paulus whether he'd felt then as Sam did now about all his women—that sleeping with one increased his appetite for the others, or maybe for women in general. During this period—which felt endless as he lived through it but was really only a month or so—he had the sense of a great **tide** of femaleness washing over him, carrying him away: flesh and smells, breasts, limbs, hair, openings. Occasionally, working in a room by himself, he would call up one of these women, or several of them, in their damp parts. Once he was aware that he'd moaned aloud. He wondered what Chase thought, hearing this animal sound from a grown man, a friend of his father's. An omnivore indeed.

It ended messily, with two of them finding out about each other—the two who cared, as it turned out, the restaurant owner and the fisherman's wife. And Sam, who had thought he was so conscientious, so careful—**he** wouldn't hurt a soul—Sam more or less sneaked out of town in the night, with apologies to Chase for not quite finishing the bathroom cabinetry.

Billy wasn't his type. At any rate, he wasn't at all attracted to her, not at first. She was so small, there was something so still, so inert in her face, so guarded in her eyes. She was pretty, he acknowledged that to himself, but pretty in a quite particular, delicate way that had never interested him—the gamine, beginning to wear a bit at the edges. So as the part of the evening that included her started, he was thinking vaguely, if he was thinking at all, that he'd just get through it—take her home, if that was called for, say a polite good night. Easy. Manageable.

So he was surprised to feel his interest in her growing, especially once Leslie and Pierce left. And not just his interest, but his attentiveness to her, to what was sexual about her, which he hadn't seen at first. When he lifted her ridiculously shapeless blanket of a coat and turned it this way and that, trying to help her on with it, he was intensely aware of her physically, the neat shining bowl of her hair cut sharply in against the white stalk of her neck, her tiny waist, the shapely triangle of her back, and the way the muscles movedunder her fitted top as she strained her arms behind her to find her sleeves. Of course, by then he was piqued—unsettled anyway—by her sudden coolness to him and the way that had made him feel.

Like a boy on a first date. Like a jerk.

But maybe, he told himself afterward, she had behaved the way she did at the end of the evening because she was responding to the strangeness of the beginning of it as much as he was.

And it had been very strange for Sam, almost all of it.

He had been early to the theater. He was habitually early. He enjoyed the vague sense of moral superiority the first arrival has, and he liked to have some time alone before any social event to settle himself, to get ready for whatever was coming. He stood under the marquee, watching what had been a chilly mist when he arrived begin to gather into real rain, and looking around at this neighborhood, which had always intrigued him, starting back when it was one of the most beautiful slums in the city. Now it had been gentrified several times over—it was not just beautiful anymore, it was expensively beautiful.

Across the street a row of storefronts took up the ground floors of the old brick town houses and, above them, like so many lighted stage sets, the apartments, one to a floor, it seemed. There were characters visible in several of them.

Around him the theatergoers arrived and milled. Sam watched them, too—another of the pleasures of being early. A group of what seemed to be students was assembling in front of the doors, almost all of the men sporting the little goatee that had become so inexplicably popular now—a half dozen Lenins. They were calling to one another as they gathered, they were talking loudly in twos and threes. One of the young women, a beautiful redhead with very white skin, said to the man standing with her, "Yeah, seventy-two hours at the max. And even then, sometimes . . ."

Family visits, Sam thought. He'd put money on it. Staying with parents, having your parents stay with you. It made him think of his oldest son, Charley, and his wife, whom he visited once a year or so for a weekend—**max**—by what seemed like mutual consent. At least they never pressed him to stay longer, and he didn't ask to, in spite of the fact that Charley lived the farthest away—San Francisco—and was the one child of Sam's with little children of his own, Sam's only grandkids.

It was suddenly quiet under the marquee when the group went inside. Sam saw an old couple coming up the sidewalk toward the theater in the deep shadow of their umbrella. They were both tall, the man bent a little over the white-haired woman. They walked slowly and cautiously. It was perhaps seven or eight seconds before he recognized them— a world of time. He felt shock when he did, and then the effort of trying to make the quick adjustment. He started to move in their direction just as they arrived under the marquee and Pierce swept the umbrella back and away to close it.

"Ah!" Sam said, stepping up to them. He felt confused by his mistake, by how changed Leslie was, but he held her face and kissed it, twice—remembering, at the moment he did it, that this was exactly the way he had held her the one time he truly kissed her, standing in a field in Vermont.

So that started it. A sense of discomfort that set things in motion, that was at work through the evening. Certainly he felt awkward talking to Leslie and Pierce for a little while after that, though Pierce, as usual, made everything easier with his energy, his loud voice.

Then there was the play, the way in which it stirred his shame about himself. It seemed to affect Leslie, too, nearly silencing her for a time. It must be hard for her, he thought during the first act. There must have been such a time for her, a time like the one in the play, when she was waiting without knowing whether Gus was alive or not.

And then after the play, just before Billy arrived at the restaurant, they were having their strange discussion about pornography, sparked by Pierce's account of a show at the MFA that he'd gone to see that afternoon. It occurred to Sam that Pierce might have introduced the subject to distract Leslie, to pull her back from wherever she'd gone in response to the play. But maybe not. You couldn't always tell what Pierce was aware of, what he just stumbled into.

Pierce had said that his first porn experience was with photographs of his father's that one of his older brothers had found and showed to him. "Beauties of the twenties or thirties," he said, "with the great blurry, silvery lighting and the makeup of that day, **comporting** themselves in various ways I would have thought shameful. But no. They were all smiling pleasantly—happily, I'd venture to say—while they diddled themselves or looked back at the camera over their handsomely displayed buttocks. And 'splayed' is the operative part of that word. That was what dazzled me most. That it wasn't shameful." He frowned momentarily. "That was, I suppose, the real revelation involved for me."

Sam had offered a movie he'd seen at college. "Pretty formulaic. The stud arrives at the door. A milkman, I think. Or a postman. Or an iceman."

"The iceman cometh," Pierce said.

"Well, exactly. The missus, without much to-do, lies down on the kitchen table, and, yep, the iceman cometh. Amply."

And though Sam had seen such a movie, this wasn't his first experience with porn. He couldn't have spoken of that, wouldn't have spoken of it in Leslie's presence. That had happened at a state fair when he was about fourteen or fifteen. He'd told his parents he was going to play some games, and instead he'd gone directly to the girlie tent, holding out the entrance fee, not looking at the man taking his money—worried that he'd be turned away because of his age.

Inside, a group of twenty or thirty men were standing around, waiting, in much the same way they stood around when they were about to look at cattle or hogs, but without the pointed interest money brought to such things. When the woman came out, their faces, like his own, he supposed, went thick and stupid.

She was naked except for high heels. She was older—she might have been about as old as his mother. She walked back and forth on the elevated platform, lifting up her breasts, pretending to squirt her nipples at one man or another, putting her hand between her legs, clearly sticking her fingers up into herself. Meanwhile the huckster standing on the ground in front of the platform was talking about what went on in an interior tent for more money. It was as shocking to Sam as anything, the secret words said aloud by an adult: **suck, fuck, asshole, cunt.**

Sitting with Pierce and Leslie, Sam was suddenly remembering it all: the dim light, a bare bulb or two suspended from the top of the tent. The smell of the men's sweat and of the stirred-up dirt under their feet. The woman turning away from them, bending over, holding her cheeks and cunt open. He remembered that she set a bottle on the stage and balanced a coin on it, that she squatted over it, that the neck of the bottle and the coin went up into her, that she stood and reached into herself, pulling the coin out slowly, licking it off.

He'd come out afterward stunned into daylight, sunshine, the crowded fairgrounds. He was still nearly speechless when he met his parents at the agreed-on place. They took him home early. His mother thought he was getting sick.

But he said nothing about this to Pierce and Leslie. Instead, when his turn came to talk again, he was making some lofty, theoretical remarks about the venality of soft-core stuff in the movies, when Leslie said, "Here's Billy!" and turned to go to the door.

So all that was in the air when Billy arrived, small as a child. And though it slowly fell away over the course of the conversation he had with her, it came back at the end of the evening when she got down from her chair suddenly and said she had to go, she had to walk her dog. Her face, which had been so animated only seconds before, had changed, had gone flat, dead. Three minutes later, standing alone on the rainy street, he watched her walk away, her small dark form seeming to disappear into the night from one moment to the next.

Did she even have a dog? he wondered. He felt that stupid about what had just happened.

But he thought about it, he argued with himself about it, and the next day he called Leslie and got Billy's number, and then on the Friday of that week he called her, and when she called him back, they agreed to meet, to walk her dog together.

As Sam stepped out into the night air, he felt how shockingly much colder it was than when he and Billy had started their disastrous walk, much colder even than when they came back to her house from the offices of her HMO. He pulled the collar of his jacket up as he walked along the brick sidewalk. From halfway down the block, he could see that he had a ticket on the windshield of his car—the ticket Billy had assured him he would get, the ticket she had said she would pay.

When he got to the car, he lifted it from under the windshield wiper and pocketed it. He had no intention of mentioning it to her. As he started the engine, it seemed to him that the interior of the car still smelled faintly of dog, a not-unpleasant odor, actually.

The car had only just started to warm up inside by the time he got home. He came into the front hall and set his keys and wallet on the stand there. Looking up, he saw that the message light on the telephone in the living room was blinking red. **Billy,** he thought, and was surprised at how boyishly happy he felt.

But even crossing the room, he was preparing himself to be disappointed. She wouldn't have called, he told himself. She couldn't have. **She was still asleep. She was drugged.**

The voice on the machine was Jack's, his middle

son's, saying he was coming to Boston for a conference the next weekend, could he stay with Sam?
"I'm sorry to call so late. I was just assuming I'd
crash with you, but then I realized I really should
check it out first, the way real people do. I think I
haven't seen you since early summer. Too long, however you slice it. But let me know."

Sam was disappointed. And then was angry at
himself for that. This should have lifted his spirits.
Normally it would have. What was wrong with him
that it didn't now? What kind of father was he?

He called Jack and got **his** recorded message, of
course. He left a warm, enthusiastic response on it.
Yes, come. Yes, it will be great to see you.

As he hung up, he was suddenly aware that the
house felt chilly. On his way to the kitchen, he
stopped and turned the hall thermostat up. He
could hear it trigger the switch, then the faraway
roar in the basement.

Though he wasn't hungry, he fixed himself dinner.
Pasta. Pasta with olive oil and some tarragon he
found in the refrigerator and chopped up. He made
himself do this, cook for himself, three or four
nights a week. A form of moral instruction. A way
to stave off the sense of fecklessness he sometimes
felt waiting to claim him. While he sat at the
kitchen table eating, he heard the wind rise outside.
One of the dining room windows rattled. He got up
and went into the dark room to latch it. He stood
for a moment with his hand on the cold metal, lost

in thought, seeing Billy pitching forward, feeling again how frightened he'd been, watching it.

But it had changed things—the accident. Things had been too polite before then, slightly strained. Their conversation, everything, was unforced and easier afterward.

Was he glad it had happened then?

He was, he supposed. In a way. He had liked taking care of her. Helping her. This abruptly struck him as worrisome. As a habit, really—a way of being with women, with people generally—that he fell into just a shade too easily. And hadn't she been irritated, a little, at his fussing? Even at his being there? She had told him so, for Christ's sake. Why hadn't he left once he got her safely home?

Because things changed again after that. She was funny, she relaxed.

Of course she relaxed, he told himself. She was **drugged.**

Still, he had liked sitting across from her in the big, underfurnished parlor, talking about nothing, talking about his house and hers, teasing each other. What he felt about her, he realized, was that she had a moral sense, a solidity, that existed apart from any of the irregular details of her life.

Could he know that about her, based on one afternoon?

And an evening, he reminded himself, looking out the window. And a play.

He thought of the way her face had looked when

he asked her idly after the play what the worst thing she'd ever done was. You would have thought homicide by looking at her. He saw again the pain in her face as she looked around at the other sad occupants of the waiting room at the HMO. He remembered the moral complexity of the Gabriel character's response to his situation, a complexity the Anita character had likened to Henry James's work.

He **could** know it, he thought.

Outside the window, the branches of the trees bent and swayed in the wind. He went back to the kitchen and finished his meal. He carried the dishes to the sink and rinsed them, loaded them into the dishwasher.

He moved restlessly around the house. He sat blankly in the living room, not seeing the family photographs on the mantel, the worn upholstery on the couch and chairs, unchanged since the boys' punishing childhood. He went upstairs and turned the television on, but nothing drew him, not even sports. He pulled on a sweater and went back downstairs and through the passageway to his office, an addition at the side of the house with its own outside entrance, too, constructed after Susan died. He'd built it because he wanted to be able to work at home, to be on call for the boys after school.

Now he sat at his desk and fooled around with the detail he was figuring out for the windows in the library job. His mind emptied out, free of Billy, of himself, of his history and his life. At some point he looked up to see what time it was. Unbelievable: midnight. This is why we have work, he thought. He got up at about one and went back into the house.

He checked the message light on the telephone—steady green. And then he stood for a long moment in the entry hall, looking around at it.

This was the grandest space in the house, really. The staircase opposite the front door rose up, took a turn to the right across the wide landing, and disappeared. The windows on the landing reached all the way up to the third floor and, in the daytime, flooded this whole area with light. The furniture here—the hall stand, the bureau that had once held everyone's mittens or winter scarves—these were antiques, from Susan's family.

He thought of what Billy had said about his house. Big, tasteful, neutral. He supposed that was true in some ways, though it was more worn than she might have guessed.

And then he was remembering coming into this hallway with his youngest son, Mark, home from college for some holiday visit. Mark, trailing him, had said out of the blue, "You ever think about moving, Dad?"

Sam had turned back to his son, startled.

Mark was looking around this very space as though really seeing it for the first time. He raised his shoulders, almost in apology, it seemed. "It's just so big."

"And empty, I know. I think of it from time to time, I guess. And then I think of all the crap—my stuff and you kids' stuff—and I lose heart."

"We'd help."

"A likely story," he said. He had started toward the kitchen. "Want a snack? A nightcap?"

"I'm pretty beat," Mark said. "But tell you what. I'll take you out for lunch tomorrow."

This was kind, and Sam felt that, as he felt how surprisingly adult Mark had sounded saying it: **tell you what.** But it made him suddenly, heavily sad. He had the awareness of himself as a possible burden for Mark, maybe for all three boys. Did they talk about it? **Who's going to be with him at Thanksgiving?**

Well. Some**body better go.**

"Fair enough," he had said to Mark.

Now he turned off the hall lights and headed alone in the dark up the grand staircase.

There was no call from Billy on Tuesday, or on Wednesday. He was tempted to call her, but he didn't, partly because it was her turn, partly because he didn't want to rush her, to push her. It was pretty clear she was not someone who liked being rushed or pushed.

But on Wednesday night at about nine, feeling that he couldn't spend another full day without human company, he called a friend, Jerry Miller, and asked him if he wanted to have dinner the next evening. Sam had known Jerry for years. They'd been in a support group organized by the clinic where their wives were both being treated for cancer. Jerry's wife had survived.

A smaller group of these husbands, six of them, had gone on meeting on their own after that, usually once or twice a year; and Sam still saw two of that group even more often. One, Brad Callender, he played tennis with regularly. Jerry, he talked to. Not because Jerry was a psychiatrist, though he was, but because their wives had liked each other, and because he and Jerry, too, had felt comfortable with each other, almost from the start.

But Jerry was busy. He and his wife were going to see the Celtics. The tickets had cost him a fortune.

"Clearly you have your priorities," Sam said.

"You bet your ass," he answered.

He called Sam back less than an hour later. Why didn't they meet ahead of time, before the game? He could get to someplace near the Common by maybe five-fifteen or so. Afterward he could catch the green line to the Garden.

Sam suggested an old bar just around the corner from the Athenaeum.

He was early. He settled in with a beer at the long wooden bar. The room was deep and noisy, full of mostly young people just getting off from work in offices in the Back Bay or downtown. As a young man, Sam had worked in an office, doing the kind of scut work—repetitive drawing—that computers did now. He'd liked it—not the job, but the people he worked with and the sense of himself as an adult person, out in the world. Occasionally he had stopped at just such a bar as this after the workday was over, but he never stayed long. He was always conscious that Susan would be waiting for him, that he should be home, helping out.

Sam looked around. Pretty girls, handsome men. The not-so-pretty ones must not venture out, must not want to risk it. Though looking more closely, Sam saw one here or there, appended to a group of more attractive coworkers or friends—someone homely or awkward, someone fat, like the girl at the end of the bar, talking too loudly, feeling a pressure to be funny, maybe. The other girls she was with, three of them, were laughing with her—or at her— but their attention was elsewhere, their sly eyes were shifty, in constant motion, appraising the room, the men. Sam, of course, was invisible to them.

He was thinking of this, his invisibility—the invisibility of age—when Jerry came in, surveying the room, unbuttoning his coat. He saw Sam, and his face, which when unanimated seemed closed in and dull, came to life. He moved through the crowd and bent over Sam, bringing the wintry, fresh air with him as he gave him a little half hug.

Sam shifted the coat he'd been using to save the stool next to him, and Jerry settled on it, complaining of the weather. The bartender came over, and he said he'd have a beer. He turned to Sam. "What are you drinking?"

"Guinness. On tap."

"Yeah, I'll have that."

By the time the beer came, he was already launched, telling Sam about his grandchildren, who were coming for the Christmas holidays, and then about a course he was almost finished teaching at the psychoanalytic institute, a course that had taken up all of his free time this semester.

When it was Sam's turn, he said he thought he'd met someone.

"Uh-oh," Jerry said.

"Hey, it's not as if I do this all the time."

"You don't do it enough. Who is it?"

"A playwright. A friend of Leslie Morse. Do you remember her—Leslie?"

"Leslie. I think I do. She's the one you were in love with after Claire and did nothing about. The married one."

"Good memory. But why do you say 'the one'? You make it sound as though there had been thousands of others."

"I don't know. 'Cause there should have been more?"

"Well, there were more. I just didn't tell you about all of them." And they blipped by quickly in his mind. Pleasantly, except for a little stab of remorse about the Cape.

"So, Leslie?"

"Well, she called."

"**Aha.**" His hand hit the wooden bar. "It begins to happen like this at our age. Her husband died."

"No, listen. Listen for a while." And he told him. That Leslie had invited him to a play and to meet the playwright for a drink afterward. How surprised he'd been by the invitation. How strange the evening was. He tried to give Jerry a sense of it. The awkwardness of not recognizing Leslie and Pierce at first, the surprise of the playwright's being a woman, then his realization of who she was as he looked at the glamorous photo in the program. "She'd been with Leslie's brother," he said to Jerry. "And . . . I don't know if you recall any of this, but he died on 9/11. He was in one of the planes."

"I didn't know. I don't remember it, anyhow."

"Well, he did. And it just seemed **off** to me that Leslie had invited me without saying anything about who this person was. First, not telling me that she was a woman, so that this introduction was, possibly, different from just an . . . **introduction,** if you see what I mean."

"I see exactly what you mean."

"But then, second, that she was a woman who'd been involved with her brother. Her dead brother."

"It is strange. There's something . . . unkind about it, I think."

Sam started to explain the rest. The events in the play, the way they affected him.

Jerry was shaking his head as Sam spoke. When he

was done, Jerry said, "That's just not the way it was with you and Susan."

"But it **is,** in a way. I wanted it done with. I did wish her dead. I . . ."

"But it's not the same. She was ill. Painfully ill, for a long time. We talked about this over and over in group. **She** probably wanted it done with."

Sam was remembering; he was silent for a moment. Finally he said, "She might have, by the end."

She had. But the kids were still so young then. She'd wanted to hold on, for their sakes, as long as she could. And she was scared, too. Scared of dying. He knew that from waking in the night to her terror, holding her as she wept. Weeping with her.

"All I'm saying is, the play really . . . got to me. And all the time, here's Leslie, here's this diminished version of Leslie, sitting next to me, wrung out by it, too." That was how she had seemed, wasn't it? Diminished. "The whole thing was kind of crazy."

"So the play is over, you get up, and . . . what?" Jerry drank some beer, looking at Sam over his glass.

"We go to a restaurant down the street, to meet this . . . Billy person."

"Billy." He looked confused.

"The playwright. It's short for Wilhelmina. I guess."

He made a face, shaking his head. "Sorry, chum. No one is named Wilhelmina."

"One person is. Apparently. This . . . this tiny, sort of funny, little person."

"Oh, you mean small! I take it she was small."

He smiled at Jerry. "Yes, she was. And wired. Because the play, apparently, went really well. Something new, something special happened in it in a critical moment that really, **changed** it for her, I guess. For the better. And that excited her. Because . . . well, **partly** because she'd slept with the guy, the main guy, the actor playing him."

There was a long silence. Jerry had hung his face forward toward Sam, squinting at him in disbelief, or confusion. "You're not telling this right," he said, after a moment.

Sam laughed. "No. I know. I'm not. The point is, I liked her. That's all. And then on Monday, this past Monday, we went for a walk. She has a dog. A large dog. We took her large dog for a walk at the Arnold Arboretum."

Jerry sat back. "See, that's better. That is pleasant. That's a nice story, about taking a walk, taking it slow."

Sam smiled at his friend. **Shut up, Sam,** he thought. "Yeah," he said. "Anyway, I'm smitten." That was it, wasn't it? As simple as that.

"Well, congratulations. On having what must be one of the best feelings in the world."

"It sure is." He had a swallow of beer and set his glass down. "But why is it, do you think?"

"I'm sure it's chemical. Brain stuff. But don't knock it." He'd been fooling around with the cardboard coaster, and now it rolled a little way down the bar toward Sam. Jerry looked up quickly. "You've slept with her?"

"No. Not yet."

"Ah!" He nodded, sagely. "Well, wait and see."

"I think I know."

"Yeah, wait and see."

Sam watched the bartender for a few moments as he mixed a drink, then poured it from his shaker, green and foaming, into a martini glass. A tall young woman in a mannish business suit carried it off. He turned to Jerry again. "What do you think it is—are we crazy?—that we can still be talking about this stuff, about dating and infatuation, at fifty, going on fifty-five? It seems wrong, somehow."

"Why?"

"It doesn't seem . . . adult."

"You're a guy who worries about that too much."

"Is that a diagnosis?"

"I don't think you can fall in love if you're worried about it, that's all."

"Maybe I don't want to fall in love."

"Why wouldn't you? Are you kidding me?"

Sam didn't answer.

"You're kidding, right?"

"I am. Kidding. I think." And then it occurred to him—was this why he had wanted to talk to Jerry?—"I don't think **she** does, actually."

"She doesn't want to fall in love?"

"Yeah. She was saying something to me about not having wanted me to come to her house, or to come to mine. Something about just not wanting to get that close."

"Funny thing to say to a new lover."

"I'm not a lover."

"Yeah, well. You know what I mean." Behind him at the bar, a couple of girls were shrieking with laughter. He looked over at them. He turned back to Sam again and frowned. "It could be it's the 9/11 stuff. The boyfriend that died."

"Gus, you mean?"

"Is he the guy?"

Sam nodded.

"That could certainly do it," Jerry said. "You love someone and he dies. Violently. Notoriously. Conspicuously. That could make you a bit . . . hesitant, one would think, about intimacy."

They pondered this. Sam had been trying to avoid his own reflection in the mirror behind the bar, but the bartender had moved away now, and there he was, looking back at himself, a middle-aged guy.

"I'm thinking maybe she didn't love him," he said.

"What would make you think that?"

He turned away from himself to Jerry again. "She said they had, I think, **difficulties.** And then there's the play." He shrugged. "The guy who isn't sorry that his wife might be dead."

"A play is a play. You think Shakespeare killed everyone who died in his plays? Or wanted them dead?"

"No. Okay."

They moved on, they talked about the Celtics game Jerry was about to see. They talked about

Leona, his wife, who ran special programs at the BPL and was mad at the mayor and the city about funding. They talked about the mayor, they tried to remember how long he'd been in office. They tried to figure out who might run against him in the next election. When was the next election? Neither of them knew.

They finished their beers, and Jerry said he had to go. As they were pulling their wallets out, Sam said, "I think I'm right about the intimacy thing, though."

He walked Jerry to the subway at Park Street, and they embraced, whumping each other on the back, an embrace that was also a parody of an embrace. He watched his friend go down the stairs, and then he turned and made his way west on Boylston Street. He was going to walk a bit, he'd told Jerry. At Charles Street, he went right, and halfway up the block, he turned in at the gateway to the Public Garden.

It was dark and still, the flower beds barren, put away for the winter. The grand trees loomed heavily, even bare of leaves. He moved unhurriedly through, listening to his own footsteps, passing only two other walkers. He crossed the bridge over the duck pond where they'd taken the kids on the Swan Boats when they were still small enough to find that exciting.

He came out through the gate onto the busy street, facing the Ritz. The Taj, it was now. He crossed Arlington and started down Newbury Street. He was thinking over the conversation with Jerry, the part about Billy. **Unkind,** he'd called what Leslie did. Maybe he meant the fact that she did it without warning him, without explaining to him what she was doing.

But would he have gone if she had? Wouldn't he have thought it sounded like a bad idea, wouldn't he have invented some excuse? He passed the store-fronts, the bars with their perpetual Christmas lights, not looking, lost in thought.

He would have found a way to say no, if he'd been warned, he was pretty sure of that. He would have chosen not to meet Billy.

Sam circled twice by the Delta baggage area, and then there he was, Jack, tall, too thin, his mother's long, lovely face translated into something gaunt and hollowed on him. His grin was a surprise in this face; it transformed him—added pounds, made him merry. He had one bag, familiar to Sam, a worn old L. L. Bean thing he'd been hauling around for years.

He was in the car before Sam could get out, so they had an awkward embrace turned slightly side-ways to each other in the front seats. Jack had about a two-day beard. This was a necessity—he got a rash if he shaved too often. Or this used to be the case. What did Sam know of his life now? At any rate, it scraped a bit when their cheeks touched.

Jack put on his seat belt, and they pulled out of the parking area. Driving into Boston, they talked about how the flight had been, about the weekend conference. Jack gave a report on Mark, the youngest brother, who was newly married and working in New York, in a job neither of them fully understood, on Wall Street. Sam told Jack about some of his cousins, the ones he'd seen at the big family Thanksgiving dinner at Susan's sister's house. He'd started going again after the divorce from Claire, occasionally with one of his sons. He'd gone alone this year.

Jack shook his head. "Why are they all so fucking accomplished?" he asked.

"We only hear about the ones that are. Not a word was dropped about Jenna, for instance. She's probably . . . a dope fiend."

Jack grinned again. "Brian. Brian . . . weighs four hundred pounds."

"Elaine got married to a bookie," Sam said. "A small-time bookie."

After a moment, Jack said, "I'm wondering if there **is** such a thing as a big-time bookie?" Sam laughed.

They agreed to stop at the house so Jack could wash up, brush his teeth, "et cetera," and then the plan was to drive out to Waltham, to an Italian restaurant they both loved.

As they pulled into the driveway, the sensor lights came on and flooded the car with light. "Here we are," Jack said. His face, half in shadow, half in light, looked suddenly older.

"Here is where we are," Sam answered. He cut the engine.

Jack opened his door. The cold night air touched Sam, and he got out, too. Single file, they moved across the paving stones from the driveway to the front door. Sam found the key on his jangling ring and put it in the lock. They stepped inside.

Jack dropped his bag and started to take his coat off. "Same," he said, looking around. "Same, same, same. It's like the museum of my youth."

"Why not?" Sam said. "It was quite a youth."

Jack made a face and then headed up the stairs, taking them two at a time. "Three shakes," he called back.

Only then did Sam let himself look at the phone. Steady green. No news there. He heard water running somewhere deep in the walls of the house. He went into his office, leaving the doors open behind him—the hall door to the long corridor, the office door at the end of it. He'd been running some computer programs on the library project, looking at the angle of the sun through the windows at various times of the year. He started to print some of these out.

Jack appeared in the office after about ten minutes. He came and stood at Sam's desk, where the elevations were spread out. "This looks cool, Dad," he said.

"Well, it's okay," Sam answered, looking over.

"What, you don't think it's cool?"

"Do people still say 'cool'?"

Jack glanced at him sternly. "Apparently so."

"I guess I'd have to say that. That I don't, think it's so cool."

"But why not?"

"Well, they wanted a certain look, and I had to promise it to them to get the job, essentially." He was thinking of the campus, the boring buildings. A few of the older ones, Victorian heaps of brick and bric-a-brac, had some character, if not beauty. But the newer ones, built in the fifties and sixties—dorms, mostly, and a science building—were gelded versions of those old eccentricities. And in spite of what the committee said about originality, about **breaking new ground,** that was what they wanted more of. The same. Slightly more distinctive, perhaps, and Sam was providing that with the fenestration on the first floor and the echoing trim above. But he knew that the reason they'd given him the job was because he wasn't going to try to do too much.

"So you compromised or something."

"Something, anyway. But that's partly what architecture is. Not an art. Not pure in that sense. You're always responsible to a client. A client's taste or ideas."

"But sometimes you push beyond that, don't you?"

"Sometimes. For me, mostly now in the really

small, private jobs, oddly." He raised his hands to make quotation marks with his fingers and said, " 'A dazzling, unique-if-not-sculptural laundry and rec room off the kitchen.' "

Jack laughed, quickly.

"I suppose if I'm honest about it I'd have to say I'm not a big-enough name—or talent, let's be clear—to be offered the opportunity to do bold, brave work on a large scale."

"God, you're depressing me, Dad. Don't say this stuff."

"I don't mean to. I like my work. I'm really not interested in that other, **glory** stuff, actually. Cal was." Cal was his partner. "But Cal didn't make it either, in that sense."

They were quiet a minute, and then Jack said, "I've never heard you talk this way before."

"I'm just being honest. Architecture is like most other things, maybe like science, even, in that there are a few people who are world beaters. Really, just a few." He picked up the sun studies and tapped them into a neat pile. "And then there are the rest of us. I'm good. Lots better than lots of others. I'm just not in the world-beating business."

"But weren't you, once?"

"Nah. I think I just didn't ever really think about it, **once.**"

This wasn't true. As a very young man, he had thought hard about it. He wanted it. Maybe up until Susan had the recurrence, he still thought it was possible—some kind of distinction, some kind of public acclaim. After that he lost heart for it. But by then the world had changed. The idealism of the early seventies had faded, and he'd stopped believing in architecture the way he once had, in any case—believing that it could have an impact socially or culturally or politically because of the way it arranged people's lives physically. The world just seemed more intractable, he supposed.

"Why?" He turned to Jack, smiling at him. "Did you think I was a world beater?"

"I suppose so."

"Well, you're a good son."

Sam put his hand on Jack's back, and together they walked to the door. He switched the light off as they left, and they headed down the corridor.

"So when do you think you changed, Dad? The way you felt about your work?" Jack was walking ahead of him, a tall silhouette.

"I don't know. I think it might have been when your mother was ill, and I . . . sort of became a kind of **mom** myself. My own inadequate version of a housewife. That just seemed more important to me than the work I was doing at the time. Plus it would have been hard to be trying to do both things."

In the hall, they lifted their coats from the newel post and put them on. Sam said, "Sometimes when I meet ambitious people now, people who are really absorbed in their work—like you—I feel a kind of envy." This was true of Jack, but he suddenly thought of Billy, too—Billy saying, "God, I love the theater." What he'd thought at that moment, what he'd imagined he might say to Billy at some point, was that she was like a man in that regard, in her passion for her work, and he was like a woman in relation to his, each attitude probably the result of a long, complicated personal history around the issue. He knew his was, anyway.

"Nah, it's not exactly envy, what I feel," he corrected himself as they went outside. "It's admiration. Not envy. I'm not even sure I'd want that kind of devotion to my work. And not having it sure made it easier for me to do what I had to do when your mother was sick. When she died." He thought of what Charley had said of him after Susan had died. Of how angry Jack had been. "Not that it meant I did a great job, I'm not saying that."

Just as they were getting into the car, Jack said, "We weren't easy, Dad."

"You had reason enough not to be."

The restaurant was packed, so they had to wait for a table, shouting back and forth at each other as they stood in the bar with drinks. Over dinner, they talked about pets. Jack had said he was thinking of getting a dog. He was sick of living alone. They discussed breeds and sizes, they talked about the two dogs the boys had as kids—one a biter that they kept anyway, the boys loved him so much. They talked about what would be fair to the dog, Jack was gone for such long hours. Several times Sam was tempted to say something about Billy. **You know, I've started to see this woman, and she has an enormous dog,** maybe even relaying the story of her sprained wrist. He didn't, in the end. He recognized he wasn't sure enough about any part of it to beckon Jack's attention to it.

As they drove back to Boston, Sam was suddenly washed with happiness purely on account of Jack. That Jack should have come to visit him, that they should be in a car going anywhere together, talking idly and easily, seemed like a kind of miracle to him.

For Jack was the child who had been the most unmoored by his mother's death. He was ten at the time, and though he was bright—Sam thought probably the brightest of the three—he pretty much stopped working in school except when he really liked a teacher. He often didn't turn up at dinner. In the last years of high school, he started to stay out all night sometimes, without telling anyone where he would be. When he was home, he kept the door to his room closed, usually locked. Even so, you could smell the dope seeping out when you passed it.

"You've got to do something about him," Claire told Sam over and over as Jack turned fifteen, and then sixteen. But what could Sam do if Jack simply wouldn't follow the rules, wouldn't accept punishment, wouldn't change, wouldn't see anything wrong with the life he was leading?

He had been furious when Sam married Claire—this, in spite of his seeming withdrawal from Sam and any kind of life at home with him and his brothers. He was fourteen at the time. He made clear in the next few years how little he liked her. After he went away to college—far away, to

California—he always had an excuse not to come back, even though Sam and Claire were divorced his freshman year: the length of the trip, a friend whose house he was invited to for a holiday, a good summer job out there. He was home for one Christmas break during these years. Otherwise, it was Sam who made the trips across the country, seven or eight times in all, to visit with his son, to see how he was doing.

And then, in his midtwenties, Jack moved back east to go to graduate school. He started to call or e-mail fairly regularly. He seemed to welcome Sam's visits to him, he voluntarily came to Boston to see Sam from time to time. He appeared to be at peace—even happy. He had work he loved. He had an apartment, occasionally a girlfriend. And Sam, who felt he'd had nothing to do with any of that, was only grateful.

Jack fell asleep on the way home, his head lolling, his knees relaxed and dropped open. As he looked over at his son, Sam was remembering him, remembering all of them, as little boys, their sleeping selves part of their beauty. He thought of Susan then, too, he had a sudden sharp, clear picture of her as a beautiful, healthy woman, a young mother. He remembered her riding in the car, coming home from some family outing. She was in the passenger seat holding the baby, Mark, against her breast. The two older boys were in their striped sleeping bags in the back of the station wagon—no such thing as required car seats then. Mark had been nursing, and he'd fallen

asleep, too. Sam and Susan were talking softly, singing along with the radio, and then they fell silent.

After a while, Sam realized he was the only one
awake. He could hear their slow breathing, all of
them all around him, as though the space itself were
inhaling and exhaling. He looked over at the baby
and Susan. Her still-intact breast was partly ex-
posed, her chin rested against the baby's head. He
had in quick succession a sense of prideful joy in
being the protector, the one who would guide them
all safely home, and then terror at this very notion.
For a moment he felt completely inadequate to the
task. He felt like a boy.

Jack woke now, yawning, stretching, groaning.

Sam asked if he was going to see anyone while he
was in town. He had friends from high school who
came over occasionally when he was home, guys
who'd been in his wild, lost group of boys then, and
seemed, like him, to have recovered. Though Sam
supposed he just didn't see the ones who hadn't
made it.

No, Jack said. He wouldn't have time. He started
to talk about the conference the next day. He'd have
to be there by eight, which meant, for him, getting
up about six-thirty. And he'd stay on through the
cocktail reception afterward. "It's supposed to end at
six, but I bet there are people hanging around even
later than that. But I could meet you somewhere at
about seven or so. Want to do something afterward?"

"Sure."

"Movie? Music? What. I'm in your hands."

"Want to see a play?"

Now what the hell was **that** about?

Not to see Billy. She probably wouldn't even be there. She had told Sam that the reason she was in the audience the first time he went was because the play was still in previews then, because there might be shifts, corrections, little alterations in the dialogue she might be required to make. Or want to make.

No, he just wanted to see it again. He was thinking about it as he got ready for bed, listening with simple animal pleasure to the sounds of Jack down the hall, getting ready for bed, too—the doors opening and shutting, the radio playing softly. His footsteps passed Sam's bedroom door. He was singing under his breath.

He wanted to see the play again because he knew Billy now. The first time around, his responses to it had been colored by everything not-Billy. Now he imagined he might see her in it, he might understand her better. He supposed this was a kind of acknowledgment that there was something about her he didn't understand. Actually, many things about her.

Certainly Leslie had thought she understood new things about Billy from the play—that was clear from what she'd said on the phone when he called to ask for Billy's number. He hadn't thought that was fair of her at the time, but now he found himself wondering what might open for him, how it might alter his thinking about Billy if he sat through the play again.

He was curious, that was all.

Jack was a little tipsy, coming from the cocktail reception. His cheeks were pinked on account of that, or maybe on account of the walk through the cold from the hotel where the conference was held. He ordered coffee, black, and a sandwich. They were at the same restaurant where Sam and Leslie and Pierce had met Billy after the play. Jack had noticed the food on display in the refrigerators as soon as he came in. "Entrails galore, I see," is what he'd said as he sat down, gesturing in their direction.

Now he looked over at them again. "Do you suppose we're meant to be reading them or something?"

"Is that something commonly done with entrails?" Sam asked. "Like tea leaves?"

"Yeah," Jack said. "You sacrifice a bird, or a goat, maybe, and pull its entrails out. I think the Etruscans started it."

"Jesus, Jack, how do you **know** things like this?"

"You mean useless things?"

"I suppose. Yeah."

"If you remember, Dad, I was your dorky kid. I

spent a lot of time reading dorky books in which ancient rituals were cool. Or so I thought."

He did remember Jack then, before Susan's death. The innocence of it! Dinosaurs. Then dragons. Then knights in shining armor, noblemen, imaginary kingdoms. All those passions. Everything that had just disappeared after she died. It was as though some sweet, younger version of Jack had been killed, too. But here he was now—kind, funny, smart. Remade, maybe. If a bit disheveled after his long day and his one or two too many drinks with colleagues, talking, no doubt, about the regeneration of neurons, or something like that.

While they ate, Sam asked him about that, about the conference. And with almost the same enthusiasm he'd evinced in the past for things like the reading of entrails, he cataloged and described the possibilities for a cure, the ideas about ways they might get the body itself to get rid of the plaques destroying the Alzheimer's brain.

"Maybe even in time for me," Sam said. "Before I start making my imaginary trips down the Nile."

"That won't happen, Dad," he said in the firm voice of the child who's watched his other parent die.

"We hope."

They arrived at the theater just in time to use the men's room side by side—now **there** was a weird thing, Sam thought, zipping up—and then to slide into their seats with less than a minute to spare before the lights went down.

Sam had expected to see the play differently, but not in the way he did. It was true that it seemed less about his own life—that sense of being ambushed by hard truths about himself was gone. But it didn't take him into Billy's life either. What opened for him were the characters themselves, particularly Gabriel, of course, and his way of looking at the world, especially in the second act. Sam gave over to it more completely this time. He admired it. He was compelled by the moral issues at the heart of it, and almost as deeply intrigued by the consciousness Gabriel had of the alternate possible roles available to him—in fact, by the notion of **roles** one played in life.

He was pleased by all this. He was pleased at the intermission, too, when Jack said he liked it, and then at the end when he heard his little intake of breath at Elizabeth's appearance.

"That was terrific," Jack said as they sat applauding.

"I'm glad you thought so," Sam answered, feeling a bit proprietorial, a bit smug.

As they were coming up the aisle, carrying their coats, Sam saw Billy standing in the middle of an almost-empty row, waiting, it seemed, for the crowd in the aisles to thin before she moved. He was surprised to feel his body react to the sight of her, a jolt of physical excitement. She was wearing a loose big sweater—black, of course—over bleached-out old jeans. Very bohemian, which he was thinking he might point out to her. He turned to Jack and said,

"I want you to meet someone." He took his son's elbow, and when they came to the emptied row in front of the one where Billy was already starting to move toward the aisle, he guided him in.

A mistake, he could tell from the way her face changed the moment she saw him.

"Are you **stalking** me, Sam?" she asked. She flashed a chilly smile.

"I hadn't thought so, no. I . . . This is my son. I brought him to see the play." He could see Jack trying to make sense of this exchange, looking with intense curiosity first at her and then at him. Sam said, "I didn't expect you to be here, actually."

But she had turned to Jack, she was holding her hand out. "Billy Gertz," she said. "I hope you enjoyed it." There was a kind of professional warmth to her manner, but she was excluding Sam even from this. She didn't—wouldn't—look at him.

"Billy wrote the play," Sam explained to Jack.

"Oh, my God!" Jack said. "Oh, congratulations. It was really, really great."

She demurred, and he persisted. Sam could see that she was softening, Jack was so sincere in his enthusiasm.

If Sam had been alone with her, he would have asked her what was going on, he would have tried to make a joke of it, whatever she was doing. What the hell **was** she doing?

But she and Jack were chatting politely, uninterruptibly. Billy was asking Jack where he lived, what he was doing in Boston, and Jack started to tell her about the Alzheimer's stuff. Her face was animated, interested. Jack grew expansive—he was talking about something called **tau,** some gunk in the brain. Sam might as well have been invisible. He stood there, feeling foolish and shifting his weight from time to time.

When finally she started moving sideways down her row toward the aisle, she was still talking to Jack, saying how nice it was to have met him, saying she was sorry she had to get going. Just as she reached the aisle, she looked back at Sam. "See you," she said, in a voice that promised just the opposite.

He and Jack were silent filing out of the empty row and up the aisle to the lobby. Only a few people were still inside, perhaps waiting to be picked up. As Sam and Jack stood at the big glass doors buttoning their coats, Jack looked over at him. "I'm not going to ask what that was about unless you want to talk."

"Fuck if I know what it was about. I wouldn't mind talking about it, but"—he raised his shoulders—"I wouldn't know what to say."

"She's someone you, what, went out with or something?"

"Something."

"What. You slept with her?"

"No. Not that. I went out with her."

"And then what?"

"Then nothing."

"Well, you must have done **something** wrong."

Sam laughed. "Yep," he said. "No doubt about **that.**"

Jack seemed willing to drop it, though Sam could feel his son's eyes on him from time to time as they walked the cold blocks to the subway stop. He was relieved to get on the rattling, screeching Green-Line car, not to be able to talk.

"I wish I were getting on a plane, or just going somewhere," Sam said, though he couldn't think where he might like to go.

"I'm not so sure I'm going anywhere," Jack said. He gestured outside, where a light snow was falling on the huddled pedestrians moving quickly through it, trying to get home. It was cold, too. Several people passing by had scarves wrapped around the lower half of their faces. **Stick 'em up.**

"This is nothing," Sam said. "You're too used to Washington. Everyone flies through this stuff."

And the snowfall **was** light, and predicted to end by midnight. But the temperature was supposed to drop through the evening. Before he'd left to pick Jack up at the hotel where the conference was being held, Sam had dug out his warm gloves, found his scarf in the pocket of his leather jacket, and slid them all quickly into the pockets of the coat he was wearing, his wool overcoat.

They were sitting now in a restaurant almost as far south in the South End as you could get before you were on the road to the airport. It was quiet tonight, a Sunday. They were at a table in the bar area, where there were only two or three couples. In one case, each was texting someone else. Jack pointed this out to Sam by rolling his eyes. There was a Celtics game on the television set over the bar, the volume off, and they'd been watching that on and off and talking about it. Ray Allen was going crazy, and Jack said, "I love that guy, the way he just, **shoots.**"

"It's pretty," Sam said.

They'd also been talking about some alternative energy stuff Charley was doing in California—he'd sent Jack a brochure about small urban-rooftop wind turbines. And about the Democratic candidates, the chances any of them would have against a Republican, the dirty tricks any of them would be vulnerable to. Clinton, they agreed, would have more stuff they could toss at her than either Obama or Edwards would. She underestimated how much the Republicans hated her, Jack said, and how much material they had to work with around the big issue of Bill, "or alternatively, the issue of Big Bill."

"Right," Sam said. He thought about Billy, about the disapproval she'd expressed of Hillary the night they talked about politics with Pierce and Leslie. But he'd been thinking about Billy all day, actually. About why she might have behaved as she did at the theater, about what must have been his grave misunderstanding of how things stood between them. He'd been unable to answer any of his own questions about it all. He was as confused and preoccupied by her as he'd been after the night she walked away from him outside the Butcher Shop, and even more uncertain of what he could do about any of it. Maybe nothing, he thought. Maybe it was over, whatever it was, before it began.

Jack had started to talk about the presentations at the conference today, about a guy working on a vaccine. When he was excited, as he was, thinking about this, Jack stammered a little, as he'd always done. Listening to him, noticing this, Sam felt a sweet, sad combination of admiration for the adult Jack and tenderness for the boy he remembered.

A man came on the television, standing in front of a weather map, making a sweeping circular gesture over the ocean and back to the coast, the universally recognized sign for a nor'easter. Jack called the airline on his cell to find out about possible delays, but everything was going as scheduled so far.

Sam handed the waitress the valet ticket and asked for the check. Once he'd paid, they stood by the door, looking out at the storm, waiting for the car.

It was warm when they got inside it, one of the nice things about valet parking, as Jack pointed out. The radio was on almost inaudibly, turned to the NPR station Sam liked.

"Will you call the playwright?" Jack said as they drove through the dark streets. As if he'd been reading Sam's mind.

"I don't see how I can," Sam said, keeping his voice as careless and easy as he could. "She pretty much blew me off."

"Yeah, she did."

"As Dick Cheney was to Patrick Leahy, so she was to me."

Jack laughed. After a few seconds, he said, "The analogy makes you so much . . . nicer than her."

"I feel I am. I feel I deserve better." That was it, too, wasn't it? He was angry about it, in part, anyway.

"No, you're right, Dad. She must have some other . . . **some**thing, going on."

They were in the tunnel. The faint conversation on the radio turned to static. Sam said abruptly, "It's unseemly, talking about this stuff with you."

"What stuff?"

"This . . . dating stuff."

"Why?"

"I'm your father. I'm supposed to be wise. At the least, not in need of your consolation. And I sure don't want you wasting any thought on this issue."

"I won't. But you'll let me know any breaking news, I trust."

When Sam looked over at Jack, he was staring out the window, his face turned away, but he thought he could see the edge of a smile playing around Jack's mouth. He supposed it was better that Jack found it amusing than that he worried about it.

He got out at the curb and came around to hold his son for a moment as they said good-bye. The snow swirled around them suddenly.

"I'll see you at Christmas," Jack said as he stepped back. The plan was for Sam and Jack to go together to Mark's house for a few days. Mark's in-laws would be there, too. Frannie, Mark's new, young wife, liked to surround herself, and Mark, too, with family. Sam was glad Mark had this with her—it was nothing Sam could offer him.

He sat for a moment or two in the car before he pulled away, watching Jack disappear into the moving mass of people in the ticketing area, just another dark figure among the many.

In the car on the way home, Sam turned the volume up on the radio. Terry Gross was talking to someone, a woman from South Africa who'd written a memoir, it seemed from what Sam gathered—a memoir about apartheid, and somehow also about the Iraq War. There was a grave quality in her whole way of being, and the combination of that and her accent, the alternately plummy and pinched enunciations, was fascinating to Sam. Near the end of the interview, she said, "I left the only home I'd known and came to America because I wanted to live in a country where the use of torture would simply never be a possibility."

Tears sprang to Sam's eyes. He was surprised to feel this about America—this sudden sense of loss, of pain. About **his** America, apparently.

There was a little silence, and then Terry Gross said, "Yeah. Well."

When the interview was over, the news came on, and Sam turned the radio off. There were hardly any pedestrians out now, and once Sam got to his neighborhood, the streets were empty. The snow was almost invisible except when the wind took it suddenly. It had started to stick, to turn even the road and the sidewalks white. **It's too early for this,** he thought. The cold, the snow.

He pulled into his own driveway and cut the engine. The motion-sensor light had come on, and the snowflakes seemed suddenly thicker and more substantial in its glare.

Sam had no wish to go inside. He had no wish to go anywhere. His own life seemed to him a small thing. He had been of no use to anyone. Not in his work. Not in himself. Not to Jack certainly, who'd made his own long way back from harm, as far away as he could get from Sam. Not to Charley, who was never in touch, or to Mark, who'd found a new family in his wife's big clan. Not to Susan, or to Claire, either.

These people, these things that you love and care about, that you make your life out of—and then they leave, they change, they die. They have no need of you in the end.

The cold gathered slowly around the car, seeped in. Sam slouched down and thrust his hands into his pockets. In the left one were his gloves, in the right, his scarf. He pulled it out now. As he started to drape it around his neck, he felt something hard against his skin. He lowered the scarf, looked at it. Just before the sensor turned itself off, he saw, glittering in its bright light, an earring. A delicate mercury-glass earring, carried on a silver stem.

Billy's earring.

LESLIE

"YOU FORGET HOW DARK IT GETS," she said softly. They were in their own bed, in Vermont.

He didn't answer. She thought he might have fallen asleep. She knew he was tired. He never slept well in hotels, and almost as soon as they got home, he'd gone over to the hospital to check on patients and stayed there for a long time, until midevening.

Finally he spoke. "I don't forget it," he said. "I'm glad to be home." His hand ran up and down her arm. "I like it dark. Dark and quiet."

"Like a grave," she said. She was resting her head against his chest and shoulder. He smelled Pierce-like. Sweat. Soap. Semen, too—she smelled it on him and probably on herself. Also a familiar, Pierce smell.

This was their secret, their improbably intense sexual life together. Perhaps someone might have guessed it of Pierce—he had so much energy to burn, it might have seemed he would bring it to this part of his life, too. She was more unlikely, she knew. But she'd been a wild girl, what was thought of as a **bad girl** when she was a young woman. Marriage had domesticated her, but she still loved what was transformative about sex, what lifted her out of herself—and Pierce was her match in this, and her deliverer. They usually made love two or three times a week. They always had. She knew from remarks dropped by friends—friends who would have liked more sex as well as friends who would have liked less—that this was unusual. Also unusual was how generous, how careful and prideful, he was about giving her pleasure.

"Is that what you think? That it's like a grave?" His voice sounded hollow, deeper than usual under her ear.

"No. I was joking. I love the house. I love how dark it is at night, you know that. But I love a hotel room, too. The sense of life all around."

He sighed, and they readjusted themselves so they were lying next to each other. She had a sudden imaginary picture of what they would look like from above, the two long figures side by side on the bed, not touching.

It was moonless, that was some of why it was so dark. They had no curtains on their bedroom windows—there was no need of them, since they faced a wooded hill that rose up behind the house. Leslie saw the windows as rectangles of a lighter black than the room. Or maybe you'd describe them as the darkest possible gray, she thought.

She turned her head to look at him, a blurry form on the light sheet. His body still radiated heat from making love. "I talked to Sam today," she said.

"Your friend Sam."

She wasn't sure of his tone, of what he meant. She said, "Your friend, too."

"Mmm," he said.

And abruptly she was wondering again, as she did from time to time, how much he had ever guessed at. Sometimes it seemed to her he knew nothing of her inner life, and sometimes it seemed he might know all of it.

He cleared his throat. "He was calling to say thanks?"

"Yes. And to get Billy's number."

"Aha. Your magic trick worked." His voice had changed. It sounded as if he was smiling.

"Apparently." She sat up now and pulled the covers over both their bodies, arranging them so they had equal amounts. She lay down again. After a moment she said, "If it had really worked, though, she would have given him the number herself, don't you think?"

"I suppose."

He sounded distant, maybe sleepy. She wondered if he was even interested in any of this. She wondered what had kept him so long at the hospital, what he was preoccupied with. He seemed preoccupied. She said, "I was awful on the phone."

After a pause he said, "I bet you weren't."

"I was. I said I thought the play was about Billy and Gus. That it revealed how she felt about Gus."

He was quiet for a long time. "Well, that'll break the spell, all right." His voice was dry.

Is that what she'd been trying to do? Break the spell? **Undo** giving him to Billy? Take it back? Take **Sam** back?

But she couldn't take Sam back. She didn't have Sam. She hadn't had Sam, hadn't had him for ages.

No, she thought. She'd never had him. She was a wish of his, a dream, at a time when his marriage was coming apart. That was all. She knew that. A younger wish at that, she reminded herself. She'd been pretty then. Her hair was dark brown; she was slender.

Well, not slender, but not like now.

And she supposed Sam had been a momentary dream of hers, too, one she allowed herself from her place in a marriage that was never going to fall apart.

Abruptly she was thinking of the play again, of the man, Gabriel. Of his marriage. He had seemed fond of his wife as he spoke of certain things. What had changed for him in his marriage, how, in order for him to feel as he did? In order for him to be glad, at least for a moment, that his wife might be dead.

Leslie looked up at the invisible ceiling. She was trying to imagine how it would be if Pierce died, how her life might change. Maybe it would open out somehow, maybe she would turn away from all the practiced routines they shared. Maybe she'd get a job. A real job.

She thought of the conversation they had with Sam at the intermission last night. He had asked her about work, and she had tried to make light of the fact that she didn't have any anymore. Standing in the lobby with the two men, she had said, "One needs love and work, isn't that what Freud said? Anyway, I guess I'm down to love." She looked at Pierce when she said this. She supposed she'd wanted him to do something. Defend her choice somehow. Say in front of Sam that he loved her. That love alone was enough.

No, she couldn't have wanted that. She knew that was nothing Pierce would ever say in front of anyone else. She had wanted something from him, though.

But he'd ignored her signal, if she'd even given one. He started talking about Freud, about the odd things one remembered he was supposed to have said. "There was the cigar, of course. Altered forever now because of Monica Lewinsky. By God, it isn't just a cigar, after all." He had grinned, beckoning Sam's smile. She had probably smiled, too, he looked so goofy, so eager.

Then he told a joke, one Freud was supposed to have liked. The old couple, talking. " 'When one of us dies . . . I think I'll move to Paris.' " He'd laughed, loudly.

Well, it was funny, but it was painful, too.

Therein, Pierce would have said, **lies the joke.**

But that's what the play was about, she was thinking abruptly. At least in part. The wish to imagine what life could be, how it could change, if you were unencumbered.

Now there was a peculiar word. **Unencumbered.**
Pierce's breathing had thickened. He was asleep.

Did everyone who was married do this from time to time, imagine an unencumbered life? She wondered if Pierce did. If she died first, he could move to Paris. She saw him there, walking—no, loping—down a narrow street, looking around avidly, taking things in, asking strangers questions in his terrible accent. He would have the energy, the vitality, to do that.

She wouldn't. If he died first, she might shed their routines, yes, but she wouldn't be able to do what he would do—start anew, make a new life.

Of course, there was grief. Pierce might be changed by grief if she died, as she had been when Gus did. Grief might waylay him. **Belay** him.

She thought of Billy again. Billy and the play. Billy and Gus. She'd been wrong to say that to Sam. Why should it matter to him whether or not Billy had for a moment—for some moments, for days even, or months—wanted to be free of Gus? Wanted to imagine that. **That** was what Billy had a right to. Whatever that feeling was. The feeling of **wanting more,** as Gabriel had said. Wanting to be free of everything too familiar in life. Wanting something new.

"We want," the man had said. "When we stop wanting, we feel dead and want to want more." Something like that.

All her life, she had tried not to want. To be content. To be at peace. Safety lay that way, she had thought. You couldn't be hurt.

Then Gus had been murdered and his death had opened a way for her to want even less, to make her life even smaller. She didn't know anymore whether she was content. Whether she was at peace.

But all she wanted was right here. Here was where she felt safe. Next to Pierce. In their bed. Here, where she lived—safe and quiet and dark.

RAFE

THE EVENING AFTER RAFE WEPT onstage for the first time, Edmund came to his dressing room before the show to talk to him. He sat down in the other uncomfortable chair there, groaning a little as he settled his weight on it, his legs splayed wide, his feet in their immense sneakers turned out: first position. Rafe wondered what size his shoes could possibly be—was there such a width as a quintuple E?

"Guess why I'm here," he said, his hands already busy in his beard.

"I know why you're here."

"Okay. Then you know what the big question is. **Are** you going to be able to do it again?"

"I think so. Or it'll be close enough."

"The tears, too? I assume they may be the iffy part."

Rafe looked at his own impassive face in the mirror. "They may not be as tough to produce as all that."

Edmund nodded several times. "That's the good news and the bad news, I guess. Handy for us that

that's the case. Maybe too bad for you that you have a reservoir to call on. As it were."

"Yeah."

"Okay then." He heaved himself up. More groaning. "I'll go talk to Faith and tell her that's how it's going to be." Faith was the actress with the ten-second Elizabeth part. "And maybe Serena." Anita. "The conversation you had with her was a little different, too. You must have had a notion about what was coming up for you at the ending."

"Yeah." He was looking at Edmund in the mirror. "I felt a little bad, springing it on everyone. But I thought she responded great. I thought it really worked, whatever Serena was doing. Both of them, actually."

"Yeah, it did." He turned at the door. "Well, onward. The last preview. And then we'll all talk tonight, after the show."

As promised, Rafe had done it again that night, and he knew that it wouldn't ever be a problem after that. It was true that it didn't surprise him, it didn't sweep over him the way it had the first time, but it worked. He made it work.

He made it work by thinking of Lauren. He imagined Elizabeth as Lauren, and his betrayal of Elizabeth became his betrayals of Lauren, all of them, thought and word and deed—and then, too, the very thing he was doing at that moment on the stage, the betrayal of using her to make himself cry. He thought of her long, slow dying and how grateful he would be if she could just come back and stand before him as Elizabeth did—as Faith did—at the end of the play. Just a little bit damaged. Only slightly wounded. And the tears came.

Afterward they all sat onstage in the living room, closed in by the lowered curtain, and Edmund gave them the pep talk for opening night. They were in great shape. This last preview had been terrific. The audience had been incredibly responsive. He said that with Rafe's new version of the final scene, "the last piece has fallen into place. It's going to be a fantastic show." He stood up and did a little jig for them. He was surprisingly graceful and light in motion, but everything wiggled absurdly, and they all laughed. When Rafe followed him backstage, he could hear Edmund's heavy breathing, the air sibilant and ragged in his nostrils.

For three weeks, for the play's run, he did it every night, summoned up his dying wife and his sorrow over his life with her. And then, almost as soon as the curtain dropped, he changed back into his jeans and T-shirt and sweater and went home.

Twice he went out with Edmund, but that was it. He turned down the other groups that sometimes formed to have a drink together, including, once, Billy. She made a kind of funny face at him as they were leaving—**Come on**—but he shrugged and lifted his hands: **How can I?**

It wasn't that Lauren was awake when he got home. She wasn't. The Round Robin, one of whom came just as he was leaving for the theater or just after he'd left, tucked her in early. When he opened the bedroom door, there was the sound of the humidifier and, under it, her breath, occasionally her light snoring.

So he checked on her, checked on the cat, sometimes he read the paper, sometimes he watched television. Politics, mostly. **'Tis the season.** They talked about it all the time at the theater, too. Almost everyone in the cast and crew was for one of the Democrats, mostly Obama or Clinton. Serena, who was a Republican, liked Giuliani, but no one was willing to discuss this with her.

Rafe had decided he liked Edwards. It had something to do, maybe, with his working-class background, his populism. Or maybe it was just that he had a sick wife. Identity politics at work.

Late in the run, he was offered two plays to read for, so there was that, too, in these solitary evenings—reading these plays, preparing the lines that might be his. It was good news, of course, probably due to the fine reviews the play had gotten. And Rafe's reviews were better than that. There had been mention of an Eliot Norton Award.

Well, Edmund had mentioned the possibility to him a couple of times.

Still, he was restless. He looked forward to Gracie's long holiday visit, coming up right after the show closed. He looked forward to sitting up late with someone else, talking, watching television. Gracie liked to play gin rummy, too, something she'd taught him. He thought with pleasure of their long series of games, the way he got lost in them. He'd bought green visors for both of them for Christmas.

For Lauren, he'd signed up for audiobooks that he could download, and bought her an iPod to listen to them on. Just as he handed over his credit card to pay for it at the checkout counter, he remembered Lauren's speaking of the miracle of her speech-enhanced computer program. "The digital age," she had said, making what passed for a wry face. "What a **fantastic** time to be an invalid."

At the party closing night, held in a windowless, dramatically lighted room at the back of a local restaurant, Rafe stood, drink in hand, and watched the group assemble and move around. The actors were all there, and Edmund, of course. Some of the sound and lighting and set folks had come, and the costume designer, Madoka, wearing something that seemed less like clothing than fabric samples pinned on her randomly. There were some unidentifiable people, husbands or wives or lovers of someone involved with the show and along tonight for the fun of it. Ellie, the stage manager, was talking to one of the backers—maybe the one who was paying for the room and the trays of hors d'oeuvres and wine in elegant glasses being passed around. Edmund had said he wasn't "at liberty" to reveal who had sprung for the party.

Bob, the actor who played Alex, came up to him

and they talked for a while about Philip Seymour Hoffman, Bob's god, perhaps partly, Rafe thought, because they were built so much like each other. But Rafe agreed, he loved Hoffman, too.

When he went to get a fresh drink, Serena cornered him. They talked about what came next. He told her about the possible plays. She said she was glad for him. She said, "It's just great to see you come into your own the way you have."

"I'm fucking forty-five," he told her. "I better have come into my own."

She looked flustered. "Well, but you know what I mean."

And because she had meant it kindly, because she'd been good in the show, he said, yes, he did know what she meant. He thanked her.

Someone had brought music, an iPod with tiny speakers. Ellie and Nasim had been dancing for a while. Now Annie was, too, with her husband. When the song ended, Bob called out, "Do your dance for us again, Edmund." A couple of people started clapping, started chanting, "Ed**mund**! Ed**mund**!"

Rafe saw Billy turn from where she was talking to one of the set guys. She stepped quickly across the room toward Edmund, who was getting ready to launch himself. She said, "Eddie and I will dance together," taking his arm. The song playing was "Such a Night," by Dr. John. Billy turned to Edmund, raising her hands to dance in closed, ballroom position. He stepped forward, towering over her even though he was not especially tall, and they began to do what might have been a fox trot, with an exaggerated stylishness.

This was kind of her, Rafe thought—rescuing Edmund from their laughter. Their loving laughter, to be sure. But what they'd wanted was to see him make a fool of himself again, and she'd shielded him from that. Rafe set his glass down and turned to Faith—Elizabeth—who was standing near him. He asked her to dance. And then a couple of others, Madoka, two of the light guys, also moved onto what constituted the dance floor—a small carpeted area next to the table on which all their bottles and glasses were set.

Later, after a few people had left and the group was smaller—split up into intense or apparently hilarious conversations among two or three people— Billy came over to where he was standing, propped against the wall watching things. He'd stopped drinking by now. He was thinking about getting home.

"You know," she said, "I never got to tell you how fantastic you were."

"Thank you for that."

"That first time." She shook her head. "That especially was the time that just knocked my socks off."

"Wordsmith that you are," he said.

Her face shifted—a kid's pleasure. She laughed her quick, snorty laugh. Then she said, "It did, though.

Even though I wasn't even **wearing** socks. And I hear you're moving on. Other stuff is coming at you."

"It may be. I have a couple of things I'm reading for."

"I'm glad. You really . . . you really made this one work, for me. You helped me know why I wrote it."

"Well, I'm grateful to you, too. For Gabriel," he said, bowing his head. "I know it's part of why I'm getting these other things now."

"I'd be pleased if that were true," she said, and she did a little curtsy back to him, holding her very straight skirt out as much as she could to each side. He thought of her body, her strong legs, opening them, and he felt a quick pang that made him aware, for a few moments, of his breathing.

"What's coming up for you?" he asked.

"Not much. More of same, more of same, as our friend Gabriel says. Or as our friend Emily **reports** that Gabriel says. I've got a play I'm working on."

"But I thought this one was going out."

"Next year, it's supposed to be. Next fall."

"Ah. So for the moment, a quiet life."

"Tomblike," she said, and she smiled. He had read somewhere once that different kinds of smiles came from different parts of the brain, that a genuine smile, a smile of real pleasure, came from one site, and a polite smile, a smile only **intended** to signal pleasure, came from another. This smile came from there, that other part.

It went away quickly, and she said, "You know, I probably shouldn't bring it up, but I hope everything was okay after our"—she looked quickly around—"tête-à-tête."

"It was. Okay."

"I mean, I was sorry . . . I **am** sorry, if it caused any difficulties, at all. It was an easier thing for me, I'm sure. In my uncomplicated solitude." She spoke the last words mockingly.

He was remembering Lauren, sitting on the toilet, lurched slightly to the side, her face wrecked, crying. "There were, just a few difficulties . . . ," he began.

"Oh! I knew it!" she said. "Ohh." She shook her head. She seemed almost tearful. She might have been a little drunk. "I am sorry."

"Don't be. It's not your fault." Madoka was leaving now, calling good-bye from the door, blowing kisses. Everyone called back. Ellie went over to embrace her. Rafe and Billy waved. Then Rafe said, "You're too quick with that stuff, you know."

"What stuff?"

"That mea culpa stuff. Not every fucking thing is your fault. I mean it. People's lives are"—he lifted his hands, palms up—"what they are. Not your responsibility." She looked so stricken suddenly that he wanted to lighten things up. "Plenty **is,** of course. Your fault. Just not everything."

She dropped her head to the side. "I know." She nodded several times. "I know. It's grandiose, actually. My own secret little psychopathology."

"Not so secret. Not so little, either."

She smiled, quickly.

"But who knows," Rafe said. "Maybe it even helped me—the difficulties. Kind of . . . helped me feel my way into the part. So I should probably be grateful for them, too. Even though I'm not."

"You know, I felt something like that, actually." A frown line of concern etched her forehead and disappeared. "That something had happened that let you feel things differently on the stage. Of course, I was just guessing. But that next time was when it was so different, I thought it might have had to do with . . . with what happened."

"What happened, yeah. And its aftermath. **And** all the things we had talked about that night, and earlier—what you said about the play, about your life. All of it, all grist for the proverbial mill."

After a moment, she said, "Everything is, isn't it?"

"For me."

"For me, too. But it's a funny way to live, don't you think?"

"Well," he said, "you **use** everything. There's that to be said for it. You use everything up, pretty much."

She looked sad. Then her face did that waking-up thing again, and she said, "The environmentally sound school of human interaction. No waste, no mess."

"I don't know about the mess part."

She laughed.

Suddenly Edmund was upon them, throwing an

arm around each of their shoulders, looking from one of them to the other. "A drink, my lovelies?" he said. "We're moving on, per closing time."

Rafe shook his head. "I've got to get going."

Billy said, "I'll have one, Eddie, if you'll promise to carry me home afterward."

"Since you are the exact size you are, Wilhelmina, it's a deal."

Everyone was standing around, pulling on coats, mittens, hats, scarves. There were four or five of them going on. Others were making arrangements for rides with Rafe, with Serena, with Nora Fine, one of the backers—all of whom had cars.

"Oh, I'm just so sad this is over," Annie kept saying, until finally Edmund said, "Life goes on, dear."

"And on, and on," Rafe said.

Outside, they stood around a little longer in the cold night, saying more good-byes, vowing to stay in touch. The usual. Across the vast empty lot where their cars were parked, Rafe could see the traffic moving along briskly on the elevated expressway, looking like so many Matchbox cars and trucks. He went over to Billy, bent down, kissed her cheek. She smelled winey. Just as he started to move away from the group toward his car, Edmund caught him and embraced him. "What pleasure this was," he said, patting Rafe's back.

"Mine," Rafe said. "The pleasure was mine."

———

Now Rafe is sitting in his car outside the dark triple-decker, the engine off—not ready to go in, not ready for it to be over, though he's also glad it is. He's living it again, the way he felt night after night.

"Beginners!" This is what Ellie, the stage manager, calls out backstage when it's time for Rafe to take his place on the set—Rafe, the actor who **begins** it all. Waiting for her call in his dressing room, looking in the mirror, he can never decide what he feels about what he's about to do. Is it the most cynical thing possible? Or is it the best use he can make of his life, of Lauren's life, of what's happened to them?

Gabriel looks back at him from the mirror, the man he's made, and made his own, the man whose grief drinks from his own grief, whose joy eats his joy, but whom he uses, over and over, to escape his grief and joy, to make them commodity, currency. For better or for worse—he doesn't know—to make them art.

BILLY

FOR A WHILE, there was so much to do. The end of the semester, with the last student work to go over, then a public staged reading of the student play that had won the Dorland Prize—she had spent the better part of a week in late November reading through the submissions. Then there was an end-of-semester party at the grand Cambridge house of one of her students, a fortyish married woman. After the first few moments, Billy wasn't surprised at its size and splendor, actually. There had been something noticeably moneyed about Angela, about the quality of her chicness, that Billy had picked up on early in the semester, though she had no idea of the source of the dough. She hadn't gotten to know the students as well as usual this year because the play was so time-consuming.

The party was boozy and cheerful—the students were relieved to be finished—and Billy felt some envy of their flirty connections as she stood at the edge of one conversation and then another. She tried to move around, to be sure she talked to everyone a little, though she doubted anyone really cared, but she ended up spending too much time with Patrick, Angela's husband. It turned out that he had made his money developing unhackable security systems for businesses. More and more, Billy felt, people were having lives, making livings, in ways that were incomprehensible to her. This would only get worse, surely, and then she'd have to start setting her plays in the nineties, the eighties, the seventies even, which she remembered very little about. In any case, she stood at the edge of the room for a while with this Patrick, asking her boneheaded questions about his work.

Then she got stuck with a student, Maddie—Maddie of the invariably tragically isolated dramatic characters. She quoted to Billy a number of remarks that she said Billy had made in class, remarks Billy had no memory of at all.

"Are you sure?"

"Yeah. You know, it was John's scene, that first one he wrote?" She was a pretty, nervous woman. After every classroom break, she returned to their seminar room reeking of nicotine. "You also said his character spoke like a 'superannuated Valley Girl.'"

"I did?" Billy asked.

"Yes. You said no one Amelia's age would keep saying, 'Oh. My. **God**!' all the time. You said, 'One would hope with age comes maybe not wisdom'—or it might have been '**perhaps** not wisdom'—'but at the **least** an enhanced vocabulary.'" A little smile played around her mouth offering these words back to Billy—she was apparently pleased to be showing Billy her attentiveness. Her devotion, it would seem.

But Billy wasn't sure of her intention, actually, her tone. It felt hostile, in some way she couldn't identify. As soon as she could decently break away, she did.

She talked for a while to the wife of one of the students, a lawyer who had just left her job to study religion at Harvard's Divinity School. She had no idea what she'd do with it, she said, but she felt a need to look at her religion and her religious impulses in a disciplined way.

"But how wonderful, to be starting over," Billy said.

"Well, it's very American, I'm afraid."

"Not the way you're doing it, I wouldn't think. The American way would be just to announce Jesus as your personal savior, your best friend, and then go on precisely as you would have anyway, in the assurance that he blessed every single thing you ever did."

"Ah, no politics now," the woman said. Her name was Louise.

Billy rounded her eyes in innocence. "Oh, I wasn't speaking of Mr. Bush."

Louise laughed.

Later she sought out John, to whom she'd apparently made her various insulting comments, and was pleased at what seemed his lack of any lingering resentment. Maybe she'd said what she'd said in a better **way** than Maddie had repeated it back to her.

By now, a couple of hours into the party, dancing

had begun in a large room off the immense entrance hall, dancing to music Billy didn't recognize. She took this as her cue. She found Angela and said good night.

She spent the next evening going over the comments she'd made on the students' work and concocting grades for them. She sent them in by e-mail the following morning, and that was that. Semester over.

Two nights later, the last performance of **The Lake Shore Limited.** It seemed a little undercharged to Billy, but it got a standing ovation. This didn't mean much, really, since everything these days did, but still, she was pleased. And afterward, the cast party at a restaurant, with everyone connected to the show along for the fun of it.

Billy had been a little concerned about Rafe the last weeks. He'd seemed to be avoiding her, and the others, too—leaving almost as soon as the curtain descended each night, turning down invitations to have a drink. But they talked easily at the party, near the end. She was able to tell him at last how pleased she'd been about what he'd done with the part.

He'd seemed stronger, tougher, refreshed by having finished, and perhaps, too, by having done so well. He'd had wonderful reviews.

Edmund came up to the two of them as they were talking, proposing they all move on to a place nearby that stayed open later. Rafe said no, he had to get going. Most of them were going to get going, it turned out, but Billy was worried about Edmund, so she told him she'd come along.

When they divided up outside, those leaving, those going on, Rafe came over to her, bent forward, and quickly kissed her on the cheek, then moved off with a small entourage he was giving a ride to. An easy good-bye, then. But as he walked away, for some reason she thought of the way his face had looked the night she saw him float past the restaurant where she sat with Leslie and Pierce and Sam— so solitary, so ghostlike.

They walked down the street to the next place, the four of them who weren't ready to go home, and Billy. Like the last restaurant they'd been in, this one was in one of the renovated old factory buildings that studded this part of the South End, the last section of the neighborhood to be developed. The streets here were still dark at night, dark and empty and a little scary. Billy was glad for the company of the others.

The bar was half full. She and Faith and Edmund sat on stools, turned around to face Larry and Annie, who were standing. They gossiped about those who'd left earlier, they talked again about the last performance, and then about what each of them was doing next.

Billy talked for a while to Faith, who'd had the tiny Elizabeth part, so tiny that she hadn't been at most of the rehearsals and didn't come to the theater until around the intermission. It was the first real exchange they'd had. Billy liked her.

She got into a longer conversation with Larry. He was short and stocky, the build of a little guy who'd consciously decided to change his body through weight lifting. She knew him from other plays—of hers and of friends. He lived with an actress Billy liked, too. Karen Blackmun.

He asked how it felt to be done with the play.

"It's too soon to know," Billy said. "I usually do have a little postpartumy thing. A couple of times in the process, actually. Once when I finish writing it, and then again, like now, when it closes. But I just can't tell with this one."

"Why not?"

"Well, I worked for a long, long, way-too-long time on it."

It had been years, in fact.

In the immediate aftermath of 9/11, of Gus's death, she was sure she would never write about it. How could she? To write about it would be to claim it in some way, and she had no claim. In fact, she had what felt like the very opposite of a claim. But then on the first anniversary of 9/11, Leslie asked her to come to a little service in Vermont, and Billy felt she couldn't say no. It was mostly just hymns and readings, but somehow it touched Billy, and she really broke down in Leslie's presence for the first time. She wept for Gus, for Leslie, for everyone who had gathered in New York on the same day at the large memorial service there. She wept for all that had happened to the country afterward, for the terrible uses that were being made of this sorrow.

The afternoon seemed endless with the reception after the service and the introductions to people who'd known Gus. Over the course of it, the feeling of **living a lie** Billy had had the year before rose in her again, compounded. As she spoke to people, she had the sense that her weeping had in some way glorified her in her grief for them. It had become essentially **who she was** to them. It gave her life a meaning for them, a particular meaning.

It made her a terrible fraud in her own eyes.

When she came home, she sat down and, in a kind of fury at herself, wrote out something she thought might become dialogue for a character in her position, a man, incapable of any true action that wouldn't also betray his dead lover. She put it aside, but kept coming back to it over the next years. She worked on it around and between other things that she finished more quickly—worrying at it, changing it, trying to find the right conflict, the right way to resolve it.

Elizabeth, the wife figure—she'd had several other names along the way—had died in several versions. In one of those versions, Gabriel's decision to stay with his lover, Anita, was understood by him as a kind of punishment. In another, he sent Anita away and was alone at the end.

What became clear to Billy as she struggled with

the material was that a happy ending wasn't possible for Gabriel if Elizabeth died. Occasionally she wondered whether that had any meaning for her, for her own life. She'd remind herself that what she wrote wasn't predictive, wasn't reflective, of anything that might happen or had happened to her, but she couldn't help feeling that what was true for Gabriel in his dilemma might also be true in some altered way for her.

She began to try out situations in which Elizabeth lived. In one, she survived but was injured. Gabriel was told this, and he went off at the end to find out how badly, how much a nursemaid he was going to have to be to her.

But that was too Ethan Frome–ish, she decided, and rejected it.

It had taken her a while to find the ending the play had, but when she'd written it, when that part of it was done, she had a little depression. She saw her shrink for a few sessions; she got some pills. And now the next part was done, too, the part where it came to life, where it had its own life and was changed again by that—by Edmund and Rafe and Serena—into another story.

So it was all over, after all these years of living with it. Billy had no idea what this would mean.

She had felt . . . what? Released, perhaps, by seeing it onstage. By what Rafe had made of Gabriel's choice, what he gave to it. But did that have anything to do with her anymore? Could Rafe's tenderness, his sorrow, speak for her? She didn't know. Maybe it was nothing she would ever have been capable of—as much a lie as the one that had been thrust on her in the first place, the one she'd felt forced to enact for Leslie's sake. For Gus's.

At the bar now, she said to Larry, "What I'm feeling at the moment is just relief, to be done. Not the usual little **drop**." She flopped slightly to the side momentarily. "So I don't know," she said. "I don't know what it will be like."

The restaurant began to close down.

Edmund had told her he would carry her home—she'd made this her joking condition to moving on to the next place with the small group—but by now he was drunk. They all had to put him in a cab, in the end. It wasn't easy. He kept climbing out to embrace someone else, braying about how much he loved them, asking over and over after those who had left already. After the third attempt to make him sit, to make him **stay** sitting, Billy leaned in and told the cabbie he should start his meter **now** and gave him twenty-seven dollars, all she had in her wallet. Finally Larry and Faith got him into the cab next to Annie, who was going in his direction and would drop him off.

"God bless her," Larry said as the cab pulled away down Harrison Avenue. "I hope she can get him out when they get there."

Billy went home by herself, wending her way the few blocks north on the dark, silent streets. She took

Reuben out for his walk and then she lay in bed, too wound up to sleep. Wound up by the play, of course, and its last performance. By the end of the kind of shipboard intimacy it produced among the people who worked on it. But that was always there. Even the affair was there, more or less, with Rafe. Often it lasted a little longer if the man was unclaimed, but usually not. So that was part of it.

But she thought it had mostly to do with what she'd talked about with Larry—the amount of time the play had taken out of her life, the years she'd been living with it, working it out. Her closeness to it. There was something in it she didn't want to relinquish this time. Something she didn't want to give up. This surprised her.

When Billy woke up the next morning, her first thought was of Sam. Not a thought, really. A memory. She was lying on her side, her view was through the opened pocket doors into the living room, and she imagined him as he'd looked setting the cup of tea down for her. She remembered him sitting in the chair opposite her, stretching his legs out in front of him. He hadn't called since she'd seen him with his nice son. And before that. He hadn't called since the day of their walk.

That was good, she told herself. It was good that somehow he had finally picked up on her wish not to start anything with him. She'd had to be a little cool to him to bring it off, but she hadn't been rude, she didn't think. In fact, having his son at the theater had been perfect, had been a godsend. He had made politeness necessary. It was her politeness to the son that had let her signal Sam her lack of interest.

The only reason she was thinking of him now, she told herself, was that she had so much time stretching out ahead of her. But she'd been waiting for this, waiting for her life to get back to normal after the play. She'd even anticipated the emptiness she felt beginning to descend on her, she'd made plans to stave it off. She was going to a concert at Jordan Hall tonight—the Emerson Quartet doing Mendelssohn. She was having dinner with a friend from BU later this week. There was a Christmas party for the faculty on Friday, and she was having drinks on Saturday with Edmund. She'd go to her sister's in New Jersey for Christmas, and then, just after Christmas, she was going to Chicago to stay with a friend and see everyone she used to know.

And with all that, she wanted to work on a new play she had going.

She turned over in bed to look out the bedroom windows. There was a pine at the back of the yard that she often thought of as consoling. Just its deep, dark green, she supposed.

She had her life again. She was glad. The sense of its slipping out of her control, the feeling she'd briefly had with Sam, that was over. And this hollowed-out feeling she had now of being accountable for every minute of the day, for all the hours to come, and to come after that?

This was temporary, she told herself. It was the postpartum feeling, something she knew very well how to deal with. "Get over it," she whispered out loud.

She sat up and threw the covers back. Reuben's head rose from the bed to see what this meant. She spoke sharply to him: "Let's go, Rube. Let's take a walk."

She did stay busy over the next days. She worked out twice at the gym, several hours each time, something she had let fall away during November. She went shopping for presents for her grown nephews, still living at home. She had her nails done and read through several **New Yorker**s that had arrived and been put in a pile on the coffee table. She read a collection of poetry written by a Chicago friend. She read it again. She cleaned up.

As she was going through the piled-up bills and notices on her desk, she decided it was time—why not?—to throw away all of her old accumulated bank statements, going four or five years back. All the old income tax filings going back longer than that. It would be nice to have those drawers free for other uses.

She went into the kitchen and got a big black garbage bag from the box under the kitchen sink.

Crouched there, she was slowed for a moment by the memory of the feelings that had confused and overwhelmed her the day Sam took her for their walk. That was done, she told herself. Life goes on. She stood up. She went into the living room, to her desk. She pulled out the first drawer and began to lift things out.

She was on the second garbage bag, halfway through the next drawer down, when she found it, a large manila envelope, not, this time, full of receipts for tax deductions. Flat, empty feeling. Not labeled, though she knew right away what it was.

She opened it, slid the photograph out, and there they were, Gus and Leslie—young, happy, beautiful. She examined it closely, all the familiar details. The blur of light and shadow that signaled the flower garden, Gus's bony bare feet in the grass, the tips of his fingers appearing at Leslie's waist from behind, his eyes, slightly shadowed by his fair hair. Leslie's strong profile looking at him, her long straight hair and pale skin.

She hadn't looked at it in several years, anyway. Would she, ever again? They seemed like strangers, these two people—whoever they were, gone now. Gone, of course, because of death—Gus's terrible end. But gone, too, because of life, because of the alterations of time, the reshaping of the self over the long years. Leslie's self, remade.

Billy's self, too, changed, worn to a new shape.

As Gus's would have been, if he'd lived. He

couldn't have stayed the sunny boy forever. If he had, how awful for him.

The line from the psalm at Gus's service came to her: **And the place thereof shall know them no more.**

No more Gus. No more Billy either. Not as they were then. Taken away—by death, by life, inexorable life. Billy felt tears at the back of her throat, but she didn't yield to them.

She put the picture back in the envelope and set it in the open black trash bag, on top of her tax return from 2002 and the spilling old canceled checks.

The snow started in the night and was already five or six inches deep when Billy went out in the morning with Reuben and set the trash bags on the curb. The sky was a pearly gray. There were so few cars moving in the street that she let Reuben off the leash, and he bounded free and then back to her again and again in his pleasure, like the puppy he'd once been.

She didn't try to work. While she ate her breakfast she had the radio on, listening to the school closings, the names of all the nearby towns' school districts, the private schools, arranged alphabetically. Later she read, she listened to the quartet she had heard the week before, and then Annie Fischer, Maurizio Pollini. She sat by the window and watched the world transform itself while the music sang to her.

The trashmen seemed to be delayed. The bags had disappeared entirely. Had become little hillocks of white, the blanketing snow like a metaphor for forgetting, she thought.

But I didn't forget, Gus. I did the only thing I knew how to do with it. I wrote it, I built it. I tried to make it come out the right way, for you. I used it. For you, this time.

Around five, the truck swung by, its clashing noises muffled by the deep powder, by the thickened air. She watched the men pull the bags out of the snowbank and toss them into the wide maw of the yellow truck. When they'd gone, when she couldn't hear the truck anymore, she felt a kind of letting down, a release of some sort. She cried for a little while.

When she was done, she went into the bathroom and looked at herself in the mirror. She splashed her face with water. Then she dried it off.

She found her boots in the bedroom closet. She put on her bat coat, her hat, her mittens, and went out alone into the twilit, reborn world, Reuben by her side.

SAM

SAM HAS SET THE EARRING in a dish on the hall stand where he also keeps his keys. Every time he goes in or out, he sees it there, winking at him, seeming to ask him something. Twice it's gotten caught in the keys as he picks them up and he's had to thread it out of them before he leaves.

What he thinks he's going to do, what he knows he should do, is to mail it back to Billy, but he doesn't have an address for her. He can't remember the street number of the house on Union Park where he picked her up the day they went for their walk. He's not sure he ever knew it. She might have said **the eighth house in from the corner,** or whatever it was. **The fifth house in.**

He could call Leslie to get the number, but for various unexamined reasons, he doesn't want to. He actually did call the theater, but whoever answered there said, quite rightly, that they couldn't release that kind of information.

So there it sits. Three or four times he's picked it up and held it, as if doing this will make it clear to him what the next step is. **A magic stone,** he had thought the last time he did this, and he put it back, smiling sadly at himself. **Idiot.**

And now he's standing over it, leafing through the mail, mostly junk. With the advent of e-mail, no one writes letters anymore. He has gotten a few Christmas cards this year, including one from Leslie and Pierce, but even that seems to be fading as a custom.

But here is a thick, square envelope, announcing the possibility of something personal. There's no return address on the front, but when he flips it over, he sees Charley's San Francisco address in the triangle of the folded-over flap. He opens it.

It's a card—a spare, simple tree, like a child's cutout, with brightly colored ornaments strung in loops across it. Charley and Emma have both signed it, in their very different handwritings—Charley's a scrawl, Emma's something worthy of the Palmer method. Folded inside the card is a typed letter. It will be the yearly summing up of their activities, written by Emma. Sam is unfolding it as he walks into the living room and sits down. There's a pure, chaste light in here, a result of the snowstorm outside, the whited air. He holds the letter and reads about Charley's small business installing solar panels and rooftop wind turbines on private homes. Emma is working part-time, running the "office" for him. The children—Sam's grandchildren, photo enclosed—are both doing well, and their activities are described.

It makes Sam almost unbearably sad. Charley is the son who's most lost to him, though he was never the cause of worry and desperation the way Jack was. But Charley turned away from Sam early on, clearly seeing him as unreliable, not adequate alone as a parent, and not doing a good-enough job of pretending to be Susan as well as himself. And then he and Emma had married when they were both so young, they'd moved so far away. Charley's never in touch. If it weren't for Emma's occasional letters and Sam's brief yearly visits to them, he would know nothing about his son or his family.

He remembers the day Charley told him he was going to get married. He'd come up on the train from college in Pennsylvania to make the announcement in person. They were sitting in this room. Sam was worried about it. He was pointing out Charley's youth, and Emma's. As he spoke he could watch Charley's face somehow shut down, his mouth form itself into a small, grim smile. "Well, you don't have to come, then," he said.

Sam backtracked quickly and said no, no, of course he wanted to be there, of course he would come, he wouldn't dream of staying away.

Too late.

The day after this—after Charley's announcement, after Sam's misstep—Sam took him to the Back Bay train station. He sat in the car and watched him walk away. He didn't turn back, he didn't wave, and Sam had the sense, as Charley disappeared in his puffy nylon parka, that he'd screwed things up with his oldest son, screwed them up beyond salvation.

It was that day he had sat in the Starbucks on the corner near the station and suddenly felt he had to do something about his life, something he translated as the need for Leslie. Surely it was the depth of his despair at having failed Charley again, of having failed in everything else, as he felt it then—as a husband, as a father—that made him reach for the solution, the answer, in such an impossible place, he thinks now.

He remembers the astonishing rain as he drove up to Vermont, several times so heavy on the windshield that he could see only ten feet in front of him. One downpour was so blinding, an opaque silver cascade down the glass in spite of the frantic wipers, that he pulled off the road entirely to wait it out, setting his emergency lights to blink. As he got farther north, it grew lighter, but it was mixed with snow. Falling slush, really. It was sticking on the grass divider like a lacy cloth.

He had the radio on. He had wanted something—music, some afternoon interview on NPR, something to fill his mind uselessly so he wouldn't have to think. He turned it off when the stations fizzed and buzzed and went staticky, but once he was past Hanover on 91, he tried it again—he thought he remembered the number of the public radio station for this area.

He was fiddling with the knob, looking down at the digital read of the numbers, so he missed the beginning of the accident—the deer leaping into the road, the car two cars ahead that slammed on its brakes and started to skid. What he saw, looking up, was the car directly in front of him turning sharply right to avoid the skidding car, and a fleeting glimpse of the deer, now on the other side of the highway, the white flag of its tail rising and falling as it ran, as it disappeared into the black woods. He braked just as the car in front of his lost control. It shot off the road, over the grass verge, and into the trees, turning slowly all the while, so it ended up facing backward, its headlights shining eerily into the woods.

Sam pulled off the road and stopped. The first car, the one that had started everything—though actually, of course, it was the deer that had started everything—that car was gone, its taillights fading to glowing dots in the dark distance.

He got out of his car and ran down the slight incline. It was an old car, big—a boat, really. The passenger side was undamaged, but the hood had buckled in. The engine was shrieking steadily, a sick noise. There was one person inside, a woman, hunched over the wheel.

Sam opened the door on the passenger side and bent in. She lifted her head slowly and turned to him, her face stupid in terror. She was young, maybe in her twenties. A girl. There was a purplish lump already rising on her forehead, blood seeping from it.

"You're all right," he said.

"I don't know," she said after a moment. Her breath was coming unevenly. "I don't know."

Sam could barely hear her over the engine's wail. He reached in and turned off the key in the ignition. Everything was silent, suddenly. And dark.

"Can you get out?" he asked her. "Can you open your door?"

She sat up slowly. She tried the door. She couldn't move it. He saw that it was wedged against a tree trunk.

Sam got into the car, out of the snowy rain, and sat next to her. Blood was running now from her swollen forehead, and he found a handkerchief in his pocket to blot it. Gradually she seemed to come to herself, to be less terrified. He asked her what hurt. Her head, she said, and her leg. He leaned over and saw that the side door had been pushed in, that her leg was stuck, somehow wedged against it.

"I feel a little dizzy," she said.

He thought that he shouldn't even try to get her to move, that she should stay where she was until someone could look at her. He told her so. He went back up to his car and called the Hanover police on his car phone. He described approximately where he was and gave them the license number of his car, which they would be able to spot by its blinking lights. He said he thought they were going to need an ambulance. He went back down the hill and sat in the car again.

She had relaxed; she was almost lighthearted now.

She had dry-looking, curly hair and a round face, nearly all in the same plane—flat. When she smiled, though, she was almost pretty. She was talking about the strangeness of the accident, the feeling that it had happened in slow motion. "I was almost more **interested** than scared," she said. "As soon as I felt it was out of my control, I was just . . . curious, I guess you'd say, about what would happen next. Do you know what I mean?"

Yes, he said. He did.

He kept wiping at the blood. The swelling itself appeared to be slowing it.

"I wonder, could you die thinking that?" she said. " 'Oh, what will I hit now, and now?' I mean, just being **interested**?" She giggled suddenly.

He saw that she was younger than he'd thought. Maybe in her late teens. He thought he should keep her talking. "Where were you headed?" he asked. "When you were so rudely interrupted?"

"Oh, I was visiting my aunt. My great-aunt, actually. She's in a nursing home."

He dabbed again, trying not to hurt her, and said, almost absentmindedly, "Well, no good deed goes unpunished."

Apparently she hadn't heard this before. She smiled in childish delight. After a minute, she said, "My aunt is pretty crazy, actually. She has Alzheimer's disease."

"I'm sorry."

"No, it's not so bad. She thinks she's doing a lot of

neat stuff. She said she was glad I arrived when I did because she'd just gotten back from her trip down the Nile." She laughed, and he did, too, in response to her amusement, but also to the prettiness of her laugh.

"I've always wanted to go to the Nile," Sam said after a moment. "Maybe that's the way I'll finally get there."

"Oh, **you're** not old," she said.

"Not yet," he agreed. It was getting colder. He might want to get his coat out of his car pretty soon.

Her face had become earnest. "Do you believe in signs?" she asked him.

"Portents, you mean?"

She looked as if she didn't understand the word.

"What kind of signs?"

"No, what month you're born. **Those** signs."

"Oh. No. No, I don't."

"Oh." She sounded disappointed.

"You do?" he asked after a moment.

"Yeah. Sorta." She leaned back. She seemed suddenly exhausted. She closed her eyes for a moment and then opened them fiercely wide and licked her lips, as though willing herself to alertness. "I mean, my horoscope today said I should stay close to home."

"There you have it," Sam said. "All the proof you need."

She looked at him. After a few seconds, she said, "I know you're kidding me. You don't think . . . that's real." She seemed embarrassed and a little sad, and Sam felt bad. She was shuddering a bit from time to time, too. He got out of the car again and went up the hill for his coat. When he came back to the car, he put it around her shoulders. He buttoned it under her chin. She was protesting, but she let him do it.

"There," he said when he was done arranging it. "Better?"

"Yes," she said. After a minute: "You're really nice. To do that, and to stay here with me."

"Anyone would," he said.

"No, that's not true," she said. After a moment, she said, "Where were **you** going? Are you going to be late for something?"

"Oh." Sam smiled ruefully. "I was going to meet my own true love."

"Honestly?" She sounded impressed.

"In a manner of speaking. **She** might not agree." And then, because they needed to pass the time, because the temperature in the car was dropping steadily, the engine ticking as it did, he told her about Leslie, a shortened, edited version of the story—he left Charley out, he left out his own feelings of emptiness and failure. When he was done, he said, "So, do you think she'll come away with me?" He smiled at her. "Would you?"

"Well, it's very romantic," she said hesitantly.

"Thank you." When she didn't look at him, he said, "I **think,** thank you."

"Well, she is married. To someone else."

"To the wrong man, obviously." Sam was joking—half joking—but he was aware, suddenly, of how he might sound to her. Like someone dangerous. Like a stalker.

They sat silently for a moment. The wet snow hissed gently outside as it landed on the trees. She said, "But I don't think you . . ." She was looking at him, worry in her plain face. "Maybe she really, really loves him, did you ever think of that?"

"I have thought of it. Often. But I think I still have to do this."

"Well, I hope it . . . I hope it's all okay."

There was something so genuinely concerned in this, so sweetly generous, that he said, "Oh, it will be okay. No matter what. Just as you will be okay, right?" He dabbed again at the blood still pumping, but slowly now, from her head.

"Yeah, I'm gonna be fine," she said.

They talked a little more—she was studying to be a licensed practical nurse, she was living with her mother, a widow—and then, in the distance, they heard the sirens. Sam got out of the car and went up the hill to the road again. They pulled up, two police cars and a fire emergency truck, and he led the five or six men down the slope. He stood back while they got her out—four or five of them pushed the car backward and then were able to open her door. They put her on a stretcher and carried her up the hill. Sam walked beside her, trying to speak to her, to reassure her through the busyness of the EMTs. He told her she'd be okay now, though before they covered her, he'd seen that her leg, the leg that had been wedged in by the crushed door, had a long gash. She must have been losing blood from there, too, while they had their polite conversation— much more blood than she was losing from the cut on her head.

He thought to ask her name just as they got to the emergency vehicle. Melanie, she said. Melanie Gruber. He asked the cops where they were taking her. He told her he'd call, he'd find out how she was, but that she was going to be fine now that help was here. She smiled at him weakly and then waved as they lifted her into the back of the red truck.

One of the policemen stayed to talk to him about what had happened. Sam said no, he hadn't got the license of the first car, but said that he didn't think whoever was driving it had been aware of what was going on behind him. The cop took his car phone number, "just in case," he said, and he left, too.

Sam was alone by the side of the road. He went back down to Melanie's car and retrieved his coat from where the EMTs had thrown it. He saw that there was a wide dark stain of blood at its hem.

He started his car, and continued on his way to Gorton.

Where he saw Leslie and Pierce in their house, in their life together. And though he **didn't** believe in signs, not even in portents, he nonetheless felt that this was the scene he'd been brought all this way, on this exact day—a day with exactly the events of this day—to see. And that all of it was connected, somehow—his sadness over Charley, his sense of being lost in his own life, the difficulty of the drive up. The accident, and then Melanie Gruber's . . . sweetness, he supposed. At that moment he couldn't have articulated the connection, but he felt it. He felt it, along with a lifting, a release, that he also couldn't have explained clearly to anyone else.

Driving back in the direction of Hanover, he hadn't been sure what he wanted to do. He was exhausted, suddenly. The lighted houses in the fields or nestled close to the road were like a call to go home, but the notion of the long drive back to Boston through the snow, through the rain, seemed impossible to consider in the state he was in.

He drove into town. He checked in at the Hanover Inn. After he'd scrubbed his teeth with a washcloth and washed his face, he went downstairs to the restaurant and had a hamburger and a beer, still in the state of lightness that had washed over him at Leslie's. The hamburger seemed to him a great hamburger, an extraordinary hamburger. He had another beer, which he drank slowly, feeling a sense of happiness, of grace, in everything he saw and touched and tasted. When he was done, he signed the bill and went back to his room. He called down and asked for a toothbrush and toothpaste from housekeeping. While he was waiting for them to be delivered, he telephoned the hospital where they'd taken Melanie Gruber. He was hoping, he realized, to be able to talk to her, to hear her musical voice, maybe even to tell her he hadn't done it, hadn't tried to claim Leslie.

She was sleeping, they said. They couldn't give him any information about her beyond that.

"Sleeping" sounded good, he thought. Sounded safe.

A young man arrived at the door with the toothbrush and a small tube of toothpaste. Sam brushed his teeth; he got into bed and fell asleep almost instantly. He slept deeply, dreamlessly, until sunlight moved slantwise across the bed and woke him.

And when he woke, he immediately thought of the girl again. Actually not her as a person so much as meeting her, what he saw in some crazy sense as the miracle of it, the way it altered how he saw everything in its aftermath. She, she was the sign, the portent, the **emblem**—of possibility, of chance, of fate. **Things arrived in your life.** They descended upon you. It was like falling in love, Sam thought, but in this case without the emotion at the center. Just the aura of it, the sense of blessedness, of great luck.

He called the hospital again and got passed around from extension to extension. Finally someone came on and said, "Who is it you're trying to find?"

He said her name.

"Oh, yes," the woman said. "She's been released. She's gone home."

He had laughed aloud on the phone, these words seemed so perfect.

Now as Sam sits in his living room, holding the Christmas letter from Emma, thinking of Melanie Gruber, he realizes that he's called her up in part because he feels the same way about Billy, about the accident of Billy's arrival in his life—exactly that surprised. That lifted up.

Clearly it had been a mistake on Leslie's part, introducing them. It shouldn't have worked. He remembers realizing from the look on her face at that moment that she was in some sense **presenting** him to Billy; he remembers being at once irritated and moved, there was something so presumptuous and yet kindhearted in this. He remembers thinking quickly about how he'd manage the end of the evening with Billy, if he got stuck with her.

But then there was the unlooked-for connection they'd made, the sense of possibility he'd felt in her presence and her clear responsiveness to him— though it was also clear that for some reason she struggled with that. Something, he thinks now, that they never had a chance to talk about. That they ought to talk about.

He needs to talk to her, Sam thinks. He thinks if they can just sit next to each other and talk the way they did in the waiting room of the HMO, or in her parlor, they can figure things out, they can get through whatever her hesitations, her fears, are.

He thinks of what he said to Jerry, that he was smitten with her. That seems exactly right, a word that suggests something's having **happened** to you, some agent's acting on you, whether you like it or not. He's smitten, he's been **smited** by his feelings for her. Wham! Like fate. Like an accident. An accident you watch happening to yourself in a kind of wonderment.

All this while Sam has been looking out the window at the snow falling. Early snows, this year. Global warming, no doubt. This one started in the night, and now it's piled up. There's probably more than a foot out there. Just before lunch, Sam moved the car to the bottom of the driveway so he wouldn't have to shovel himself out.

What he'll do, he's thinking, is mail the earring back. He'll write a note to send with it, he'll persuade her to see him again. He feels, not hopeful exactly—he remembers her face when she saw him in the theater, the way it shuttered itself—but excited. Excited to be acting, to be doing something.

He'll go now, he'll walk by the house and see what the number is—he's sure he'll recognize it: her desk in front of the curved tall windows, the lamp on the desk. There was a small, bare tree in the little yard at the front of the house, he remembers that, too. Maybe a dogwood.

He goes into the hall, pulls his coat off the newel post, grabs his keys. It's cold out, but the air feels soft, as it often does in a windless snowstorm.

The ride over is slow. End-of-day traffic is thick, and everyone is driving carefully, lights on, because the roads are so slippery. Sam is going slowly, too. Even so, the car fishtails several times when he's applying the brakes, and he's never entirely sure he'll come to a complete stop when he needs to. Nothing is plowed yet in the city. Probably all the trucks are out on the highways, trying to get them cleared for the commute home.

He turns onto Mass Ave by Symphony Hall, headed south. There's a policeman directing traffic at Huntington Avenue, bundled up, wearing an orange safety vest and thick mittens. When he signals for Sam to go forward, Sam feels beckoned personally, given a gift. He crosses Columbus Avenue, and then turns left on Tremont Street. The traffic is instantly easier here. He drives the width of the South End, going very slowly after the halfway point, reading the street signs. He's not quite sure how far in Union Park is.

And then he passes it, too late to turn—but it's one way in the wrong direction anyway. About a block and half beyond it, there's a parking place at a meter. He takes it. As he pulls the keys out from the ignition, he sees that Billy's earring is hooked through one of the smaller rings dangling from the big, central one. He untangles it and puts it in one of his coat pockets. He puts the keys in the other pocket and gets out of the car.

He walks back toward Union Park. He passes the restaurant where he sat with Pierce and Leslie waiting for Billy those weeks ago. It's packed with people sheltering from the storm, feeling cozy and safe and festive, no doubt, looking out the glass at the falling snow. He passes a real estate office, a café, less full.

As soon as he turns in to Union Park, he's in another century. It's still and silent, and the grand old Victorian brick houses seem serene, remote. The snow is falling slowly and evenly. It's almost invisible in the air, just the blur through which Sam sees everything. What lingers of the light is opalescent. The sidewalks are covered with a blanket of white, the cars humped shapelessly. The black iron fence that circles the oval park in the center of the block is traced in white. Each of the fountains has a rounded, jaunty cap.

He walks in on the left side of the park. Lights are on in some of the houses. From his pedestrian's angle, he can see the ornate ceilings, the heavy curtains held to the sides of some windows—here the back of a chair, there a piano lid, opened. Sometimes a chandelier. Somewhere a lone shoveler is prematurely at work, the metal striking the brick sidewalk with a sound that carries distantly through the windless air.

Sam's breath is loud in his ears. She was somewhere near the middle of the block, he remembers.

His hands are in his pockets; he's holding the earring. He thinks he recognizes the tree a few houses ahead—the gray bark, the arching shapely branches.

And then he sees what seems a child in a black coat almost at the end of the block, standing next to a large animal, a black dog. The dog is stopped, too, his nose down in the snow, digging at something under it. Sam takes some steps toward her to be sure. He can see the shape of her face now, the full cut of the coat he remembers.

He is walking toward her, faster now. He calls her name. His voice is muffled in the air of the park.

She turns her head in his direction. She sees him.

Her mouth opens, and then it moves, as though she's speaking. Now her hands in their outsize dark mittens rise slowly and cover her face. The dog sees him, too. He looks up at Billy, wanting to know what to do.

Sam has stopped. He waits for her.

After a moment, her hands come down, they drop to her sides, and he can see her face clearly now, even through the scrim of the snow—the sorrow, the relief, stamped on it.

One of them steps forward first, but later neither of them can remember who.

ACKNOWLEDGMENTS

I want to thank the Corporation of Yaddo for a fellowship that launched me into this book, and Smith College for the Elizabeth Drew Professorship, which gave me time to work on it while I was teaching. I owe thanks also to Joy Carlin for allowing me to watch her work as a director at the Aurora Theater in Berkeley; to David Auburn, playwright, who patiently and generously answered a list of tedious questions; and to Barbara Gaines, artistic director of the Chicago Shakespeare Theater, for her help and cherished friendship.

ABOUT THE AUTHOR

Sue Miller is the best-selling author of the novels **The Senator's Wife, Lost in the Forest, The World Below, While I Was Gone, The Distinguished Guest, For Love, Family Pictures,** and **The Good Mother;** the story collection **Inventing the Abbotts;** and the memoir **The Story of My Father.** She lives in Boston, Massachusetts.